The Alice Series
Book 2

Angel
of
Time

E. Graziani

ISBN: 979-8-88653-173-2

Fire & Ice Young Adult Books
An Imprint of Melange Books, LLC
White Bear Lake, MN 55110
www.fireandiceya.com

Published in the United States of America.

Cover Design by Caroline Andrus

Thank you, Nancy and everyone at Fire & Ice for rebranding and publishing this series.

For my family: Nanni, Julia, Alicia, Michaila & Chiara, for your support.

For anyone who has read any of my books...thank you.

Chapter One

Boston, Massachusetts
September 2029

"My phone has a new function—it's taking a 3D shot of everything around it—including us...voice and everything."

Gracefully, Ali backed away from the little device and sat down beside Claudio. "Smile!" she ordered, placing her cheek against his to pose for the video. "It plays back in high-res 3D—it's awesome," she added proudly. Claudio, a broad smile on his face, took her slender wrist and stood, pulling her to her feet.

"Well, we cannot just sit here then, let us see what it can do...come on. Dance with me." He took her hands in his and improvised a loud song, singing uninhibitedly off-key as he stepped forward, left and right, guiding her in his spontaneous dance. Alice laughed without reservation. His silly steps were totally out of character—she was pleasantly surprised at Claudio's openness and ease around her.

"Right now, big finale—" He scooped her up with a final swaying motion and dipped her gracefully, guiding her arms and holding her tightly at the waist. Lifting her back up with no effort, he kissed her hand, his eyes never leaving hers. Ali's world stopped for an instant. She allowed herself the pleasure of gazing into his eyes and then broke contact, walking briskly to retrieve the device.

With an abrupt wavy click, the image stopped transmission.

Alice Ferro stared at the blank room around her—she reached over to her device and pressed the hologram control again as she swallowed the lump in her throat.

"My device has a new function..."

Ali watched the hologram again and again, losing herself in the one minute and forty-seven-second recording. Sitting, with her knees gathered up under her chin, she smiled wistfully at the transmission. "Right now, big finale—" *This is my favorite part. He looks unbearably beautiful, too beautiful for words.*

Their images undulated and then faded again.

Ali scooped up her phone, minimized it, and placed it back on her bedside table. Zombie-like, she walked to her desk, rummaged vaguely through the drawers for something, and pulled out a black, hardcover journal, beat up and worn. Ali's journal had been her best friend on days when she couldn't talk to anyone else. So many doubts and feelings were swirling around inside, and she needed to express them before she either lost her mind or burst. She had no one else to turn to because what happened to her last summer was...impossible.

Ali poked around further and discovered a thin-tipped marker. With her eyes downcast, she walked to her bed, settled onto it, and opened the book. She poised her pen over the first page, and began to write—carefully at first, then progressing to a furious pace—her hand unable to keep up with her brain.

Even though she and Claudio had only been together for two weeks, she had a lifetime of emotions stored up inside her.

She should have known that it was a doomed relationship from the beginning. As much as she ached for him, there was no alternative to their end.

Yet, she couldn't stop wondering what had become of him. Maybe, one day, she would have the courage to research Count Claudio Moro—just to make sure he was even real in the first place—but not now. The hurt was still too much, still too raw.

Ali lifted the marker off the page. Sticking it between her teeth, she flipped the pages back and forth to check over what she had written—a habit that had been fixed firmly into her by her English teachers.

Ali closed the book, placed it beside her on the bed with the pen resting on top, and flopped down, her face emotionless, staring at the ceiling. The gnawing feeling in her stomach was back. Every time she allowed herself to think of him, it came back. She walked into his love with her heart wide open, and now grief and despair tore at it piece by piece.

She turned her head. Outside her window, the maple tree swayed in the late summer breeze. September—ugh!

There was already a crisp nip in the air at night, and before long the leaves would turn their brilliant autumn colors—a last valiant show before the drab nakedness of winter. The last of the humid heat, reminiscent of the Tuscan climate and the endless summer rides on the Vespa, would fade, leaving only the cold and snow. Slowly, she rolled herself up into a ball and lay sideways on her bed, staring at the lazy waving maple, reliving the pain of that final scene.

"Ali!"

Alice shot up, startled. Her mother stood at the door to her bedroom, looking impatient and annoyed.

"Oh my gosh!" Alice put her hand to her heart. "Can you make a little noise before creeping up on me like that?"

"Creeping up on you?" Barbara's brows were furrowed, an incredulous look on her handsome face. "I called you three

3

times from downstairs! When I come up here to check on you, I find you rolled up in a fetal position on your bed. Didn't you hear me?" Her Italian accent thickened as it always did when she became agitated. Barbara sat herself down on the edge of the bed and gently cupped Ali's chin in her hand. Her tone softened. "What's wrong? You look as though you've lost your best friend."

Ali sighed and remained silent. The words to describe what she was feeling hadn't been invented yet.

"Ever since you came back from Italy, you've done nothing but languish around the house. Half the time you don't even answer your phone. You don't go out with your friends, and I would be surprised if you've seen Caleb more than once or twice since you've been home. Not that I'm pushing you to see him or anything—he seems too perfect to me, but...talk to me, sweetheart."

"I'm sorry, Mamma." Her attempt at a smile produced a grimace instead. "Maybe it's just the letdown after a great trip. You know, back at school, the same routine." She didn't look directly at Barbara. "Don't worry. I'm fine."

"Really?" Barbara asked again, gently squeezing her chin and turning her back around so that she could see Ali's eyes.

"Really," Ali repeated. Her eyes widened, and her head exaggeratedly bobbed up and down. "Stop worrying! Hey, what's for dinner?" *That'll change the topic fast enough*, thought Ali.

Barbara's beautiful smile slowly crept back on her face. "One of your favorites," she answered, "stuffed peppers. Now come downstairs and eat—don't stay up here by yourself a minute longer. Papa and I have to leave soon to meet Doctor Spencer and his wife for dinner."

Barbara rose and walked to the door, but hesitated for a moment, her hand resting on the doorjamb as if deliberating on whether to continue her stride. When she turned around, her eyes paused briefly on the journal and then met Ali's gaze. "Ali, there is something I need to ask. Did anything unusual happen over there? With that boy?" Her mother's head had that familiar angle to it—the suspicious angle.

Ali gulped and wondered what Leda told her.

"Mom, really, stop worrying," Ali reassured her with a grin. "Nothing happened, and I'm okay. Just hungry and tired."

"Good. I'd better see you eat more than a sparrow's share of the food tonight." Barbara grinned back. With a fluid movement, she turned and headed to the stairs.

Slowly, Ali got to her feet and grabbed the journal from her bed. As she walked to her closet, she thought of what her mother said about Caleb. Barbara was right—she was totally avoiding him. She had to make things right. Caleb had been good to her and deserved to know the truth. Inasmuch as Ali felt she had betrayed him, she realized that because she fell so easily for Claudio, her feelings for Caleb must not have been genuine to begin with.

She stuffed the journal under some sweaters high up on one of the shelves in her closet and turned to make her way downstairs. As she walked by her dresser, she glanced at her reflection from the ornately filigreed princess mirror above it.

"Well, Ali," she mumbled to her reflection, "you talked your way out of a death sentence—you should be brave enough to break up with Caleb."

Chapter Two

Morning—the part of the day Ali dreaded—getting off the school bus and having to pretend all is well. Cornered, with nowhere to go but straight ahead, she would have no choice but to speak to people.

They're going to ask why I didn't answer their texts last night, Ali thought as she spotted a group of three girls on the front steps chattering, browsing, and texting in a multitasking finger-frenzy on their little devices, their thumbs dancing like butterflies over the extended screens on their phones.

"Hey, guys. What's up?" she said as she approached them, trying to sound upbeat.

"Hey," Mina and Jelsy chimed simultaneously.

"Hey, girl," answered Kiana as she finished off a text. "By the way, where were you last night?" Her eyes narrowed as she adjusted the backpack strap on her shoulder. "You didn't answer any of your messages. No texts, no posts, no 3Ds—" She leaned in close and kept her eyes on the other two girls, feigning secrecy. "Did you sneak over to Syracuse with Caleb, to his dorm, or something?" She snickered, shooting a sly side-glance at Ali.

Mina and Jelsy giggled as they stepped into the school, their voices instantly drowned out by the loud chattering of hundreds of teenagers that reverberated against the endless rows of lockers.

"C'mon," coaxed Jelsy loudly as she looked back at Ali, an all too innocent smile on her glossed lips. "You can tell us." Her lips puckered as she blew exaggerated kisses.

"Yeah," echoed Mina, her brow furrowed in frustration. "Where were you? Last night wasn't the first time you dropped off the face of the earth. Can you at least post your status or something, so we know what you're doing?"

Ali sighed. "I'm sorry, okay? You're right." She shrugged and halted at her locker. The friends had managed to secure four lockers in close proximity. Before the summer, these girls had been her closest friends; they'd been inseparable, but Ali had barely spoken to them while she was in Italy, and now she was sure they sensed she was avoiding them. "I've just been really tired lately. Sometimes, I can't sleep at night," Ali said in a matter-of-fact tone as she set to work on her locker combination. "Sometimes, I just need to be alone, that's all. And no, Ki, I was not at Caleb's." Ali slammed the lock against the metal door as it failed to open. She reset it to zero and started again.

"Okay. Touchy," snapped Jelsy. "I'm going to class." She spun around and walked briskly in the opposite direction, her hand in the air, waving. "Ciao!"

"I'm off, too," said Mina. "See you guys at third." Her parting glance was aimed at Kiana with an arched brow and a roll of the eye.

Alice turned so that she was leaning against the lockers—she hadn't missed Mina's eye roll. Was she really that insufferable? That annoying? Thinking of the summer made her pine with nostalgia, despite the obvious stumbling blocks that went with it. She rubbed her forehead and thought of Caterina and her unconditional friendship—she missed her.

"Wow," said Ali, "I guess no one's allowed to be less than perfect." She spun around and attempted once again to crack her locker combination and failed. "For God's sake, get me out of here." Her words dragged out in an exaggerated drawl.

"Hey, what is up with you?" asked Kiana sincerely. Kiana had been Ali's best friend since grade three. They'd met when Ali had transferred to Holy Trinity Elementary after Christmas vacation. Ali recalled how the kids in class had looked at her like she was an insect while whispering, "Who's that girl?" as they strolled past her and hung up their coats.

Kiana was the only one who had taken pity on her—the poor wretched new girl—and tried to make her feel welcome. Ali never forgot that.

"Nothing, Ki," Ali lied.

"It's Caleb, isn't it?" Kiana grimaced. "Like I say: if it has tires, testicles...or a microchip, you just know it's going to be trouble...just sayin'."

"Oh my God, Kiana!" Ali burst into laughter. Kiana never disappointed her. "You always know how to make me laugh." She took in a deep breath, leaning up against the lockers. The morning crowd in the hall was beginning to thin as the hundreds of uniformed students entered their first-period classes. The two girls stayed put, silently agreeing that it was time for Ali to give up her secret.

When the national anthem and opening exercises were over, Ali slid slowly down to the floor and sat, her legs crossed, fiddling with a loose thread on her backpack. Kiana watched her for a while, waiting for a signal. A full fifteen minutes passed and then the hall was just too quiet—it was well past the start of the first period.

Finally, Kiana leaned down close enough to whisper, "So, Alice—are you ever going to tell me what's wrong?"

Ali thought about her options as she continued to twirl the black and purple thread up and down and through her fingers.

It crossed over her forefinger and twisted about her thumb in a rhythmic pattern of coils and loops.

What the hell am I supposed to do? I can't keep talking to my journal...I need to tell someone. Maybe if I share the load, it'll be easier to carry...just for a while, anyway. Ali looked up at her friend and nodded slowly. "I think I need to." But unquestionably, not every detail.

Kiana nodded back, relief spreading across her features. "Okay, well, we'd better move someplace else unless we want detention. We should be in Classics right now." She stood.

"The library study carrels?" proposed Ali, offering up her hand.

Kiana grabbed it and helped her up. "Let's go."

Chapter Three

Ali felt like crying, but she didn't dare. Her guard was still up, and under no circumstances would she let Kiana know the depth of the emotions swirling inside her. But she knew that something—anything—had to be given to her best friend to ease her worries regarding her behavior. She owed her that much.

Alice led the way to the school library; her eyes downcast and her mind reeling, trying to figure out how much she could tell her friend. Her heart longed to tell her everything, to let Kiana in and allow her to help.

I need to be careful at how to play this out, Ali thought as she approached a set of carrels that were in a relatively secluded part of the library. "Okay." She flopped her backpack down on the inside of the desk and sat down on one of the blue leatherette chairs.

"It's weird, but I think I'm nervous," Kiana said as she pulled a chair from one of the other desks closer to her friend. She slipped her arms out of her rucksack and haphazardly threw it on the floor beside her chair. "Okay, Als—I'm listening."

"So...well...last summer when I was in Italy, I kind of met someone there. Someone special—"

"I knew it!" Kiana cut Ali off in mid-sentence, her voice at a decibel level that cut through the silence of the library like a javelin.

"Ki—shhh!" Ali hissed. Her hand reached for her friend's wrist and squeezed it hard.

"Ouch!" Kiana wailed. "What the hell was that for?"

"Jeez, can you keep your voice down, please?" Ali put her fingers to her lips and peered about surreptitiously. "I don't want anyone hearing this."

"Well, you don't have to take my skin off."

"Well, you don't have to attract all kinds of attention by yelling your head off!"

"Now you're being loud—"

"Kiana, please."

"Okay, sorry." Kiana exhaled and settled herself down. "Tell me everything—go." Her friend's expression was intense, her eyes narrow, and her head tilted attentively toward Ali.

Alice sighed, then continued, "This summer—in Italy—I met someone."

Kiana nodded. "Go on."

Ali licked her lips. "We-we became very good friends, and after a while...we...he was so...he's my soul mate, Kiana." Her eyes began to sting. *Damn, I promised myself I wouldn't.*

Ki took her hand gently. "He's your soul mate, and you're here and he's there."

"Yeah," Ali nodded, her eyes welling up. "Basically, that's it."

"So, you're in love with—what's his name?"

"Claudio. Claudio Moro. And yes. Deeply in love." Ali brushed the tears away with her shirt sleeve.

"Does Caleb know? Are you and Claudio still communicating?"

"No to both." Ali sniffed. She glanced back up at Kiana, a

matter-of-fact expression taking over her features. "Claudio and I broke it off. And as for Caleb, I'm breaking up with him, too. I didn't have the heart to tell him when I came back. He looked so happy to see me when I got home. Then he had to pack, move, leave for school...anyway, next time he's home I'll have to tell him it's over between us."

"Wow. No wonder you're walking around like a zombie." Kiana furrowed her brow. "Poor Caleb—he'll be crushed." She moved her head slowly from side to side in disbelief. "But I don't understand. If you and this guy are in love, why stop communicating? I mean, you can still talk, right? It's not impossible if you love him. He's as close as your phone—you can Facetime."

Ali knew this conversation would hit a snag. "We had to stop...it's complicated."

"Complicated? Why is it complicated?" She threw Ali a look of astonishment. "There are lots of people who have long-distance relationships. You two wouldn't be the first."

Ali marveled at this last statement. *If you only knew how distant he is, my friend.* "This is different. It's not possible."

"Come on, Ali. If you can dream it, you can do it. Remember that? Nothing is impossible if you want it badly enough. Make it possible. You're the author of your own destiny. That's what we've always told ourselves." Kiana had a look of definite satisfaction at her wise words.

"And to that, I say easier said than done." Ali let out a sigh and gave Kiana a sad smile. "That's why I've not been myself." She reached over the side of the study carrel and groped around for her backpack. "I might as well message Caleb right now—I'll have more courage if you're here. I think he'll be home for the weekend. We can get together then, and I can break it off in person." She pulled out her device, extended it with a swish of her thumb and forefinger, and voiced Caleb's number. One ring, two rings...

"I still don't understand why you and the Italian guy can't—"

"Trust me, it's not happening," Ali interrupted. Caleb's voice mail. Damn! "Hi, Caleb—it's me. Can you call me back when you get a chance? I need to talk to you. It's important." Ali contracted the phone. The gloomy, worried look in her eyes expressed what her words did not—a genuine guilt at having to hurt Caleb.

Alice's best friend wobbled her head. "I really don't envy you this, Ali—or Caleb—he loves you, you know."

"Yes, I know."

Kiana shrugged and looked away.

Ali sensed an undercurrent of mild disapproval, but she didn't care. "Look, Ki, I may feel guilty, but I will never be ashamed of what Claudio and I shared. It was the truest emotion I've ever felt for anyone." Her tone took on a cool confidence. "You know, I was hesitant at first—when I started to really fall for him, and I don't just mean teenage infatuation...I mean falling deeply, madly in love. I hesitated to let my feelings boil up to the surface. And you know what he said to me? He said that a few days with me were worth a lifetime to him. And that falling in love has no timetable or schedule...you just know that it is good and right. Ki, I have to tell you that I still believe that because of the kind of man that he was." Alice held her head up and nodded slowly as her gaze fixed on her friend. "A few days with Claudio were worth everything. Only now he's always, always in my mind..."

Ali's last words hung in the air like a stifled speech bubble in the dusty library stacks.

"All right, Ali—love is love. And this one sounds like you should never have let it go."

Glad that Kiana had finally found it in herself to offer sympathy and support, Alice reached over and hugged her friend. "Thank you," Ali said softly. She glanced at her phone and grimaced. "We'd better go since first period is almost over."

Chapter Four

The extended tech device sat on Ali's bedside table, its power light blinking idly as she sat on her bed, her legs drawn up under her chin and her arms wrapped around her knees. She stared at it, trying to muster enough courage to dial Caleb up again and set up the date for the unavoidable meeting to end their relationship. Her guilt was strong, but her need to set this right was stronger. In a snap, she reached for the phone and said, "Caleb Fenton," before she lost her nerve.

As soon as the phone dialed, he picked up. "Hi babe." His usually warm voice hesitated. "Why isn't your screen on?"

"I just didn't activate it," Ali responded, trying to maintain an even tone in her voice. "No big deal."

Caleb sighed. "I guess not, but it would be nice to see your face while we're talking, which hasn't been a lot lately."

Ali flinched and ignored his last comment. "So, I was wondering if you're coming home for Columbus Day long weekend next week. Can we catch up, then?"

"Absolutely! I'm counting on it. Driving down from Syracuse on Friday afternoon, so I'll pick you up around seven. Sound good?"

"Yup. And let's just make it coffee somewhere—nothing fancy, okay?"

"Sure, see you then. Love you."

Ali hesitated. "See you then. Bye." She folded her device and tossed it on the bed, her stomach churning.

She didn't relish the prospect of their upcoming date. She knew Caleb loved her, but it would surely be worse to let him hang on and believe everything was fine. This had to be done— she had waited long enough.

In her reverie, Alice's peripheral vision caught a red glow emanating from the top of her device. She turned to glance at her phone—it indicated that a memo she had logged had matured. It read: Get papa at univ. lab.5:30—car's in garage.

Ali sighed heavily. "Oh, crap!" Positively the last thing she wanted to do right now was drive all the way into the city to pick up her father at the university. "Crap, crap, crap!" With a hearty roll of her eyes, she dragged herself off the bed with exaggerated frustration and stomped to her closet door where her satchel hung on the doorknob.

Ali glanced up and spotted her journal. A corner peeked out from the pile of sweaters where she had hidden it. Not wanting anyone to read it, she reached up to push it further under the cardigans and pullovers. Once she fixed the sweaters, she glanced away, battling the urge to gaze at a remote corner of the closet, fighting the need to reach up and grab the treasure hidden beneath. But alas, the longing was much too strong.

On tiptoe, Ali reached up while holding the crossbar and grabbed the keepsake box. The container was unremarkable— just an old hatbox she had decoupaged one rainy afternoon with her mother when she was eleven or twelve.

Looking at it hungrily, her hands swathed it. Slowly, almost reverently, she removed the lid and pulled aside an old prayer book, a handmade tenth birthday card from Kiana, her First Communion gloves, and an old pink tiara. At the bottom of the box was a small plain silken gift bag with a drawstring. Carefully, Ali picked up the sack and tossed the hatbox on her bed. She drew the strings open and delicately reached inside to find Claudio's handkerchief—the cloth she had taken from his neck in the last few moments that they were together in 1512.

Ali closed her eyes as she brought the fabric to her nose and breathed in. She filled her lungs, taking in his wonderful, delicious scent that still lingered in the handkerchief. Her eyes remained closed as she touched her cheek with it, pretending it was his hand, which had so frequently caressed her face. "I miss you so much," she whispered. "I didn't think that it would be this hard to get over you."

Claudio's scent brought back vivid memories and intense feelings. Her last few hours with him made their connection stronger, as though traveling back to 1512 had permanently set their relationship. She doubted that anyone else would, or could, have this effect on her.

But reality came crashing down and drew Ali back to 2029. She couldn't stay there clutching Claudio's scarf indefinitely. Tenderly, she tucked the last link to her soulmate back into the drawstring pouch. After placing it at the bottom of the hatbox, she meticulously arranged the other articles over it, hiding the only physical memento of his existence. Once the keepsake box was in her closet, she picked up her device, grabbed her satchel from the doorknob, and walked somberly down the stairs to pick up her father.

Chapter Five

Traffic from the Boston suburbs to downtown Cambridge was an unspeakable evil. The glinting, endless lanes of cars and trucks were moving at a snail's pace, making Ali extremely anxious—she hated things beyond her control.

"Time." Alice spoke clearly to the dashboard.

"The time is four fifty-seven." An impassive woman's voice spoke back.

"Damn," Ali mumbled. She bit her lip and checked the mirror. The lane next to her was clear, so she flicked on her signal and turned her wheel deftly to the right, making a quick turn onto a side street. Ali headed north to the university, ignoring the tree lined side streets and halting obediently at each stop sign, all the while tapping her impatience on the steering wheel.

The closer she got to the university, the more evident the presence of student life became. Frat houses and student residences took over from urban family dwellings, turning the avenues and boulevards surrounding the Massachusetts Institute of Technology into a giant beer-kegging academic village.

To top off the cliché, there was old, drenched toilet paper hanging from one of the trees outside the Alpha Epsilon Pi house.

Vaguely, this made her think of Caleb's residence at Syracuse University, which in turn made her think of Friday. She was not looking forward to Friday. Caleb was just a poor unsuspecting soul, caught up in a situation created as a result of a scientific anomaly produced by Leonardo da Vinci.

The thought of da Vinci brought back memories of last summer and her short time in 1512, where Claudio had told her that he worked as an apprentice with Leonardo in his Galluzzo Abbey studio. One of his wild experiments to harness the power of the lightning bolt had gone awry. Leonardo didn't know it, but he had created a time portal to different places and times. The two worked on it to create stability in the moving pictures within the currents of the spirals, and as the Fates would have it, Claudio fell in love with the Ali of 1512—otherwise known as Elisa, a scullery maid who worked at the palace.

Meddling by the Medici to keep the two apart had produced a final standoff with Bruno, the duke's nephew, who fancied Elisa and vowed that she would be his at all costs. Claudio feared for Elisa's life, so he and da Vinci decided to take her to the Abbey, thinking her safe there. But due to a battle to get at both her and Claudio, the maid panicked and inadvertently stepped through the time portal in the chamber and was reborn to the present as Alice. When her adoptive parents decided to take her on holiday back to Italy, Ali's past and future collided in ways she could never have imagined.

She made a quick right onto Audrey and then another right onto Vassar Street, where her father's office was, in the Department of Temporal and Astrophysics just beyond the main building.

While she drove, she thought of Harvard just up the street

and the Widener Library. She hadn't driven by it in a while. As one of the biggest libraries on the Harvard campus, it held everything you'd ever want to know about Social Sciences and Humanities.

Perhaps she would try again soon. Maybe this time she would enter. It wasn't the first time she had driven by the library while pretending to ignore it. In fact, she wanted to be close to it. Inside that structure, on one of those naturally lit floor-to-ceiling windowed aisles, nestled in one of the wood-on-metal stacks, sat an old dusty book that might hold information that was precious to her. So valued and so wanted that she felt if she cast her eyes on it, she would die.

Ali hungered to know more of Claudio. To learn of his accomplishments and of his life. But in her mind, if she were to postpone the acquisition of that knowledge indefinitely, she would remain close to him. If she were to stay uninformed—if she pushed back the finality of that irrevocable knowledge—her awareness of his plight would be suspended and that would mean that he had not lived and died without her. That he was not buried and dust.

So, she maintained her course to her father's office, anticipating that one day she would have the strength to quench the thirst of the curiosity inside her.

Once beyond the imposing main building, the astrophysics department was just up ahead. She turned onto the building parking ramp, grabbed her father's faculty card from the cup holder, and inserted it into the ticket machine. The barrier arm lifted, and she drove through, navigating easily into her father's parking spot.

'Reserved for Doctor Reno Ferro'

She slipped the car into park, turned off the ignition, and waited. "Time," she asked the dashboard.

"The time is five thirty-eight."

"Not bad," she whispered to herself. "Call Papa," she

ordered. Within seconds, a gentle ringing tone floated out of the dashboard controls.

"Alice?" Her father's voice drifted through the speaker.

"Hi," she answered. "I'm here."

"Uh—okay. Can you be patient for a few minutes? I'm in the middle of something."

At this, Ali groaned—she knew what "a few minutes" meant. It could stretch into a half an hour, or even longer.

"Ali, did you hear me? Do you mind waiting just a couple of minutes?"

Ali exhaled noisily. She paused for a moment and thought about the promise she made to Claudio—one of the last things she said to him—that she would learn more about the science that had brought them back together.

Biting the inside of her cheek, she decided. "Maybe I'll just come up," she said, unbuckling her seatbelt.

"That's a great idea." His voice took on a chipper tone. "I can show you what I'm working on."

"Sure," she agreed. "Be there in a minute." Grabbing her satchel, she slid out of the Volkswagen and closed the door, depressing the lock mechanism on the key ring. As it chirped its connection, she turned toward the glass door of the building and strode in. Standing alone and looking at the elevator button, she remembered Claudio, waiting at the lift in the Villa in Tuscany, struggling with suitcases—this made her smile. She pressed the up button.

A short ride up brought her to her father's floor. Ali exited and briskly veered right to the end of the hall. She grabbed the doorknob and turned, walking into a large white room with a reception desk front and center. The receptionist had already left, and there were only two people at their desks, absorbed in their interactive 3D touch screens, researching and reconfiguring the calculations on some star system or other. Alice tucked her honey-brown hair behind her ears and smiled at them, but they didn't acknowledge her presence.

She stopped in front of her father's door, knocked softly, and entered without waiting for a response. "Hi, Papa."

"Hello, darling." Reno sat behind his desk, gazing into one of the 3D touch screen models which surrounded him. "Just one minute," he mumbled. Several worktables bearing slab size 3D tablets comprised much of his office space. Reno was extremely reliant on the latest technology in order to further his scientific experiments, save for an old-fashioned telescope which was strategically positioned at the window to view the stars. Currently, he was absorbed in a virtual model that looked like a curvy cone of varying colors, upon which were a variety of algebraic equations, grid patterns, and timelines. He grasped, modified, and moved these equations, which gave rise to changes in the cone model.

"What's that?" Ali asked, fascinated.

"This," he gazed at her, while pointing at the floating object, "is a newly revised model of my Dark Matter Theory. My improved theory relates to the accelerated expansion of the universe and the concrete correlation between its extension and its effect on forming visible formations, like galaxies."

"Wow," Ali said, impressed. "I have absolutely no idea what you just said."

"Yes, wow!" Reno laughed at her comment. "Why, not twenty-five years ago there were not many who believed that Dark Matter even existed. Now we know beyond a doubt that it is instrumental in the continued expansion of our universe."

Alice listened to her father and nodded politely. "Interesting, Papa. Dark matter, huh? So, is that anything like dark magic?" She raised a brow and a corner of her mouth.

"You can make fun, but experiments based on trial and error like this make scientific advances possible. Do you have any idea how long it has taken us to reach this level of understanding? We can discover things in one evening of observation that would have taken us months, or even years, just a few decades ago."

Alice admired her father's passion for science.

"I'm just teasing. I know how important this is to you. In fact, maybe I can come back when we have more time, and you can tell me more." She was about to turn to sit in his office chair to wait when something occurred to her. "Papa, has anyone ever looked into how we can capture a lightning bolt—like use its power for electricity?"

"Good question, albeit rather out of the blue. Ha-ha. Get it? Lightning bolt? Out of the blue?"

"Yeah Papa, I get it." Smiling, Ali rolled her eyes.

Her father sighed. "Well, I tried. There have been studies—I can't mention where because they are being commissioned by a multi-national consortium—but the research is promising. Maybe one day..." His voice trailed.

Alice smiled at the possibility of one of Leonardo's and Claudio's experiments coming to fruition in the 21st century. Turning her gaze to several other models swirling about on her father's work tables, Alice cleared her throat to ask the other question that had been swimming around in her mind for weeks. "Dark matter. So, do you know anything about black holes and singularities?" She allowed a quick side glance to weigh her father's reaction to the question.

"Of course," he answered. He minimized his model and shifted his gaze from his work to Alice. "Black holes are an important part of temporal mechanics and physics." He rose from his work stool, massaging his neck. "Why do you ask? And didn't you learn about this in astronomy?"

"Just curious to know more," she said evasively. "And you can explain better than anyone I know."

Reno shrugged, strode to one of his worktables, and proceeded to maximize desk-sized 3-D tablets. He chose an icon and spread his fingers over it to increase the image so that it occupied his entire desktop. A model of a sun blinked to life over Reno's desktop, and once he tapped the image, it began to burn and shimmer.

"Watch the image. It's easier to understand if you can see it." The sun began to shrink. "You see, a black hole is what is left over when a star runs out of fuel and collapses in on itself until there is nothing left but a powerful point of gravity smaller than an atom. This center of the black hole is called the singularity. The area around that is the inner event horizon, and the outermost layer is the outer event horizon. A black hole is defined as a region of space-time from which gravity prevents anything, including light, from escaping. Black holes are spherical and spin around, dragging and confusing the space-time continuum like thick syrup around a spoon."

The image transformed into a tiny dot where the sun had once been with arms emanating from an outer ring.

Freaky, thought Ali. *It felt like I was in syrup when I stepped into the chamber.* "Wow, Papa, that's amazing." As fascinating as it was, the image didn't look anything like the thing in Leonardo's chamber—those strings weren't spiraling like the ones in the chamber. "Can black holes exist with spiraling arms?"

"Yes, in that case, the space around them is not being vacuumed in, if I can use that analogy. What you are describing is a wormhole—different from a black hole, but in many ways, the same."

"Okay, now you lost me."

"Wormholes are theoretical." Reno minimized the black hole model and scrolled through several others before stopping and extending an image. While the image loaded, Reno continued to explain. "Scientists think that since space-time is flexible, two distant points in space could be connected by a pocket of really high gravity. Some scientists theorize that they may also connect different points in time."

"Like a time portal." Ali's stomach jumped. *Space and time are flexible*. Her parched throat made her voice sound like a croak.

"Right. But unlike black holes, wormholes have no singularities, no core, and no massive gravity. Think of it as a friendlier version of a black hole." She stood immobile as the image finished loading, and what Ali saw was beyond her wildest expectations. The match was perfect—she may as well have been staring at the inside of da Vinci's chamber.

Her father continued. "We need to stop thinking that everyone and everything is at the same point in time." He removed his lanyard and laid it on his desk, lengthwise. With his finger, he drew the ends close together. "Think of this lanyard on the desk as time. If I move it up and down, it is still the same length. But see the edges? They are closer together. In theory, wormholes are portals in the space-time continuum that allows for jumping from one point in time to the next. Of course, this is all theoretical, but time is definitely not linear. We are getting closer to unraveling the mystery every day."

"Of course," was all that Ali's small voice could manage. *Theoretical, he says; boy, could I tell him a thing or two*. She stared into the strings, the brightness at the center of the array taunted her like a winking eye.

"Ali? Alice?" Her father edged his face between the image and her line of vision. "What's the matter?"

She shook her head and turned dazedly to her father.

"It looked like you were a million miles away," he said, scooping up his jacket. "You okay?"

Ali felt the beginnings of a headache.

"Oh, yeah. I'm okay." Her face flushed with excitement. "It's just so interesting." She rubbed her temples and nodded, smiling her appreciation. Her father didn't appear convinced.

"You're sure?"

"Yes, absolutely—could not be better." The stunned realization that her father had a viable hypothesis about how time portals worked resulted in a feeling of euphoria rising up from the pit of Ali's stomach. "Oh my gosh, Papa, this is amazing. Do you know anything else about time travel?"

"Interesting stuff, eh? If you want, you can come back the day after tomorrow. I have a late afternoon class—you can read up on some theories like the Penrose–Hawking singularity theorems." He minimized and powered down the tablet.

"Darn, the day after tomorrow is Friday, Papa. I have a date with Caleb—sorry. But, another day for sure, okay? Very soon— I really mean that."

"Hmph! Caleb," snorted her father. "There's something about that kid."

Alice was mildly surprised at her father's reaction. "Caleb— you think so?" She grimaced and grabbed her satchel from the chair as her father was almost ready to go. Reno smiled and picked up his portfolio case.

"I'm just being facetious. He seems nice enough." Reno picked up his lanyard and waved his security card at the door. The alarm light switched on, and the silent countdown to exit began. "But be sure to come back up here—whenever you wish." He ushered Ali out of the office. "It was nice talking to you about my work."

"The word, 'interesting' doesn't do it justice, Papa. Don't worry—I'll be back soon."

Chapter Six

Friday arrived, and Alice was drained from not sleeping. Dichotomous images of Leonardo's time portal and breaking up with Caleb plunged her mind into overtime.

Ali tried to watch some television as she waited for Caleb, but she couldn't focus. After waving off the media center, she sat in silence, checking her device constantly for the time.

7:10, 7:12, 7:15. Where was he?

Finally, there was a knock at the door. *Body language is everything*, thought Alice as she arose from the couch and tensely walked to the front door. She swung it open, and there he was, looking perfectly handsome—sculpted face, bronze-tipped brown hair, and a body that fit very nicely in denim.

"Hi, babe," he said cheerfully as he crossed the threshold and hugged her. His lips tried to find her mouth, but she turned her head. He kissed her temple instead.

"Hi, Caleb. You're late." *Damn, I sound icy.* She laughed a little to downplay her response and pulled away.

"Well, late? Not really. I think we said seven*ish*, right?"

"Yeah, you're right." She bit her lip. "Never mind."

He flashed a dazzling smile and leaned toward her, his hands reaching for her hips. She stiffened noticeably and clasped her hands on his wrists.

"God, Ali. I miss you. It seems like I never see you anymore." He leaned his head in until their faces were close, his eyes latched onto hers, and their mouths almost touched.

"Don't be dumb, Caleb." She pulled away again, and he released her. "I just saw you a couple of weeks ago, and I talk with you at least two or three times a week. You're in college, remember? You're busy, and away from home. You're not down the block anymore like when we were in high school." She sensed his confusion. "Come on, let's just go. I need some air."

Looking exasperated, Caleb threw up his hands. "Whatever you say. Let's go."

They walked silently to his car. The sun had just set in the early October sky, and there was a thin line of cobalt blue on the horizon over the Boston suburbs. He opened the door for her, and she climbed in.

"Thanks." The door slammed closed as he circled to the driver's side.

"So, where to?" he asked as he slid into his seat and buckled his belt. His voice was bordering on irritated, and his gaze was fixed straight ahead.

"Let's just drive," Ali said, wrapping her sweater a little closer to her body. There was a definite chill on her side of the car. "Can we grab a coffee and just talk?"

Caleb nodded slowly. She felt he knew what was coming. How could he not—her attitude was screaming 'break-up.'

"Sure, we can do that. There's a coffee shop just over there. We'll go to the drive-thru and then park at the Fields."

The 'Fields' was an old cornfield that had long been abandoned. Some awesome bush parties had transpired in that field, most of them eventually broken up by the police cracking down on underage drinking.

The drive to the overgrown space was silent, and Caleb had taken on a brooding air. They pulled up to a spot away from the road. When Caleb's gaze met Ali's, she didn't look away. He carefully picked up his coffee from the cup holder, pulled back the tab, and sipped slowly.

"So, we're here, Ali." He took another sip. "Do you mind telling me what's happening with you? Since you came back from that vacation, you're like a different person. I can't even touch you anymore. It's like I repel you or something. Like, I'm repulsive to you. What did I do? Did I do something or say something?" His tone was even and calm. "I don't know, it's like you—you won't talk to me anymore, and when I ask you what's wrong, you ignore me or change the subject."

"I-I know, I'm not being fair, and I'm sorry for that," Ali spluttered. "It—it's just that I respect you so much, and I feel so, I want to say vested, but that is so cold sounding. You know what I mean? We've been together so long and all our friends are the same—it's so, so comfortable. But..." She swallowed hard. "But not anymore, Caleb." She licked her lips. Her mouth felt like a desert in a drought. She reached for her coffee and took a gulp, letting it burn her throat.

His gaze swept from hers to the dark abandoned field beyond the windshield.

"When I was in Italy, I realized that I didn't feel the way you feel about me. I-I'm not in love with you, Caleb...and I believe with my whole heart and soul that I never really was. I thought I was because everyone assumed that we were perfect for each other. But I know now—I know the truth. I have to end it. I respect you too much to continue this."

Emotionless, Caleb nodded, which Ali thought was strange. She waited for a reaction, but he only sat there, sipping his coffee, thinking, staring.

At least anger, she thought. *Something.* "Caleb?"

"So," he started, his voice cold and exact. "You just came to this realization in Italy? Just out of the blue. You just woke up one day and thought, 'Hey, that idiot back home? Don't want him anymore.' Is that how it went down?" His voice took on a shallow, cold quality.

"Truthfully," Ali looked away, letting her mind remember her time in Italy, "I felt that something wasn't right before I left. Actually, going there, and...and well, just going there crystallized what had been kicking around in my head for a while. It's not you, Caleb, honestly. It's me. I know that sounds cliché but—" she raised her eyes to find him watching her with disdain.

"Oh, that's classic." He cut her off. "'It's not you, Caleb, it's me.'"

His tone had a mocking quality that she didn't like, his face a callous expression she didn't like.

"Do you really expect me to believe that you just came up with that idea in your own little head? That you didn't have help from one of your stupid friends? They're jealous of us, Ali, don't you see it?"

"What are you talking about?" Ali grimaced. "And don't you dare call my friends stupid. That is offensive!"

"Oh, excuse me for offending you." He threw his coffee out the window, and some landed on his jacket and upholstery. "Shit! Look what you made me do."

"Look, I told you I'm sorry. Do you think I wanted this to happen?" Ali tried to reason, but he interrupted.

"I don't know—did you? I drove in from Syracuse for you. To see you. Why? What happened to change things between us?"

"I couldn't help what happened in Ital—" She stopped dead in mid-sentence. She didn't want to kick him when he was down, but it just slipped out.

"What happened, Ali?" His voice was even, but his jaw was clenched. He was furious. "Tell me."

Ali felt fear rising from her belly to her throat. "Caleb, please calm down."

"You met someone over there, didn't you? You met some greasy, low-life who fed you a line, and you fell for it." His mouth took on an unpleasant twist. "You cheated on me."

Ali felt icy fingers seep into every pore as she moved her back against the car door and tightened her grip on the steaming cup of coffee. "Do not speak to me like that. No one speaks to me like that." Her jade green eyes held more rage than alarm. "It's obvious that you can't handle this. Please take me home."

"You know, you're right. We are vested, as you say. I've invested a lot of time in you." He turned his head and gazed out into the blackness. His voice was flat. "But now that you've decided to end it, I owe you nothing. Get out." He reached over her lap and roughly opened the car door. "You heard me—get out. Walk!"

Ali sat, dumbfounded. "What? We're in the middle of nowhere?"

Caleb reached over again and violently unlatched her seatbelt, almost slapping her with the buckle. "Out!"

She gasped. Her coffee cup went flying out of her hands and splashed to the ground outside as her hands protected her face from the flying buckle. Ali looked at Caleb in disbelief. Was this really what he was made of? Had he fooled her so easily this past year?

She didn't speak her words; she spat them out as if they were poison. "Don't you ever, ever speak to me again!" Ali scrambled out of the car and backed away, prepared to sprint if need be. Looking around with a wild vengeance for something to throw at him, all she found was the empty coffee cup, so she snatched it up and pitched it violently at him, clipping him in the head.

"Hey—that's assault," he said seriously as he pointed to the coffee cup rolling in a circle on the passenger footrest. While he was distracted, Ali reached into the car and grabbed her satchel from the floor. "You would do this to me? Leave me here?"

"You cheated on me—remember?" he said coldly.

Ali was on the verge of tears but didn't dare give him the satisfaction of seeing her break. "I may have, but that's no excuse for what you're doing!"

"You leave me no choice. I don't want to lose you, but I—"

"I've got news for you—I was never yours to lose! And for your information, he is worth twenty of you, if not more. He is a gentleman, and he is brilliant—and a kind, loving person." She spoke with determination as he started the car. "Don't ever talk to me again. If you see me on the street, cross to the other side —we are through, you sorry excuse for a man!" Angrily, Ali slammed the car door shut.

Sniffing and still in disbelief over Caleb's immature behavior, she began her trek through the darkened field toward the streetlamps. In a final moment of anger, she spun around once more and bellowed at him as he drove off, "You are so lucky you're not in 1512 right now, 'cuz he'd run you through for this!"

As she walked to a safer place, Ali called Kiana to come to get her and kept her phone handy, just in case Caleb decided to make another appearance. Once she was safely back in a neighborhood, she found a bus stop and sat on the bench to wait, not daring to call her father or mother.

As she waited for her friend, she thought of how she almost gave up Claudio for him, wasting time fretting and feeling guilty instead of spending time loving the man who deserved her.

Her need to cry came back with renewed intensity. She didn't fight it. Her tears softened her temper and opened her lungs to the breath of fresh air, freeing her from the guilt that had weighed her down. All she wanted was to move forward.

～

Kiana rescued her from the bus stop with Mina and Jelsy in tow, after which they decided to go back to Kiana's to consume copious amounts of ice cream.

"Jeez, Ki—I didn't want anyone to know," Ali whispered to Kiana as the other two, well-meaning girls swooped down on Ali to console her.

"Why are you stressing about this?" Kiana asked, hands on her hips and eyebrows raised in surprise. "He's the one who should be embarrassed."

"Wow, what an insect," agreed Jelsy. "He had no right to strand you like that. Who knows what could have happened."

"I still can't believe it." Mina shook her head slowly from side to side. "You think you know someone—"

"Look, if my parents find out that he kicked me out of the car in the middle of an abandoned field, they'll freak on him. This stays here, between us. Promise me."

Assurances given, and hearts crossed, Kiana disappeared into the kitchen to gather up as much ice cream and caramel sauce as she could carry.

Much to Ali's surprise, the heart-to-heart chat with her friends did her good. She missed leaning on them for encouragement because she felt she couldn't disclose her reasons for being miserable. She realized, in a roundabout way, that she could still pour out her pain to them—at least partially.

"So, Als, what are you going to do now?" asked Mina between spoonsful of chocolate chocolate-chip ice cream and butterscotch.

"Holy crap, Mina, come up for air." Jelsy gave her a disapproving glance.

"Just focus on school, I guess. I have math, science, and history this semester—an insane combination, but maybe that's a good thing. I've got tons of labs due already and a history paper on the Iraq war I have to work on."

Ali glanced at her friends and smiled as she offered her hands to all of them and squeezed theirs in gratitude. "Thanks so much, you guys, for being here for me. I missed you. I missed this."

"Well, hello! We missed you, too. Don't disappear again, okay?" Jelsy laughed.

"Not a chance of that happening again," she promised. As the conversation turned to other very important topics, like figuring out a destination for spring break, Ali's mind wandered. As she scraped the last of her cookies 'n' cream from the bottom of her dish, her thoughts settled in their usual place; she thought of Claudio and the chamber in Florence and of how Luca had probably already begun taking it apart to dispose of it. Then just as suddenly, with a herculean effort, she pushed them away and smiled back at her friends. She needed to get some distance between her and last summer.

Chapter Seven

As the bus pulled into the school driveway and made its way to the south doors on Monday morning, Ali spotted her friends waiting for her under the overhang. Her rose-colored glasses were off, and she was seeing the world from a wider, harder perspective. She waved to them and got up to disembark.

Not a second after she was clear of the bottom step, they surrounded her like a pride of lionesses around a stray cub.

"Hi guys," Ali smiled at the three of them.

"How are you doing, Ali-girl?" asked Kiana. Mina angled her head to peek around Jelsy.

"Yeah, how're you doing? Why don't you check your phone anymore?" Jelsy echoed, a pouty look on her face. "We were worried about you after what happened Friday."

Mina nodded in agreement.

"I don't even want to think about Friday night." Ali opened the glass door and strode through. "Wasting time thinking on it gives him more power, and there's no way I want to do that." She stopped at her locker. "I just want to focus on school. I need to get started on my history paper today. Anyone for the library tonight?" Ali thought for a moment, then arched her brow. "The university learning commons? My dad has an evening lecture once a week this term—I offered to pick him up after class, so I could have the car. Widener is close." Her voice lilted.

"Sure, if that's an invitation, we'll keep you company, Als." Kiana smiled. "I could use some time in a library myself— English paper."

"Mmm, me too," Jelsy agreed.

"I guess we're all in," chimed Mina.

Harvard's Widener library's main entrance was located on the south side, graced by its cascade of granite steps, and its tall oak doors which were guarded by Corinthian columns. The library dominated the block, and an inner automatic double-sliding door greeted the girls. It opened to the entrance lobby, where the side-by-side passageways led them through the anti-theft security sensors. The Technology Circulation Desk was to the left.

"Let's see," mused Ali. Her finger trailed down the manifest on her phone. "Retrieval services, digital archives, reference, and research, special projects... Ah! Here it is—stack access and stack guides—sections nine to thirteen. Come on."

The quartet headed to the stairs. When they reached the top, they were met with signs pointing left to the stack guides, where they would find the automated digital search service. "Look. This way," said Ali.

"History, Iraq war, causes and timelines," Alice spoke into the receiver, her device aimed at the terminal. In seconds, a red LED light shone, and the book locations were uploaded and at her fingertips. She peered about to orient herself regarding the locations of the corresponding numbers. "Okay,

Mina, you and I are this way." She motioned straight ahead with her device.

"English, Margaret Atwood, The Handmaid's Tale, themes throughout," Kiana requested. "We're three sections over." She held up her device.

"Okay girls, keep in touch." Mina turned and walked, looking at the guide numbers on the tall shelves which lined either side of the main access hall.

"Remember, I have to pick up my dad in an hour," said Ali, her brows raised in warning mode.

"No worries," said Jelsy, with a sarcastic grin. "The topic isn't so interesting that we'll lose all track of time." They disappeared into the stacks, and Alice set off, trailing after Mina.

"So, I think...we are...here." Mina's words punctuated her glances.

Ali stopped behind her. The two drew a dozen or so books from shelves and sought out a table where their finds could be evaluated. Within a half-hour, Ali found that she needed more.

"I'm going back in. You finish those up, okay, Mina?" She walked back into the stacks, checked for titles under the guide numbers, and meandered up and down the rows. Angling her head to read the vertical titles, she found something and pulled four more books that looked promising.

She turned and headed out to the main hall to inform Mina of her find. Ali was surprised at how far she had walked—conveniently, she was standing directly across from the digital server. Slowly, she took a few steps toward it. Clenching her teeth, she deliberated as she shifted her weight from one foot to the other.

Do I dare to read about Claudio in the context of a historical figure—and can I handle the facts I'll unearth in doing so? I'm supposed to be distancing myself from all that. But what became of him? Did he marry, and if so, who? What did he accomplish? And the most melancholy of all, when and how did he die? That will be a hard one.

These questions swirled in her head. Just thinking of what she could discover made the back of her throat tingle. *Do it,* she thought, forcing herself. *Do it while you're here. What are you afraid of anyway?*

Ali approached the terminal. Her mouth set to work, yet she wasn't sure what to ask of the server. "History—" She halted. Bringing her hands to her mouth, she covered her lips, puzzling over what terms to use to encompass all the relevant references that could possibly involve Claudio yet narrow it down enough so as not to bring up every book in the library that had da Vinci mentioned within its pages.

She swallowed her disquiet and spoke softly, satisfied with her decision. "History, Renaissance, Italy, Study of Nature, Leonardo da Vinci, Count Claudio Moro." Her heart raced as the words left her mouth. Not long after her information request, the server's LED blinked.

Her heart leapt, and she gasped—it had found something. She scrambled, searching for her device, dropping the books as she frantically felt her pockets. "Damn," she mumbled. "Damn, damn, damn, it's on the table." Ali dashed to the study area, her adrenalin pumping wildly, as a thousand thoughts raced through her head. Breathless, she screeched to a stop, startling Mina who was beginning to pack up.

"What the hell are you doing?" Mina twisted her body around to see a wild-eyed Alice making a bolt for the table. "Where were you? Look—it's almost time to go. Your dad, remember? Kiana and Jelsy are already downstairs." Mina waved her tech device at her as evidence. "And I still have to check these out." She motioned to the two books she had chosen. "I guess you didn't find anything," she said, as she glanced back at her friend who had returned empty-handed.

Ali looked at her hands—only then did she remember that she had dropped all the books.

The excitement drained from her body like water through a

funnel. Her heart fell into her stomach with the anti-climax of having to leave, knowing that somewhere, here, in these dusty volumes, she could find answers to questions that had plagued her for weeks. "But I-I think I might have found something...something that we can use."

"But your dad—remember? We're going to be late."

Alice grasped her phone and looked back at the machine. "Just let me get this code and then we'll go. Grab your stuff, I'll upload it on the way out."

Tomorrow, Ali thought. *Tomorrow, I'll come back*. She held her device to the server as if it held the secret to the Holy Grail, allowing it to upload the codes, and wondered how she would ever make it through the night and the next day.

Chapter Eight

Alice felt that she might jump out of her skin with anticipation.

Deep in her heart of hearts, she knew if she freed herself to hope and dream, and to let her wild imagination fly unfettered, everything she had tried so desperately to keep bottled up—all the pent-up desire to know, confined, repressed, and stored deep inside her these past weeks—would bluster full throttle into a surge of unbridled emotion.

She wasn't used to thinking impetuously, but she felt herself on the brink. Seeing her father's model of the wormhole was unsettling enough; add to that possibly discovering what became of Claudio...the thoughts in her mind swirled out of control.

The night crawled by mercilessly with Alice repeating the ritual of glancing at her device's clock a thousand times.

11:40. 12:52. 1:19. 1:42. 2:02...

Her mind was a never-ending muddle of questions, suppositions, self-imposed caveats, and admonitions. Finally, guarded approval for 'just this once' seeped into her thoughts.

When she did manage to nod off for a brief time, the vivid

dreams of Claudio at the City gates, the hearing in the Guild room, and Bruno's hateful snarls were enough to violently rouse her awake, panting and soaked with sweat. All this from a tiny LED blinking red.

She was too curious to resist. She would do it.

Alice skipped happily down the stairs, her fingers tapping lightly on the banister as she descended. "Good morning!" she announced, unusually chirpy.

Startled, Barbara and Reno responded in unison, "Good morning, Ali."

"Coffee, sweetheart?" asked Barbara.

"Please. And a croissant with Nutella." Reno glanced at Barbara over his coffee. "You seem to be in a good mood today." His voice held guarded optimism. "It's rather refreshing."

"It certainly is," agreed Barbara, placing a steaming mug within Ali's reach.

"So, I just wanted to let you know I have to go back to Widener today—after school—it's for a history thing." *Technically I'm not lying*, she thought. "Okay? I'm taking the bus. I know the way."

"I can swing by and pick you up when you're done," said Reno. "It's close by."

Ali nodded and smiled broadly as she took a generous bite from her croissant.

The digital wall clock finally blinked 2:45 pm and mercifully, the dismissal bell from her last class sounded. With no small degree of haste, Alice hustled to her locker, grabbed her bags, woolen sweater, and scarf, and disappeared out of the double doors, walking briskly to the bus stop down the block. She had managed to avoid her friends, happily circumventing the inevitable third-degree about where she was going and why wasn't she taking the school bus. She had no patience to field questions when she could not be entirely truthful. Not to mention, someone may want to accompany her, which she absolutely did not want.

Gliding smoothly along, the bus found its stop just in front of the imposing library on Harvard Street. Ali sidestepping through the door ran up the treelined path, leaves crunching under her feet. With phone in hand, she retrieved the bar codes for the books, only then realizing she hadn't even bothered to check the titles. Ali strode quickly through the front doors, through the security turnstile and up the stairs.

She headed to the stacks, on a mission. The list of possible titles on her device was endless. Her lips moved as, under her breath, she recited the first few:

The Civilization of the Renaissance in Italy by Jacob Burckhardt.

Humanism, The Study of Nature and Early Science, Ormond Patterson.

Journal of Medieval and Early Modern Studies: Leonardo da Vinci as an Agent of Historical Change by Elliot Trundle.

Leonardo da Vinci—The True Renaissance Man, Audrey Tonnos.

"There must be at least forty references here," she whispered. "Maybe it was too broad." Ali thought of narrowing down her search parameters, but she didn't dare run the risk of missing a possible mention of Claudio in any of the library texts or periodicals.

"I'd better get started." She feigned annoyance, but she was overjoyed. Anything remotely involving him, in some small way, brought her closer to his spirit, allowing her to cling to his very essence.

She set out to devour the books one by one, however long it took; hours, days, weeks, months, she was determined to find something—anything, regarding Count Claudio Moro.

~

Tired and bleary-eyed, she massaged her eyelids. So far, she had skimmed and scanned six volumes, with no trace of Claudio's name anywhere. Plenty of references to da Vinci: his innovatively advanced designs, his patrons, and his art, but no Claudio.

Her device was signaling. She extended it to read a message from her papa. <Are you ready? I'm leaving now.>

Ali texted back. <Sure—will meet you outside.>

She arose and swiftly ran her fingers along the stacks with her device window open to the references it held. Further on down the aisle, she found and pulled additional books for further perusal at home. *These will do for now.*

Reno pulled up on the street adjacent to the front door as Ali exited the building.

"Did you find what you needed?" he asked.

"I think I'm on the right track," she responded confidently as she buckled up. "Hey, when do you think I can come back to your lab and talk about wormholes and dark matter?"

"Anytime you like." Reno was positively glowing at his daughter's interest in temporal physics. "The door is always open to you."

"Tomorrow?"

"Why not."

Chapter Nine

Christmas was on the horizon, and holiday decorations had sprung up all over the city like weeds in a garden. Mild anticipation for the holidays took over the usual frenzy of school and Ali's continued library investigations that might uncover anything about Claudio.

Ali noted Bruno's and Clarice's names pop up a few times when she queried general searches involving Renaissance advancements and the Medici family. Each time she saw them, she shuddered her disgust. Once, her heart almost stopped beating when she read an entry regarding another pupil of da Vinci's, Francesco. According to the source, Francesco was one of Leonardo's favorite students. He traveled with the old master to France and remained there with him until his death in 1519, but there was nothing about Claudio.

How could there be an entry for Francesco and not Claudio?

Just the same, Ali resolved to keep looking—she reckoned that if she gave up, there would be no forgiving herself if she overlooked even the smallest detail.

Every Monday, Alice was permitted to use Reno's car for

school, provided she picked him up after his night class. While she waited for her father, she visited the university library, and sometimes city libraries, for schoolwork assignments—once done, she habitually scoured the history sections for any books or periodicals that had anything to do with Leonardo. Her search usually resulted in a few extra books in her backpack and some additional pages of reading on her tech device. The mention of Francesco gave her renewed hope.

Ali's visits to her father's lab also became a weekly event. Wednesdays, Alice took the city bus into the city after school and would meet Reno, usually with dinner in hand, as Barbara had a lecture that night. Ali and her father would eat at his desk while one of his 3-D models floated above them, providing a view of a galaxy or satellites flying over the earth in time-lapse photography, displaying the brilliant spectacle of the Northern Lights dancing overhead.

"So, what did you learn in school today, my darling?" He asked the same question every day.

"Nothing special," she replied. "How about you? Did you learn anything today?" Expecting his usual answer, Ali was paying more attention to her dinner than her father.

"Actually," he paused to chew his salad, "today, some colleagues of mine learned something significant." He smiled with a twinkle in his eye and took a swig from his bottled water. "No, I'm going to say discovered—that's a better word."

Ali angled her head between bites and waited. "Let's hear it."

"Mmm...today, my team received data of results regarding some important experiments we've been conducting from two different sites—that, in itself, is promising. You may find this interesting since you had asked me about the possibility of harvesting the power of a lightning bolt."

Ali stopped chewing and looked up.

Reno continued. "My associates found that the ability to

recreate the power of lightning may well be a possibility by using very powerful precision lasers. And I'm not talking mimic on a small scale, I mean a real lightning bolt. These lasers could heat and ionize the air much like a lightning strike, except we can control the lasers—unlike a bolt of lightning."

Alice blinked at her father. "Do you mean that you can harness a lightning strike?"

"Not yet, but if they are able to replicate it, study it in a controlled setting, they may be able to study how to harness a lightning bolt."

Ali smiled at this. She knew someone who had already done that—da Vinci. "Can you imagine the energy at our disposal? Do you know that a lightning bolt's energy has the ability to heat its surrounding air temperature greater than that on the surface of the sun?"

Ali nodded with raised brows. "Pretty powerful." She thought for a moment as she wiped her mouth. "Papa, do you think that a bolt of lightning could...um, I mean, if you could trap it somehow, and knowing that it has such great and intense power that when its energy collapses into itself, it could somehow create a—let's say a black hole or wormhole on the earth? And suppose the wormhole creates a time portal between two time strands? Let's say our time and five hundred years in the future—and on one end of the wormhole, time passed much slower than at the other end. What do you think would cause that?"

Reno blinked, his expression surprised. "Alice, that is a highly sophisticated theory. Where did you hear this?" Her father studied her seriously, his lips pursed. "Have you been poking around in my tech devices?"

"No, why? I'm not three, Papa." Ali's expression was innocent, but inside she felt like kicking herself. *Tone down the enthusiasm.*

"How could you possibly know about something so advanced, so unusual?"

Ali licked her lips. *Think. Where. Where could I...* "I went to the movies last week with my friends. The new Star Trek movie. That was one of the things in the movie." She made herself busy by gathering up the remains of their dinner and putting the containers and other accoutrements back in the bag for disposal.

"Oh, I'm impressed." Reno smiled and handed her his empty container. "In truth, my team is working on a theory that is strangely similar to the scenario you just described—minus the time portal existing on Earth that is—which is highly unlikely. But, yes, there are a few theories kicking around about why the difference in the passing of time may exist."

Ali stopped fussing with the plates and looked intently at her father, ready to receive the information.

"We've created a term for it—The Digression Paradox." Reno smiled proudly. "We know that when molecules and particles are exposed to energy, they become hot, so they move faster. Alternatively, they slow down when they are cooled. That is just basic physics. Time speeding in progression the further one ventures into a wormhole reflects that basic principle. Think of it as time twisting in space. The originating event thrusts itself out into space-time with so much energy that it creates a cone. The larger end of the cone is at the origin, and the smaller end at the other." Reno took the last gulp from his water bottle and tossed it into a recycle bin in the corner of his office.

Alice nodded as she tried to contain her excitement. When she had looked inside the chamber, it had been like looking into a giant black funnel that went into infinity. Was her father describing the phenomenon at the monastery?

"Why did—er—why would this happen? And how can it be

corrected so that the progression of time is equal?" Her tone bore more than the usual level of excitement.

Reno smiled with a corner of his mouth and arched a brow. "You do realize, sweetheart, that these are just theories."

"Ha! Sure, I do. This is just conversation, Papa."

"Well, we think we know why it happens. Picture a funnel—a giant one, massive. Now, stand at the top of the funnel at its widest end, and toss a ball down its side. Watch as it slowly winds around the top portion—the widest part—and then starts making its way down. As it goes further down, it starts to travel faster and faster on the sides of the funnel until, finally, at the bottom, it is spiraling around the funnel at its fastest. Time at the origin of the event is the ball at the widest end of the funnel. Time moving faster is the bottom portion. That is the Digression Theory."

"Of course," Ali whispered. She saw everything clearly. She knew exactly at that moment, that her father was right. "But, Papa, how can we correct it?" Ali gulped.

Reno burst out laughing. "It is absolutely gratifying to hear you so interested in astrophysics and quantum mechanics, and I wish I knew how to correct a telescoping wormhole, but... that I don't know." Reno reached for his coat and scarf from the coat hook. "Come on, Ali—your mother is probably on her way home by now. It's late." He picked up the take-out bag and tossed it in the garbage. "The cleaners need to get in here, and they won't come in if we're here."

Ali pushed herself to a standing position. "Sure, but..." She bustled around him like a puppy as he busily donned his coat and gathered his devices to go home. "Do you have a theory—even a guess as to how to stop this digression thing?"

"A very basic one, but we'll never know if it will work because we don't have a wormhole handy to try it on." He chortled at his joke as Ali weakly laughed along. "Let's go."

Chapter Ten

"Come on Ali, it's Friday night," begged Kiana. "There's a party at one of the frat houses. Jelsy's cousin is a pledge there—it'll be fun. We're all going." Her face and voice strained to convince her friend to attend the traditional celebratory end of MIT's first term.

Ali jostled her extended phone on her lap, trying to think of an excuse to back out. Sleep had eluded her the past two nights, though she had promised herself that she wouldn't dwell on the information her father had shared with her over dinner on Wednesday.

Surrendering, she had pulled off her covers and padded softly to her backpack to grab one of the sixteenth-century history books she had borrowed from the city library. As she searched the pages for information, the faintest hope of making any discoveries about Claudio's fate was slipping away with every page she flipped. If there was nothing here, where could she search next? She had exhausted all the possibilities from her own school library, the university libraries, and all the city libraries.

"Um, I don't know, Ki," Ali stalled, a glum expression in her eyes. "I didn't get a lot of sleep last night. And I wanted to get a head start on my history paper."

"On a Friday night?" Kiana grimaced.

"Yes, on a Friday night." Ali shrugged impatiently. "What am I going to do at a frat party, anyway? There's just going to be drunk, loud kegger-huggers there, on the verge of tossing up their dinners because they've had about ten too many."

"You're turning into an old woman as we speak. Come on! Last month, your excuse was that you were too busy working on your college applications. We've got two weeks, and it'll be Christmas break—it's done!"

"No, I just don't find partying enjoyable anymore."

"You never found that kind of thing enjoyable."

"So why do you keep asking me?"

Kiana took a deep breath, exasperated. "Because you're my best friend, and I hate to see you wasting away, pining for Fabio—"

"Claudio."

"Whatever. Pining away for Claudio for the rest of your life. Wait. I'm getting another call from Jelsy. Putting her on split screen with me."

Jelsy's image phased into view alongside Kiana's on Ali's device.

"Hi, my girls," Jelsy said, smiling sweetly. "Okay, what are you guys wearing tonight?"

Ali started, "Hi, Jels. You know, I don't think I—"

"She says she doesn't want to go." Kiana was too fast for her.

"Why not?"

Kiana responded by shrugging and rolling her eyes.

Jelsy clicked her tongue, *tsk*. "Again, with the Claudio thing?"

"Ki, I asked you—"

"Really, Ali?" Jelsy said, her eyebrows shooting up in disapproval. "You couldn't tell me yourself about this amazing guy you met, and now you give it to Ki for telling me?"

"I'm not giving it to Ki—she promised to keep it quiet."

"And you believed her?" She snorted. "Just never mind that. I'm picking up Mina and big mouth over here at nine, then we're coming to get you."

"But—"

"No buts. Convo over. Done. That's it. Nine o'clock. Be ready." Jelsy nodded to Kiana, after which her hand swept over the screen, and she phased out.

"Well," said Kiana, spreading her hands innocently and shrugging. "I guess that's that."

Alice's shoulders sank, knowing it was pointless to argue any further.

Rummaging in her closet, she finally settled on a black scarf to top her off-the-shoulder gray sweater, a nice touch with her honey-brown hair, which as much as she tried, was still untameable, so she opted for a loose ponytail.

Nine-fifteen and still no Jelsy, mused Alice. She grabbed her satchel, swung it over her shoulder, and plodded downstairs to wait by the door, thinking they couldn't possibly be much longer. Once there, she tossed her purse on the couch and began digging around in the closet for an appropriate pair of boots.

"Oh, hi sweetheart." Reno poked his head out from the kitchen, a slice of pizza in his hand. "You want some?" He held it up.

"Too late at night for that, Papa. Thanks, anyway."

"Feeling confident about Harvard? The application and all?"

"I don't even want to think about it—I'll end up jinxing myself if I do."

Reno chuckled. "You look nice. Where are you off to?" he asked vaguely, walking back to the kitchen table, which was covered in papers and tablets.

"Out with my friends," she said cryptically. She was sure her father wouldn't approve of her attending a kegger tonight. "Wow—looks like your office exploded in the kitchen." She set her satchel down on the counter, and took out a lip gloss, using her phone as a mirror. "What are you and Mamma doing?"

"Mamma is at a faculty social tonight for Christmas. I'm going to catch up on some work." He pointed to the mess on the table. "Where are you going with your friends?"

"Uh...visiting Jelsy's cousin."

"That's it?"

"Yeah." *Technically, not a lie.* Wanting to change the subject, Ali asked, "So, have you found out anything else about our 'little project?'" She kept it light, not expecting much of an answer.

He chomped back the last of his double cheese and veggie, then wiped his mouth. "I guess you could say that." His expression bordered on the mysterious.

"Hmm...like what?" Reno's tone piqued her interest, distracting her from the berry lip gloss she had been applying.

"Well, darling, to be truthful—this thing has turned a corner." Gathering up what was left of the pizza, he placed the box on the counter near the sink. "Information Security has classified this experiment as confidential, and that means any of the data elements collected cannot be shared. Not even with my lovely daughter. Sorry, Alice."

Bee-de-bee-de-beep Ali's device chimed.

"Sounds like your friends are here," Reno said, leaning against the counter and motioning the phone still in her hand.

∼

There was a definite bounce in Ali's step when she sauntered out to the car after her friends signaled their arrival; she could tell it wasn't lost on Kiana, Jelsy, and Mina. She was smiling and wearing lip gloss—Ali knew there would be comments.

"Hey there, Als. Look at you, girl—all smiling and everything." Jelsy giggled, her creamy white face sticking out of the car window.

"You look so nice." Mina smiled and leaned over to get a better look at her from the passenger seat.

"Mmm…" agreed Kiana, "but your hair is still a disaster."

Ali laughed softly and rolled her eyes at her very best friend. "Oh, my God, Ki. Stop, you're so mean."

"Yeah, be quiet." Mina laughed as she re-focused and scrolled through her feeds. "She might turn around, run back in, and hide in her books again."

"Go ahead," Ali grimaced as she entered the car. "Laugh all you want—but I will do awesome on my essay, and I plan on acing all my exams. These marks count the most, you know."

Kiana waved her hand in Ali's face. "I don't want to hear about school tonight, okay? Let's just have some fun."

"You know what, Ki? You're absolutely right." Alice felt better than she had in weeks. It felt good not to be brooding for a change. "Thanks for being so patient with me these past few months—I know I haven't exactly been the life of the party and…I really do love you guys."

The three girls let out a loud, "Aw!" in unison.

"Ali, that's what friends do," Jelsy cooed in a silken tone.

"Yeah, no matter what. We stick together," Mina chimed in.

Kiana stuck her hand up again. "All right, enough. All this sweet stuff is giving me a toothache."

Jelsy was just about to slip the car out of 'park' when Ali yelped out, "Oh snap! Wait!"

"Now what?" asked Jelsy, pulling back on the transmission.

"I forgot my purse," Ali grabbed the door handle and before

anyone could protest, she was halfway up the walk to the door. "Two seconds, I promise!"

Ali tore into the house and checked the couch for her satchel. "What the hell? Where did I..." Then she remembered she had it in the kitchen when she was talking to her father. "Oh, hey Papa, I...oh...Papa? Where are you?"

"Alice?" Reno's disembodied voice floated down to her. "I'm just upstairs. What did you forget?"

"I just came back in for my...oh, there it is." Her satchel was sitting right where she left it, on the kitchen counter. She grabbed her purse and turned to leave. "'kay—now I'm really going. Bye."

"'Bye sweetheart, be careful."

Ali was nearly out of the kitchen when her eyes swept over her to father's tablet...and she had a horrible thought.

'This thing has turned a corner.'

What does that even mean?

'Information security?'

There was a low conversation happening upstairs. Reno was talking to someone. His tablet was right there, and he had left it unlocked. She craned her head to glance at it, then stopped, pausing to listen for her father's steps. The horrible thought in Ali's head became a strong urge.

He left his email open. You know this is going to drive you insane if you don't peak. He's probably on a call up there. This is just too tempting.

Gingerly, she stepped in front of the tablet. It was opened to his email—his encrypted account. She bit her lip as her eyes scanned the text.

<Hello Reno—sorry to bother you on your weekend but Switzerland has been trying to get you on your phone for a conference call—the Washington and Geneva groups are anxious to talk—can you get to your phone? seems lightning has struck twice...>

"Alice!"

"Ahh!" Her father's stern tone made her spin around, startled. "Oh my God Papa—you scared the living—"

"What are you doing?" His eyes darted to his tablet, which he scooped up and held against his chest. "These are confidential sweetheart."

Ali grimaced and sputtered. "Pfft! I—I came back to get my purse." She held it out for him to see.

"I have to get back upstairs—I'm on a conference call. I just came back down to get some specs." He began gathering up some loose papers, and another tablet—this one significantly larger. "Not too late now," trailed behind him as he took the stairs two at a time.

Alice wanted to press him, but as she opened her mouth to pose a question, two distinct blasts of a car horn reminded her that her friends were waiting outside.

Chapter Eleven

The parking situation on the street was a nightmare. Because of the party, they had to park blocks away and hike to the frat house with the freezing cold winds nipping at their ears.

"Nice going, Als," grumbled Kiana. "If you hadn't taken forever to get your dumb little purse, we may have been able to park in the same city."

Jelsy's cousin, Kevin was at the door with a beer in his hand monitoring the guests—Jelsy had confided to the girls that the house had been busted in the past, and he had to be extremely careful not to let things get out of hand.

"Hey, Jels." Kevin smiled, giving Jelsy a hug.

"Hi cuz," she replied, hugging back. "Looks like the place is rockin'."

"Hi, ladies." Kevin nodded his acknowledgment to the other three girls. "Yeah, it's pumping. Everybody's winding down—end of semester." His face took on a stern expression. "Hey, remember what I told you," he wagged a finger at them. "No drinking. You guys are underage."

"Sure, no worries, Kevin."

They all nodded their compliance and walked into the zoo-like atmosphere.

Ali crinkled her forehead and leaned into Kiana, yelling to be heard over the thunderous baseline. "If he's worried about us being underage, why would he even let us in?"

Kiana raised a brow. "Ali, you think too much. Let's mingle!"

Dozens of people were packed into the common rooms, gathered in groups of four or five conversing raucously while beer pong happened in the basement. Ali stuck to a corner with a Coke in her hand, watching her friends socialize. Some of the boys—or rather, men—were Claudio's age, and she wondered if any of them could manage to accomplish one-third of what he had in his teen years alone.

"Hi!"

"Ah!" Ali jumped out of her daydream, almost spilling her Coke all over her sweater. She spun around—it was Jelsy's cousin, Kevin.

"God. You almost gave me a heart attack." She placed a hand over her chest.

"You look like you're a little lost, so I thought I'd check in," he said, his brows furrowed. "I don't think Jelsy told me your name."

"Ali—Alice Ferro."

"Your last name is Ferro?" He shifted his weight and took another sip of his beer, never taking his eyes off her.

"Yeah."

"Are you related to Professor Ferro?" His finger pointed at her as his eyes narrowed while his mind put it all together.

"He's my dad."

"No freakin' way!" Kevin's voice shouted above the din in the room. "Like, he's my freakin' hero."

Ali arched her brows. "Wow, what a coincidence." Ali half-smiled and tried stealthily sliding away from him.

"Hey, your dad is a very cool professor. Brilliant. His

research is impeccable, almost ingenious. He teaches one of my fourth-year classes." Kevin's demeanor changed and appeared to take on a serious air when he spoke of his studies.

"Thanks. Yeah, I guess he is pretty talented."

"Yeah, talented. Like a virtuoso of astrophysics." Kevin chortled heartily over his joke.

"So... you're in astrophysics?" Ali asked with a grimace.

"Yeah, I am. Hey, you know your dad is like working on some awesomely unreal stuff. Like, I went to his office last week to get an extension on my lab assignment, and there were like these weird dudes in his office. And after when they left, he let me in, and he looked like really happy but like, flustered." Kevin took another gulp of his beer, draining it down to the last drop.

"So, did he say why?" Ali's eyes were wide.

"No." He burped loudly. "Excuse me—no. Like I just said, I'm glad I caught you in a good mood professor because I need to ask for an extension on my term paper. He just said something about it being a *really* good day and that something turned a corner. And then he gave me an extension."

"Oh," Ali pursed her lips and baited. "Does my father ever mention anything about his work, like science work that he does—to you guys—in class, I mean."

"Uh, no." Kevin had a starry-eyed quality about him that made Ali want to laugh. "But talking to him one-on-one was so cool—cryptic, but cool."

Ali's thoughts echoed Kevin's—cryptic was right. The 'turning a corner' thing intrigued her. Papa said the exact same thing to her earlier that evening, right before his strange behavior with the tablet. The email she spied must have been referring to the lightning experiment. But what did that have to do with Washington and Geneva?

"Hey, Als. Sorry to break this up, but we gotta go. Jelsy needs to get the car home." Mina's tone was flat as she scrolled through her messages. She looked up and noticed Kevin. "Hi. Nice party, Cousin Kevin—see ya."

"Nice talking to you, Kevin." Ali smiled, then looked beyond him to Mina. "I am definitely ready to go."

While the girls ruminated over the evening on the drive home, Ali thought a little more of what Kevin had said. It was a major discovery, that for certain she had figured out—some connection to the laser and lightning experiments, but what did that have to do with Geneva? She resolved to delve further, but between chatting, laughing, and finally enjoying herself on the way home with her friends, the topic was relegated to an out of the way spot in back of her mind.

Chapter Twelve

Alice turned onto the Widener Library building parking ramp, grabbed her mother's faculty card from the cup holder, and inserted it into the ticket machine. The barrier arm lifted, and she drove through. Only one last week of scheduled tedium to endure before the Christmas Break.

As she walked to the library entrance, she breathed in deeply, filling her lungs with the crisp clean night air. Snow was on the way—she could smell it. The trees had nothing left now but drooping gray branches and soon another winter would sweep over Boston—all the warmth of the summer long gone.

She slogged up the steps, through the heavy oaken doors, and beyond the security checkpoint. The curvy stairs to her right brought her to the familiar humanities wing in the vast library. Ali casually tossed her things in one of the few available study carrels and pulled out her tech device.

Her last history paper this semester was on the effects of twentieth-century technology on the economy of North America. Not one of her favorite things to research, but she had to come to terms with the reality that she couldn't focus all her time and energy on her father's temporal physics lab.

Ali figured, all things considered, that she was doing relatively well, and had settled back into a routine after her bout with a broken heart. She knew that she had done the right and noble thing for everyone involved. Staying in 1512 with Claudio would have had terrible repercussions, not only in terms of the timeline but for her life here as well, especially her life here. Her family and friends were here.

It was time to let go.

Keeping her mind busy was what got her through the day—most days. Of course, sometimes, that was easier said than done. Some days, everything reminded her of him.

Her finger ran down the references on her device, and she found a good place to start—the automobile—she smiled as she thought of how Leonardo had sketched images of that long ago.

She chose a few e-books and searched the stacks for some print editions. Once satisfied, she sat and began pouring over the books for information on her topic, but she was distracted. Her eyes began to wander around, peering at the other students. Next September, she mused, she may be here as a first-year student, just like them.

Or somewhere else. Regardless, she needed to focus on good grades in her last high school year.

Damn, she thought, *I forgot to get articles.*

Ali rose and stepped to the sign indicating the periodical section. She strode to the stairs and up to the proper section in the mammoth library, counting out the steps like she did when she was a little girl: one, two, three, four...

She crossed the unusually quiet foyer and veered left, walking by a series of darkened conference rooms and habitually peeking into each one as she went by. The doors were closed, but she could see through the windows that each room contained some very old books. In fact, there were some that were displayed on pedestals—those books looked positively ancient. She came to the second-last room, and the light was on. Inside, a lady wearing white cloth gloves was bent over a very old leather-bound book.

The lady must have sensed someone staring because she looked up from her intense study of the volume. She smiled, and Ali smiled back.

The woman walked over to the door. "Can I help you?"

"Oh, no. I was just admiring the book." Ali pointed to the manuscript on the table. "It looks ancient."

"It is, by our standards—seventeenth century."

"Wow," marveled Ali. "That's old."

"Did you need something from the rare book section?" She raised an inquiring brow.

"Are you a librarian?"

"I am, but not from here. I'm from New York on a rare book exchange program." She looked very pleased with this last statement.

"How very interesting," said Ali, biting her lip. "Do you just have books from the seventeenth century or do some date further back?"

"Oh yes, we have a few dating back to the fourteenth century. We have journals, city records, poetry books—some from figures in history you would probably recognize." She gave Ali a perfunctory smile. "Well, I'd best be getting back."

"Uh, wait!" Ali's 'wait' was much louder than she had intended it to be. "Do you have anything from early sixteenth-century Florence? It's kind of a hobby of mine...Renaissance Florence." Ali was secretly praying, all the while ignoring her promise to herself. This might be her last chance to have the questions answered about Claudio that had been awash in her mind for months.

"We do have something. I think..."

"You do!" Ali's heart jolted. "Please, may I look at it?"

Her expression revealed mild astonishment at Ali's enthusiasm. "I could help you look at it. I couldn't let you handle it, but I can hold it for you and flip the pages."

Ali's stomach tightened. "Oh yes, please."

"I think it's in the next room." She slipped out of the small space and closed and locked the door behind her with Ali trailing close behind. Once inside the adjacent conference room, the librarian reached for a book on one of the pedestals. It was small, bound in brown leather with gold gilded lettering, and somewhat tattered.

"This collection of letters was composed by an early sixteenth-century courtier who had associations in Florence for a time. He was a prominent figure, a diplomat, courtier, and author. Back then, the Medici—I'm sure you've heard of—"

"Was his name Claudio Moro?" Alice almost pounced on the book, which prompted the librarian to take a step back.

"No, I don't believe so. I think his name was Baldassare Castiglione. But the author of the letters does make some references to other courtiers in his correspondence." The librarian's device signaled. She set the book down and removed her gloves. "Hello?"

Alice's mind raced, and her heart hammered against her chest. Could this be it? This inadvertent detour to the second floor? Had this diversion brought her to an answer about Claudio's history?

Ali gestured to the librarian. "Can I look at the book?" She mouthed the words as the woman was still on the phone.

"No—wait! No, not you—there's a girl here who...can I call you back? Thanks." She contracted her device, looking a little annoyed. "I'm sorry, but I cannot let you handle it."

"Can you please hold it for me, then? Please, this is very important." Ali clasped her hands together.

The librarian deliberated. "I suppose I could, but you mustn't touch it."

"Oh, I promise I won't." Ali nodded excitedly.

The lady put on her gloves again, and they began. Page by page, Ali quickly perused each piece of scratchy correspondence. Some of Castiglione's letters were lengthy, others short, but all in the same calligraphy and written in an old Italian vernacular.

"Wow, this guy was all over the place...Milan, Rome, Spain... here's Florence." Ali checked every line carefully, searching for Claudio's name as the librarian turned the pages.

"What did you say the name was? The name of the person you mentioned earlier?" Her gloved hand held onto the thin paper very gently as she flipped it over.

"Count Claudio Moro," Ali said proudly.

"I think I see a reference to just that person, a brief one, but..."

Alice couldn't resist. She touched the book, her heart pounding so wildly she thought it would burst.

"Please, I will hold the page for you." The librarian protectively grasped up the little book.

"Of course, I am so sorry." Ali breathed deeply and managed to compose herself. It took everything she had not to rip the book from the lady's hands and run with it. "May I see the reference, please?" With full focus, she managed to understand most of it, as some of the language was difficult. Slowly, she read each word, carefully translating the meaning. But as she read the letter, Ali felt her soul chill with grief and her expression go from the flushed heat of excitement to cold desolation.

She backed away from the book, her breathing shallow, and her vision blurred. This could not be. Of all the endless possibilities, this could not be the one. All her sacrifices and his gallant return had been for nothing.

"Are you all right?" asked the librarian, her mild annoyance now turning to concern.

"No." Ali's tone was flat, robotic. Her eyes didn't stray from the yellowed parchment in the old book. "Can I get a picture of that with my phone?"

"I suppose." The librarian held the manuscript while Alice, her hands trembling, recorded the image on her device.

In seconds, Ali had the page securely stored. For good measure, she took a picture of the cover and inside title page, then left the library conference room without a word to the woman who still held the book.

The librarian, sporting a quizzical look, quietly closed the door to the conference room, flipped the lock, and continued her preparations for the rare book exchange program as Ali walked away.

In a daze, she walked back down the stairs, through the foyer to her study carrel, and sat down hard, causing people to turn to see if she had fallen. Ali looked down at her phone screen and extended Baldassare Castiglione's letter to Giuliano de Medici. After activating the translate option, she reread the letter in English three times, just to be sure.

Oh no, God please, no. Am I too late? Will I get there in time?

Ali stood and shoved her books into her backpack. She stuffed an arm into her coat sleeve and ran to the marble stairs, hardly breathing as she sprinted out the front doors and into the night air, not for one moment stopping to catch her breath, and dashed to her car.

In the car and out of earshot, Ali's instincts kicked in. The first person she thought to call was Luca—she still had his number on her device. It signaled on the other end for what seemed like centuries. Finally, she heard a click followed by muffled shuffling sounds.

"Luca? Luca, this is Ali!" The urgency in her voice increased with each syllable.

"Ali? What's wrong?" He sounded groggy.

"Did you and Father Donato start disassembling the chamber yet?"

"Ali, it's three in the morning here."

"I'm sorry, but this is really important. The chamber, did you start taking it apart?"

"We started, but there were several complications. The aperture into the sixteenth century has to be neutralized before we can—"

"Don't do anything to that chamber!" Ali shouted. "Leave it alone. I repeat—do not neutralize the aperture. I read something tonight about Claudio...in a history book."

"What did you find out?" Luca's tone had changed.

"I'll explain later. Right now, I-I have to get there, somehow. I have to think of something. Anyway—don't do anything else to that thing, please! I'm coming back. I have to go back in."

Chapter Thirteen

Alice sat in the car, staring at the steering wheel, unaware of the passage of time, but she was pulled back to reality when her device signaled. Her father was ready and waiting for her to pick him up at one of the MIT lecture halls.

Her hands had steadied a little, and she hoped she would be okay to drive, though she still wasn't certain of her frame of mind. Castiglione's letter explained everything: why there was no reference to Claudio Moro or his association with da Vinci or his success as a noble in the Medici banks, even though he'd had incredible potential to outshine any Renaissance figure of his age.

Claudio died shortly after she came back from their hearing. Not only had he died—he was murdered. Her beloved Claudio had suffered a violent death. Unfortunately, there were no details in the letter as to why or how or who had killed him.

Ali was beyond tears—beyond emotion. All she could think of was how stupid she had been. Was there no way to have researched this before making their decision to go their separate ways and return to their former lives?

What a waste, she thought. *What a complete and utter waste. If I had known, he could have just stayed here. He dies anyway in 1512.* His life ended before he had a chance to do anything else. He might as well have stayed in the present and lived his life in 2029.

Ali knew that her first instinct to call Luca was right—the wormhole could not be destroyed. Claudio had to cross back before he was killed. She needed to get word to him. But how? How could she send a message back five hundred years? Sending a letter into the future was easy—it was just a matter of time, Leonardo had proven that—but back?

Beep-de-beep-de-beep-beep.

It was her father again. <Hey, where are you?>

"Crap! I forgot about Papa." She looked at her hands—they were steadier. Ali started the ignition and gripped the steering wheel. But before she put the car into drive, she opened the window wide and breathed deep.

Looking up at the cloudless night sky, with the moon full and high in the heavens, Ali knew there was no other way. She had to go back to Italy and figure out how to get Claudio back before he was killed. Exactly how she was going to convince her parents to let her go and how she would do it, were unknown variables.

∾

"Hi, Papa." Ali tried her best to sound normal, despite the turmoil happening within.

"Hi sweetheart. Hey, what took you so—"

"Do you mind driving, Papa—I'm really kind of shaky." Her belt was undone, and she was out of the car before he could answer, walking around to the passenger side.

Reno halted in mid-step and rerouted to the driver's side.

"Of course." He placed his things on the back seats and

climbed in. As he buckled up, he glanced at Ali. "What's the matter—are you sick?"

"No, just...uhm...just really upset. I got some really bad news." Totally on the fly, she seized the opportunity. What did she have to lose?

"Really? I'm sorry. What is it?" he asked with concern in his voice.

"A very good friend of mine—in Italy—he's not well."

"Oh, that's too bad. What's wrong?"

"I'm not sure, but he's not going to live very long. It's actually someone that I care about—a lot."

Reno's eyes held empathy. Ali hated herself for not being entirely truthful, but she had run out of choices.

"Is this that boy your mother told me about? Claudio?"

Ali nodded. Just hearing her father speak his name pushed a button inside her, releasing a dam of pent-up emotion that gushed forth with a loud, rasping sob.

Taken aback by Ali's reaction, Reno reached out and took his daughter's hand in his, squeezing it tightly. "Alice, darling, come now, don't cry."

Ali covered her face with her free hand and let herself cry as Reno held on clumsily.

"Alice, let's go home and talk to Mamma about this."

She was inconsolable.

He gently let go and drove, soon pulling into their driveway. There had been a dusting of snowfall in the suburbs, and the asphalt was covered in a fluffy white topping.

Ali looked over at him as he pulled up on the emergency brake. "I'm sorry about all this," she said after regaining some control, but her eyes were red and puffy.

"Are you a little better now?" asked Reno.

"Yeah. A little." Ali hiccupped in response as she dabbed a used-up, wilted tissue at her eyes.

"So then, let's go inside. Mamma's home—she's better at

these things than I am." He looked relieved to be getting out of the car.

As she pushed open the passenger door, Ali took a deep breath to steady her hiccups, gratefully taking in the cold to cool the flush she felt inside. She grabbed her stuff and followed Reno through the side door, dropping her backpack and coat in the mud room.

"Barbara?" Reno called out as he watched his daughter walk like a zombie into the living room and flop onto the couch. "Barbara!" He yelled out louder.

A muffled, "Yes," was heard, and soon Ali could discern Barbara's footsteps descending the stairs.

"Why are you shouting?" she asked, breathless. "I was just upstairs changing and I—Alice, what is it?" Her eyes shifted from her daughter to her husband. "Did you two have a fight?"

Reno shook his head. "No, it's not that at all," he replied. "Alice has learned some devastating news. A friend of hers in Italy has become very ill. The young man you told me about— from last summer." Reno furrowed his brow. "You know the one."

Barbara *tsk*ed. "Oh dear, that's too bad. Well, maybe you can call him and wish him well." Barbara moved to Ali's side and sat beside her, draping an arm around her shoulder.

"It's more serious than that, Mamma. He's going to die." Ali's lips trembled as fresh tears spilled over onto her cheeks. She sniffed, closed her eyes, and pinched the bridge of her nose, hoping to stop a new round of sobbing. "I'm not sure what to do. I want to go, I really do, but I know you guys won't like it. I'm almost afraid to ask."

At this Reno, waved his hands in the air. Motioning to Barbara, he shook his head and mouthed 'No!'

Barbara peered at him with confusion and shrugged.

"Well, sweetheart, this is so sudden. How did you find out?" Barbara asked.

Lying was loathsome—but through her tears and pain, Ali had to think of a way.

"I found out at the library tonight. I spoke to Luca, Dario and Anna's son." Neither were untrue, she tried to justify.

"Leda and Roberto's friends, yes. Oh, dear. What to do?" Barbara bit her lip and shifted her gaze to Reno. He rolled his eyes and crossed his arms over his chest—clearly, he was about to be voted down.

"Alice, I feel for this kid, but aren't you in the middle of an important assignment—are you going to leave school and fly over there? You were just there, for God's sake. And when you get there, who will look after you?"

If only he knew how independent I can be, Ali thought.

"It is a bad time, Papa's right. But then again, if it's that serious—I could call Leda and Roberto—give them advanced warning and ask them to help," Barbara offered.

"And her assignment?" Reno sputtered. "School comes first."

"I promise I'll finish my history paper by tomorrow night. I have all the sources and references. And I won't be gone long. Just over the Christmas holidays, I swear. I'll be back as soon as I can—before school starts up again, for sure."

"But what about Christmas?" he asked, shrugging, his hands raised in a last effort to sway the women.

"Oh, darling, I don't think Ali would be very merry here. I can see that this is very important to her. Besides, the odds are that in a few months she will be off on her own at university. We may need to start giving her some credit that she can take care of herself."

Her mom's words were logical and said with grace and love —and Ali loved her for it. Barbara was in her corner on this one, and it made her take heart, so she could be strong.

"Oh, Mamma. Thank you." Ali hugged her mother tight, in true gratitude. Barbara always supported her when she needed it the most. The maelstrom in her mind was a little easier to bear.

"I don't know. It just doesn't feel right." Reno scratched his head and sat across from his wife and daughter, clearly unconvinced. "I want to go with you, Ali, but work is so critical now. Barbara, why don't you go with her?"

"I could, but I really don't think she needs me there."

Alice marveled at her Mamma.

"She will be eighteen in less than two months. I have faith that she knows what she's doing. But I will call Leda," then to Ali. "You can stay with them."

Chapter Fourteen

"Luca, it's Alice." It was three in the morning in Boston—9:00 a.m. in Italy.

"Alice, thank God you called. I just talked to my mother and father, and they are beside themselves. They don't know what to do. Talk to me—tell me what you know about Claudio." Luca was breathless.

"Your poor parents. I'm so sorry, but I had to call you right away to find out if the chamber was intact, then I had to pick up my dad and, well, look all I know is what was written in an old journal. I found it in a library here, in Boston. It's a book of letters written by some guy named Baldassare Castiglione. He was a high-level courtier or advisor or something for Duke Giuliano. In a letter he wrote to the duke, he told him that..." Ali had to stop. She cringed, nearly unable to get the words out. "That Claudio had been killed."

Silence prevailed on the line connecting Ali to Claudio's good friend, nearly four thousand miles away.

"No." Luca finally broke the silence. "No, that can't be. It must be someone else."

"I wish it were someone else, Luca." Ali let out a rattled

sigh. "But I read it with my own eyes. He referred to Count Claudio Moro. Here, wait." She extended her device to produce the saved document. "I have it here in my phone. I'll send it to you." Ali scrolled through the documents, chose the text, and sent it to Luca.

"Hold on, I have it... 'several of the most chivalrous of courtiers have passed to their demise, as in the person of acquaintance, Count Claudio Moro, who has recently been killed in a most violent manner.' " Luca stopped, his voice shaky. He glanced briefly at Ali, then continued reading. " 'I would have given the task of portraying Count Moro as one of the most perfect courtiers. Alas, 'tis Messer Fregoso, who is acquainted with the young courtier's mother, the countess Maria, who incidentally I have discovered shall soon wed the said advisor of His Grace, the Illustrious Giuliano...' "

Luca continued reading to the end of the letter. Claudio's name was only mentioned twice, but the gist was all too clear. Claudio had died that same year—the letter was signed and dated at Rome, 1512, but with no month or day. Ali's hands were shaking as she listened to Claudio's friend speak the words. She didn't know how it was possible, but it was even worse coming from him. When he finished, there was only silence on the line.

"Luca?"

A deep sigh floated from the tech device into Ali's room.

"Luca!"

"Yes," a barely audible voice replied. "Yes, I'm here." He drew a heavy breath. "I can't get over this. How can this be?"

"Listen, Luca. We have to do something."

"What? What can we do? It's done. The chamber will be neutralized soon, and the entire room will be sealed. Claudio left instructions outlining the deactivation. He wanted it that way."

Ali's frustration was growing.

"Think a minute. He didn't know that things would play out

this way. Do you really believe he would have stayed in 1512 if he knew he was going to die? He would have come back with me—with *us*. I know it in my heart."

"It was his decision to return. The tainting of the timeline was at the top of Claudio's mind. He was worried that—"

"I know, Luca, blast the timeline! He's going to die anyway —don't you get it? There was no point to him staying since there is no timeline to mess with. If he's going to die, he may as well come back. And—and I am going back to 1512 to get him."

"What!" Luca's voice was shrill. "No, you can't, Alice. That goes against everything Claudio wanted."

"Is the portal neutralized yet?"

"Not yet, but we only just found the instrument recently to be able to counterbalance the wormhole."

"What instrument?"

"It's a near-absolute zero temperature compartment. It would neutralize the residual energy of the lightning strike."

"When is it happening?"

Her question was met with silence.

"Luca, for God's sake, when?"

"Soon." Luca sounded cryptic, yet he was sharing this information with her, which had to count for something. She was convinced he saw things her way. It was barely there, but Ali could sense his willingness to be persuaded.

"Even if you could go back, we don't know that he isn't already dead."

Ali winced at the words.

Luca continued. "Besides, how are you going to do it? How are you going to go back to 1512, find Claudio—hopefully still alive—and convince him to come back with you? On top of that, you'd have to do this all within a few hours because of the time difference. Won't your parents wonder where you are?"

Ali raised her brows at Luca's questions and bit her bottom lip. She pondered how to respond to him. He had presented her with the faults in her plan, however, defeat had not found Alice yet. Her mind worked to unravel the puzzle Luca had placed at her feet.

"There must be a way around this," said Alice, her fingers on her forehead. "There must be a way to adjust the time difference, so I have more time to make this right." Her mind wandered. "Hey! I just had this idea." Her hands moved to her temples and massaged furiously, as though this would tease out the thoughts chasing each other around in her mind. "My father's been working on this...this lightning simulator. He told me a while ago that they were experimenting with it. This thing is supposed to replicate the effects of a lightning bolt. He also said that his team is working on a theory about wormholes in space, like the one in Leonardo's chamber. He called it the Digression Paradox."

Ali explained her father's theories to Luca, his face on the device conveying wonderment and awe.

"Fantastic," Luca whispered. "The Digression Paradox—of course. It is so simple, so perfectly elegant."

Alice nodded enthusiastically. "Funny—that's exactly what my father said."

"Let me think on this, now. This lightning simulator, if I'm on the same track, you are thinking of using it to—"

"Simulate a lightning bolt on this side of the chamber and adjust the disparity in the passage of time!" Alice's voice rang with excitement. "What do you think?"

"I think this whole thing is making you a bit crazy—that's what I think!" Luca shook his head in disbelief. "Have you thought of what tampering with a wormhole, a time portal, could do? Not only to us in the chamber, but to the space-time continuum? We don't have the knowledge or expertise to even attempt something of this magnitude. And what even is this experimental...whatever it is?"

"It's a laser. A very powerful precision laser. My father said that this device is supposed to be able to heat and ionize the air like a lightning strike, except lasers can be controlled—unlike a bolt of lightning. Get it?" Her voice took on an exasperated tone. "Luca, we have to try. Ask your profs about this. For God's sake, you're a scientist—a student of science, anyway. Aren't you supposed to look beyond what is probable today and create what is possible for tomorrow? Please, help me." Ali cast her eyes down and ran her fingers roughly over her scalp and through her mane. When she looked back up at Luca, her eyes were watery. "He's going to die—soon. I'll go in, with or without adjusting the time discrepancy. I leave here in two days." Her voice softened to a whisper. "I'm going to get to him, whether you help me or not."

There were no words from Luca, only a worried expression. Then, finally, he spoke. "All right—you win. I'll talk to some of my profs today and see what they know...what they think. Heaven knows they will probably think I am a raving lunatic."

Alice breathed out a sigh of relief, and her expression softened. "Thank you, Luca. Thank you—"

"Don't get too excited, Ali," he interrupted. "I'll tell you right now, it is highly unlikely that what you are suggesting will work—even if we could get our hands on one of these lasers—"

"I know. All we can do is hope and not give up. And if we don't find one, or if it doesn't work, then I'll have to deal with the fallout when I come back home."

"Right. I will call you back when I know more."

Luca was about to minimize his phone when Ali had a sudden thought.

"Wait. Before you go, I just thought of something else. It may be nothing, but I came across one of my father's emails, and don't ask me who it was from, but it said that 'lightning struck twice', and from the context of the email, I think it meant once in Washington and again in Geneva. And he mentioned that he was very satisfied with the result of an experiment. He told me his work had 'turned a corner' and in a moment of elation, he uncharacteristically said the exact same thing to someone from his class. I don't know. I think it means something. I have a gut feeling it may have something to do with the lasers. You know—lightning?"

"Washington and Geneva. I'll see what I can do," Luca nodded. "I will keep that in mind when I make some inquiries. Good night, Ali." Luca broke the connection with a troubled look in his eyes.

With this minutely encouraging thought in mind, Alice minimized her device and drew her covers up around her chin. The plan was outlandish, but it was better than no plan at all.

She was keenly aware that the only sure thing was her ability to get back to Italy. She knew that Father Donato would probably allow her into the chamber room and travelling to 1512 was simple enough—it was basically a short walk—but the need to adjust the time discrepancy, so as not to arouse suspicion if she was unable to get back within the allotted few hours, was paramount. If her parents were at all suspicious, they would activate her sub-dermal chip. If she were still in 1512 when they activated it, there would be no locator beacon—and that would make her parents panic.

Ali was sure she would need at least a few days to convince Claudio of his inevitable fate. He would need time to get his affairs in order before travelling back to 2029 so he could live out his life where he belonged, by her side. She had it all figured out in her mind, but deep inside she knew nothing was certain.

Sleep finally found Ali, but it was a troubled, restless slumber.

Chapter Fifteen

"Oh my God, are you for real? Again? When are you leaving?" Kiana's jaw dropped open at the news.

"Tomorrow afternoon." Alice juggled the device as she face-timed with Ki and held a hot cup of cinnamon tea in the other hand. "My flight leaves at 5:45 pm."

"But, why? You're going to miss Christmas—and New Year's? What about school?"

"I popped in today and handed in the last of my assignments for this term. My mom and I needed to take the day to arrange a few things."

Kiana nodded slowly, with an air of mistrust in her expression. "I thought you sounded sketchy today when I asked you why you weren't at school." She puckered her lips and raised a brow.

"Sorry. I didn't want to get into it right then." Ali's eyes drifted from her friend's gaze. "Just trust me that I'm going back for a very good reason."

"Mmm...I'm sure you are." Kiana's voice dripped sarcasm as her face contorted into an uncharacteristic grimace. "Come on, Als. You're going back because of him. It's Claudio, isn't it?

What, are you going to live there now?" Her eyes narrowed into slits.

"Look, Ki, can you please not judge me and question me right now? He needs me. I need to help him."

"Unreal," she said as she shook her head and looked away. "What's wrong with him?"

"Let's just say it's a matter of life and death. I can't say anymore."

"More sketchiness. So, when are you coming back?"

"As soon as I can. I just wanted to tell you I was going. I'll text you when I get there, but I don't think I'll be able to check in as often as I'd like. So, if you don't hear from me for a while, everything's all right. Don't worry."

Kiana's skeptical expression transformed into concern. "Ali, are you sure everything's good?"

"Yeah. I called the others earlier to wish them a Merry Christmas. Merry Christmas, Ki."

"You too, Als. You'd better get back here, soon." Kiana angled her head, her eyes piercing Ali's soul.

Ali sensed Kiana was doubting her honesty. "Promise." Ali dipped her head and minimized her device.

She rose from her bedside and opened her closet doors to try to choose some things for the trip. The first things she packed were her stable boy clothes—the clothes she was swathed in as a baby, many years ago when she was found at the monastery and the same clothes that the brothers had saved for her when she returned with Claudio last summer. Her gaze meandered up to the decoupaged box with Claudio's scarf in it.

As she reached up to retrieve the box, she prayed that she was not too late.

～

"Do you have everything you need, darling?" asked Barbara at the security gate.

"Yeah, Mamma. I have my phone, of course, and everything I need is either in my phone or in my bag, which is a carry-on anyway, so I can't lose it." Ali stood with her device in hand, ready to scan it on the airport ticket tracker. Her passport was her face and right thumb, which would be scanned by separate devices once she passed the security checkpoint. Barbara and Reno gazed at her apprehensively and nodded.

"And you'll be alright in finding your connecting flight in London?" Reno asked, furrowing his brow.

"I did it in August. I'll be okay." Ali smiled, thinking of how she believed at the time that it would be a while before she saw Italy again.

"I should go in." Ali motioned to the ticket tracker; its little laser light flickered weakly in the sun splashed terminal.

With a natural movement, Barbara and Reno both wrapped their arms around their daughter. A minutely framed Alice was almost swallowed up by her parents' huge bear hug.

Barbara whispered in Ali's ear, "Now, try not to let things get to you. He may not live, but remember, you have your whole life ahead of you. Try to keep that in mind. And let your aunt and uncle help you." Barbara kissed Ali on the forehead and pulled away.

Though her mother wasn't in on the full story, her words rang truer than Ali cared to admit.

"And if you need anything—call us," Reno said, his expression troubled. "You know, Alice, I still don't like the idea of you traveling alone with this whole thing weighing down on you."

"Don't worry, Papa." She wrapped her arms around his neck and kissed his cheek. He stooped to accommodate. "I'll be careful," she whispered and then loosened her hug, but he hesitated before letting go.

With her e-ticket checked and her identification verified,

she was set to proceed to the gate area. Ali walked determinedly toward the entrance, then stopped. Hoping that her plan would work and that they would be spared unnecessary worry, she turned to blow a last kiss to her mother and father. Reno and Barbara waved back with sad smiles that betrayed their misgivings about the entire situation. Ali turned and walked through the checkpoint; a gentle buzzer signaled that she was clear to continue to her gate.

Once Ali boarded the plane, found her seat, and plugged in her earpieces, she let herself take on the full extent of the anxiety over her imminent task. Her stomach was in knots. Essays completed, school commitments put on hold, and last-minute plans in place to arrange for her aunt and uncle to retrieve her from the airport in Pisa had all served to distract her from the real possibilities of the dangers involved in this rescue mission—of the reason for her trip—to travel back in time to save her soul mate's life.

"Alice! Over here, Alice!" Leda waved at her niece from behind the barrier, just past customs.

Ali heard her name and followed the sound with her gaze, which came to rest on a familiar face. Though the airport at Pisa was much less hectic than it was last August, there were still plenty of people in the terminal, making their way to and from a winter's holiday in Italy.

"Zia!" Ali waved back. Impatiently, she waited until it was her turn to speak to the customs agent.

"Reason for your stay?" the agent asked, poker-faced.

"I'm here on holiday—to visit." Alice stammered. The guard scrolled through a screen as he spoke to Alice.

"Thumb, please."

Ali complied, allowing her finger to be scanned. He double-checked it with the passport imprint on her device, then smiled.

"Enjoy your stay." The light over the door went from red to green, which meant that the laser detectors had been lifted and she could proceed. She thanked him, picked up her carry-on, and advanced.

Alice was barely through the barrier when Leda threw her arms around her lovingly. "Ali," Leda greeted her with a smile of complete understanding and empathy, "so good to see you again, darling, despite the situation."

"Thanks, Zia," Ali said, returning the hug. "It's so good to see you, too."

Leda pulled away and grabbed Ali's carry-on. "How was your flight?"

"Okay, but—don't worry about that, I've got it." Ali tried to reclaim her carry-on.

"No, I insist." Leda squeezed Ali's hand and headed briskly toward the doors, bringing Ali along with her as if she were a small child.

Alice smiled and thought of how much Leda and her mother were alike. "Zia, I can't thank you enough. I mean—you know—hosting me again after such a short time."

"Nonsense. I just wish that it wasn't under such gloomy circumstances." Leda pressed her lips together and shook her head from side to side. "We called Dario and Anna. They are obviously concerned about Claudio. He is not well, they tell me, the poor young man."

Ali took a deep breath and nodded, though it was barely perceptible.

Leda guided Ali to an interior elevator which brought them to the multi-leveled parking garage. "Over here, darling." Leda motioned to the familiar Citroen, as tastefully elegant as Ali remembered it.

As she moved toward it, Alice couldn't help but sense that

with every step she took—with every conscious action she made—she was moving forward to her destiny. It felt good and right and though she had no idea if the scheme would work, she had to try.

Leda steered the auto lithely into the sun-drenched Tuscan afternoon. A smile crept involuntarily across Ali's pale, wintry face. *Wow. Won't be long until the freckles make their appearance in this sun. Don't they ever have gray skies here?* Ali mused as she glanced out the window, lost in her thoughts, thinking of her next step.

"You look tired, darling. And you have such a worried air about you." Leda took Ali's hand and squeezed her fingers tightly. "It's almost the opposite of the Ali we were used to last summer. I'm so sorry about your friend. Anna tells me that they have the best of care for him. He is at a private clinic in the Alps. If you like, I can bring you there tomorrow—I just need to confirm where it is. Anna was vague as to exactly which clinic, and for that matter, where in the Alps it is."

"Yeah, sure, Zia. Whatever you like." At this point, Ali wasn't sure how to respond. "Maybe I'll give Luca a call when we get to your house, so we can, you know, coordinate."

"Of course, as you wish." Leda glanced briefly at her niece with an understanding smile obviously aimed at easing some of her stress.

"So how is Zio?" Ali tried to make pleasant conversation to avert some of the focus from the web of lies she was spinning.

"He is well working hard, as usual. He is in Switzerland right now. He flew out this morning for a meeting with some people from the Department of the Environment there. About the final phase of the carbon emissions policy. He is particularly involved in…" Leda's voice faded into the background like white noise. As Leda chatted about Roberto's work projects, Ali nodded politely, but her mind was a million miles and five hundred years away.

Chapter Sixteen

"Hey, Luca." Ali was on her phone in the guest room while Leda prepared a little something for them to eat.

"Hey, when did you get in?"

"A couple of hours ago. I had to call my parents first, to let them know I arrived safely."

She heard Luca inhale a deep breath. "Wow. I still can't believe you are really going through with this. I must tell you Alice, this is a crazy idea at best. And at worst—"

"I know what I'm doing." Ali cut him off, unwilling to convince him all over again that she had made up her mind. "Did you talk to Anna and Dario again?"

"Yes." Luca paused. "My mother spoke to your aunt, and she offered to let you stay as long as you need to—all you need to do is ask."

Alice sighed with relief. "Right. That's perfect. Thanks, Luca, and thank your parents for me."

"They are just as skeptical as I am, but I think they understand where you're coming from. I think they are hoping that you can help him—they grew fond of him the year that he was here."

"Yes, he does have that effect on people." A smile was playing around the edges of her lips. "So, my aunt has offered to drive me to Claudio's clinic tomorrow." Her voice took on a hushed tone. "I'll just ask her to drive me to the villa instead. You're there, right?"

"Yes, Christmas holidays," Luca said flatly. "Olivia is on holiday, too. We will be going to Milan tomorrow to visit her." His voice took on an optimistic tone. "I was telling Olivia about our situation—you remember Olivia—she's my girlfriend, although I don't think you ever actually met, but anyway—"

"Luca, I can't go to Milan. Not now."

"Hear me out—I think we have a remote chance at a solution to our problem with the laser. I may be able to get one."

"You what?"

"One of Olivia's professors is a regular advisor for CENA-Corp—in Milan. She does consulting work for the prototype engineering and product development team."

Alice wondered what that had to do with anything but refrained from interrupting, so Luca could finish his explanation.

"I suggest we take a drive to Milan tomorrow. Try to get here early. If you are going to do this, we need to make certain you have as much time in 1512 as possible. Otherwise, the questions will fly if you are weeks late getting back. We cannot risk the chamber being discovered—that was Claudio's ultimate caveat. The time difference must be adjusted, and Olivia and I think we have figured out a way to get a laser like the one your father tested."

"Luca—you told Olivia about the chamber?" Ali hissed, grimacing in disbelief.

"Listen—I trust Olivia as Claudio trusted you." His voice

grew edgy for a moment. "She may hold the key to the Digression Paradox."

"Alice, dinner will be ready in ten minutes." Leda's voice filtered in through the closed door.

"Be right there, Zia. I'm on the phone with Luca."

"Of course, take your time, sweetheart."

Ali turned her attention back to the device. "I'll get there tomorrow as early as I can, okay? I hope you know what you're doing."

"Right. Sleep well." With a click, the conversation ended.

The two women had a quiet dinner—empty space hung between them and conversation. All the niceties had been hashed out, and there was only the rawness of silence. Alice was exhausted.

"Zia, Luca told me that it would be alright if I stayed at the villa—to make it easier to get back and forth to the clinic." Ali's eyes shifted to the food on her plate, which she had been pushing from one side of her dish to the other.

Leda folded her hands and drew them pensively to her mouth. "I suppose that would be all right," she responded, with the slightest hint of wariness in her voice.

Ali exhaled in relief.

"You've got a couple of weeks. Then, either way, your parents want you home. Do you understand what I'm saying?"

Ali understood completely and nodded in agreement.

"Yes, of course." She desperately hoped that two weeks would be enough.

Chapter Seventeen

L eda worked her way through the busy Siena streets in the cold early morning. In contrast to the sweltering heat of August, the weather had turned to a frosty chill, and the ancient avenues were dressed up for the Christmas season. Wreaths, lights, and ribbons were hung on wires criss-crossing above the streets, while the shopkeepers showed off their holiday treasures in a last-minute attempt to lure late shoppers.

"You see this shop here, Alice—they carry genuine panforte, still handmade using an ancient recipe by local monks. And that one over there..."

Alice knew that Leda was trying to cheer her up. She obviously mistook Ali's hushed mood for the sadness she would have been feeling for her ailing love. Instead, Ali was struggling with the anxiety of what was to come.

Not long left until Christmas, mused Alice, her eyes sweeping over the festive red, green, and gold decorations in the Siena city center. Normally, this would have evoked warm feelings of family and security for Ali, but not this year. Her mind was on Claudio and the looming danger he was facing at the hands of an unknown aggressor.

Leda drove from her condo to the highway on ramp, and before long, they were speeding along on their way to Chianti via the Florence *autostrada*.

"How about some music, sweetheart? You look so sad." Leda spoke into the dash, and the radio turned on. The song was a familiar Christmas carol, only it was in Italian. Leda hummed along as Ali watched the countryside rush by in a white and grey blur.

"Alice, please let me know if you would like for me to come get you for Christmas day. I really don't mind, you know." Leda glanced at Ali as she sped closer and closer to Chianti and the villa.

"Thanks, Zia. But I really think I'll prefer to stay there, with Claudio." Her gaze broke from Leda's. "I want to spend every minute I can with him."

"As you wish, *tesoro*. You can always change your mind."

Had she really thought this through? Had she logically measured the benefit of her actions with the possible repercussions for the past, present, and future? She imagined the scene—his wavering between the happiness of seeing her again and the anger at her having risked traveling back, contrary to his wishes.

Then again, when had she ever done anything he had asked her to do? A flash of humor crossed her face.

Leda steered the car onto the next roundabout ramp, which held familiar signs: San Miniato, Greve in Chianti, Firenze.

"Almost there, darling," said Leda, nodding to the signpost.

Ali took in a deep breath and exhaled, her chest feeling as if it would burst. She shook her head and laughed silently at her own silliness in the face of what she was about to do, as the radio played softly in the background. The song ended, and the radio host chimed in.

"It is minus two degrees here in Florence, and we expect a little more snow in the forecast for the next few days—as much as two centimeters—so it should make for a picture postcard Christmas. In other news, we have further word on earlier reports that the last known direct descendant of the Medici family, Prince Carlo Gregorio de Medici, has died suddenly at his winter retreat in the south of France. He is not survived by any immediate family, though there are distant relations in Italy and the United States—" Ali's heart jumped at the name announced over the radio.

"There are still Medici around, Zia?" Ali asked, surprised.

"Yes, there are," her mouth quirked with humor. "But the name doesn't really carry the fear or the influence it once did."

"Fear and influence are right," mumbled Ali.

"Pardon?"

"Nothing—I'm just surprised to hear that they still exist."

"Well, they don't rule Florence anymore, but they still carry much wealth. There is land and property all over the country, and beyond, I think, that still belongs to them. Though it sounds like one of the last of them has passed." Leda spoke to the dash again. "Rewind thirty seconds. Increase volume."

The announcer's voice was crisp and clear in the little car. "It appears there are several parties claiming the Medici birthright, but the lineage has been so watered down that experts are already saying it will be necessary to carry out DNA tests to determine the closest ties to the very private and reclusive Prince Carlo. It is..." Ali listened and wondered if Carlo was anything like Bruno.

As they made their way up the familiar incline to the villa, the winter landscape sped by Ali's window. Snow covered the mountains like a carpet, hiding the greenery. Only the occasional majestic cypress jutted out of the rolling fields of bare olive trees and grape vineyards. Picturesque villages in the distance stood quiet and still, each chimney displaying a curl of smoke gently puffing out from their warm hearths.

Alice breathed in the delicious smell of burning wood from village fireplaces wafting into the morning air, as Leda wound the Citroen up the snow-covered cobblestone driveway and stopped it in front of the double-door entrance. The villa stood as it had just a few months before, only now it was adorned with Christmas trees on either side. Alice felt that Claudio would appear out of the back and come around to greet her with a huge hug and a delicious kiss at any moment.

"Here we are, Alice. Are you ready to go in?"

Ali shook herself out of her reverie and gazed dazedly at her aunt.

"I'm ready."

"Leda, are you certain you won't stay for lunch," Anna implored as she wrapped her sweater around her, the chill in the mountain air making clouds from her breath. It felt as though the temperature had plummeted in the time it had taken Alice and Leda to bring Ali's carryon into the villa.

"No thank you, darling. I must get back. I have some last-minute details to take care of at the studio before Christmas." Leda smiled and affectionately hugged her friend, then let her eyes wander over to Alice. "Besides, I think our girl here is anxious to visit someone." Draping an arm over Alice's shoulder, she pulled her close and kissed her forehead.

"Yes, we should be off soon," added Luca, who stood behind his mother, stuffing his hands in his pockets as he gave the slightest shiver.

Leda peered over Ali's head to Anna and Luca. "If you need anything, let me know."

Ali hugged her aunt tightly. But for a reason she wasn't quite sure of when Leda loosened her embrace, Alice hesitated to let her go.

"Everything will be all right," Leda said, smiling down at her. After a final hug, she turned, opened the car door, and got in.

Anna, Luca, and Ali watched silently as she wound her way down the driveway, through the gates, and out of sight. Alice felt a finality in that image that was hard to describe. It was time to go forward.

"Right, now, Alice?" Luca's voice was even and direct. "Shall we?"

"Do you have to leave right now? She just got here." Anna motioned to Alice. "She hasn't eaten."

"No, thank you, Anna. I'm not very hungry." Ali's voice croaked as she buttoned up her jacket.

"Olivia is waiting for us, anyway, Mamma. We have a three-hour drive ahead of us—maybe some sandwiches for the way?"

"Of course. I will get a little something together while you fill Alice in. I'll be right back." Anna turned as she spoke and bustled into the rear door of the villa.

"Fill me in on what?" Alice angled her head toward Luca.

"Have I ever mentioned that Olivia is very impressive around a computer." Luca's mouth produced an impish grin that reminded her of Claudio.

"Not that I can recall." Alice raised a brow.

"That is her major at the university in Milan, where Claudio and I attend—er—where I attend, that is." Luca headed toward the villa. "Do you need anything from your carry-on, before we go?"

"Are we staying overnight?" Ali called out to him as he nipped swiftly inside the building. Moments later, to Ali's surprise, he sauntered back out with a guitar case.

"No time. We drive to Milan, get Olivia, go to CENACorp,

hopefully, print what we need, and come back. Father Donato is expecting you to cross tomorrow morning."

Tomorrow morning—that soon, Ali thought. Her nose crinkled, and she furrowed her brow as she watched Luca stuff the guitar case into the back seat of Luca's Fiat Uno.

"What do we need that we have to go all the way to Milan to print? Can't we find paper somewhere around here?" Ali grimaced. "And why are you bringing a guitar if we're coming back tonight? Are you going to break into a song by the side of the highway?"

Luca flashed Alice a smile as he shut the rear door of his little car. "The case is for what we are bringing back with us." His gaze turned to the villa as Anna bustled out to them with two lunch bags and a couple of bottles of mineral water. "I'll explain on the way."

"Here." Anna handed the lunches to Luca. "Now drive slowly. It's best you get there late than not at all."

"I will." He gave his mother a kiss, then turned to Ali. "Ready?" With a wave of his hand, he invited Alice to get into the car. The women said goodbye, and within minutes, Ali and Luca were on their way to Milan.

Chapter Eighteen

Luca's Fiat bobbed up and down as they sped over the imperfections on the autostrada. New England was not the only place in the world to experience potholes in the asphalt from the weather. Alice was silent until they were well established on the highway heading north.

"Thanks for doing this, Luca. I really appreciate everything you and your family are doing for Claudio and me."

"Don't mention it." Luca signaled and steered to the left lane, then shifted into fifth gear and let the car fly.

Ali stared into the distance, the hilly scenery covered in white. She would have to ask again, as Luca was not obliging. "So, can you explain why we need to go to Milan to get something printed?"

The corners of Luca's mouth turned up in a smile. "My girlfriend, Olivia, is very skilled in computer sciences—I believe I told you that much?"

"Yes, that you told me."

"You recall when you spoke with me about your father's recent discovery? The Digression Paradox?"

"Yes?"

"And the lasers—the experiments? How we could perhaps modify the portal to align the passage of time between the two apertures?"

"Yes, of course." Ali's eagerness grew as she waited for Luca to get to the point. "Did you ask your professors if they knew anything?"

"In fact, I did." Luca chortled, sounding very proud of himself. "I told them that a very good friend of mine in Boston was studying with Doctor Ferro and that she had mentioned quite unintentionally that a certain laser had been tried in two separate locations. I took a chance and said that the experiments in Washington and Geneva were successful. They knew exactly what I was referring to. And when they were satisfied that I wasn't a spy or something, bent on using the information to destroy the world, they made me swear to not divulge the location of the lasers—one of them at the University of Geneva."

"But we didn't know that it was at the University—" Ali gasped. "Luca, you're not thinking of breaking into the university and stealing it, are you?"

"No, I would not go that far. But Olivia has figured out the next best thing."

"I'm listening."

"My professor confirmed that the test results were positive —the experiment worked—they triple, and quadruple checked the findings, and it's a little rough around the edges, but essentially, the laser used in the trial worked. They were able to simulate a controlled lightning strike and at least partially take some readings as to a type of containment field required to test a real one."

"And we already have a containment field!" Ali squealed.

"The chamber!" Luca and Ali blurted simultaneously.

Ali clapped her hands together, overjoyed at some good news for a change. A sign posted on the shoulder indicated a cut-off for the A15 to Parma and then the A1 to Milan. Luca exited via the ramp, entered the flow of traffic on the A15, and continued at top speed.

"Oh my gosh, Luca—this could work...this could really work." She was energized with renewed optimism. "I am almost positive that we have a chance now. If I can stay long enough, I'm certain that I can get him to come back." Then, she remembered the print. "But wait, back to Olivia and—what did you call it? ZENACorp? How do we get the laser?"

"Not ZENA, CENACorp. In addition to being a very clever student, Olivia is also an assistant to a brilliant U of M professor. Doctor Torosin has worked with CENACorp in their prototype engineering and product development labs. She has access to one of the most sophisticated three-dimensional printers in existence. CENACorp creates prototypes for organizations like NASA and Virgin Galactic. It has been used to print complex systems for the University. This printer is able to replicate almost anything using multiple layers of materials— metals, rubber, petroleum-based products, even organic substances."

"That's incredible. We have a 3D printer at home, but this one sounds light years more advanced. But, to get the prototype printed, don't you need plans for it?"

"Yes, naturally you would have to have the specs." Luca shot a nervous glance at Ali. "Olivia is working on that as we speak."

An involuntary smile crept across her lips. "Luca—I thought you were going to tell me she already has them."

"I-I have total confidence in Olivia. Of course, it's a very delicate process. She tried to hack into the University of Geneva's database, to download the specifications for the laser from their engineering department, but their firewalls were too sophisticated, and she was nearly discovered. She ended up sealing the breach without being detected, though. She is amazing."

Ali bit her lip and her smile disappeared. "I'm pretty sure that's illegal," she said in a guarded tone. "I mean, it's pretty risky, isn't it? We're going to break into CENACorp to borrow their printer...and without specs for the device even?"

"Don't worry. We'll figure it out. Somehow." Luca grimaced and held up his hand, palm up. "Look, do you want to even out the time discrepancy or not? Besides, we're not breaking in. We are visiting Olivia's professor and taking a detour while we are there."

Ali nodded slowly. "Sounds like a good plan, or at least a start to one." She studied him. "Look Luca, I'm sorry about being so sanctimonious. I should talk—I'm the one who got you into this, and now Olivia is mixed up in it, too."

"No time to worry, Alice." Luca motioned to the post up ahead.

Aı Milano, the sign read, an arrow indicated the exit was imminent. "Almost there," he said as he flipped on his signal light to exit right.

Chapter Nineteen

A cloud-covered sky produced a steady drizzle as Luca pulled into the driveway of Olivia's condominium complex. Located in the Milanese suburbs, the buildings were more reminiscent of the condos in downtown Boston than most of the structures present in this ancient Italian city.

Luca stopped the car in front of the sleek glass double doors, took his phone from his pocket, and fired off a quick text. Then he sat back and waited as Ali peered through the windshield up to the top of the building.

Not two minutes afterward, a young woman with chestnut hair and almond-shaped eyes opened the door on the left and started down the ramp.

Luca exited the car and walked briskly to greet her with a hug and kiss on the lips. Alice smiled wistfully to herself as she watched the two exchange words and walk arm-in-arm to the car.

Alice opened her door and instinctively walked over to Olivia, her hand extended. "Ciao, Olivia. I'm Alice. Pleasure to meet you."

Olivia started to extend her hand but must have thought better because she reached over and hugged Alice instead.

"So nice to meet you, Alice."

Olivia's spontaneous response made Ali tear up. She felt a burst of emotion that she had been successfully keeping bottled up. Ali hiccupped and tried to pull away, but Olivia held onto her.

"Don't cry, Alice," Olivia whispered in a comforting tone as Luca stood uneasily by, busying himself with shifting the guitar case around in the back seat to make room for a passenger.

Ali gathered up her courage, swallowed her tears, and let go of Olivia to search for a tissue in her satchel. "Olivia, I don't even know you, yet you've already helped me so much. I could never thank you enough for this," Ali said, as she dabbed at her eyes.

Olivia shrugged. Her eyes, a brilliant blue, smiled of their own accord. "Anything for love. Besides, I adore a challenge. Getting to the specs for the Y17 Laser—" she held up her tech device, "well, that has been one hell of a challenge. The University of Geneva has some pretty tough firewalls against hackers."

"Any luck?" asked Luca.

Olivia shook her head and handed Luca her phone, who immediately went about scrolling through it.

"How was your flight?" asked Olivia, as she stuck her hands in her pockets.

"Grueling," groaned Ali. "I couldn't wait to land. Usually, I enjoy flying but—"

"These are CENACorp's records," remarked Luca, holding up the phone.

"I know," said Olivia, with a teasing lilt in her voice. "I had a gut feeling that if CENACorp did work for the University of Milan, that maybe they've also had business with the University of Geneva. All I had to do was Google that one. I found tons of literature on it. I checked their database to see if they've manufactured prototypes for Geneva—and guess what?"

"They have?" asked Luca.

Olivia confirmed with an air of pleasure. "They have."

"How does that help us get the specifications to our laser, though?" asked Ali.

"CENACorp's firewalls are even tougher than the University of Geneva's," explained Olivia. "And I'm pretty good with computers, but I'm no expert hacker."

"So, what do we do?"

"We visit my professor. It just so happens that she is working on a consulting project over the break, and I have asked her for a tour of CENACorp."

"Come on, Alice." Luca had Olivia's hand in his as they walked to the Fiat. "Let's go. I'll explain on the way."

Ali circled to the rear passenger door and got in while Olivia entered the front passenger seat, closing the door behind her.

Once in the car, Luca pushed on the clutch and set the car in motion. He turned to Ali. "So, when we are in CENACorp, Ollie's professor will need to bring us in as access is restricted. Ollie has explained to Doctor Torosin that you are visiting from the States, who your father is, and that your aunt and uncle and my parents are friends, but that's about it. Ollie asked her professor if she would mind taking you for a tour of CENACorp. Now listen carefully because this is where it can get tricky. Once we are in her office, we..."

Alice listened intently to Luca and Olivia's plan. If she didn't know better, she would have thought she was in a high-tech spy movie, stealing plans for a rogue government. The fact that they were stealing was not lost on Ali. The entire operation put them all at risk and could have serious repercussions for everyone. Then again, Ali reasoned, where else could they find this laser? More importantly, Claudio's life was at stake.

"Olivia, Luca—I need to ask before we go in." Ali's voice took on a grave tone. "I don't care about me. I mean this is my choice. If I get caught, I have to face the consequences, but this situation—it doesn't involve you. Are you sure you want to risk this?"

"That's where you are wrong, Alice," said Luca. "Claudio is our friend, too."

"He's right." Olivia agreed. "We attended university together—just a few kilometers from here." Olivia nodded toward the city and looked at Ali once again, her eyes honest. "It's not only about you and him. We care about him, too."

Ali felt the lump in her throat creeping back. She would have to hold it together and stay alert if this scheme was going to work. With fresh resolve and blind faith in her new friends, she cleared her throat and squeezed her lips together. It would be alright.

"Okay. Let's do it."

Chapter Twenty

The trio entered the modern-looking building and strode to the front desk. "Olivia Neri for Doctor Torosin, please," Olivia said to the reception security, as she massaged her temples. "I'm one of her students—she is expecting me."

"Of course, miss," the guard responded cordially. He buzzed the doctor's code and waited. "Doctor Torosin, Olivia Neri is here to see you." A few words, and a click on the other end of the line, signaled that their presence had been acknowledged.

As the three stood waiting, Luca with the guitar case in hand, Ali's eyes scanned the lobby. The furnishings and architecture of the CENACorp lobby were pristine white and minimalistic, with the clean palette of color broken only by the imposing metal detectors just beyond the security desk.

The elevator doors pinged, then opened wide, revealing a tall woman, lithe and graceful, with nearly black shoulder-length hair and deep brown eyes.

She strode toward them, wearing an impeccably tailored gray pantsuit with very expensive-looking black pumps. She was all smiles for Olivia.

"*Grazie*, Riccardo," she said to the security guard. "Hello, Olivia." Her demeanor was as dignified as she was distinguished-looking. With a fluid gesture, she grasped Olivia's hand.

"*Ciao*, professor," Olivia said, wincing, rubbing her forehead.

"Hello, Doctor Torosin. How are you?" offered Luca.

"Ciao, Luca." Though she extended her hand to Luca, her gaze reverted to Olivia with apparent concern for her discomfort. Luca accepted, jostling the guitar case into his left hand. Doctor Torosin now shot a puzzled look at Luca as she eyed the case.

"I would rather not leave it in my car. It has a lot of sentimental value—you understand."

"Of course." She furrowed her brow in a puzzled fashion and then her gaze darted back to her student. "What's the matter, Olivia? Are you in pain?"

"I've got a terrible migraine, Doctor—but don't worry, I'll be fine. By the way, this is my very good friend from America, Alice Ferro." Olivia gestured to Ali.

Ali flashed an enthusiastic grin. "A pleasure to meet you, Doctor Torosin. I'm your biggest fan." Ali thought that may have sounded a little over-the-top and bit her tongue to keep from commenting further.

"Alice, meet Doctor Torosin, one of Italy's leading computer systems engineers."

"A pleasure, Alice." Doctor Torosin tipped her head. "So nice to meet you. I'm glad you are here, but..." She turned back to Olivia. "Do you really feel up to doing this today?"

Olivia winced again. "We have to do it today, professor. Ali is only here for the holidays, and she must go back to Tuscany tonight. She's interested in an engineering career and is so looking forward to a tour. In fact, she is even considering studying in Italy next year, so this is the perfect time for her to see the best in the field." Olivia tried to smile at Ali but grimaced instead.

Alice's face broke into an open, friendly smile.

The security guard, who was watching the exchange, kept a curious eye on Luca's guitar case. He finally stood and leaned over the carved alabaster counter. "Can I get you something for your headache, miss?"

"I took something already, thanks," Olivia said gratefully. "I'm sure I'll be all right soon enough. If you don't mind professor, can we get started?"

"Certainly, come on." Doctor Torosin walked ahead and guided them through the metal detectors. Ali cautiously glanced back at the security guard, who only sat down again after the metal detectors flashed a green light.

"This way," said Torosin, waving them forward onto the elevators. The doors closed behind them after the doctor pressed a backlit button to an upper floor.

Doctor Torosin held her access control card over the scanner and the lock to her office gave way. The lights flickered on automatically. She opened the door to a spacious, comfortably furnished room, which contrasted with the rest of the minimalist décor in the building.

"Please, come in," she ushered the three friends in, with Olivia quietly groaning in pain as she crossed the threshold. Torosin watched as Olivia gave the performance of a lifetime. Finally, she motioned Olivia over to the couch on the opposite side of the office space. "Uh, maybe if you sit a moment or two…let the medicine work."

"Oh, yes. Good idea." Olivia sat down, massaged her skull, and closed her eyes. "Oh…the lights. I think it might be getting worse."

"Try putting your head back," suggested Torosin, after which she glanced at her phone, then at the digital clock on the wall. "So, Alice," the doctor sat on the edge of her desk and crossed her arms over her chest. "I must say that I greatly admire your father's work. His newest published paper on quantum entanglements and photon beams was fascinating."

"Yeah." Ali's eyes appeared mesmerized by the topic. "He worked really hard on that one."

"I must have missed it," announced Luca.

After the brief exchange, there was a marked silence in the air.

Torosin chewed the inside of her cheek. "Uhm. Can I get you some water, Olivia? I have some in the little fridge."

"No thank you." It looked as though Olivia was down for the count.

Torosin glanced at her phone again. "Oh dear, it's getting late. Maybe we can go on without you, Olivia," she said anxiously. "I do need to get home...the holidays, you understand."

The doctor got up and started for the door, her access card in hand.

"No—I wouldn't miss this for anything," Olivia said weakly. "Maybe I'll just grab some water for the way if you don't mind, doctor?"

"Help yourself," said Torosin, then pointed to the guitar case. "Luca, you can leave that here."

"Thanks. It was getting heavy," said Luca. "Might as well leave our coats here, too." Ali and Luca peeled off their layers of winter garb, which for Ali was all too reminiscent of the harsh Massachusetts winters back home.

"Maybe we can go see the labs first? Alice, I hear you are interested in seeing the 3D printer—the one we use for engineering prototypes?"

"That is a perfect start, doctor." Luca made his way toward the door, opening it and waving the doctor through.

"Yes! I cannot wait to see the printer." Ali exited just ahead of the doctor. "I'll be making notes and telling my dad all about it as soon as I get back to Boston."

"It must be very exciting to have one of the world's leading astrophysicists as a father."

"I guess so, but to me—he's just my Papa."

"Very good." Torosin walked down the hall, her access card in hand. "Here, Alice, we'll take the elevator up a few floors to engineering." But seeing only Ali and Luca trailing behind, she looked back, craning her head, and called out, "Olivia?"

But Olivia was on the couch in her office, fast asleep, her rhythmic breathing slow and steady. Torosin shook her head and walked briskly back to the office, looking in on her. "I guess she thought the better of it." Then, after a moment's pause to deliberate, she pulled the door closed behind her. "Honestly, you kids need more sleep. We might as well get started. When she wakes up, she will have to catch up with us."

Ali heard the door lock automatically as she exited, the lights dimming to blackness behind her.

"Anyway," started the professor. "Back to what I was saying. You know, it's so gratifying to hear that you are thinking of becoming an engineer. Any thoughts as to which field?"

"Not yet, Doctor Torosin. I'm pretty much open to all possibilities right now." Alice knew the script. They had gone over it several times during their drive from Tuscany. All Ali could do was hope that the professor wouldn't detect anything suspicious in her tone.

The elevator button dimmed, and the doors opened allowing them entry. Torosin pressed the fifteenth-floor button. They were on seven.

"We'll stop by the development labs first," said the doctor. "That's where the magic happens—where our engineers design the prototypes from customer specifications. From these specs, we can create working trial products. CENACorp applies the principles of science and technology to create aircraft components and support equipment, researching and developing—"

Alice watched the lights on the floor indicators as they ascended.

Nine, ten...fourteen, fifteen. The doors whooshed open.

"...undertaking systematic manufacturing, involving the assembly and modification of components," the doctor said proudly. "In fact, we have an office in Geneva, too. After this, we can pay a visit to the printer that creates these working prototypes, yes?"

"Amazing," Ali whispered as she and Luca exchanged nervous glances.

"Here we are." Torosin swept her card over the scanner and pushed the door open. The space was deserted. "I'm afraid that everyone's left for the Christmas holidays." She glanced back at Alice as she led them in. "This is where our engineers work to bring client inventions to life—as well as other interesting things."

A pristine white lab gleamed with high-tech gadgets, desk-size 3D tablets, and other things that Ali did not recognize.

The tour of the engineering lab would have interested Alice immensely, had it not been for her ever-present worry. *Oh, my gosh, I hope we can pull this off. Did we miss anything? What if we overlooked some important detail? What if we all end up in jail?*

Alice nodded and gushed at all the appropriate times. Finally, Torosin ushered them down the corridor to another room, this one with a set of double doors wide enough to fit a car through.

"Now, Alice," the doctor stood with her card in hand, poised to swipe it over the security scanner, "in here is the printer you've been asking about." She waved her card over the red LED light and pushed the handle down. The lights flickered on, and in the center of a relatively unremarkable, but immaculate space, was a sleek metal object about the size of a small automobile.

"This is it," Torosin said proudly. "We call it the Wizard ST20 Replicator." She strode over to one side of it and opened its lateral compartment. "You can see inside, here."

Approximately a hundred separate packets made of Mylar-like material lined the inside wall. Some were large and still others very small and from each of these sacks, thousands of thin optic-like fibers emanated. They were fed into a computer panel the size of a filing cabinet that was attached to the side of the component, and then into the printer.

Ali heard a distinct gasp come from Luca's direction.

"Fantastic," he said as he stood open-mouthed, marveling at the intricately set filaments.

"We can manufacture anything in here, even organic-based objects. We are working with experts in various health sciences fields so that one day it can be perfected to produce a perfectly matched human organ."

Alice was mesmerized.

"It works by a process of layering. It layers an object from digital information, using multiple materials. It does require detailed specs, but really it should be able to reproduce just about anything."

The feeling Ali got from looking at this marvel of human technology was like the way she felt looking into da Vinci's chamber for the first time. In her reverie, she had almost forgotten why they were there.

As the doctor disappeared behind a computer panel, still pointing out features of the device, Ali turned to Luca and whispered in her softest voice, "So, do you know what to do?"

"Absolutely," Luca responded with barely a murmur. Nervously, he grabbed his phone his pocket, moved around to the lateral compartment and scanned the printer serial number and code descrambler with his 21.0 app. If they were to transmit secret information through cyberspace, the newest iPhone was the only device with enough encryption capabilities to keep that information from inadvertently being lost in the wild.

The printer came to life with a low hum, and the doctor reappeared from behind the panel. "Now, most things that we've produced have been a combination of plastics and metals —these materials call for a certain degree of calibration—and a specific amount of layering to create a nice smooth prototype— probably with a layer of less than ten thousandth of a—"

Luca checked the time on his device as they followed the doctor around the printer.

"Did Olivia find the extra security card?" asked Ali, speaking from one side of her mouth.

Luca nodded. "It was in her desk—just as she said it would be."

"And the laser specs?"

"Not yet." Luca licked his lips as he glanced at his phone again. "She's trying to get into Torosin's tablet. We need to keep her busy for another hour or so. You try to keep her talking so she won't notice the time, meanwhile, I'll stay in touch with Ollie and let her know where we are."

Chapter Twenty-One

"Did you get your fill of checking out the printer, Alice?" Doctor Torosin asked as she secured the door to the printer room with her access card.

"Positively. Yes, it's like nothing I've ever seen before. Very advanced technology."

"That it is." The doctor nodded in agreement. "If you're ready, we'll proceed to the third floor. We can peek at what the technicians are putting together in our little aerospace testing department."

Into the elevator and then, Ali and Luca followed Doctor Torosin to an open-concept floor where the windows were floor to ceiling. A handful of men and women moved briskly about, their footsteps echoing against the sterile marble floors.

"Once the prototypes are created," explained Doctor Torosin, "they are put through a series of tests to determine their ability to function for our clients. If they don't work according to client specs, then..."

Anxious for the minutes to slow down to a deliberate crawl, Ali prayed, intentionally lingering in each space and asking multiple questions as the doctor toured them through the CENACorp facility.

Olivia had to hack into Torosin's tablet, find the laser specifications, download them into her device, break into the printer room using Doctor Torosin's access card, upload them to the printer, create the laser prototype and return to the professor's office, all without being discovered.

To add to the frustration, Olivia wouldn't be able to communicate with them after positioning her phone's receptacle adaptor into the printer to allow it to upload and initiate the painstaking layering process if she was able to get to the specs at all.

Meanwhile, Ali felt totally inadequate simply having to do her best to keep Doctor Torosin engaged and talking.

"Next, we can visit our executive offices, top floor of course."

The penthouse, as Ali would have described it, was entirely different from the rest of the building. They entered from the elevator into an atrium with a glass roof that gave way to the cloudy sky overhead—it was late afternoon. Torosin walked to a mechanical door and waved her card over the sensor. It parted to reveal a long hallway, darkly decorated with deep green and black marble floor tile and cherry wood paneled wainscoting.

"These are our executive offices. Since this is our flagship branch, management uses it as a hub."

"How very old and distinguished looking," commented Ali, *oohing* and *awing*, listening intently to the doctor as they entered the board room, while glancing at Luca so often to confirm the time. Over sixty-five minutes had elapsed since they boarded the elevator from Torosin's office.

"How is she doing?" Ali mouthed to Luca.

He shrugged. "She hasn't messaged me." A glistening line of perspiration had appeared above Luca's upper lip.

"Well, I guess that's about it." Doctor Torosin grabbed her

phone from her jacket pocket and peered down at it. "Is that the time? Oh dear, I wonder how Olivia is doing." She turned on her heel and headed back to the door. "I am positively notorious for losing myself when I talk about this place."

She stepped back into the atrium from the offices and held the door open wide for a dawdling Ali and Luca as they meandered by the workspaces, looking in and taking their time. Once through, she made certain the door was secure behind them.

"Can you see the stars here at night from the glass roof?" Ali pointed up to the ceiling as she walked to the elevator. The doctor was standing inside, holding the OPEN button. "It must be amazing—like being outdoors—only you're...indoors." *God, I must sound like an idiot.*

"Yes—I guess you could say that," Torosin replied, with a hint of impatience in her voice. "Now, if you don't mind, I really would like to get back to my office." She remained cordial, but her manner was hurried. The lift doors closed on them when she pressed the seventh-floor button.

Ali looked at her phone; barely seventy-five minutes had elapsed. She glanced sideways at Luca, who had just finished wiping the beads of sweat from his forehead. Fifteenth floor, fourteenth, thirteenth...

What if Olivia couldn't hack into Doctor Torosin's tablet and get the specs? And Olivia said it would take at least sixty minutes to complete the print if she got them. What if it hadn't finished and Olivia wasn't back in the office? How would they explain that to the doctor? She went to the washroom—yes, that's it. But with a guitar case? A guitar case that had been fitted with flexible foam to protect a 3D-printed laser? Ninth floor, eighth, seventh—stop.

It could go either way, Ali thought as the elevator *pinged*, and the doors slid open.

Ali watched as Doctor Torosin approached her office door

with long, steady strides. With a deft wave of her security card, and a gentle push on the door, she was in the office; Luca and Ali nervously followed close behind.

"Oh dear, she's still in so much pain that she's breathing hard," said the doctor, her brow furrowed with pity for her student. Olivia's wrist rested on her forehead with the rest of her hand shading her eyes. "And you didn't help yourself to water after all, I see."

As Torosin strode over to the mini fridge in the corner of her office, Luca inched to the guitar case resting horizontally against the wall and lifted it slightly. He glanced at Ali and nodded—an impish look in his eyes.

She got it, thought Ali. *Okay, breathe now, just breathe. This is the easy part.*

"Still pounding, eh, Olivia?" asked Luca.

"Oh, yes. I feel like I need to go home." Her voice was low and uneven. "Go home right now."

"Then you must get home," said Doctor Torosin, helping her up. "Where did you park?"

"Luca parked in the underground lot," said Olivia wistfully.

"Do you want to bring the car around to the front?" asked Torosin. "It might be easier than walking to the car in the underground parking. You two can go ahead and use the front doors—the way you came in?"

"No, doctor," Olivia said, perhaps a little too emphatically.

The guitar case thought Ali. The laser contained titanium, which would be picked up by the metal detectors at the door.

"No, we parked close to the elevator. Let's just go straight to the underground lot. I think I need Luca to help me down, and Ali doesn't know her way around, so we can all leave together." She sighed, then lay back down and covered her eyes with her hand.

The professor raised a brow. "Fine, then. I'll walk you to the elevators."

After Luca grabbed his coat, he helped Olivia with hers.

Gingerly, with Luca and Torosin on either side of her, Olivia walked to the door. Ali hoisted up the guitar case, expecting it to be heavy as lead, but it wasn't that bad at all.

The four made their way to the elevator. "Here we are," said the professor.

"Thanks so much for the tour, Doctor Torosin." Ali shook the doctor's hand in gratitude. "Systems engineering is definitely at the top of my list, now that I've seen all this."

Torosin folded her hands in front as they waited for the elevator. "You are most welcome, Alice. Anytime." She smiled politely, then turned to Olivia. "I hope you're feeling better soon."

Olivia slowly nodded her head. "I think I may be feeling better already, professor."

"Oh, that's good news." The entire casual conversation at the elevator was surreal to Ali, just knowing that in the guitar case was a newly printed prototype worth millions of euros made her head spin.

A soft ping and the LED arrow pointing 'down' announced the lift had arrived. The doors slid open and the three strolled casually onto the elevator.

"Enjoy the rest of your holiday," said the doctor pleasantly with a final wave. "And *Buon Natale.*"

The three waved back and with a swift motion, the doors *swished* closed. As the elevator descended smoothly to the underground parking lot, the trio dared not to even breathe too loudly. They would not be safe until they were out of the underground lot. Ali had to fight back an overwhelming urge to jump up and *whoot* with joy.

Ali and Olivia stood by the rear of the car while Luca picked up the guitar case and hoisted it carefully into the trunk of the Fiat. He secured the hatch closed and walked around to the driver's side, then Olivia got into the passenger seat and Ali scrambled into the back seat.

Once everyone was in, Luca hit the ignition and slipped the car into gear. They wound their way out of the underground lot, through the security barrier, and out of the building into the crisp, late afternoon, with the state-of-the-art laser prototype hidden safely in the trunk of the car. As they drove to Olivia's condo, Ali placed her hands on Luca and Olivia's shoulders and smiled at them with deep gratitude.

"Holy, holy crap," Alice let out a huge sigh. "Olivia, you are a goddess!"

"I don't know how you did it, Ollie," remarked Luca, wiping his brow. "I thought I was going to pass out from worrying if you'd get caught in the printer room."

"How did you pull it off?" asked Ali.

"With this," Olivia produced her phone. "Getting into the Doctor's tablet was easy enough—finding the specs—a little more difficult. But nothing I couldn't handle. I uploaded the plans to my phone then used the doctor's access card to get to the printer. After that, it was a matter of having enough time to complete the prototype."

Luca swiftly pulled into the guest parking area of Olivia's building, pulled on the brake, and held out his hand. "May I see the specs, my gorgeous one?"

Olivia handed him the phone.

"This is fantastic!" Furiously, Luca scrolled through the device. "Brilliant!" He smacked the side of his own head and pointed to the phone.

Olivia shook her head and smiled at his reaction.

"Why didn't I think of this?"

Alice angled her head, so she could see the equations that looked like hieroglyphics. "That's the laser?"

"Yes," confirmed Olivia. "I had some time to look them over as it was printing. This laser works on basic principles. It has been modified, but in short, it is electricity based, which means we can use a portable energy source to power it. From a cursory look at the plans, it works by releasing fifteen million amps of electricity into an array of very fine high-temp alloy wires. The wires dissolve into a cloud of charged particles, creating a channel of plasma through the air. The plasma releases energy in the form of a high-intensity, super-short duration laser pulse which uses air like a lens."

"Genius," whispered Luca, as he scrolled through the specs again. "The surrounding air focuses the beam, keeping the laser pulse tight rather than scattering it all around. In other words, the laser creates the path of least resistance between the power source and the target. This is, essentially, a lightning bolt, and a damned powerful one at that."

Alice was quietly decompressing in the back seat, but Olivia gave Luca a hearty high five.

"Isn't it beautiful science, my love?" Olivia cooed. She reached for the back of Luca's neck and pulled him close, kissing him passionately, obviously overjoyed at their discovery.

Alice smiled at their enthusiasm before awkwardly looking away. She only looked up again when Olivia opened her door. "Okay Alice," she said as she stepped out, and opened Alice's door so they could trade spots. "I will be going down to Tuscany later. I'm driving my parents to the airport first. They are vacationing in the Dominican over the holidays."

Alice exited the back of the Fiat and immediately hugged Olivia tightly. "I will never be able to thank you enough for this. I hope this whole thing doesn't end up getting you or Luca into some kind of trouble."

Olivia hugged Ali back and then released her, holding her by the shoulders. "You don't worry about that. Just focus on getting Claudio back."

Ali got into the front seat as Olivia walked around to Luca's window and stuck her head inside. To Luca, she said, "See you tonight. Love you," and blew him a kiss. To Ali, she flashed a 'thumbs up,' and headed to the condo, disappearing through the glass double doors.

With a burst of power from the Fiat, Luca and Ali sped off again, on the road toward Tuscany.

Chapter Twenty-Two

The traffic from Milan to Florence was light.

After Alice checked in with her parents, Anna and Dario invited her to their Christmas Eve feast at the villa. There were only a handful of patrons staying over the holidays.

Olivia arrived just in time to join them for midnight mass in the little village of San Miniato. The angelic voices of the choirboys singing Christmas hymns made Ali yearn for the security of her parents, yet also made her realize how much she wanted to share it with Claudio.

As Ali lay staring at the ceiling, counting the seconds until 5:30 a.m., when her phone alarm was set to go off, she decided she had better talk to her parents one last time. After extending her device and softly speaking her mother's name, she propped up the phone on her lap. The screen glowed a ghostly green as it worked to complete the call.

"Hello?"

"Hi Mamma," Ali spoke in a hushed voice. "*Buon Natale*."

"*Buon Natale*, my darling. How are things going?"

"Not that great. I'm not going to be able to call you for a

few days. This new clinic that Claudio is in is way up in the Alps, so there may be some interference. I may not be able to call you or Zia. But if you need to get in touch, call Anna at the villa. I will let Zia Leda know, too—so you won't worry if you don't hear from me."

"That sounds a bit cryptic, Alice. What kind of interference could there be—there are signals everywhere now—it's not like when I was young."

Ali's hand went impulsively to the locator chip embedded in her right forearm.

"Because this place is a very exclusive clinic. They don't allow electronics in there because people may copy their...technology...and equipment." Ali winced at her excuse.

"What's the clinic called?" Suspicion was creeping into Barbara's voice, but Alice was ready.

"It's the Floris Group Hospice and Clinic, in the Apennines." Ali sensed from the silence that her mother was checking out the clinic on her device.

"Looks like a nice place," Barbara finally responded. "I do hope they can help him there. And I'm sure that having you near him is reason enough for him to fight and perhaps overcome this."

Tears welled up in Ali's eyes and spilled over onto her cheeks. "I wish the same Mamma—that he survives." She wiped the tears with her pajama sleeve. "Can you call Zia and let her know that you are okay with it and that Anna will call her tomorrow? I just don't want to talk with anyone but you and Papa. Is he there?"

"Yes—here he is." Barbara handed the device to Reno.

"Alice? Hello, sweetheart." His smile turned into a grimace. "You're crying and that worries me."

"It's just a little stress, Papa. I'm fine." *If he only knew what I was planning, he'd be on the next plane over here.*

"Can I wish you a Merry Christmas?"

"Of course, and a Happy New Year." Ali's smile was forced. "I'll have to maintain radio silence for a while, but, like I told Mamma, I promise I will call as soon as I get back—I mean as soon as I can." She cleared her throat. "Mamma will explain everything. I love you both so much." She felt the tears want to come again, but fought them back.

"And we love you." Both Reno and Barbara were in the screen now.

"Be careful and stay safe," said Reno.

"We're sending lots of positive thoughts your way, and for Claudio, too." Barbara blew her a kiss.

"Ciao." Ali disconnected and then texted Kiana, Jelsy and Mina.

<Hey guys—just wanted to say Merry Christmas and I miss you all. If I don't message you for a while, don't worry, I'm safe. I'm giving you Claudio's cousin's number just in case something happens. But whatever you do—do not give it to my parents unless it's a complete emergency. Love and miss you. See you soon. Ali>

Despite everything, Ali did eventually fall into a chaotic sleep that was peppered with vivid dreams, rich with images of the chamber and the laser poised directly at the center of the aperture, ready to be fired. She was staring dazedly into the spirals, waiting for the laser to fire, but it never did. Panic rose in her throat; her breath was quick, and her heart was pounding. She would never be able to find Claudio, convince him of his destiny, and get him out in just an hour or two. She was thinking this, but her mouth wouldn't work. Suddenly, there was a knock at the tear-shaped door—a sharp knock that roused her and made her recognize that she was still in her villa room.

"Ali? Are you awake?" It was Olivia. She peeked her head into the room, her silhouette against the light in the hall giving her an eerie quality.

"Uh—yeah," Ali said groggily. How could she have slept through her alarm? "Yeah, I'm awake."

"Good. Luca wants to leave in half an hour. Is that doable?"

"Entirely. I need to shower and get my stable boy clothes on. I'll put on a coat to cover it, just in case." Ali felt around on her bed for her sweater—the room was chilly, and it was still inky dark out.

"Meet you downstairs." Olivia started to close the door.

"Wait," said Ali. "I want to thank you again for doing this. For giving up your Christmas to help me."

"Stop thanking me," Ollie shrugged. "My parents knew I would be visiting Luca for the week—and that's exactly what I'm doing." She softly closed the door.

Ali reached for the table lamp and switched it on, crawled out of bed and walked determinedly to the panel heater, pumped it up, and then strode into the shower. *Who knows when I'll be able to do this again?*

Alice felt surprisingly comfortable in her sixteenth-century clothing. Her wild mane was tamed in a tight bun at the base of her skull, with a stable boy cap hiding it and her face. The ancient fabric of her outfit felt rough and scratchy against her skin, and her shoes were nearly worn clean through at the toes.

There was just one adjustment—she wore Claudio's handkerchief around her neck. As she felt the smoothness of it, she closed her eyes and pictured him in his brocades and riding gear. The idea that she would soon see him again sent her spirit soaring.

A soft knock at the door produced Anna carrying a tray with a steaming cappuccino and a brioche heavily slathered in butter and apricot jam.

"Oh, Anna, thank you." Ali smiled appreciatively. "But I don't think I could eat anything right now. I'm too nervous."

"Nonsense." Anna pursed her lips. "You need to eat. Lord knows when you will eat again once you—complete your traveling."

Alice succumbed to Anna's caveat and accepted.

"Please be cautious and have the least amount of contact possible with people in 1512. Once you find Claudio and have explained things, get back fast. Make your stay short and exercise the greatest caution in not tainting the timeline." Anna's words were wise and surprising to Ali. She had not thought of Anna as involved in this venture as she seemed to be.

"I will." Ali wiped her mouth as she chewed on the last of the brioche, gulping down her coffee as a chaser. "And I won't." She eyed Anna as she took Ali's empty cup and rose to leave. "So, I'm guessing you know about everything? Claudio, his death, how much in love we are?"

Anna laughed softly. "It's not every day you get to meet your nineteen-times great uncle. One day, Alice, you and I will sit down and have a long chat. But today is not the day. Come down now—Olivia and Luca are ready. And by the way—*Buon Natale*." Anna held the door for Ali, and they both turned toward the elevators.

When the lift doors opened on the main floor, her friends were waiting for her at the double doors, ready to go. The deep winter darkness still had a grip on the small town and though her jacket was usually enough to keep her warm, she felt a chill from the inside out.

"You look great, Alice," said Olivia, with a warming smile.

"Ready to go?" Luca appeared a bit on edge himself.

Ali breathed in and released, stuffing her hands in her pockets. "Yes—let's do this." She turned to Anna to say goodbye, who unreservedly gave her a great motherly hug.

She placed an antique wooden rosary in Alice's hands and folded her fingers around it. "Take this and keep it with you always—to watch over you. Good luck," said Anna, wrapping her sweater around her shoulders.

Chapter Twenty-Three

Luca pulled the car up directly in front of the monastery doors. With mechanical efficiency, he extracted the power sources and equipment needed for the chamber adjustments from the trunk.

After sending a quick text, they waited patiently at the door. Despite the early hour, the abbey was aglow with lights, indicating the brothers were already at service to usher in Christmas Day.

The door slowly opened, and one of the brothers waved them in. "Wait here please," he whispered.

"I thought Father Donato was coming," Ali murmured to Luca.

He shrugged and peered down the marbled hallway. "He'd better hurry," said Olivia. "It's going to be light soon."

A tall figure appeared from across the courtyard, hurriedly making his way toward them. Alice watched as it approached. "I think that's him," she whispered, hearing the jangling of keys as he got closer.

"Alice, how good to see you again. Luca, Olivia, good morning, and *Buon Natale*. A blessed Christmas to all of you, my young friends." Father Donato was winded and appeared frazzled. "Sorry about the wait. I had to go to my office to get the keys."

"*Buon Natale*, Father," said Luca with an incline of his head. "And thank you for allowing us in this morning. I have everything we require for the chamber modifications."

"We're so sorry for taking you away from your Christmas services, Father," Alice said apologetically. "I wish there was another way we could do this."

"You are not taking me away at all." Donato motioned for them to follow. "The bishop was kind enough to say Mass for the brothers at dawn, and I will say a community Mass later this morning. But, before we get started, I want to speak with you about this...venture."

Everyone grabbed a piece of equipment, and he led them down the familiar path to da Vinci's former living quarters. They stopped at the first landing in front of the planked wooden door. "I think it is commendable that you are attempting a rescue, but are you aware of the possible dangers that await you? Not only from the modifications you two are planning on the portal but the dangers in 1512?"

"I understand your concern, Father," replied Ali as the monk started to work on the lock of the first door, "but I don't plan on being in 1512 for long. That's why we're making modifications to the portal. I can't be gone that long and expect not to have the cavalry descend on your little corner of the world. Plus, the longer Claudio stays there, the greater the chances of his deadly fate coming true."

Once he released the last lock, Donato opened the door into the hallway, lined with more barred-up open-air windows, revealing a steep drop to the valley below. At the end of the hall was the door to Leonardo's antechamber. He approached it briskly, and once in, the abbot turned to his right. The windows were sealed with brickwork. He reached for the battery-powered lantern and switched it on, lighting up the entire space. Ali shivered. The closer she got to fulfilling her task, the edgier she became. Briskly, they followed Donato to the antechamber, and then to the tear-shaped door.

"I cannot say, in good conscience, that I approve. I believe it is a very dangerous and unnecessary risk, not only for you but also for the abbey. We are not sure if the laser will work. All you have is one experiment that suggests it works to emulate lightning."

"Father," Ali responded, intensely concerned that Donato wouldn't let this go forward. "It is, in fact, more controlled than with an organic bolt. The energy from the laser is manually calibrated. It won't damage the abbey or put anyone in danger. The energy will flow into the chamber and through the wormhole. It is proven science—my father and his team have a theory."

"A theory, Alice," interrupted the Abbot. "Just a theory."

"But if it worked once, it will work again. Right, Luca, Olivia?" Ali turned to her friends for confirmation.

"Theoretically—yes," Luca replied feebly.

"There's no reason to think otherwise," affirmed Olivia.

At this, Donato raised an eyebrow and sighed heavily. "I remain unconvinced."

The space was as barren and cavernous as Ali remembered it. "This is the last door to the chamber," Ali said, her voice echoing against the stone.

Shaking herself back to her task at hand, Alice placed her bundle on the floor as Luca plodded in with his equipment. As she watched her friend, she could envision Claudio the first time he had brought her here, remembering how he had brushed his hand against the wall of the room, as if to feel and grasp hold of events that the walls had absorbed. He had been deep in thought as he stared at the door, walking toward it with a transfixed look on his face. The same look that he had the moment she first saw him. The knots in Alice's stomach were back.

Luca stopped in front of the teardrop door and lightly traced its molding with both hands, starting from the tip of the point at the top to the bottom. Thrusting both palms of his hands against the molding, the door popped. It stood just barely elevated to the molding flanking it. With a gentle nudge from his hand, it revolved open with a whoosh.

"I'll go in first Ali, then Father will let you in."

Ali nodded. He picked up the guitar case and the heaviest bag and proceeded in.

"It seems we have been here before, Alice." Father strode to the door and copied Luca's motions. The door popped open to reveal Luca already setting up the contents of the guitar case. "Promise me that you aren't making a hasty decision."

"I'm not, Father."

"Somehow, I already knew that," he said, letting out a long, audible breath.

Olivia stepped through with more bags, then Father approached to open it again for Alice.

Ali gazed at the door intently. "Let me do this, Father." She moved closer to the door Claudio created for the chamber room. Slowly, she felt for the raised dots under her fingers just as Luca had taught her. Once she felt the nearly imperceptible Braille-like embossments under the frame, she squeezed gently, and the sensors in the doorjamb released the airlock. It popped open, allowing them in one by one. When Luca told Ali the secret of the mechanism, she realized that it only appeared to be magical, but it wasn't magic at all, just good engineering and exceptional construction.

"You seem to have gotten the hang of that quickly," quipped Luca as he moved toward the chamber and released the door, revealing the infinite space beyond the simple copper box.

Gingerly, Ali strode over the threshold into the chamber

room, her vision instantly drawn to the center of the chamber, to the paradox of the infinity inside its walls. She felt herself moving toward it, mesmerized by its power. Just on the other side of the chamber was Claudio's world—five hundred years in the past. A shudder shook Ali's body, her nerves raw at the prospect of her imminent time traveling.

She turned her attention back to Luca and Olivia. They had to set up the laser with a portable power source—in this case, the greatest portable power source available was a suit-case-sized unit capable of generating up to 20 million amps. This extremely expensive piece of equipment had been "borrowed" from the university lab by Luca. His position as assistant to his professor was proving to be highly instrumental.

"So where do you think we should place the laser?" Ali asked as she unpacked the bags filled with provisions for Luca and Olivia. They would have to stay and monitor the aperture once Alice entered, and the laser had been discharged.

"I would suggest ten point five meters from the opening for optimum efficiency. According to my calculations, based on Claudio's description, that was the length that the bolt had to travel in the copper rods from the rooftop to the inside of the chamber."

Once the cables from the power source were attached and Luca had set the dials on the laser, they were ready to go. The only fly in the ointment was the fact that it could not be tested. A Y17 laser randomly pointing and firing in a monastery would not do.

"All right, Alice." Luca's breathing was ragged as he looked over the laser and the power source, making last-minute adjustments. "I think we're ready. Olivia and I will monitor the laser. Now, if something happens with the laser," he locked his gaze onto Ali's, "I will need to call up re-enforcements—the likes of my professor and others who have greater knowledge than me, but that is a last resort—we must respect Claudio and da Vinci's wish that this stays a secret."

Father stepped forward. "And most importantly, don't take any unnecessary risks. Try to blend in—vernacular and all. You are Elisa now, not Alice. Think back, use every shred of memory and experience, every recollection and knowledge that you have of past events—you will need them to play your part as the person you once were."

"I understand. Don't worry—I did it before," Ali reassured him. "And I know we talked about this, but I-I need someone to be here at all times, just like the last time." Ali stammered out the last part.

"We already have our shifts planned, and lots of provisions, pillows, and sleeping bags." Olivia smiled. "We won't leave you —we promise."

"I'm leaving my device here, in my bag, but I've got a hard copy of Castiglione's letter to Medici to show Claudio. I can't bring much else."

A defined silence hung in the air, like they had reached the top of a summit and were looking to the other side. It was the *do or die* moment. Ali took a deep breath.

"Well, I guess it's time then." Her words split the silence.

Father raised his hands to gather them together.

"Let me give you all a blessing." He closed his eyes and whispered a prayer as he made the sign of the cross over the three friends. "Go now with God's blessing." He sent a sincere, fatherly smile to Alice.

"Thank you, Father." Ali reached up to hug him. "Luca, Olivia—" She turned to her friends and drew them near.

"We know," whispered Olivia. "Please, be careful."

With a final nod, Ali turned and walked with measured caution to the copper chamber, wishing with all her heart for Claudio to be on the other side, to be working in the master's studio as she walked through. He would be stunned and surprised at first, but then he would be overjoyed to see her again—of this she was certain.

With these thoughts in mind, her hand impulsively gripped the scarf around her neck. She closed her eyes and walked toward the spiraling strings and into the infinite darkness.

Chapter Twenty-Four

Ali's skin tingled, and a pulling sensation overtook her—each cell in her body was drawn into the center without any effort on her part at all. Her limbs moved in syrupy darkness, her ears muffled with the sound of a million stars bursting around her. As she walked through a wall of thick honey, colors abounded, but it did not offer any resistance. Instead, she was drawn through the darkness as if she were falling backward, while an unseen force propelled her body forward. Ali opened her eyes to another world of fiercely glowing energy inhabiting the chamber, fleeting cones and overlapping spheres and crescents and jagged spirals.

Slowly, with her hands in front of her, she emerged into da Vinci's studio feeling like she was coming out of one of her fainting episodes with a foggy feeling and stuffiness in her ears.

Ali shook her head to try to clear the pressure in her ears and looked around the room, her eyes adjusting to the immersing darkness, save for a strip of moonlight shining through the translucent stained-glass windows.

Nighttime—and no one is here—talk about anti-climactic. The smile on Ali's lips vanished.

"Hello?" she whispered. Nothing. "Hello?" Still no answer. She padded to the window and opened it, allowing the warm breeze to wash over her. She breathed in and looked down at the drop from da Vinci's window. Too far to jump, she thought and latched it closed.

Now adjusted to the darkness, she moved around with only the moonlight as her guide, dodging articles that were strewn about the space. She tiptoed to the antechamber door. The intricate locking mechanism had been activated from the outside. Hanging her head back and closing her eyes, she bit her lip, trying to remember the sequence of cogs and wheels to press that Claudio had shown her. Ali pictured his movements. Her hand repeated his gestures, and the locks clicked and whirred and popped open.

"Yes!" she hissed. As she stepped into the antechamber and closed the door behind her, she noted that the window was ajar. It bore a lovely stained-glass image of the Baby Jesus staring back at her, his eyes a paragon of innocence.

Ali wondered briefly when the window had been replaced by secure brickwork, but her thoughts were whisked away like smoke in the wind when she heard a loud snore accompanied by noisy breathing and whistling coming from a room off the antechamber.

She gasped and whirled about to face the direction of the snores. It had to be Master da Vinci. Padding ever so softly, she stepped to the door, gripped the knob tightly, and held her breath as she turned it. The lock gave way. Ali opened it a quarter of the way, and by the light of a single lantern, she discerned the covered shape of a person on a small plain bed.

Okay, now—you are Elisa Beatrice de Povri—speak in the Floren-tine vernacular. She drew in a breath and whispered, "Master, wake up."

The snorting stopped, and rhythmic breathing took over.

"Master da Vinci—it is Elisa—wake up." Her whisper turned into a hiss. "Leonardo, it is Elisa, I have—"

"What? Who is there?"

Ali caught sight of his disheveled white hair as he poked his head out from under the thin bedcovers.

He propped himself up on one elbow and reached for the knob on the lantern, increasing its intensity. "Who is there!" His voice echoed in the large space.

"Sir, it is I, Elisa." Her voice quivered at da Vinci's thunderous demand. "I have come back, Master. It is of ultimate importance that I speak with you, sir."

"Elisa?" da Vinci's voice was filled with wonder. It was plain to Alice that he was thoroughly perplexed. Gingerly, he rose from his bed and reached for the lantern, then plodded across the floor in his bare feet.

Ali smiled as he drew nearer, already feeling more at ease. "Yes, Master, it is me. My sincerest regrets for awakening you, sir. But it is of the gravest consequence."

As he drew closer, his face softened and split into a familiar, fatherly smile. "In Bacchus' name, child, you seem to delight in awakening me from my deepest slumbers." He chuckled, hugging her shoulder to shoulder while holding the lantern close to her so he could see her face. "It *is* you, my dear. Such a sight for old, tired eyes you are—but, alas, unless my mind is playing on my senses, I believe you were to stay in your time."

He let go of her and looked gravely into her eyes. "I do not begrudge you your visit, however, there is the matter of this blasted timeline and its integrity. It was my understanding that young Claudio had spoken our concerns on that rather delicate matter with you."

"Yes, dear Leonardo, this is an important thing, but I do not come here for a visit. I come as the bearer of terrible news." She reached into her pocket and took out a piece of pristine white paper—too processed to perfection for da Vinci's time.

His brow furrowed as he grasped the paper.

"I was in our library and discovered this letter about Claudio. This is a copy, taken from a book filled with letters from Baldassare Castiglione to various nobles—"

"Castiglione, yes, I am acquainted with him," said the old master. "Let me see now." Leonardo began reading the letter with an air of confusion. The old master suddenly stopped and looked at Ali, his expression dumbfounded. "But how can this be?"

He shook his head in disbelief as he continued to read. "My dear Elisa, this is most distressing news. Indeed, terribly disquieting." He looked over the letter again.

"There is no indication as to when this shall transpire. Only the year it is written—this year." Ali pointed to the date on the copy paper.

Da Vinci turned to a nearby footstool, still staring at the paper, set the lantern on the floor, and sat down hard. Ali went to the master's side and gently retrieved the letter from his grasp.

"It is for this precise reason, sir, that I have returned."

He looked up at her, his eyes clouded with grief. "That is very admirable, Elisa, but sadly you cannot change history—it is done. You cannot let him know of this lest he knows his fate and be allowed to live. If he saves himself, the entire course of what is to be may change. I fear there is no way out of this dreadful quandary." Leonardo's tone was empathetic and sad, yet firm. "The boy must die."

"No, sir." Ali's voice was small, but just as firm. "I assumed that at first, but then I thought, or rather, I know there is a way he can be spared." Ali's small hands were clasped palm to palm, while Leonardo listened. "He can come back to 2029 with me. He will live his life there. Claudio would be gone from here, fulfilling his destiny in 1512, but he would still have a chance at happiness in the future, with friends that care for him. History will be satisfied, but he will be safe...and alive."

Leonardo deliberated for what seemed an eternity, and then he spoke in a doubtful tone. "You make a good argument for this however, your good judgment is clouded by love for this young man."

"Master, my reasoning is logical. Yes, I love him, but my judgment is sound and based on rationality. In a very short time, Claudio will die. He will be gone from this time. I cannot find a thing in my research that will make any difference as to how he leaves this era. Unfortunately, he makes no significant contribution in the short time that he has left here, so he can leave at any point with me—the sooner the better."

"And what of Countess Maria? How will he justify this sudden disappearance to her Ladyship? And for that matter, the entire court?"

Ali took a deep breath. She had no answers for these questions. "That, sir, I shall leave up to the count." She took da Vinci's hand and locked her pleading eyes to his. "Now, Master Leonardo, will you help me? We should at least give him the choice. Where is he?"

His face softened, and he nodded. "I will help you, my dear. Who has the power within to refuse that angelic face?"

"Thank you, sir!" Ali hugged him and her confidence in the ultimate completion of her task doubled. "Now, according to my calculations, it has been approximately twenty days since I departed. Correct?"

"Yes."

"Good. And he is still attending as your apprentice? When will he be back so we may speak?"

"He no longer arrives here on a regular basis but happens here on his examinations of the chamber. He is very anxious as to why it has not been neutralized and disassembled yet—he related to me that in your time there was sufficient science to enable its safe deactivation."

"He may have been overconfident on that point, but we were fortunate that there was a glitch."

"A what?"

"A problem. The method of counteracting the passage was not effective—it did not work. Also, we discovered a way to offset the time progression discrepancy between our time and—"

Leonardo's expression changed from a man listening intently to one with deep concern. He moved closer to the door of the room housing the chamber. Ali heard it too—a distinct, high-pitched hum, accompanied by an eerie light emanating underneath the door.

"They're doing it now!" Alice exclaimed.

Leonardo's brow puckered. He grasped the handle and tore open the door, revealing the chamber aglow. There were no spirals, no colors, no infinite darkness into eternity—only a light so bright he and Ali had to turn away.

"What is this? What are they doing to my chamber?" bellowed Leonardo.

A torturous, high-pitched sound escaped the chamber, making them grimace in pain and hold their ears for fear of having their brains split in two. It was the last thing Leonardo and Ali heard before they both collapsed on the cold stone floor, like marionettes whose strings had just been cut.

Chapter Twenty-Five

Alice awoke to the muted light of day streaming in through the stained-glass window in the chamber room; her ears were still buzzing. Da Vinci slowly began to move his head about, trying to reach consciousness. Her head pounded like someone had taken a hammer to it, but she spun herself around to look at the chamber. What she saw knocked the living breath out of her.

The chamber was empty.

It was an ordinary copper box. No darkness, no light, just an empty space taunting her with its open door. The reality of what this meant hit Alice with a crushing force; there was no passage to her world. The bridge to 2029 was gone.

"Master," she croaked. "Master da Vinci, wake up." She nudged him gently, her eyes now brimming with tears.

"Ah!" He let out a yell and shook his head, sticking his fingers in his ears to clear the buzz left in the wake of the attack on his senses. "What in the devil happened?"

"Sir, look at the chamber." Ali stood slowly, tears on her cheeks, her hands on her head.

"Why, it is no more." Leonardo's voice was barely audible.

"It is gone. What evil form of Nature is this?" His voice cracked with emotion.

Alice did not know what was worse: the disappointment in Leonardo's voice or the fact that it appeared certain she was stuck in 1512.

"Sir, I am so sorry—it was supposed to work—everything pointed to the theory that a simulated lightning bolt would bring the two timelines into sync. We assumed the idea would work."

"The word 'assumed' troubles me, Elisa. You cannot assume things will work if they are not tested first. This is a thing I am discovering more and more as I work to understand Nature. You and your friends have destroyed the portal because you allowed your emotions to cloud your judgment." He stood with a look of defeat in his eyes.

Leonardo's stark words struck her to the core. The Master was right—she had forced Luca to help her with something beyond both their understandings, and now she, her family, and Claudio would pay the price. Her thoughts were a turbulent grey whirlpool of regret, shame, confusion, and fear. How would she fix this? Could she fix this?

"I do not know what to say, Master," she said quietly.

"It does not matter, now." Da Vinci's voice was lifeless. "We need to send word to Claudio that he must come to the monastery immediately. Together, with Francesco, we may be able to repeat the miracle of the time portal. I cannot say that it will be possible, though."

"I understand," said Alice, gulping. Her mouth felt like sandpaper. "Can we send word now?"

"Yes, perhaps we should. First, I shall dress, and then I shall get us both something to eat. After which, I shall saddle my horse and proceed to the palace in search of Claudio. You, however, will stay here and wait until we decide how to proceed."

Having to wait was torture. Ali detested delaying action because of someone else, even if it was Leonardo da Vinci. But there was no option; she could not leave the room, roam about the abbey, and take a chance on being seen. So, she sat on Leonardo's study chair, her bread and ale untouched, with her chin on her knees, and her arms wrapped around her legs, waiting.

She thought about where Claudio was and about whether he was still alive. Had he gotten into an argument with Bruno that afternoon? Had they engaged in a duel? Was she too late? She wondered how she would introduce the subject of his looming death and how he would react.

With her angst permeating every cell in her body, she ripped off her cap and threw it across the room, untied her hair, and massaged her scalp. These reflections kept coming back to her, playing out in her mind as her hand made its way to her forearm and rubbed the microchip under the skin.

How long had he been gone, she wondered. Through the window, she could see the sun lower in the sky. The master had probably been gone at least two or three hours. Ali strolled around his study, peering at sketches and into glass containers that she hoped held animal parts.

None of the sketches were familiar, though she had seen enough of da Vinci's art in textbooks, art galleries, and museums to know these were from his hand. As she took another frustrated, impatient walk around the studio, she heard the unmistakable clicking of boots on the stone floor, outside the apartments.

"Crap. I hope that's da Vinci," she murmured.

As the steps moved closer, she could tell whoever it was had a quick purposeful gait—too youthful for Leonardo. Next, she heard the sounds of metal clanking against the wall. A sword? Her stomach coiled tight with anxiety. This isn't Leonardo.

To Ali's horror, the footsteps stopped right outside Leonardo's door. There was a sharp knock, and she covered her mouth to keep from yelping.

Ali dashed to hide in the chamber room—a cold shiver ran down her spine as she secured the door and engaged the locking system. "Crap!" she hissed. She found a space behind the shelves that held an assortment of timekeepers, flasks, and clay pots filled with pigments.

"Oh my gosh, oh my gosh," she chanted in the smallest whisper. Ali held her breath behind the shelves and stood still, praying that whoever it was would go away. To her chagrin, keys began to jingle on the other side of the door.

There was silence for a long moment—it seemed to Ali an eternity. Whoever it was, they were probably surveying the place, checking it out. She stood stone still and waited.

"Sir?" The word echoed in the room.

Ali gasped.

"Master Leonardo?" The voice was like music. It was her beginning and ending, her heart and soul, her body and spirit and sun and stars.

Chapter Twenty-Six

"Claudio!" Ali could not get out from behind the shelving fast enough. "Claudio!"

"Alice?"

His familiar, throaty voice spoke her name, and she nearly fell over the pigment pots, as she momentarily tangled her feet in a canvas. She looked up at him and stopped. Never was there a more beautiful and welcome sight. All her worries, fears, and doubts were cast away with his presence like smoke in the wind. Claudio's bewildered expression turned to a glorious smile, and her breath caught in her throat. Would she ever become accustomed to his charms?

"Yes, it's me—it's me." A dazzling smile flashed across her face, and she ran to him.

"Oh, my God." He was rooted to the spot. "Alice?"

She had almost reached him when he darted to her, finally able to move. There was one step between them, and he took it to close the distance. In an instant, they were holding each other, his hands in her hair, pressing her face close to his heart. Alice freed the emotions that had been struggling inside her and let her tears flow. She was home—in his strong embrace.

Claudio swept his arms under hers and brought her up close to his face, lifting her off her feet. Her arms wrapped around him, and her fingers knotted in his hair as she drew closer to him, letting his kiss spin gloriously through her body. After savoring their long-awaited moment, they opened their eyes, still close enough to feel the warmth of each other's breath on their mouths.

Claudio slowly set her down, not taking eyes off her, looking into her soul. It was an endless moment filled with indescribable happiness, wonder, and pure love.

"My darling—it is you!" He smiled as he held the backs of her arms. "You have come back to me." He tucked a lock of her hair behind her ear, then kissed her again gently. "I love you so," he murmured against her mouth. "You have made me so happy."

Her skin tingled under his touch as he gently skimmed his thumb over her lips. Alice returned his kisses, then, with cherished familiarity, she hid her face in his neck and chest as he held her tightly, his strong arms like a blanket around her tiny frame.

"I love you, too." Her voice was a deep whisper. "I always have. How could I ever have believed that I could live without you?" She took the palm of his hand and placed it on her cheek, thinking that this perfect fit could never be replicated with another. Breathing in a satisfied sigh, she let her skin revel in his touch.

Claudio spoke first, his strong hands still holding her. "How long have you been back? How? I do not know what to ask you first, my darling, but I love you so, and I am overjoyed that you are here!" He swept her up once again in his arms and cradled her, as though hugging her was not enough. "You, in your stable boy garb as before—I feel I must pinch myself. Is this all a dream from which I will awaken and suffer certain devastation afterward? These twenty days may as well have been twenty years, I have yearned for you so."

Ali giggled, unable to control the joy inside her. "For you, it has been only twenty days—for me, it has been four months—which may as well have been four centuries." All this talk of time made her remember the reason why she came back. "Claudio, as much as I love being in your arms," she reached up and tenderly kissed him on the cheek, "you must put me down, and you need to listen, okay?"

"Why? Just let me hold you."

"This is serious. Now listen."

"Whatever you want," he said, setting her down. "I will listen to you morning, noon, and night, for we are never to be separated again." His mouth curled into an irresistible smile as he slipped his hands down to hers, linked their fingers, and pulled her close to him.

"Okay, this is important, my love." She looked up into his dark eyes. "Claudio, do you trust me completely?" Her gaze was intensely serious.

"Of course, I do." Claudio's smile faltered, and his brow furrowed. "You know I trust you with my life. Why do you ask?"

She bit her lip and sighed. "Listen carefully." Ali pulled one of her hands free to take the piece of photocopied paper out of her pocket. "My love, you need to brace yourself because it is not good news. There is something very important you need to know. I found this passage in an antique book in 2029—the book is by Baldassare Castiglione—do you know him?"

Claudio's expression resumed a lighthearted quality, and he took the paper from Alice, glancing at it briefly. "Castiglione—yes, I know him—he is one of the duke's advisors. What does he say?"

"This is serious, Claudio," she interrupted. "Read it."

Chapter Twenty-Seven

With a large dose of coaxing on Alice's part, Claudio brought himself back down to earth. She watched his expression change as he read the letter, his face growing serious, his eyes narrowing at the place where Castiglione expressed his regret to the duke regarding Claudio's death.

"And you said you found this where?" Claudio asked, holding up the piece of paper.

"In a rare antique book—at the university library. I copied it to show it to you because I figured you would probably scoff at the idea of such a thing happening. But it says right there, you will be killed violently this year." She pointed to the date on the page. "See—1512."

The line of his mouth tightened as he slowly moved his head from side to side. "This is most troubling," he finally uttered, his voice calm and even.

"Troubling? You're going to be killed, and you call that troubling?" Ali raised her open hands. "Are you kidding me?"

Claudio paced as he read the letter again. "I need to think

this through rationally and weigh all possible variables before deciding on a course of action."

"What do you mean 'think it through?'"

"First of all, I would like to know who will...murder me."

"If you wait around to find that out, won't it be too late?" Ali laughed without humor. "My love, your fate is right there in front of you—you die within four months—no variables." Exasperated, Ali put her hands on her hips and paced stride for stride alongside him.

"Perhaps it does not have to be this way—perhaps I can—"

"I know what you're thinking and no you can't. Remember the timeline? Events must be maintained, or the future may be affected. Think about it rationally." She grasped both his hands in hers and looked in his eyes. "Look, I understand your skepticism, but you can't argue with history. You are coming back with me, Count Claudio Moro, and that's that."

"You are brilliant, Alice." He took her chin in his hand, smiling down at her. "And very noble for attempting to come back to rescue me." He pulled her close and kissed her eyes, then traced the bridge of her nose with his lips and worked his way to her mouth. Her knees weakened under his spell. "But, is that your only reason for seeking me out once more?" His eyes sought hers for answers.

"I was strong," she admitted breathlessly. "I was very strong until I discovered this. Then I couldn't bear to think that you were being so righteous and decent, to think that you went back because you thought you would be tainting the natural occurrence of events—and then to have your life snatched away from you so senselessly and without meaning. I couldn't bear to live with myself if I didn't at least try to warn you. Then I thought, since you would not exist here anymore, you could come back and live your life in 2029—with me, if you want to." The condition of the chamber came back to Alice's mind. She swiftly put her hand to her mouth to keep a gasp from escaping. "Oh, and I almost forgot—there is something else I have to tell you—Master da Vinci already knows."

Alice took his hand and led him to the chamber room.

When he saw the gaping, empty space where the time portal once spiraled into eternity, he dragged his hands through his hair and uttered, "What?"

"Claudio, I am so sorry."

"What the devil happened?" He turned to look at Ali, a look of profound disbelief on his face.

"Well, Luca and I had an idea that—"

"Luca," Claudio hissed.

"Well, actually, it was my idea," conceded Ali. Guilt overtook fear at Claudio's reaction should he get hold of Luca again. "I thought if we were able to get a laser to mimic a bolt of lightning, it would allow us to harmonize the passage of time in our world with the world of 1512. Then I could come back to get you, with time to spare, before people realized I was missing. You see, my father had told me about a discovery that he and his team had made called the Digression Paradox." Ali explained everything to Claudio, including the caper at CENA-corp and how she got Luca and Olivia to help her, then finished with how there was a blinding light from inside the chamber and its resulting darkness.

Claudio could not speak, he only looked from Alice to the chamber and back again. "Now I am afraid, but not for me." He wiped his mouth with his sleeve. "For you. What will happen if the Master and I cannot re-establish the portal? If we cannot get you back to your time, your risk was all in vain. What will we do then?"

Alice had never considered the possibility that they may not be able to restore the chamber. The thoughts flooded into her mind like a breached dam. Was she to spend the rest of her life here, in a world now foreign to her, five hundred years in the past? And what if they were not able to avert Claudio's death? Would she have to face the possibility that she must live her life in Renaissance Florence alone?

Chapter Twenty-Eight

"My love, why would you ever risk coming back here for me?" Claudio gave Ali a long look. "We talked about all that the first time. Why will you not ever do as I ask?"

She raised a brow at his statement. "Are you seriously asking me that?" She tried to lighten the situation, though she was still worried about what her future held.

He allowed her a half-smile and took her hand once again. From down the hall, voices could be heard, deep in discussion.

"...and you do believe that the letter is genuine—that Castiglione speaks the truth about Claudio's fate?" The speech was slightly muffled, but Ali was certain it was Francesco. Keys were inserted in the door, but it swung open—Claudio had not locked it when he entered, due to the immense distraction on the other side.

"Hmm...most odd," da Vinci mused out loud. "I was certain I had secured it. Oh, dear, I do hope she has not taken it upon herself to—" Leonardo looked up and saw the two of them hand in hand. "Ah, I see why my searches were in vain, Francesco. The young count has preceded us to the monastery."

"Good evening, sir. Francesco." Claudio nodded his acknowledgment. "I came here, quite by happenstance, and found a particular young lady awaiting me." He slid his hand around Ali's waist and drew her closer, so her shoulder was under his arm. It was a perfect fit, like Cinderella's foot in her glass slipper.

"Claudio." Francesco bowed slightly to his friend, his face beaming a grand welcome for the girl at Claudio's side. "Elisa, how wonderful to see you again." He gently took her hand and lightly brushed his lips against the back of it. "The grace and beauty you lend to those stable boy garments are unsurpassed by any other wearer. Of this, I am certain, my lady."

Ali giggled. Claudio grimaced.

"Wonderful to see you again, Francesco. How is Caterina?"

"I dare say, she misses you. She speaks constantly about you and how she wishes you well."

"Is she still with your family?"

"She is—and very happy to be at service there, I might add. Though she still maintains friendships with some of the maids from the palace, I think."

"My friends," interrupted the old master, "we shall speak niceties later. Now we have a very important matter at hand— or rather two important matters: the quandary confronting us about Claudio, and, of course, the chamber and its apparent malfunction. What say you, gentlemen?"

Claudio's gaze swept from da Vinci to Francesco. "If lightning worked before, can it not work again, sir?" asked Claudio. "We shall fashion another proper copper rod on the roof to draw lightning to the chamber. The plates shall trap it as before, and the portal shall return."

Da Vinci's hands grasped the velvet lapels of his day jacket as he turned to face the copper structure, nodding slightly. He gazed pensively at it for a long moment as the three listened for his concurrence. When he spoke, his eyes focused on Ali. "I suppose it is possible, however, my first thought is that there is no assurance that a portal will open at the same time or place as where you come from, my dear."

That possibility had never crossed her mind, nor, it appeared, Claudio's.

"There are many irregularities that may affect the outcome of a similar trial." The wise old man shook his head in doubt, his kindly eyes looked at Alice with obvious empathy. "I do not wish to alarm you, child, however, I fear that the likelihood of you returning to your proper place in time is at best uncertain. You must prepare yourself for this possibility."

The words reverberated in her head like echoes in a chasm. A strike to the stomach would have been easier for her to take. "Oh, my God," Ali whispered the words, her hands covering her mouth. "What if I cannot get back—my parents—oh no— it was not supposed to be like this. Everything was supposed to work out. What am I going to do?" Her eyes filled with tears and brimmed over.

Claudio held her, her face against his heart. "Master da Vinci, I realize you are being realistic, but can we please maintain a positive outlook?" Claudio's eyes widened, and he looked down at Ali's quivering frame before glaring back at the old master. "We must try to recreate the portal right away, sir." To Ali, he whispered, "We shall replicate the results, Alice. I swear I will get you back home."

"But do you not see, the longer we are here, the more likely it is that you will be killed," said Ali.

"I am afraid we have no choice, Elisa. It is as Claudio has said." Leonardo spoke with a resigned tone in his voice. "Whilst we pray for a storm, and a fierce one at that, we should look for a proper place for you to stay. As welcoming as the brothers are, a monastery is no place for a girl."

Francesco stepped forward. "That is simple—she will stay

with my family. Caterina is there, and she will be pleased beyond reason to see you return."

"Caterina?" Ali turned her head to face Francesco, wiping her eyes. "I would like to see her again. I missed her." She dabbed her sleeve against her nose, which caused Claudio to scan the room for a handkerchief. Seeing none handy, he proceeded to innocuously untie his old one from around Ali's neck.

"Here." He handed it to her. "Use this." He motioned to her nose.

"No," Ali answered. "I am rather attached to that." She swiftly grasped it and retied it, then accepted another, which da Vinci produced from his pocket.

"You must not fret, child. I did not say we would not try, only that it shall be a difficult go of it," Leonardo said apologetically.

"I have full confidence in Master Leonardo," Claudio said, gently taking her hands into his. "We have one of the greatest minds of ours, or any age, in our midst."

At this, the old man chortled. "We will prevail, my dear. Of this, I am abundantly certain."

"And, Elisa, do not fear for Claudio," Francesco said, his hand on his rapier. "I will do my utmost to keep him out of harm's way for you." Ali, feeling slightly more comfortable with the ordeal, looked up at Claudio and offered a feeble smile, after which she strode to Leonardo and Francesco and kissed them both on their cheeks.

"Thank you both so much for helping us. How can we ever thank you?"

"By staying out of trouble until we can safely send you both home."

She thought how Leonardo's words were innocently stated yet could be powerful harbingers of what lay ahead.

"Before we do anything else, I believe it prudent our young

visitor be settled into her temporary dwelling and that she is provided with dress appropriate for her situation and gender," Leonardo added.

"Francesco, perhaps it is appropriate that we depart from the monastery together," suggested Claudio. "I shall accompany Elisa to your home. When we arrive, I am sure that Caterina should be able to find a suitable dress for her. Perhaps it is best that I stay at your home this night, Francesco."

"Claudio, as much as it would ease my mind to have you there, I do not wish to raise your mother's ire. Are you entirely certain you wish to proceed in that manner?"

Claudio narrowed his eyes.

"Well done, my lady, Elisa. I believe you shall pass for a Renaissance woman yet." Francesco clapped his hands in delight.

Claudio chuckled and wrapped his fingers around her hand. "If this girl is not a Renaissance woman, then I do not know who is."

Ali blushed beautiful roses on her cheeks.

"You are exceedingly kind, my lord. Did you ride Spirit here, sir?"

"I did, and I do believe that she has noted your absence."

"Now you are teasing me."

"Nay, I do not. You shall see forthwith."

"Shall we go then?" Francesco prompted.

The master pointed to her cap, which she had thrown against the wall and had landed on an easel. "I shall remind you, Elisa, cap tight about your face. Here," the master grasped a worn velvet cape from a hook beside the door, "take this cloak and wrap it about you. Father Federico has been very patient with us, but I dare not test him again. The fewer eyes that see you here, the better."

Chapter Twenty-Nine

"You did very well in slipping back into your old self today, 1512 Florentine vernacular and all," Claudio shouted back to Ali as they were carried with strength and effortless grace on Spirit. The mare, black as a moonless sky at midnight, galloped with a steady stride through the Tuscan hills, following Francesco's horse to his family's home just outside of Florence.

The heat had dissipated as evening settled in, leaving behind a cooling breeze that swept playfully through Claudio's hair. Alice held him tight around his waist, loving every moment of the closeness to her one true love. She had not fully realized how much she had missed his hands gently holding hers, and the security of knowing that he would always love her. She knew in her heart and soul that he would always be hers, and she, his.

"Thank you, my lord." Her happiness at being with him was ridiculously evident. "I think I shall try to maintain this speech, even when others are not around. Otherwise, I shall run the risk of slipping up and giving myself away."

"Ha! 'Slipping up' is a colloquialism not yet in use, my love."

"Cut me some slack, will you?" Ali laughed, her cape flying in the gentle wind raised in Spirit's wake. She felt lighter and more relaxed than she had for longer than she could recall. Ali decided she would allow herself the luxury of enjoying her reunion with Claudio and worry about what was to come later.

"Here we are," said Claudio, guiding Spirit through a hamlet. Peasants and townspeople were tilling the lands and tending their flocks of sheep and goats. At the top of a small summit was a stone house, surrounded by a looming retaining wall. Against the one side, which sloped down to the houses below, was a grove of olive trees and the occasional lemon tree. On the other, flatter side, a pergola was fixed to the wall of the manor home, shaded by ancient grape vines entwining endlessly. As the three rode up to the house, Ali saw a corral with several horses and a stable.

"This is Francesco's 'house'?" Alice's eyes were wide. She would never have given a thought to Francesco being a proper country gentleman. "This is a manor house—an estate."

"It is a grand country manor. Francesco's father is a baron and owns this entire estate and all the lands with it."

As Spirit gently wound her way to the stable, Ali took in the pastoral scene: fresh green hills dotted with lavender and rosemary, fields of wheat undulated like the sea, bordered by trees of at least a dozen different species.

Claudio guided his mare into the corral and dismounted. He reached up to assist Ali and held her by the waist, much as he had done on the last day they were together outside the monastery doors. She slid between his hands until they were face to face. He took full advantage of this by stealing a loving kiss, which was followed by Spirit gently nudging Alice from behind with her nose.

"Oh, how could I forget about you, Spirit—good girl?" Ali gently stroked the mare's nose, thoroughly enjoying the moment, when she heard a cry from the manor house.

"Elisa!" The shout was clearer now. "It is you! You have come to visit."

Ali whirled around to see Caterina running down the slope from the house to the stables, pebbles shooting up from under her shoes. When she arrived at what was considered a respectable distance, she hurriedly curtsied to Claudio and then Francesco, after which her face focused entirely on her friend. "Oh, how wonderful to see you." She threw her arms around Alice and hugged her tightly. "It has not been a month since last I saw you, yet it feels like an eternity—I have missed you so."

"So have I, my dear friend." Ali's smile gushed her joy as her friend held her at arm's length to appraise her.

"My dear! Why in God's holy name are you sporting boy's clothing? And you are so thin. Are they not feeding you in Prato?"

Ali leaned into Claudio for an explanation as to why she would be in a city nearly a day's ride away.

"We told interested parties that you are now in service at a manor in Prato," he whispered.

"Of course." Ali nodded, then turned to Caterina. "The count suggested I wear comfortable clothing in consideration of the long ride, and naturally, I have forgotten to bring a change more suitable for the situation. Might I impose, dear friend, and ask you to lend me your change of clothes for the short time that I shall be visiting with you, the count, and our most kind and generous host, the Baron?" Ali curtsied to Francesco, indicating her thanks.

"Heavens to Bacchus, you are here for a visit—and a lengthy one, I do hope. Done and done, but I fear you shall be drowning in my clothes." Caterina looked down at her own healthy proportions. "I shall fix it for you—never you mind. And now, with Master Francesco's permission," Caterina took

Ali's hand and led her to the great stone house, "I shall get you fed while I make some adjustments to your garb."

"Adjust away, Caterina." Francesco nodded his approval.

As Caterina grasped her hand, Alice looked back at Claudio, his beauty enhanced by the simplicity of his clothing, though she was certain that as a count he could have dressed as ostentatiously as any courtier. His tousled dark hair was offset by a simple tan linen shirt, loosely fit, which brushed playfully against his strong tanned arms. He sported riding breeches with worn leather equestrian boots to the knee. His sword, concealed in its scabbard at his side, glinted in the setting sun —he was irresistible.

Claudio spied Ali watching him as Caterina led her up the stone path. "I shall be in forthwith, Elisa." He smiled broadly and motioned to the manor. A stable hand emerged from the side of the house and swiftly took the reins of both horses from the two men. "Francesco and I should like to have a word or two before joining you."

Ali nodded and engaged Caterina in conversation.

As the two women reached the door, Alice turned to look at her love again and noted that his broad smile had disappeared. He and Francesco were having a rather serious conversation.

"Come with me, dear, and let the men talk. They have matters to discuss—I am sure of it." Caterina led her through the kitchen door on the pergola side of the manor. "In the meantime, we shall get you a dress rightly fitted."

The entire space smelled heavenly. The instant the delicious aroma hit Ali's nose, her mouth started to water.

Caterina scurried to a room off the kitchen and reappeared with garments draped over her arm. She held up a day dress against her friend, assessing the amount to take in.

Ali looked around the kitchen. Stone floors scrubbed clean and shining, whitewashed walls, with ancient wooden beams adorning the ceiling. The hearth was the center of the kitchen, an iron spit stretched across it for roasting meats over the open fire. On the large harvest table, there were pottery and wooden bowls, a few spoons, and a knife. In the corner of the kitchen rested a plunger churn for transforming cream into butter. Alice recognized all this in the form of a memory akin to a dream.

On the other side of the hearth was a door that Ali guessed led to the main portion of the house. There was no oven, but she spied crockery on shelving beside the hearth and recalled that to bake bread, pastry, or other dishes, the cook put a covered pot or food wrapped in clay into the fire embers.

"You must let me see what I am able to do with this. I certainly hope no one from the village saw you looking like that —it would be a scandal. Now, perhaps this." Caterina held up the bodice, complete with lacings, then the apron. Using her fingers, she measured the rough fabric. "Very well, I should have this ready for you tonight." She smiled, putting the clothing aside. "Now, it is time for you to eat. We have a delicious potage for supper—a stew of legumes, oats, and barley, onions, greens, and herbs, with the meat of wild boar. It was Cook's specialty—she taught me, you know."

"With much appreciation, Caterina. I did not realize how hungry I am." Ali's mouth watered at the delicious smell, not having eaten since that morning—in 2029. In the cavernous hearth, a small fire burned cheerily within it, and an intensely aromatic pot of stew bubbled over it in a three-legged pot. Footsteps on the stones outside made the women look up to find Claudio and Francesco chatting amiably as they stepped in.

"I do believe," Francesco breathed in deeply, "yes, that is Caterina's wild boar potage. Have the maid set for supper in the dining hall, Caterina. Father shall be dining with the duke this night."

The Duke. Ali shuddered. The memory of the hearing a scant few months ago still haunted her. Thinking of how close she came to living out her days in the Medici prisons made her shudder.

Chapter Thirty

"Honestly—is it as bad as Master da Vinci is intimating?" Ali asked, her forehead crinkling with concern.

Caterina had excused herself to alter the borrowed dress, leaving the three of them to discuss the situation. Ali had tried to be strong and positive, but as the setting sun sank deeper behind the hills to the west, she realized her first day in 1512 was almost over, and she was no closer to getting back home than when she first stepped through the portal—further, in fact.

"I suspect that he was attempting to prepare you for the worst, but I think there is a good chance we can re-activate the wormhole. We will need to replace the copper rod." Claudio grasped her hand under the table.

"I am acquainted with a man who works with copper," Francesco said as he finished off the last of his ale. "He should be willing to smith one for me. Ambrosio is his name, and he is just within the city walls. I shall go to him on the morrow and enquire how long it should take."

"Thank you, Francesco," said Alice. "You are a true friend and gentleman."

"To this, I can attest, my love," Claudio agreed. "I shall go with you, Francesco, with the necessary measures and requirements for the attachment." He returned his attention to Ali. "In the meantime, you should stay in this hamlet with Caterina. You are not acquainted with anyone here, so you should be safe."

"Have you given thought to what you shall do, Count?" Francesco's tone had turned grim. "Will you depart our Florence forever or will you gamble and remain here, hoping to stay one step ahead of the Reaper for the rest of your days?"

Claudio winced at the last few words. "My thoughts, at the moment, are a maelstrom, my friend." Claudio kept his eyes on Ali as he spoke. "I will consider all things, when my mind clears, however—"

"There now, Elisa." Caterina peeked her head in from the other room. "This should do. Come into my room and give it a try."

"Very well," replied Alice. She squeezed Claudio's hand discreetly under the table, rose, and headed to Caterina's room.

The maid led Alice to her bedroom to try on her newly altered dress. Once Ali had it on, Caterina put her hands on her hips and surveyed the maid's garb, positively beaming at her work. "There now. You look much better."

Alice glanced at herself in the small mirror and smiled. "Beautiful, my dear friend. You really do have a talent for this."

Caterina blushed at the compliment. "Oh, go on. Now give me those old things, and do not dare don boy's clothes again," she said, scooping up the stable boy clothes. "It is simply not proper." Caterina led Ali back to the kitchen, where Claudio and Francesco were speaking in hushed tones.

"Here she is, my lords." Caterina chortled her approval. "And looking every bit the lady, now."

Ali stepped timidly into the kitchen, her bonnet tight around her loosely braided hair. Caterina's dress was still a bit roomy, which allowed the light fabric to billow and gently caress her limbs. The brown bodice, strings drawn tightly about her waist and ribs, accentuated the curves of her delicate figure. With her hands folded demurely in front, Ali felt like she was ready to attend a Renaissance festival. Having this thought in mind, she nearly burst out laughing and had to bite her lip to keep from blurting out a chuckle.

"Nicely done, Caterina. You have golden hands with a needle and thread." Claudio's smile made Caterina blush. His eyes gave away his appreciation as his gaze danced on Ali's every lovely detail.

"Now that I am properly dressed and will not create a scandal in the village, shall we venture out for an evening walk, my lord?" Ali wanted desperately to have some time alone with the man she loved.

"Shall I accompany you, my lord?" Francesco asked gravely, his hand on the hilt of his sword.

Claudio shook his head. "Not necessary, however, I offer you my thanks, friend." Claudio offered Ali his hand, and she took it appreciatively. "We shall not be too long." His words were for Francesco, but his gaze was fixed on Ali.

Chapter Thirty-One

Ali ran her fingertips along the fence of the horse corral as they strolled leisurely along the dirt road. Above them, the sky darkened to a lavender twilight. Dotted with the occasional cloud, there was just enough contrast to offer the brilliance of another perfect dusk.

"What were you and Francesco talking about—when I went to change?" Ali asked.

"Our best plan of action." Claudio smiled down at her. "Francesco asked what I intend to do. He said I should take your warnings very seriously, considering the enemies I have made of late. I am concerned of course, however, you are my priority, and you must return to your time as soon as possible. But let us not speak of that now. There is quite a view from the plateau of the hill behind the manor house, let us go there instead. We can descend to the village on the morrow. It is better then and will be brimming with life. It will give you a true picture of life here, as I am accustomed to living it."

Alice laughed quietly.

"You find that amusing?" He smirked and extended his hand

to help her over a rock. She held it tightly, twining her fingers in his.

"Yes." She nodded, her eyebrows raised. "Your life as you are accustomed to it? Perhaps you experience village life whilst you are on Spirit on your way to the monastery or some other place." She bumped him affectionately on the hip. A long pause followed that he filled with a weak smile. "I am sorry that I have come back to complicate your life, but I thought I was doing the right thing."

Claudio turned and took her shoulders in his hands, so he could look deeply into her eyes. "Do not ever think for one breath that you are inconveniencing me, Alice. I could no more begrudge you your return than I could begrudge my heart for beating in my chest. You are my soul—my very breath. Do you not know? I am afraid for you—that is why I am not mad with happiness as I would be if there were no dangers here. I am accustomed to life here—you are accustomed to your orderly, class-sensitive, politically correct society."

Ali bit her lip and nodded. "I know." They started up the incline again, but Ali had a thought. "Speaking of which, are Bruno and Clarice still being troublesome? And what about your mother? Oh, hey! Your mother—it says in Castiglione's letter that she... she..."

"Yes. The countess is keeping company with Court Counselor Filippo. Dare I say that she is—more than tolerable? Filippo is a good companion for her. She has been alone too long."

With a twinge of anger that colored his eyes, he continued, "Bruno has been sulking about the palace since the incident at the Great Hall and avoids me at every opportunity. I still believe he thinks I am a threat, as I have decided to take my mother's advice and at least pretend to have an interest in the Medici Empire. As for Clarice..." Claudio gave the tiniest shudder. "Clarice was very happy to hear that you were at service in

Prato. She is, unfortunately, as insufferable as ever, although she tends to retreat if I ignore her or look at her sternly. Otherwise, all is the same. Remember, it has only been a few weeks here, as opposed to your four months. And you? Your parents, aunt, and uncle? How did you manage to get away for an extended period, such as this?"

"First of all, parents, aunt, and uncle—they are well. I told them you were ill, and I had to be by your side. Basically, I lied —for which I feel like a snake—but at the time I was fresh out of ideas."

"And the young man, Caleb?"

Alice stiffened at Caleb's name. "Ugh." She groaned and rolled her eyes. "Do not ask."

"What? Tell me."

"When I told him I was breaking it off, he kicked me out of his car...abandoned me in a deserted field—in the dark."

"He what?" Claudio's face twisted into an angry grimace, his eyes smoldering with fury.

"Caleb turned out to be the complete opposite of you. I should have known he was too perfect, just like my father said—"

"If he were here, I would throw him a sword, and we would have it out—man to man."

Ali took his hands in hers as she threw her head back and laughed. "Ha! I yelled out to him just as I walked away. 'If he were here, he would run you through!'" She thrust her fist in the air to punctuate her words as they reached the uppermost portion of the plateau.

"Brava! It is a pity I was not there. The coward! He dares to put a woman in a perilous situation such as that, the son of a jackal." There was a little clearing at the edge that looked like it had been sculpted out of the hillside, showcasing the glowing village. Claudio pulled her close and wrapped his arms around her waist.

"Calm down. I threw an empty coffee cup at his head. He will think twice about doing something like that again." Ali's infectious laughter echoed through the dell, and Claudio laughed along with her.

"I truly believe that I have missed your laughter and sense of humor the most." Gathering her into his arms, he held her snuggly, so that her lips were close to his. "May I show my affection for you, my lady?"

Alice smiled at the familiarity of his question. "You asked me that once before—I remember," she murmured, her lips barely a breath from his. "In the palace garden. The first time we kissed... I knew then that I had fallen in love with you." Her head was spinning, and her limbs grew weaker, but she had the strength to close the gap between their lips.

The shadows in the darkness contrasted with the brightness of the waxing moon, playing with his dark features. Claudio opened his eyes, his gaze soft as a caress, and she wondered how he could make her feel so many things at once.

He slackened the ties on her bonnet and slipped it off her head.

"You are indescribably breathtaking in this light." He wrapped his hands in her curls and pulled her close once again. "We shall think of what to do on the morrow, my darling. For now, just hold me, and let me hold you. Wherever we are going —we shall get there together."

Alice could not have felt more at peace, more secure, and more treasured as she did with Claudio under the perfectly quilted blanket of a starlit sky. She knew, unequivocally, that returning to him was the right thing to do.

Chapter Thirty-Two

"I feel as though I have been transported into a life-size diorama of a medieval village," Ali said, basket in hand. It was the next morning. She had been sent by Caterina to fetch some provisions for the daily meals, and Claudio was only too happy to escort her.

"I am pleased that you are enjoying your glimpse into your past," Claudio said.

"I confess that I am feeling rather anxious, my lord. You have not given me an answer as to whether you are coming back with me," she gulped, "or not."

Claudio breathed deep and focused his gaze on the children a few steps ahead of them running after a loose dog. "Elisa, you will need to allow me an opportunity to speak with my mother —for obvious reasons." He grasped her elbow and pulled her over, pointing in front of them. "Careful there."

She nodded and sidestepped a cow pie in the middle of the street. Life was seething around them with vendors yelling out the virtues of their wares, animals loose in the streets, women bustling about with baskets of food, and men working at their crafts in the marketplace.

"Does Francesco own all this?" asked Ali as she took in the shoemakers, blacksmiths, tanners, and toolmakers all jostling for places alongside millers, vintners, and olive oil makers.

Claudio nodded. "Many of the villagers work his land, some produce is given to him, but the villagers retain a portion to sell so they are able to live a decent life. Some of the men are guildsmen and operate in accordance with their art."

"Fascinating. Tell me about the women. What do they do?"

Claudio cleared his throat. "Some women in higher society have taken on a greater role, but do not wield power directly, such as you witnessed with Duchess Filiberta. You may say that she is the so-called 'power behind the throne.'"

"But what about these women?" Alice whispered to Claudio, staring at the humanity surrounding her. There were no women working in the trades, although they bustled about with children. On the way into the village, Ali had seen many women working in the fields and carrying loads of olives and wheat.

Claudio hesitated. "Elisa, you are in a different time. I shall be honest—the predominant role of women is to take care of the home, marry, produce sons, and raise healthy and educated men. For many in the lower classes, a daughter is not looked upon as the infant of choice. A dowry must be provided at the time of marriage, which is a hardship for many families."

"How positively infuriating." Ali's lips flattened into a thin line. "I thought that they were allowed a little freedom."

"Yes, but only the upper classes—they are allowed to form an opinion—to a certain point." Claudio looked at Ali with an apologetic eye. "Do you remember our talk in Fiesole?"

Ali nodded. "I do. And I do understand that we are in a different time, but I do not have to like what I am seeing."

Claudio and Ali were on their way back to the Baron's home when Francesco intercepted. "Good morning, Count, Elisa. It is another fine day—a fine day to visit a coppersmith, I think."

"Yes, my friend," Claudio smiled. "I shall escort Elisa back to your home, saddle Spirit and we shall be off."

"Once we are done, we may need to consult with the Master," said Francesco.

"Agreed. Come, Elisa. I shall not be long—the coppersmith is just in Florence proper—" Claudio stopped suddenly mid-speech. His attention was caught something in the distance.

"What is wrong?" Alice asked as they approached a small stone house.

Claudio shook his head slowly from side to side. "I thought I—" He opened the rickety gate to the house and strode to the garden, looking about the small plot of land.

"What is it, Claudio?" Francesco dismounted his horse and pulled the sword from his scabbard.

"Nothing," Claudio said distractedly. "Nothing. I thought I saw someone I recognized, but I suppose I was mistaken, as there is no one here." Claudio narrowed his eyes as he thought. "Francesco, is there anyone from the palace living here?"

"Not that I am aware of. Why?"

Claudio licked his lips and smiled at Alice, brushing a lock of hair from her eyes. "Nothing." He shook his head. "My darling, I would ask that you stay with Caterina in the manor house and do not venture out alone."

Francesco had a puzzled look on his face. "My friend, I shall meet you at the stable after I ensure Elisa is safe inside."

"What is concerning you, Claudio?" Ali repeated.

"Probably nothing, but it does not hurt to be cautious. We should both try to stay safe—for each other's sake."

As the old woman lugged the pails of slop for the pigs, she cursed that she had been ousted from her previous employ. She was tired of milking cows, tending the vegetable garden, brewing ale, and washing clothes to pay for room and board in her cousin's home.

Her previous position at the palace as a washerwoman might have been lowly, but it fed and clothed her, and provided a place for her to sleep without the headache of listening to her cousin grumble about being a midwife.

She thought of how her mother and father—poor as dirt and long since dead—had turned her over to her aunt and uncle. They fed her for a while but in the end, sold her to the palace as a servant.

Being forced from the only place she had known comfort, festered a hatred in her that made her already worn-out body feel more sluggish and drained.

"Yes, but only the upper classes—they are allowed to form an opinion—to a certain point."

I know that voice. Slipping into the shadows, she strained to hear more.

"I do."

Yes, I know that voice, too.

"And I do understand—"

The sound of horse hoofs camouflaged their words.

"Good morning, Count, Elisa."

Count Claudio and Elisa! So, this was where she has been hiding!

The old woman had expected the young scullery maid to travel to some distant kingdom—away from those mischief-makers, Clarice and Bruno. Instead, she was in the hamlet with the Baron and Count. How very interesting...and convenient. Unable to resist her curiosity, she allowed herself to peek around the post where she was out of view. A sly smile crept across her thin parched lips as she thought about how she could use this knowledge to her benefit.

Heavens to Bacchus, the count had caught sight of her!

Spotting the large container, the family threw their rotting vegetables in for the pigs, she sprinted toward it faster than she had moved in decades. Quietly, she opened the cover, slipped inside, and laid down in the slop, closing the lid overtop.

The old woman held her breath as she heard the squeaky gate opening.

There was a thump, then a scraping of metal against metal as though a sword was being pulled from its scabbard.

Her heart was pounding against her chest. She was barely breathing for fear of being discovered. If they saw her, she would be banished from her cousin's farm, too.

"Francesco, do you have anyone from the palace living here?"

He did recognize her. Thankfully, the Baron would not know her—she had only been in the village for a little over a fortnight.

"What is concerning you, Claudio?"

"Probably nothing, but it does not hurt to be cautious. We should both try to stay safe—for each other's sake."

Yes, darlings, try to stay safe.

The old woman almost gave herself away by snorting out a laugh. The swing of a creaky gate followed by footsteps and the sound of horse hoofs signaled their departure. The woman held her breath for a moment longer, unwilling to take the chance of being discovered.

Slowly, she extricated herself from the rubbish, feeling even more defiant at having demeaned herself in such a manner. She swore to herself that somehow, she would use this situation to her advantage.

Chapter Thirty-Three

"Good afternoon, Mother." Claudio entered his apartments and greeted his mother, brushing her cheek with a kiss. He had just completed the visit to the coppersmith with Francesco.

Countess Maria was deftly playing her harpsichord, signaling that she was in good spirits. Claudio could attribute her good mood to one thing; the attention that Counselor Filippo had been bestowing on her. At times, it made her positively giddy. On these occasions, Claudio had to smile to himself and be glad that she had found a companion.

"Good afternoon, darling," Maria replied, after receiving his kiss. "You have been with your friends again?"

"Yes, Mother," Claudio confirmed as he took a seat on the settee. "However, I do wish to tell you that I spoke with one of the duke's counselors on my way into the palace. I have an opportunity tomorrow to meet with one of his business advisors on the new alum mine in Tolfa, near Rome. Dare I say, this intrigues me more than a position as an accountant."

At this, the countess' expression brightened. She stopped

playing and gazed at her son with wide eyes and a surprised smile. "Claudio, my dear, that is wonderful news."

"Yes, I thought you would say that." He decided to take the opportunity to mention another important point. "You do understand that a position such as this would take me to another part of the country—out of Florence."

The countess pursed her lips and furrowed her brow. "I suppose I must prepare myself for such an occasion." Her eyes shifted to the window as she paused in thought. "As much as I detest to admit it, you should make your own life. It is a natural thing. "

"I am glad that you are willing to entertain the possibility of that happening, Mother."

"But not alone, darling. You should have a suitable wife at your side. A wife can take care of you. Look after your household."

"I see your point, but do you see mine? The Medici's hold on their banks is dwindling, and with only recently coming back to claim the throne, it may not be wise to do that. This place in Tolfa is a position more attached to Nature, making it more appealing to me. But it might be difficult for you, as I would not be able to visit as much."

"Why do you speak so much of this now, Claudio? Do you know of something you are hesitating to tell me about, lest I be troubled?"

Telling her the truth about why he had to leave Florence was not an alternative. He must flee not for a position with the Medici business empire, but before he is murdered. Tolfa was as good a place as any to start the conversation about his imminent departure.

"No—not at this moment, Mother, yet you should be prepared. One day I may have to leave Florence and go elsewhere to make my own life."

His mother sniffed and straightened her posture, placing

her fingers on the harpsichord.

"Let us hope that day shall be indefinitely postponed." A soft knock sounded at the door. The countess' lady-in-waiting scurried in from the salon to answer it.

"Good day," said the voice at the door. "I have come to visit the countess if she will allow me the pleasure of her company on such short notice."

Claudio recognized the voice. It was Counselor Filippo Fregoso. The young woman curtsied and opened the door wide, allowing him entry.

The moment that Filippo saw the countess, his eyes lit up. He strode over and gently took Maria's hand, which she held up, ready to receive his kiss. Claudio stood and bowed respect-fully, extending his hand to greet his mother's suitor.

"Your servant, my lord," said Filippo.

"Your servant, Counselor Fregoso," replied Claudio. "How is the duke, sir? I take it he is occupied in his affairs as always." Claudio was being polite, as he was not in the least bit inter-ested in the duke. The only thing on his mind was speaking to da Vinci to inform him that the copper extension would be ready to use within ten days.

"That he is, my lord." Filippo took a seat on the opposite side of the room, smiling pleasantly. "He was meeting with your teacher and, incidentally, another courtier. I believe you know him—Baldassare Castiglione?"

At the sound of this name, Claudio's heart sank to his stom-ach. This was too unnerving to be ignored as a coincidence. "Baldassare Castiglione? He is back?"

Filippo nodded casually.

Claudio tried to appear relaxed about the topic, but inside he wanted to dart out and interrogate Castiglione about where he had been, how long he was planning on staying, and where he would be going when he departed.

"Yes. I think he is to stay for a short time before making his journey south to Rome. He is to serve there as the ambassador from Urbino."

The lady-in-waiting placed a tray bearing goblets of wine and a plate of figs and goat cheese on the table.

"Ambassador? How impressive," remarked the countess, a goblet of wine in hand.

"Indeed, sent by His Holiness the Pope, nonetheless—and he was bestowed the title of count by the Duke of Urbino." Filippo raised his glass to Countess Maria. "To your health, my lady."

"To yours," Maria returned.

"To yours," echoed Claudio. "He will go to Rome, you say." The letter that Elisa had shown him was dated and posted from Rome. Claudio's mouth felt like dried parchment. "Did you, by chance, happen to hear when he would be leaving for Rome, Counselor?"

"Why, yes. I believe he mentioned that once he had completed his business here, he would be departing in less than a fortnight."

Claudio swallowed hard, his blood pounding in his ears.

A feeling of urgency overtook him. Having only just taken a sip of refreshment, he set his goblet down and rose to take leave of his mother and Counselor Fregoso.

"Mother, I shall see you later tonight." Claudio took her hand and brushed his lips against it, then turned slightly to Filippo and bowed. "Counselor, always a pleasure."

"Wait," said the countess, her hand still raised. "There is a banquet tonight. All of Florentine society shall be attending—that should include you."

Claudio's mouth worked to try to find an excuse not to be present, to flee to Alice, to talk of this new development.

"In fact," Filippo, nodded in accordance with Countess Maria, "Castiglione is the guest of honor and I believe da Vinci is attending as well. It may be to your advantage to attend, my lord."

Claudio tried to slow his thoughts as they raced in his mind. The logical thing would be to return for dinner and speak with Castiglione, but his heart told him otherwise. He wanted to spend every moment with Ali, to feel the touch of her delicate hand in his. The thought of her made his face split into an involuntary, idiotic smile.

"I think he agrees with you, Filippo. See—he is smiling with anticipation." His mother raised a brow at her son with wisdom only a mother could possess. She knew him too well to think that it was the prospect of dinner that made him grin like a schoolboy.

"Indeed, I shall be there this night," Claudio responded to his mother, then glanced at the counselor. "Mother is well aware of how much I enjoy these events." His voice dripped with sarcasm as he backed up toward the door.

Filippo looked questioningly at the two and stood up as Claudio bowed to his mother. "Then it is settled—we shall dine together this night."

"Good afternoon." Claudio bid his mother and her suitor goodbye, left the apartment, and headed straight away for the manor house.

Chapter Thirty-Four

Taking the servant's stairs and exits, Claudio swiftly departed the palace. The last thing he wanted was to encounter any of the nobles—he would have his fill of them at dinner, which meant a heart-wrenching evening away from his love. Claudio's hand grabbed the post on the fence encircling the outside of the courtyard and swung through the gate as he had done since he could remember. He exited to the stables and found his mare, Spirit, harnessed in her stall. She stomped her hoof and whinnied as her master entered, startling the groom in the stall next to her.

"Prepare her, please," Claudio said to the stable boy, who nodded and bowed.

"Right away, my lord."

"Come, Spirit, old girl," Claudio said as he stroked her nose. "We are off for a ride to Francesco's before dinner." The instant the saddle was adjusted, and Spirit was ready, he mounted the horse and eased her gracefully out of the stable. As time was short, he raced to the manor house, hating that every precious hour he spent with Ali had to be measured to the absolute moment. There would never be enough time with her, even if he lived to a hundred years.

As he raced through the hamlet, he drew stern looks from the villagers who were tending to their early evening chores of rounding the animals back into their pens and closing shops and lower guild trades for the night. Chickens and ducks squawked and flew clumsily out of the way as Spirit galloped by.

Before long, they came to the start of the higher path, which wound its way to the manor house. The candles inside had already been lit, and the late hour gave Claudio even further urgency to speak with Alice about Castiglione's presence in the palace. He halted just outside of the front door, tied the mare to a nearby post, and sprinted up the steps, entering without knocking, unwilling to waste precious moments.

"Elisa!" he shouted into the cavernous great room, his voice bouncing off the ceiling as though it had been sent back with a slingshot. "Elisa?" he repeated. "Francesco. Caterina?" Odd. Where could they all be?

"Good evening, my lord," a rather old and rickety man emerged from the interior of the house with a cheesecloth slung over his shoulder. "Pardon, my lord. I was just in the kitchen when I—"

"Yes, good evening. Where is your master? And the maids— Caterina and Elisa?"

"The master has departed for a function at the palace. A letter came this afternoon with an invitation for all the noble landowners having business with the duke. My lord, young Francesco, is attending with Francesco the elder." He bowed and then stood awaiting other questions from the count.

"And the maids? The little one with brown hair and Caterina?"

The manservant shook his head as if suddenly remembering a long-lost thought.

"Begging your pardon, my lord—yes, the maids. Uhm..." He

put a finger to his lips and again descended into deep thought. "Ah, yes." The elderly man waved his finger and Claudio held his breath, anticipating the answer. "The young ladies were in the kitchen with Cook, but I do believe the little one has gotten herself to the barn. She is oddly fascinated by the animals, it seems—helping the hands with the stock."

A smile crept across Claudio's lips. A picture flashed in his mind of Ali feeding pigs, milking cows, and gathering eggs.

"Thank you," said Claudio. "And your name is again?"

"Nestor, my lord."

"Thank you, Nestor." He inclined his head to the old man and exited the house. At once, he mounted Spirit and was off to the rear of the manor, halting her in front of the barn. He descended and tied her to a post, patting her neck firmly when she whinnied and snorted in protest at a barking dog.

"Shh! Silence Loki!" Claudio warned with an authoritative voice, prompting the dog to back up into the barn, but not before Alice almost tripped over him to get to Claudio.

"My lord, I thought I heard Spirit." Ali reached up and stroked the horse's nose. "And you, of course." She opened her arms to him, and they embraced. "I missed you today," she whispered in his ear.

"And I missed you," he whispered back as he breathed in her earthy aroma. "Hmm. I take it Caterina has put you to work today."

Ali pulled away, held his hands at arm's length, and smiled a mocking grin at him.

"Very funny. In fact, I have rather enjoyed myself this afternoon. There is nothing wrong with a little manual labor—not that you would know anything about it, Count Claudio."

"My lady, shall I remind you that I am your social superior, and you must respect me and afford me a certain degree of—"

She placed a finger on his lips and stopped him in mid-sentence. "Do not even go there."

Her smile was playful and teasing, and it was all Claudio could do to keep from scooping her up and carrying her away on Spirit right then and there.

"My darling," he took her finger and kissed it, then held her hand to his heart, "I wish I could stay, but I just came to give you some news. First, the smith has confirmed he shall have the extension ready in ten days' time. And please do not be alarmed at this second bit of news."

"All right, I will not."

"Baldassare Castiglione is at the palace."

Ali's mouth dropped open and her eyes widened. "What!"

"Shush now."

"Do not shush me—"

"Excuse me, I meant, please not so loud—"

"Is that the count I hear?" Caterina emerged from the rear servant's entrance of the house, wiping her hands on her apron, and dashed to where they were standing. "Good evening, my lord." She curtsied and smiled. "Nestor told me you were here. Are you not attending the function at the palace this evening, my lord?"

Indeed, he was quite late.

"Yes, Caterina, thank you for reminding me. Elisa, I shall make this short. We plan on speaking to Master da Vinci tonight about the matter at the monastery. I also plan on speaking to Castiglione about his immediate plans, which should give us an indication of how long we have left."

"Left for what?" asked Caterina. "Are you departing again, Elisa?"

Ali offered a weak smile. "I must take my leave soon. Please, go back to the house. I shall take my leave of Count Moro and join you directly."

Caterina nodded half-heartedly. "Good night, my lord." She backed away to a respectable distance and went back inside the manor house.

"For God's sake, Claudio," Ali admonished. "Be careful. It sounded in the letter like he had first-hand knowledge of what happened to you."

"Yes. And, from what I hear, the duke shall be leaving Florence for the hunt soon—perhaps within a day or two. I am thinking that Castiglione will be on his way soon after that."

"That does not give us much time. That copper extension needs to be operational soon—not in ten days. Tell that smith he needs to hurry up."

Claudio nodded. "I shall—tomorrow I will pay him a visit and demand he work day and night on it."

"And what about your mother?" Alice shifted her gaze to the ground for a split second, clearly uncomfortable. "Have you talked to her about leaving?"

"The bug has been placed in her ear—so to speak. I need to make certain that she is comfortable with the idea. But for now, I fear that I must leave you again."

"Off to the party?" Ali smirked.

Claudio rolled his eyes. "Unfortunately, yes. But I promise I shall be back all the earlier in the morrow."

"You had better be," she whispered, then reached up and gave Claudio a quick kiss.

"Do not work too hard, my love." He bowed and grabbed Spirit's reins. "Until tomorrow." He climbed on the mare, and clicked his boots against her sides, sending Ali a conspiratorial wink before he set off to the palace, raising a cloud of dust in his wake.

Chapter Thirty-Five

Back at the palace, Claudio bounded to his apartments, cleaned up, changed, and made it to the Great Hall just as dinner was about to be served. Everyone was seated, and he made a distinct impression being the last to enter.

Bruno was there with his newest collection of sycophant friends, as was an icy Clarice, seated near the duke and duchess. The ever-present, brooding nephew of the duke muttered a few cuss words as Claudio passed by. Feeling Bruno's hateful eyes on him reminded Claudio of the incident at Fiesole and the monastery. He had only seen Bruno a handful of times since the hearing at the palace when his and Elisa's innocence was restored. Since then, Claudio had consistently been ignored, as if pretending not to see him would make the entire ordeal go away.

Yet, Claudio could not help but wonder when Bruno would lose control of his composure and let his envy and hatred take over his common sense again—if he had any common sense to begin with.

"Blast," he muttered as almost everyone in the Great Hall turned to watch him make his way in. He nodded politely to the courtiers and nobles, bidding good evening when appropriate. Naturally, he would be seated next to his mother, who in turn would be sitting next to Filippo. He wished that Castiglione would be close by, so he could gather some intelligence regarding his itinerary and imminent travels.

"Ah, there you are my friend," Claudio muttered to himself. Baldassare Castiglione was seated as the guest of honor at the head table, next to Duke Giuliano de Medici and Duchess Filiberta.

Francesco, who was also seated at the head table, nodded his acknowledgment, as did da Vinci who then tipped his head toward Castiglione, clearly encouraging Claudio to speak to the man. At the same time, his mother caught sight of him and waved him over. Claudio nodded and raised a hand indicating that he would be there shortly.

Stopping a respectable distance from the duke and duchess, Claudio bowed deeply. Bruno continued to ignore him.

"If it pleases Your Grace," said Claudio, holding his bow, "may I take this opportunity to bid Your Grace Giuliano and Duchess Filiberta a good evening."

"Good evening, young Claudio," drawled Giuliano as Filiberta inclined her head toward the count in acknowledgment. "Good of you to come." There was a hint of sarcasm in his voice. Claudio arose to face him.

Bruno's face screamed satisfaction at his uncle's acerbic tone.

"At the very least, Your Grace, I have not waited until the middle of the meal to deliver my greetings."

At this, Filiberta chuckled quietly. Giuliano had admonished him for his behavior at the last great banquet when Clarice had kept him talking so long that he had not paid his respects to the duke and duchess until well into the meal.

"Indeed." Giuliano bristled at Claudio's comment and Filiberta's reaction. Recovering, he smiled at the young man in front of him. "On a more favorable note, I hear you are making inquiries regarding a serious position at Tolfa."

Claudio saw, from the corner of his eye, that Bruno's smug smile had disappeared.

"Why Count Moro, that is wonderful news." Filiberta smiled. "We can greatly benefit from a clever youth such as yourself in Tolfa."

Claudio inclined his head at the compliment, and as he did, his eyes strayed to where Castiglione was sitting. "My lady is too kind, I am sure."

"The alum business is a lucrative one for the Medici. It would please us to know that we have a person of integrity and good moral character there, to look after our interests."

"I am certain, Your Graces, that if I should be so fortunate as to attain the position, I would do my utmost to prove my worth to the great house of Medici."

At this, Giuliano smiled. Bruno's face was becoming redder by the second. He leaned across the table on his elbows and whispered something to one of his friends.

"Now, if Your Graces will pardon me, I shall deliver my salutations to the guest of honor." Claudio bowed again and held it until he was properly dismissed, then he walked the short distance to Castiglione. Dressed in a dark crimson velvet suit, complete with a hat embroidered in gold thread, he looked the part of an ambassador.

"Good to see you again, Count Moro," said Castiglione as he held out his hand to greet the young count.

"You as well, Count Baldassare," said Claudio with a sincere smile and a hearty handshake. "It is with great pleasure that we have the opportunity to speak again. You are here for some time, I hope?"

Castiglione held onto his jacket lapels as he spoke. "Alas, I am here for all too short a time. I leave in less than seven days, after the duke and I return from the hunt."

Claudio's heart sank.

"A mere week, and you shall leave us?" Claudio tried to maintain control. "That is hardly enough time for the court to enjoy your presence, Count Baldassare, much less for us to talk of art and politics, as it were."

"Oh, you are too kind, count, however, my new appointment in Rome beckons." Baldassare's eyes gave away his excitement at the prospect. "But if you so wish, I am certain that the duke would be pleased to have another hunter in the party. We shall ask him." Baldassare motioned to Duke Giuliano.

"No, sir." Claudio stopped him. "I would not think of interfering with your time with the duke."

"Really, it is no trouble. There is only me and a few other courtiers."

"I thank you, sir, but I fear that I have business to attend to in Florence that shall keep me occupied in the next few days. Perhaps next time."

"Agreed. And if you are ever in Rome—"

"I shall, sir. I would enjoy calling on you immensely. Enjoy the remainder of your stay, Count Castiglione." Claudio bowed to the new ambassador to Rome, who inclined his head in return. "Good evening."

Though he could not bear to face an evening of shallow conversation, Claudio had to grit his teeth and put up with the rest of the nobles. It was time for him to join his mother at her place in the Great Hall. "Good evening, Mother." He kissed her hand, then turned and bowed to Filippo. "Counselor."

"You are late," the countess ground out through clenched teeth, which had been disguised as a smile. "Why must you always be late? Everyone is already seated."

"I am sorry, Mother. I admit to being behind my times. But I am here, nonetheless." He took his place after acknowledging the other nobles at the table. The countess was not at the head table this evening, due to all the dignitaries present, and this suited Claudio just fine—he could let his mind wander between extravagant courses of food and silly conversation.

As anticipated, Claudio's thoughts kept drifting to Alice throughout the evening. He excused himself, deciding he needed a breath of fresh air. Passing casually by the rows of dinner guests, he reached the elaborate double doors of the balcony. He opened them and strode through, welcoming the cool evening air. Directly above, he heard the unmistakable sound of male laughter.

Claudio instantly recognized one of the voices as Bruno's. He and his friends sounded like they were having a rousing good time.

"I tell you as I stand here when the throne comes to me, I shall make significant changes. My uncle wishes the goodwill of the people, but if he were to ask me, the only way to control the Florentine population is with fear," Bruno announced.

"Come now, my lord. Do you think that your method would prove a better government than your uncle's? He appears to take a great stake in what his court thinks, as was evident not too long ago at Moro's hearing?"

Claudio recognized Horatio's voice, the son of a wealthy noble. Instinctively, he leaned into the shadows of the balcony above, lest he be spotted by the rowdy group.

"Yes, the duke did revel in the afterglow of his releasing the two young turtle doves." Great, raucous laughter followed Bruno's statement.

Claudio rolled his eyes.

"Hmph! I do not know who is more of an ass, Moro or my Uncle!"

Claudio raised an eyebrow at this and listened harder.

"If he continues in this form of governance, he will surely be ousted by a family in Florence who craves the power of the throne, much like the Pazzi did years ago."

A pause overtook the conversation, creating an awkward

lull. Claudio walked silently to the side of the balcony to get a better position for listening.

"But we know that will not happen again," offered Horatio. "You are merely playing at the notion." Silence followed the last comment.

In the ensuing quiet, Claudio strained to hear the conversation.

"Am I?" Bruno's voice hung in the still night air. "One can never predict what the future will bring, can one? My uncle is of an old model of governing. His time has passed. Florence needs someone strong to lead it to its former glory—someone like me."

"Do not joke about such things, my friend. Though you are the duke's nephew, you are not immune to his punishments. Why, even the thought of such a rebellion would serve to—"

A hushed quiet was all around.

Who does he think he is, the fool? thought Claudio. The thread of the conversation was unnerving. Even thinking of doing such a thing to his uncle would raise suspicion in this precarious climate so soon after the Medici's return to power.

The silence was shattered by a crash, which was followed by cussing from the balcony above, startling Claudio. Then all was quiet again.

He tried to keep his mind off what he had heard, but his thoughts drifted back to what Bruno had slurred. Was it the wine speaking, or was he delusional? Did he really intend to usurp his uncle? When it came to Bruno, one really could not predict.

I will not think on it. Claudio decided to temporarily ignore the conversation and mind his own business. The last thing he needed was further complications. He paused and took one last breath before returning to the dining hall.

❧

The conversation between Moro and his uncle Giuliano had been enough to sicken Bruno—Tolfa, the alum mines, and now even Castiglione was singing the count's praises—it was so very tiresome. He knew that he had to act quickly, perhaps as soon as the morning. Leaning across the table on his elbows, Bruno spoke to his friends softly.

"Come, let us make haste. I require respite from this dreary dinner." As he arose, he grabbed a bottle of wine and his glass, and with his friends in tow, headed upstairs to his apartments.

The balcony overlooking the palace gardens was a welcome reprieve from the large crowd at this evening's event. Bruno thought about his uncle and how simple it would be to take what he wanted. He had the support of a few key players in the nobility, to whom he had promised some lucrative positions if they assisted him with his plans. All he needed was the element of surprise, and he would be the new successor to the throne in the Duchy of Florence.

Sneering, he looked up at the heavens, considering how wonderful it would be to sit on the throne as the next duke, ignoring his friends' concerns. "I tell you as I stand here when the throne comes to me, I shall make significant changes."

An awkward lull overtook the conversation as Bruno assessed his friends' reaction.

"But we know that will not happen again," offered Horatio in the form of a lightly veiled warning. "You are merely playing at the notion." Silence followed the last comment. Bruno began to pace, walking towards the inside of the balcony parapet.

"Am I?" Bruno's voice hung in the still night air. "One can never predict what the future will bring, can one? My uncle is of an old model of governing. His time has passed. Florence needs someone strong to lead it to its former glory—someone like me."

"Do not joke about such things, my friend. Though you are

the duke's nephew, you are not immune to his punishments. Why, even the thought of such a rebellion would serve to—"

Bruno walked to the side of the balcony as his friend spoke and he happened to look down. His heart sank into his stomach—that was Moro hiding down there in the shadows. Blast him! He had been heard.

Horatio proceeded to caution his friend at his flippant words, but Bruno swiftly waved to Horatio to be silent. His friends watched him as a mix of rage, embarrassment, and regret at being so careless settled on his face. In his anger, he grabbed the door and flung it against a planter, smashing the glass to bits as he skulked back into his apartments. Silently, his friends followed.

"What is it?" Horatio asked when they were safely inside.

"My intentions have been heard by Moro. I thought my uncle would be the only one to sacrifice his life for my rightful succession to the throne, but now—" Bruno pinched the bridge of his nose. The only option for him to deal with this unpleasant turn of events was highly inconvenient. "I have no choice but to dispose of the count, as well."

Chapter Thirty-Six

The next morning, Claudio made a point of arising early to ride out to Francesco's manor. Bruno's conversation with his friends the night before was relegated to a spot in the back of his mind, having to wait as there were more pressing matters to attend to. He was able to steal a moment at the banquet to exchange a few words with Master Leonardo and Francesco about the latest news.

Claudio gathered up Alice and brought her back to da Vinci's Florence studio. There, they met with the master to discuss what to do next.

"Do not lose heart, my darling," said Claudio to an increasingly worried Ali over her morning meal at da Vinci's city residence.

"I hate it that I have no control over what is happening." Ali sighed, looking at her breakfast of bread, dried beef and goat's milk. "I am constantly worried about what will happen to you. Every time you leave me, I feel as though it will be the last time I will see you. I am worried about what is happening back home. Are my parents aware that I am gone? Have they realized that I have disappeared?" She pushed the beef out of the way and settled for the bread and milk. "And I cannot become accustomed to eating beef for breakfast."

"I am sorry that you feel that way." He reached over the table and took her hand. "About your parents, not the beef."

She laughed softly as Claudio squeezed her hand.

"I have fresh milk for you, my child." Da Vinci announced as he entered the kitchen via the courtyard. He plucked a cup from the shelf and held the large ceramic vase over it, pouring the cool liquid.

"Thank you, Master," Alice said to the old man as he went into the other room. She turned her attention back to Claudio. "Please do not misunderstand me. I would not change anything. I did the right thing coming here. My only regret is that I did not plan for the return with more care." She leaned in closer to Claudio. "Now we are both stuck here with no way out."

Claudio started to answer her but was interrupted by da Vinci as he came back with an hourglass timekeeper.

"Do not worry yourself any further, dear. Francesco and I have only just returned from the coppersmith—he will set both his apprentices to work, smelting the rod for the chamber."

Ali looked up at da Vinci as he picked up a timekeeper and plunked it sand side up on the table between the couple.

"Where is Francesco now, Master?" asked Claudio, then motioning to the hourglass. "And I assume we are to be somewhere soon?"

"Right you are, my young friend. Francesco has returned to the monastery to begin preparations on the chamber. I had a few thoughts on how to make the structure more efficient, and he is starting to implement the fortifications as we speak. However," Leonardo made it a point to fix his gaze on Claudio, "we will need to assist him at our earliest convenience if the chamber is to be fitted and ready within a week's time. You should begin praying for the elements of Nature to oblige us with a hearty storm." Leonardo's voice had an urgency to it.

"I shall be on my way to Galluzzo once I have the necessary copper pieces from the smelter. They will not be ready until the sand has run its course. After that, Claudio, we should be on our way." Da Vinci bustled into the adjacent studio.

"Very well, sir," Claudio responded, but he had a distinct reluctance in his tone. "Nevertheless, I must have some time with Elisa before I depart for the monastery. I shall carry a portion of whatever materials you require with me and meet you there directly—after I bring Elisa back to Caterina." Claudio turned to Alice, his gaze softening. "I am sorry, my darling, but we shall have to wait."

Ali shrugged, looking like she was fighting hard to keep from crying. "You have nothing to be sorry about, my lord."

Claudio's worries still lingered in his dark eyes. "I wish I could bring you with me, but it would be too much to ask of Father Federico. He has done so much already that—"

"Do not even say it." She put a finger to his lips. "I understand. It has to be done."

Claudio covered her hands with his own. "We shall ride out together to the hillside and look at Florence in all her splendor before I take you back—though I wish I could do more."

Da Vinci hurried back in with rolled parchment and rudimentary tools in his hands. "Excuse me—if I may interrupt." He placed the things on the table. "I shall impose on you but one more moment, my young friends." He was out of breath from scurrying about the residence.

"Sir, our apologies. Do you require assistance?" Alice stood to offer the old master a hand.

"Yes, sir," Claudio cleared his throat, "shall I help you load up the horse?"

"That would be very kind of you," da Vinci answered, with a slight nod. "I shall meet you in the central stables." He glanced at the timekeeper. The sand had run out. "I see that it is time to see my friend the coppersmith." He took Ali's hand from Claudio's and with a fatherly quality that had a calming effect on her, said, "My child, do not fret. We shall get you home."

A voice in her head forced her to at least sound optimistic. "Thank you, Master da Vinci—for everything."

"We shall leave with you, sir," Claudio said, taking Ali's hand anew. "Elisa and I will ride with you until the Porta Rossa."

Chapter Thirty-Seven

Clarice de Medici was still smarting from the small matter of a certain Count Claudio Moro, who had spurned her in favor of a scullery maid who had, until a little less than a month ago, labored in the palace. Her plan to be rid of the servant had succeeded. During the hearing, the maid had spoken with surprising eloquence for a peasant. Aunt Filiberta had certainly been impressed with her words. The way the girl spoke of herself as if she were a person of worth was almost admirable. It had given Clarice food for thought—but only a small morsel.

Drawing nearer to the looking glass on her armoire and admiring her profile, Clarice could not help but reaffirm that she was everything a noblewoman should be—pale skinned yet rosy cheeked, always impeccably dressed, intelligent, well-versed, and able to play several musical instruments. And, yes, terribly wealthy.

Yet, her thoughts kept wandering back to that day and how utterly frustrated she had felt at how Claudio had refused her delicately subtle advances. She could not understand why Claudio did not love her. No matter, if he did not return her feelings, there were plenty of other nobles who would fall over each other to love her and to be her husband. Though the fact that Moro had rebuffed her had bothered her immensely at the time, she would rise above it all, somehow.

Her brother, Bruno, was no help at all. He had sunken even further into his world of wine and women. His one true friend, Enzo, had been killed, and he had been the only one who came close to supporting and tolerating Bruno. As these thoughts floated like flotsam in Clarice's mind, there was a subdued knock on her apartment door.

"What?" Her tone gave away her annoyance at having been distracted from admiring herself.

"Begging your pardon, my lady. It is Gabriela. I would beg to have an urgent word with her ladyship."

Clarice tilted her head toward the door. Gabriela, her lady-in-waiting, was not usually in the habit of disturbing her and did not typically speak unless she was spoken to. "What about?"

"If my lady, pleases, the old washerwoman, Paolina...the one that was banished from the palace by my lady, on account of what happened—"

"Yes, I am quite aware of why she was dismissed—because of her ineptitude and uselessness as a servant, and that is all. What of it, Gabriela?" Clarice's voice was matter of fact and impatient.

Gabriela paused, then exercising the greatest self-control, continued. "My lady, she is outside the palace and has sent word that she is in possession of a piece of information that my lady Clarice would find interesting and exceptionally useful."

Clarice scowled at the thought of what information the old woman could possibly have. "Very well. Enter. You might as well prepare me for dinner as you share this 'interesting and exceptionally useful information.'"

The maid entered and curtsied deeply. "Paolina says that she will only speak of it to you and that, in exchange, she wishes to resume her position in the palace as the washer woman."

Clarice considered whether she should hear out the laundress. "What is it concerning?"

"The laundress said she has knowledge of a certain maid, who, until a few weeks ago, was Lady Clarice's adversary in love."

At this, Clarice rolled her eyes. "And that would be?"

"She will not tell me, my lady. She will only see you."

"Tell that creature that I have grown tired of her cryptic messages. If she bothers me again, I shall have her arrested and thrown in the dungeon." Clarice was satisfied that the washerwoman's story was nothing but rubbish. "Now, assist me with my hair."

"I told you she will not hear of it, Paolina. She does not believe you are useful anymore," snapped Gabriela, who had returned to the servants' entrance after dressing Clarice. Paolina was in the palace courtyard waiting to hear of Clarice's decision. The supercilious maid sniffed at the smell of the old woman and swiftly pinched her nose. "What is that horrid smell?"

Paolina had only bothered to remove the larger chunks of rotting food from her person in her haste to get to the palace. "That horrid smell is my life now, miss. My life in the pens of my cousin's farm, not a half a day's walk outside of the city." Paolina's lips curled in anger, thinking of how she had to hide in the rubbish to avoid being seen by the count and the maid. "Did you tell her that it would be very useful?"

"Of course, but she still refuses to see you." Gabriela tilted her head and leaned in to whisper, keeping her fingers tightly on her nose. "If you were to tell me what you know that is so intriguing about this girl and the count, I may be able to pass it on to milady."

Paolina snorted and wagged a finger at Gabriela's suggestion. "Miss, I may be a lowly uneducated washerwoman, but I know a trick when I hear it." She shook her head vehemently from side to side, causing bits of food to fly about. "You will tell milady, then you get the credit and the florins. I shall not forget the way you walked away when those two hellcats pinned me down in the servants' quarters." The old woman thrust her gnarled fisted hand in the air. "Nay, ma'am. By hook or by crook, I shall find someone else in the palace who shall pay me for this information. And I will tell you, when it is heard, that person shall know that it was worth it." Paolina turned to walk away, taking her desperation with her.

"Wait!" Gabriela haughtily raised her chin and waved at Paolina. "I may be able to bring your information to someone else in the palace, but should he choose to ignore you, you must give me at least a tidbit about who the information concerns."

Paolina deliberated. Then, with a grimace, she decided to tell. "Very well, ma'am. It is about Count Moro and the scullery maid, Elisa de Povri. I shall not say else."

Gabriela's eyes lit up at the news. "Listen to me. If I am to bring you into the palace, you must go home and come back tomorrow—presentable, understand? In the meantime, I shall tell the certain-to-be-interested party to expect you at this time tomorrow. Do not disappoint me, woman."

A roguish grin crept across Paolina's lips as she rubbed her hands together, hungrily anticipating the great reward she would receive. "Yes, miss, as you wish." She turned to leave again, but stopped in mid-stride, and called over her shoulder. "One more thing, miss, if you please. Who shall you be telling about this?"

Gabriela grinned, but her smile did not reach her eyes. "Lord Bruno, of course."

Chapter Thirty-Eight

The next day, not far from da Vinci's home on the other side of the murky Arno River, Paolina was on a determined quest. Her objective: to return to the washing halls of the palace, to the only life she trusted. The washerwoman's meeting with Gabriela had given her the renewed hope that she would be allowed to return if she could prove her worth and her loyalty to the Medici.

Paolina was to meet Gabriela in the courtyard, at which time she intended to whet her curiosity about the information concerning Count Moro and the scullery maid, Elisa.

Excited and anxious to impart her news, Paolina passed through the Porta Rossa at the walls of the city and entered the bustling streets of late-morning Florence, scurrying through the laneways like an old rat through a maze.

Thoughts of leaving her cousin's farm in that horrid little hamlet drove her old, tired legs to move faster. If her cousin discovered that she had left her chores unattended—she had not collected the eggs, fed the chickens, or milked the goat—she would be very angry.

As she made her way through the throngs of people in the

winding avenues, she eventually discerned the outline of the palace. *Not too far now*, she thought, breathless and sweating from the long walk and quick pace.

Excitement rose in her throat, and before long, she crossed into the portico at the rear of the palace, rushed past the stables, and arrived at the servants' courtyard where she would wait for Gabriela. By the time she arrived at her destination, it was time for the servants' afternoon rest—which worked to her advantage; the fewer people who saw her lingering about the palace courtyards, the better.

Paolina chose the only shady spot there was to sit and rest, under the cool shelter of an ancient chestnut tree. She snagged a bucket that was left by the well and carried it under the tree to sit on, creaking bones and all. As she leaned against the tree, tired and stiff from her journey, she thought about her mission. She did not know why my lord Bruno would appreciate the news when my lady Clarice could not care less, but she had an idea that it was because lord Bruno liked the ladies—and most certainly Elisa was a grand-looking girl.

But Paolina did not care that she would likely cast Elisa and Count Moro's love for each other to the wind—all she wanted was to return to the palace. She thought briefly of what Bruno might do, and even felt a tiny pang of guilt for a moment, but that went away as soon as Gabriela peeked her head out of the door and hissed Paolina's name.

"Come here!" Her whisper was harsh and commanding.

Paolina complied, arising slowly as her gnarled and swollen joints ached. "I am here, miss, just like you asked. I did what you asked and—"

"Hush! Say no more," Gabriela said sternly. "My lord Bruno will be coming from the stable. I told him of your information regarding the count and the scullery maid. He was quite inter-ested. If I were you, I would not linger too long. Give him what he wants to hear, and then be gone. If he is satisfied, he said he will think about allowing you to return. If not, I would find a very remote corner of Italy in which to hide, and I should never return—these are his words."

Paolina nodded slowly, her eyes narrowing in the mid-afternoon sun. "I do, miss." Though nervous at the prospect of being banished from Florence permanently, she was confident that Lord Bruno would not be disappointed. "I do."

Gabriela's eyes shifted from the old washerwoman to the far corner of the yard, and the stern glare she directed at Paolina changed to a gentle, submissive gaze. Paolina heard horse hoofs in the distance, and a few moments later, a great dark giant of a horse stomped its way to where the two women were standing, raising choking dust in its wake.

She recoiled at the thundering sound, and once recovered from coughing at the unpleasant dust cloud, she looked up to see a handsome, but disdainful, Bruno scowling down at her. Gabriela was already in a deep curtsey, and Paolina emulated her, not daring to look up at him again until she was spoken to.

"Well?" he said with a bored drawl. "I do not take kindly to being dragged out of the palace into this Godforsaken yard for trivialities. This had better prove to be worth it, Gabriela." He did not even acknowledge Paolina's presence.

"My lord is indulgent and generous, I am sure," said Gabriela in a silky tone as she arose, allowing herself a quick glance at the royal on his mount.

"Yes, I know," he said as he fixed his eyes upon Gabriela. "Now, do not test my patience. The duke has departed for the hunt, and if what you are telling me has merit, I have precious little time to act." His gaze swept from Gabriela to Paolina. "Old woman, what say you?"

Paolina noted his condescension, and she hated him for it. She hated the lot of them, but she also needed to eat. "My lord, if I may address him directly." She remained with her head down.

"Yes, yes, get on with it." He spat out a large projectile, which landed with a splat a mere foot length from Paolina, then wiped his mouth with a delicately embroidered brocade sleeve.

It looked as though he were quite accustomed to spitting wherever he pleased. "Yes, sir, if it pleases my lord, though I should like to ask his graciousness if he shall let me—"

Gabriela smacked Paolina on the arm, hard. "Be silent about that. The only thing you need to concern yourself with is to tell my lord Bruno what you know."

Gabriela's lips curled, and it looked to Paolina as though she wanted to give her more of the same. Paolina nodded slightly, her hand rubbing where it smarted. Bruno rolled his eyes in an exaggerated fashion.

"Now!" he bellowed and lowered his face close to Paolina's —so close, in fact, that she could smell the stench of wine and ale on his breath.

"My lord, a thousand pardons." The words tumbled out of her mouth. "I wish to tell my lord that I have seen Count Moro and the scullery maid, Elisa de Povri, together in the village where I have been living since my banishment from the palace."

At this, Bruno resumed his upright position on his horse, stiff as a plank. "And why do you think this information will benefit me?" He tightened his grasp on the reins so forcefully that his knuckles turned white.

"It may or may not benefit my lord at all. But I should think that any nugget of knowledge about a former enemy would be useful at one time or other."

"Continue."

His tone was flat, but Paolina noted that his breathing had deepened, and his jaw was clenched. She smelled his weakness and surmised that he did not give a fig about Moro. After all, the count was still living in the palace—he had only started coming around to the village the last few days. It was the girl he wanted—because she belonged to Moro.

"They were together, sir, and very friendly-looking, I might add. They were talking with the young Baron—I think his name is Francesco—about how Duchess Filiberta was the real power behind the throne and how Elisa wanted the count to go away with her and—"

Bruno held up his hand to halt her. "Hold your tongue." He then turned to Gabriela. "Leave us."

Gabriela curtsied, glanced at Paolina, and departed into the darkness of the servants' stairs. Paolina looked deep into the shadows of the staircase, and when she was certain the maid was well into the bowels of the palace kitchens, she looked slyly back up at Bruno.

"She is gone. If it pleases my lord, may I go on?"

Bruno took a deep breath and looked directly at the old woman. His eyes had changed, Paolina noticed, from boredom to fury. If it was possible, they held even more hatred and malevolence than before. "Tell me everything," said Bruno, his lips pressed together so tightly they were gray. To further entice Paolina, he pulled three gold florins from his doublet pocket and held them just out of her reach.

Chapter Thirty-Nine

As Elisa and Claudio made their way up a tree-lined, pebbled road just above the left bank of the Arno River, the mid-afternoon sun was still high overhead. It was well into September and the stifling heat of the summer had given way to the delights of early fall, making the Tuscan countryside more comfortable.

Alice, in her servants' dress, blended in rather well. Being a realist, Ali tried her hardest to keep her unease about what was going on in her time in the furthest possible place in her mind —but the worry always came back to cloud her thoughts.

Spirit clopped up the hill at an easy pace as Claudio guided her to a spot on the hillside that offered Alice an eerily familiar panoramic view of the city. "Do you recognize this spot, my lady?" he asked, turning his head slightly. He steered Spirit off the pebbled path to a clearing.

The view was unmistakable—she had seen Florence from this vantage point numerous times before. "I could be mistaken, but is this the future site for Piazzale Michelangelo?"

"Right you are. Is it not beautiful like this? Unspoiled by cement and bronze?" He halted Spirit and gracefully dismounted, tethering her reins to a nearby shrub, then turned and held up his arms to help Alice down. As she swung her leg over to dismount, their eyes met. She lost herself in his gaze. Old Florence, in all her Renaissance grandeur, lay before her like a giant tapestry, but Ali's attention was elsewhere.

As Claudio's hands wrapped around her waist to help her off Spirit, she let her arms slide around his neck. He set her down and eagerly accepted her kiss, embracing her tightly. When they released, they looked deeply into each other's eyes, their foreheads still touching.

"Claudio, I love you so much." Ali brushed her nose up against his and murmured softly. "Will Fate ever let us live in peace? Without some crisis looming over us, or us having to work around temporal rifts and broken time machines, or whatever else is going to come next to keep us apart?"

Claudio's smile faltered, but just for an instant. "I have complete confidence in the master. He will get us back to your time."

Ali's expression brightened. "So, you have positively decided to come back with me? You have accepted, without reservation, that you are in danger here?"

Claudio nodded as he took hold of her hand and kissed each of her fingers lightly. "I have, and believe me, my darling, I never doubted your information that I would soon perish." He breathed out a sigh. "But I had to be sure, for my mother's sake. I had to ensure that all the pieces were set as written...and they are. Castiglione will leave for Rome in a week's time. Shortly after that, I shall be killed."

Alice winced at the words; they may as well have been blades cutting her skin. "Look," she took a deep breath, "we need to figure out a plan—a contingency plan, you know—in case the machine is not ready, so you can just disappear." She snapped her fingers. "Gone."

Claudio furrowed his brow at her suggestion.

"We have discussed that, Leonardo and I, but I would rather not just disappear. I feel that my mother deserves closure."

Alice, her eyes downcast, nodded in agreement. Of course, his mother deserved to know he was alive and would be for a very long time—just out of touch, as it was for so many in this era.

"Of course, that goes without saying." She bit her lip before daring to bring up the next thought in her mind. "I wonder if there is a way to spare your mother the heartache. There must be a way she can know you are safe but can recognize you will not be returning."

"Yes, I have thought of that as well. Nothing would please me more than to know she has peace of mind upon my departure. Francesco and I have a few ideas on how to proceed, but they shall have to wait." He smiled down at Ali and rested his chin on top of her head. "It does please me, however, that you think of her feelings even though she never approved of you."

"She is a product of her time—you cannot fault her for that."

"I am a product of my time, and I fell in love with you despite who and what you were."

Ali leaned her head back. "But you are in love—and that changes everything."

His eyes looked deep inside her, and she felt as though he saw everything about her, all she was made of, and she was not reluctant to share her love with him.

He kissed her forehead and face, tenderly caressing the tip of her nose with his lips, and then he let his mouth find hers. Alice's heart burst with love for him. She stood on her tiptoes and returned his kisses, savoring every second with him—eons would not be enough.

Claudio breathed between their tender murmurs, his arms grasping her around the waist and lifting her off the ground. He placed her gently back on the leaf-covered ground, and she felt him pull away. He rested his head on top of hers as she listened to the pounding of his heart. Claudio's hands skim over her back, down her arms, and back over her shoulders until they rested on the sides of her face.

She felt a safety and love in his embrace that she knew she could not surrender a second time. It was as Claudio had said on the hillside at San Miniato while they watched the sunset; she was for him and him for her—they were soul mates, and without each other, life was not complete. Life would still be there, but it would be a fragmented existence.

"Sometimes," she breathed out a long sigh, "I think I was an idiot to leave you...to think that I could ever find happiness in a world without you beside me."

Claudio cupped her chin in his hand and caressed her lips with his thumb.

"You did the noble thing, Alice. You thought of everyone else before yourself. And that is one of the reasons why I find you irresistible."

Savoring this moment of calm, these ordinary few minutes when they could enjoy one another, they knew that their time was short.

It was time to return to Francesco's manor house and be on his way to the monastery. The repairs to the chamber would require both his and his master's expertise. "Pray, my lady, that this pleasant early autumn weather turns to its usual stifling heat that will lend itself to another raging thunderstorm, which we absolutely need in order to replicate Leonardo's wormhole," Claudio said.

"I will go to the abbey this evening and Francesco will accompany me. There is no event planned at the palace for dinner, as the duke is away hunting. It will give me the advantage of being able to work without having to make excuses to my mother for not being there. We shall try to labor through the night to complete as much as possible. That way, when the coppersmith completes the attachment, all we will need to do is affix it to the chamber."

Ali listened as Claudio explained his plans. Hearing him speak of his mother made her think of her parents. She wanted to tell him she missed her mother and father and that she was worried about how much he would miss the countess once he stepped through the portal for the last time. But she thought the better of it.

"Let us just enjoy this moment," she interrupted. "Can we just live it in the here and now? You, with me? Hold me."

Claudio stopped talking and wrapped both arms around her, so they could share one more kiss before heading back.

As the warmth of their loving kiss lingered, Alice suddenly felt an unexplainable sense of foreboding. *Oh my gosh, not again.* Though a shiver crawled down her spine, Ali shook it off. Nothing would spoil this moment. Nothing.

Chapter Forty

Bruno had not felt this intensity of anger in weeks.

The old woman better not have been playing him for a fool, or he would think nothing of running her through with whatever was handy. She had insisted on having her old washer place back as payment, in addition to the florins he had provided.

Stupid woman—he would not be providing employment until he had seen the girl in the hamlet with his own eyes, so he set off in a rage to do just that. The impromptu visit to the hamlet proved unfruitful, as he did not spot the girl, however he still believed that the woman was telling the truth—no one would dare lie to a Medici.

Bruno needed to work off some of his anger. On his way back from the hamlet, he had screamed at the top of his lungs and attempted to lunge his withdrawn sword at a few peasants walking on the road along the way, but they had leapt to safety —pity, as it would have relieved him of some of the fury that was eating at his belly.

He was not in the habit of being made a fool, but Moro and

his scullery maid had done just that. Bruno had always thought himself as passionate: about his plans for himself, his likes and dislikes. But this business of uncertainty was particularly enraging.

In his mind, he had resigned himself to think that Claudio would not pose a threat anymore, as he continued to fritter away his time with that madman, da Vinci. Bruno had convinced himself, spurred on by Moro's declarations that the count was not in the least interested in excelling within the Medici business empire. Consequently, making him no threat to Bruno. But in these past few days, all that had changed.

By the time Bruno arrived back at the palace, his anger had subsided, and his mind was working to rationalize his twisted thoughts. Events around him, circumstances and snippets of conversation, served to fuel his beliefs about Count Moro.

First, the exchange between Moro and his uncle, discussing the position at Tolfa—that was to be a key position in the Medici business as the use of alum in pigments and dyes was growing.

Then, the conversation between Moro and Castiglione crystalized what Bruno had initially suspected—that despite his protest to the contrary, Moro intended to usurp Bruno's rightful place at his uncle's side. Castiglione was Udine's ambassador to Rome: Tolfa was just outside of Rome. It would be easy for Moro to gain supporters in Rome, within the circles of high-ranking officials and dignitaries.

Last, the information given to him by the old maid in the courtyard served to bolster his suspicions. The scullery girl had returned from her self-imposed exile to most certainly assist that sycophant, Moro. She was probably encouraging him, so she could increase her status. In addition, the conversation regarding the partiality of Duchess Filiberta—it all made sense to Bruno. That is how Moro would take away his birthright to

Florence's throne—not by a scheme or plot, but by worming his way into his uncle's good graces.

Initially, Bruno only thought of Moro as a nuisance, but now he knew better—now that Moro knew of Bruno's plan to overthrow his uncle, the count was truly a threat. Bruno was not accustomed to having his supremacy challenged—not in his desire to conquer whichever woman he set his mind to having, nor in his desire for power—and Moro and the maid were upsetting that reputation. A month ago, he had sent his inept friend, Enzo, and a few guards to attend to Moro, but he knew now he had to do this himself. But how?

He sat in his apartments, stiff and straight, his hands grasping the armrests of his tufted goldthread embroidered chair and thought. He could not bring his accusations to his uncle. The duke would think him mad after the last fiasco when he had sent Enzo to collect the two runaways in Fiesole. That and the entire business in the monastery, which should have worked to his advantage, but had actually made Claudio appear more a courtier and nobleman than before—and had made him look like a bumbling buffoon. At this memory, Bruno seized a Murano glass serving bowl, filled to the brim with sumptuous fruits, and threw it angrily against the frescoed wall of his sitting room.

Staring at the stained Wood Nymphs portrait on the wall, Bruno tried to think of a way to foil Moro's plan. His eyes were drawn to the scene playing out on the walls of his room, and he studied the nymphs intently. They were captured in a moment of great distress. The hunter in the scene had taken one of their sisters, plucked her up from the forest and carried her away.

Thinking always made him hungry—he grasped the rope hanging behind his chair and rang for his footman. Bruno decided that whatever he did, it had to be soon, as his uncle would soon return from the hunt with that fawning old fool, Castiglione.

His eyes were drawn back to the wood nymphs and the hunter. Taking in the scene and inferring the fate of the struggling Wood Nymph in the Hunter's firm hold, an evil, cold smile found its way to his lips.

He had his plan.

Chapter Forty-One

Dawn had barely broken, but da Vinci and his apprentices were already awake and busily carrying out the repairs and modifications to refit the copper rod extension. It was a tedious task, requiring the utmost patience and precision for the chamber to work successfully.

"The bellows has been damaged." Leonardo stroked his beard as he peered down at the visibly charred metal attached to the rear of the chamber. "It must have happened when Elisa's friend fired the—what did you call the device, Claudio?"

Claudio paused before answering his teacher. "I think it is best if you know as little about the future as possible, sir."

Leonardo pursed his lips and allowed a look of surrender to cross his face. "Yes, perhaps you are right," he said, putting his hands on his hips as his gaze went from Claudio to Francesco. "Do you anticipate your smith would be agreeable to letting go of some of his copper for the bellows, Francesco?"

"I do not see why not, sir. Anything is possible for the right price—at least for that fellow."

"Right then," Claudio added, "I have enough florins for such a purchase. I shall go today before I visit with Elisa. In the meantime, let us get back to work. This chamber will not repair itself."

~

At the same moment that da Vinci and his apprentices were pondering about the coppersmith, Bruno and his posse of guards exited the Porta Rossa, their thundering horses on their way to the hamlet. Speed was of the essence, and the fewer people who saw them, the better.

Bruno's plan would be carried out during the early morning hustle of the peasants' busy day—the ideal time to find the maid outside of the manor house. He was willing to gamble losing everything if it meant Moro lost the chance of securing a position at Tolfa. That situation was too coveted to surrender to him, to allow him to take advantage of his uncle's naïveté.

Also, the girl was the perfect leverage to keep Moro in line until he fulfilled his plan to take the throne by force. Later, if he had to—if she still would not comply to be his woman even after he had disposed of Moro—he would get rid of her, too.

Bruno held up his hand, ordering the guard company to halt as they came upon the hamlet. "You are to approach the manor house just above the village in silence," Bruno whispered as the men gathered around him on their mounts. "You shall leave your horses here and proceed on foot to the corral. The maid is a small woman, slight of stature, with brown hair. We must find her before the sun rises. I am willing to wager she will venture out at some point to fetch water or go to the barn or whatever it is that they do. If she is alone, take her. Bind her hands and mouth and put a cloth over her eyes so she cannot see. You will bring her to me unharmed. And if anyone sees you, kill them."

The guards nodded.

"Do not disappoint me," Bruno whispered to the men through clenched teeth.

They saluted without so much as blinking an eye to the task they were about to undertake.

As Bruno watched, the men quietly dismounted and stealthily approached the corral behind Francesco's family manor house. They crept low to the ground and silently made their way closer to the looming house clearly outlined in the distance by an ever more cobalt blue sky.

Chapter Forty-Two

"Time to awaken, my dear," Caterina chirped. "All in the household will be up and about, and we must hurry to the morning meal."

"Mmph," grunted Alice. "Five more minutes." She had, for the moment, forgotten where she was.

"Five more what?" asked Caterina.

Alice could hear water being poured into the basin for Caterina's morning wash.

"What are you dreaming about, Elisa? Come now. It is time to rise and ready yourself for the day."

What I wouldn't do for a shower. Alice turned her head and slowly opened an eye. A lantern burned brightly on the night table beside the wash basin from which her friend was squeezing a clean but rough-looking cloth. She proceeded to wash her face and neck.

"There she is," Caterina smiled. As they had in the palace, they were sharing a room in the elegant manor house. The space was comfortable and roomy and positively luxurious according to Caterina, who was used to the meager and cramped accommodations at the palace. "Finally awake, are we?"

Alice wondered what on earth she could be smiling about at this unholy hour of the morning. Caterina finished washing and bustled to the window to dispose of the water—no taps and drains here.

"' Morning, Caterina," mumbled Alice. She pushed her covers off and swung her legs over the bed, yawning widely and stretching. Her friend walked behind a screen and proceeded to dress for the day.

Groggily, Alice arose from the bed and poured some water into another basin. The initial splash of water on her face produced a gasp and goose flesh on her arms—it was definitely not warm. Quickly, she finished up, washing as many body parts as she could, and dressed for her day.

Gathered for their morning meal in the kitchen, Alice took note of all the servants—ten in all, including Caterina, the cook, the farm hands, the old groom, the steward, and the footmen. There was a definite chill in the early morning air, so they sat by a cheery fire burning in the hearth. The mood here was much more positive and familial than what Alice could recall from her previous experience at the palace. There was laughter and joking, conversation and banter—all friendly and polite.

"His Lordship is still on the hunting trip with the duke. He shall not return for a few days, I dare say," offered the old groom. "You were not required?" he added as he turned to one of the footmen.

"Obviously," the footman snickered. "The Baron decided to forego the conveniences of his usual day-to-day. The duke has enough footmen to wait on the entire city."

"Do not be so cheeky," Caterina said with a frown. "You have no inkling of how lucky you are to work for the Baron. If you knew where she and I came from." Caterina motioned to Alice.

"Do not go off on us now, Caterina," said the cook as she brought steaming bowls of hot milk to the table. "Just eat."

"Yes, and be pretty as the cherubs on the basilica ceiling, my dear." The old groom chortled at his quip.

"Oh, silence, Nestor." Laughing, Caterina took a bowl of milk.

Ali smiled and followed suit, sipping the warming liquid. Being surrounded by friendly people made her miss her family. In fact, pretty much everything made her miss her family. And she missed Claudio, too, even though she had only seen him the day before—a moment without him was like time without end.

"Right, then, time for chores," Nestor, the old groom, said. "Let us get to them." He stood and slapped his hands on the table, jarring everyone around it.

The old footman, Sergio, rolled his eyes before taking the last sip of his wine. Alice could not stomach the breakfasts of bread, cold boiled meat, and wine. She had asked for milk and eggs the last morning, and Cook had complied.

"I shall be upstairs, tending to the Baron's things. I would hazard to say that it is quite boring without the two lordships here." Sergio was already dressed in full livery, though the house was void of any nobles to tend to. "You may come with me." The older footman pointed to the steward, a young man of about fifteen. "I am certain we shall find something upstairs to clean or to put in order."

The steward complied, trailing behind the footman.

"I should best be out to the horses." Grunting, Nestor rose slowly from the table. "I shall see you, ladies." He ambled to the door, rubbing his lower back and straightening his legs out as he walked.

Ali smiled as she thought how the poor man needed to retire. Her smile faded when she realized that in these times, retirement was probably out of the question—she doubted they had pensions.

"Be careful, Nestor," Ali called after him. "Let me assist Caterina in clearing the crockery, and I shall come out to help you."

He stopped and looked back at her bewildered.

"A housemaid? Assist me in the barnyard?"

Caterina shrugged. "She says she likes the animals."

He chuckled as he closed the door without looking back.

"Such a nice man." Alice handed Caterina the serving plates.

"I believe he has worked here since he was a young man. All his life, really," mused Caterina as she prepared the crockery for cleaning.

"This is a harsh life for you, Caterina," Alice blurted out the thought. Not so long ago, as the true Elisa of the Renaissance, she had endured such a life.

"No more unkind than it is for you, my dearest." She smiled at Alice with a quizzical look. "Whatever made you say such a thing? I should think that here is an infinitely better situation than the palace. Master Francesco and Baron Tondini are so pleasant." Caterina blushed, her cheeks turning a rosy pink. "Baron Francesco, especially. He is quite a handsome man, is he not?"

Ali giggled. "Yes, he is. Quite handsome." She handed Caterina the remainder of the dishes from the table. "Perhaps, one day, he and you may find love as Count Claudio, and I have."

Caterina laughed heartily as she deftly poured the heated water from the pot near the hearth onto the crockery in the barrel.

"Oh, my goodness—I doubt that very much." She straightened up and became serious. "It is not every day that one finds love such as yours and the count's. One can discern that it is special only from watching the two of you together. It is," she paused, "the truest form of love. Unselfish and pure devotion to each other—it is a joy to watch you two when you are in each other's company."

Ali felt color rush to her face. "Why, Caterina," Ali tipped her head her head to the side and grinned, "you are making me blush." They both laughed and continued to work until the dishes were done.

Alice looked out the window at the cobalt sky as she changed her apron, the faintest hint of light rising from the eastern horizon.

"I will start out to assist Nestor. See you shortly?"

"Are you certain, dear? You are not expected to, you know."

Ali nodded. "I know. I want to. He is elderly, and I do not mind at all." She pushed the door open and walked out to the kitchen courtyard. It was barely light enough to see without a lantern. Walking with purpose, Ali crossed the cobblestone courtyard. It had trellises abounding, with figs and grapes ripe for the picking. She grasped a ripe fig as she walked by, pulled it open, and sunk her teeth into the juicy sweetness.

Ali was nearly finished with her fig when she entered what they called the 'chicken yard', but it was not only for chickens. In fact, she could hear the ducks and other poultry in the barn. It sounded like they were already up and ready to eat. Tossing the fig rind aside, she quickened her pace.

"Where are you, Nes—" Ali stopped in mid-stride just outside the barn door. It was wide open, but the animals were still in their pens, secured from the night before. He had been out here for some time already; she wondered what on earth he could have been doing? "Nestor, are you taking a nap?" She laughed softly, entered the shadowy barn, and paused again as her eyes became accustomed to the light—or rather lack of it. Gradually, on the far side of the barn, she spotted a pair of cobbled boots lying on the ground, sticking out from behind a bale of hay.

"Nestor! Oh my gosh! He's had a heart attack." She ran to

where Nestor was lying face down—his body lifeless and still. She gasped and paused, thinking she should go inside to get Caterina or one of the servants, but she had to see if he was still alive. Perhaps she could do CPR and revive him.

Ali reached down to turn him over and gasped again, putting her hand to her mouth—his eyes were still open, but there was no life in them. It was obvious he had not died of a heart attack, but from a hard blow to the forehead. He was bleeding horribly, his cranium smashed so severely that pieces were visible through the skin.

"Oh my God, Nestor." She backed away, preparing to run to the manor. But before she could even turn to run, an arm wrapped mercilessly around her neck, and she felt cold metal on her back as a dirty, stinking hand covered her mouth.

Screams struggled to escape Ali's mouth as her hands tore at the chainmail on the massive forearm around her, but she knew that no one could hear. Behind her, someone growled. She heard scraping metal and felt a sharp pain on the back of her head before the world faded to black.

Chapter Forty-Three

The repairs to the chamber were not progressing as Claudio had anticipated. There were portions that had unsealed when Luca had used the laser to adjust the time discrepancy. Some of the materials were not of similar caliber to what da Vinci had initially used—it was obvious the merchants had attempted to hoodwink the master's apprentice.

"This mixture is useless, sir. We shall require another order of resin. This time, perhaps you should go yourself to get hold of it. That crooked villain tried to dupe us with this substandard rubbish. Blast!" Claudio cussed. His head and torso were wedged behind the structure in order to get a better position to work, but the sealant for the bellows was stubbornly uncooperative.

Carefully, he extricated himself and wondered how Leonardo could have gotten himself back there, as he was considerably larger around the middle. While Claudio's mind darted from one thought to the next, there was always one that was top of mind—his next opportunity to see Alice.

"Calm yourself, Claudio," replied da Vinci. "Perhaps you did not give it enough time to set. These things cannot be rushed, and I find that you are most impatient of late—though I cannot fault you for being so." The master was assisting Francesco to carry in some fresh rope required for the extension.

"Agreed," Francesco motioned to Claudio with a tip of his head. "All this will be but a fond memory for you one day. Your life in the other realm will continue as you and Elisa left it. But for now, do the task patiently, and do it well," he said, as his face gave way to a smile.

"When did you sprout such wisdom, Baron Francesco?" Claudio's voice oozed irony.

"Since it appears I am compelled to rescue you yet again, count," Francesco replied, affecting a thoroughly exaggerated world-weary air.

"Hmph!" Claudio was in no mood for Francesco's deprecating humor. "Do not test me this day, Francesco, lest I hurl this chisel at your—"

"That is enough, lads," interrupted da Vinci, his usually kindly eyes rolling with impatience. "Carry on working, the both of you. Let us not allow our frustrations to escalate in the guise of jest so far that we cannot bring ourselves back from the edge of exasperation."

The two paused, then exchanged apologetic smiles. *The old man does have a way with words*, thought Claudio.

As the three men went back to their work, loud knocks at Leonardo's apartment door cut through the space.

"Who is there?" Leonardo called out as his apprentices carried on closing doors and locking cupboards.

"B-begging your pardon, sir," the familiar voice replied, "it is Brother Antonuccio. I have come at the request of Abbot Federico to tell you that a m-messenger awaits the three gentlemen in the abbey c-courtyard." The little monk's voice did not have its usual shy, unassuming quality. Instead, it was filled with urgency.

"Do you know who the messenger is?" asked Claudio, bewildered.

"I-I d-do n-n—" Antonuccio could not make his mouth work.

"Calm down now, brother. Who is the messenger, and where is he from?" Claudio wasted no time in getting to the point. He headed for the door, worked the locks, and opened it. The two other men followed, dashing out of the apartment close behind, with Antonuccio in tow.

"I-I do not know s-sir."

Claudio wound his way down the halls to the open-air passage. "Is he from the palace? Is he dressed in a guard's uniform?"

"N-no sir. I-I think he is a peasant. Abbot Federico was in the courtyard, speaking with the messenger, and he was very troubled, distressed if I may say so, sir."

Messenger. Distressed. What could have happened now? Could it be Alice? Mother? Claudio cleared the long outside walkway from da Vinci's apartments to the north stairs in a heartbeat and jumped the steps, two at a time. Poor Antonuccio, his belt rosary flying in the wind, had to run to keep up with him, as did da Vinci and Francesco.

The closer Claudio got to the courtyard, the more the feeling of foreboding increased. He saw Father Federico in his familiar habit, his hands folded in prayer. Unknown fears began to crystalize deep within his belly. The messenger was one of Francesco's stewards.

"What the devil? Dioneo? What is all this?" Claudio heard Francesco mumbling behind him. "What has happened?"

The steward, cap in hand, tried to sputter out his response.

"Speak. Out with it!"

"Calm down, for Bacchus' sake, Claudio!" snapped Francesco.

"Let him speak, and he will tell you," urged da Vinci.

Claudio paused, gathering himself.

"This is where I intervene, Count Moro." Abbot Federico's eyes were grim, his hands still wrapped around his rosary. "I must appeal for calm."

Claudio's breath was shallow, and he felt what was left of any color drain completely from his face. His heart beat like a drum in his throat. The steward stepped back a safe distance from Claudio.

"Dioneo, what is it?" asked Francesco.

Dioneo bowed to Francesco. "If my lord pleases..." His voice cracked as his gaze darted back and forth from one man to the other. "Miss Caterina sent me. Something terrible has happened, sir. This morning after our meal, the servants all went to their chores—me and the other stewards were upstairs tending to yours and the elder Baron's things—the maids, Miss Caterina and Miss Elisa, were in the kitchen with Cook. Old Nestor went to the barn to tend to the animals." The steward choked at this last comment, and his eyes began to redden. "Well, the next thing any of us knew, Miss Caterina came running into the house, very much beside herself, crying and shouting that Nestor was dead in the barn, and she could not find Elisa."

"Nestor, dead?" Francesco questioned.

"What do you mean, she could not find Elisa?" interjected Claudio, newly agitated.

"Calm now." The old master raised his hands to settle everyone down. "Slowly, now, lad. Tell us everything you know."

"Miss Caterina said she stepped out to the barn after calling out for Miss Elisa, on account that she was not returning to her inside chores. When she did not answer, Miss Caterina went out to the barn to look for her. That is when she found Nestor. And, my lord," he directed this to Francesco, "he was murdered, sir—a killing blow to the head is what did it. So, then Miss Caterina tried to find Elisa, but all she found was this." He pulled a red, crumpled cloth out of his cap—it was Claudio's scarf.

Ali kept the ridiculous thing with her all the time, tied around her neck like an amulet—and now here it was almost ripped in two. Claudio's eyes grew wide, and his breath quickened.

"Caterina said she ran all about the old place and in the fields and the hamlet...nobody has seen her, my lord. She screamed out her name for a long time, but she never answered. Caterina thinks that bandits must have done it."

Though he fought to control them, tears were flowing down the adolescent's cheeks. "Apologies, my lord...Nestor was always kind to me. In any event, Miss Caterina fears that Elisa is in danger. She says Miss Elisa would never leave for long without telling on account that Caterina worries so much about her."

"This is hers." Claudio grasped the torn piece of cloth from the steward and brought it to his mouth, gripping it until his knuckles were white. "Bandits, yes. I can feel that there is something terribly wrong. I know her better than I know my own heart, and she would not do this of her own accord. She weighs her every action by whom it will affect, and whom it may hurt. Oh, no...this is not her at all." Claudio's eyes were distant, as his mind raced to calculate his next move.

"Claudio, what shall we do?" da Vinci's voice was even, but his eyes betrayed his alarm.

"We will go to the manor house." Claudio's jaw clenched as tears welled up in his eyes. "We will start from there—see if we can find her. I pray that she has taken temporary leave of her senses and just wandered away into the hills, but I doubt it. We must search for anything we can find to indicate where she may be, where she may have gone...or who may have taken her. And we shall not stop until we have found her. Mark my words, if someone has harmed her in any way if they have so much as caused one drop of her blood to be spilled—I will kill them."

Chapter Forty-Four

Clarice had just awakened from her mid-afternoon nap, and already she was annoyed. She had rung three times for Gabriela, and there was no sight of her. Not being accustomed to waiting, Clarice proceeded to pull the rope that rang the servant's bell again and again. She had worked herself into such a state that by the time her lady-in-waiting did arrive, Clarice burst into an unseemly tirade.

"Where were you hiding instead of coming when I called for you?" Clarice asked her maid with a dismissive sniff, then looked her up and down. "Where have you been?"

"I have been assisting her ladyship's brother, my lady," Gabriela said as she attempted to adjust her untidy coif and tweak the folds in her day dress.

"Hmph!" Clarice puffed out with a sideways glance. "Help me with that." She motioned to the dress lying on the settee. "And this." Her corset was loosened and required re-adjusting.

"Yes, my lady."

Clarice held onto the bedpost as her maid tightened her corset strings. "What in Bacchus' name were you assisting Bruno with? Really, I must speak to him about constantly ravishing the maidservants." Clarice felt a particularly harsh pull of the strings. "Ouch!"

"I am sorry, my lady," Gabriela said unconvincingly. "It was not that. He required assistance on another matter."

Clarice's curiosity was aroused. "With what matter?"

Gabriela paused, pulled the corset strings tight to the center and tying them swiftly.

"I asked you a question." Clarice turned to glare at Gabriela.

She was flushed but stone-faced calm. "If it pleases my lady, his lordship insists it remains a secret."

"No, it does not please your lady, and I do not give a fig what Bruno has told you. You are my maid, and you shall answer my question. Now, what is Bruno up to that requires the assistance of my lady-in-waiting?"

Gabriela curtsied deeply. "My most profound apologies, my lady, however, I fear that I have said too much already. Lord Bruno made it very clear that no one is to be privy to it, and I fear I shall feel the full force of his ire now that her ladyship's suspicions are aroused."

Clarice squeezed her lips together to keep from shouting her admonitions at her maid. She thought perhaps this was a matter better dealt with using the utmost diplomacy and sweetness.

"My dear Gabriela, you need not fear Bruno's reprisals." She tapped her maid's hand in a feigned gesture of comfort, which only served to elicit a recoil from Gabriela. Clarice continued, despite Gabriela's reaction. "I shall protect you from whatever he threatened you with—torture, prison, whatever he said—do not heed him, for I can wield an equally potent measure of power."

Clarice paused a moment and waited—perhaps the longest she had ever waited for anything in her life.

Finally, her lady-in-waiting spoke. "I fear that the information from the old washerwoman, intended for her ladyship, has made its way to Lord Bruno."

Clarice let out an annoyed breath and raised her brows. "How would he have known about that unless you wanted him to? Did you not realize what that would bring about?"

Gabriela squeezed her lips together as her eyes wandered about the apartment walls, perhaps hoping to find an answer to her quandary. "My lady," she licked her lips as a wave of apprehension swept over her face, "there are many things I may have done for which I am not proud, but this...I fear that this is too much for my conscience to bear."

She paused for a long moment, at which Clarice's impatience once again rose to the surface. "Out with it, then."

Gabriela shrunk back. "Oh, my lady. Mercy, please." The maid sunk to her knees in desperation and held up her hands, palm-to-palm, begging to be spared.

What in the devil's name could I have done to invoke such fear? And for that matter, what has my brother done that is so wretched as to illicit such guilt from her? As awful as it may be, it is apparent she does not intend to share it with me.

"Gabriela, you are wasting my valuable time. Make haste and assist me in dressing." Clarice motioned to her burgundy velvet dress on the settee. She stood with her arms outstretched, waiting to receive it as a knight awaits his squire to help him don his armor.

Gabriela scurried to collect the gown and held it in place for her ladyship to step into. "It is abundantly clear that I must investigate this for myself." At this declaration, Gabriela let out a small noise and lost all the flush in her face.

"My lady, wait!" Gabriela gulped in a great breath and let all of it spill out like a breached dam. "Your brother received word from Paolina that Count Claudio and the servant girl were seen in a nearby village. According to the washerwoman, there was talk of the duke and of his questionable governing. Bruno believes that the count would take Florence for himself. He captured the servant girl and has designs on using her captivity to control Count Claudio."

Clarice paused for a long moment, then rolled her eyes at Gabriela. "Has my brother lost his mind? That old woman would say anything to obtain favor to gain access to the palace." Delicately, she slipped her feet into her silken mules. "He cannot be serious in drudging up those ridiculous accusations again."

"My lady, I am privy to other conversations as well, conversations throughout the palace. Maids and valets talk—there was talk of a conversation between your brother and other nobles that revealed an entirely different plan—one that I only learned of after assisting Bruno with the maid. It is not Count Claudio who wishes to succeed His Grace. I can say nothing more, only...after hearing it, I feel the burden of regret on my soul at having anything at all to do with this situation."

With great depth of thought, Clarice mulled over what her maid said after which everything became as clear as Murano crystal. She believed Gabriela. Her mind raced as she imagined her great city being ruled by her despot brother and reducing all that her uncle had tried to build in the short time he had during his return to Florence.

"This cannot be allowed to happen," declared Clarice, setting her chin in a stubborn line. Angling her head and surveying her lady-in-waiting, Clarice allowed her the fact that she had been given the opportunity to speak to the old washerwoman first. Could she blame Gabriela for passing the information to Bruno? "Tell me everything, Gabriela."

Gabriela hesitated, then shifted her gaze back to her ladyship's. "I am at a loss, my lady." She halted briefly. "I will tell you what Paolina shared with Lord Bruno, only because I will not be a party to our great city's ruin. I can do no more—his actions are his own. But I beg—nay—I implore of milady

Clarice to protect me lest Bruno discovers how you gained this knowledge. Please." Her hands came together again, clasped palm to palm.

Clarice felt something—a flicker of tender warmth in her stomach, like a butterfly fluttering its wings against her insides. This twinge she felt, this brief something of a sensation—was this what they called mercy?

Chapter Forty-Five

Not too far away, Ali awoke in pain.

The throbbing in her head caused her to cry out even before she opened her eyes. Alice, barely conscious, tried to move her body. Her muscles felt like stone, tight and weak, and she could not make her hands work until she realized she was lying on them.

Her lids fluttered open, and she found herself in a darkened room. The initial reaction was confusion. In the fleeting moments of first consciousness she wondered if it was all a dream, but when she lifted her head, the pain made her realize it was very real. She remembered. The barn—and Nestor. The hand over her mouth. The metal against her back. The hit on her head.

She was on something soft and spongy—she smelled it—it was hay. Was she still in the barn? Struggling to a sitting position, Ali scanned her surroundings. She was in a shadowy stone room, with a barred wrought iron door and no windows. It was clear she was not in the barn anymore. Pain lingered in her skull relentlessly as the fear of imminent danger boiled inside her belly and up to her throat where it released into a weak cry.

An anguished shout coming from somewhere in the place made her start and then just as swiftly, faded into silence.

"God no," she whispered. Her tongue moved, and she spat dirt out of her mouth. She wiped her tongue with her sleeve, all the while battling the basic instinct to panic.

Still wobbly, she arose and went to the door, gripping and shaking the bars, hoping the door would swing open.

"Hello?" She winced, sticking her face between the bars, and waited for a response. Nothing. "Hello!" This time with more conviction. Still nothing. "Help me! Help!"

As she rubbed her head and tried not to go to pieces, she looked down at herself. Her clothing was different. Someone had changed her dress. She no longer wore the clothes of a servant but the clothes of a noblewoman—a dress made of soft green velveteen and woven with gold threading. She inhaled deeply to stave off the feeling of horror swelling in her throat. The tingle of a strangled cry was trying to escape as she ran her hands over the velvet day dress. As she closed her eyes to try to think, a feeling of realization swept over her like a wave.

She must be in the Medici palace prison. Where else could she possibly be? Though she had never been a witness to this place, even in her former life, the presumption was undeniable. But why the dress?

It took all she had to keep from crying as she sat and held herself, her arms around her shoulders, rocking back and forth on the cold stone floor like a little lost child. But she could not sit there forever. Chances were that no one knew where she was. She had to do something.

Ali opened her eyes and breathed deeply several times to settle the need to scream. *Stay calm, stay calm. You can't think when you're panicking.*

She stood slowly to assuage the dizziness she felt coming on and craned her neck to look across the stone laden hall into another cell. No one. No windows, either, but from her position she could tell there was a lantern burning somewhere nearby.

Is it even the same day? How long have I been unconscious?

Whilst in her thoughts, another distant shout pierced the eerie quiet. "Guard, I am innocent! Water...give me water," yelled a disembodied voice. That was followed by the sharp clatter of metal on metal and the clanking of keys. Faint at first, but then the sound drew closer. She listened carefully to the noise of someone with a heavy stride getting closer—then the noise ceased. Whoever it was had stopped relatively close by.

Ali licked her lips. Her tongue was as dry as withered corn-husks. Grasping the bars, she tried to decide if she should be quiet and pretend she was still asleep or ask for the water that her body craved. She forced her courage to break the surface of her fears and finally spoke.

"Hello?" The soft echo of her voice hung in the air like vapor on a cold day, and the clanking of keys began again. *Step, clank, step, clank.*

Ali instinctively stepped backward until her hands hit the wall of the cell. A guard emerged on the far side of the hall, sword at the ready. From his approach, Ali thought he may be anticipating a confrontation, but when he saw her, he sheathed his weapon. He could not have been more than twenty years of age.

"You are awake, then." The guard's words held no emotion.

Alice could not find her voice to answer him.

"Well, what is it you want?"

She tried to make her mouth work. "I-I..." She licked her lips, but her tongue stuck uncomfortably to them. "Please," her voice wavered, "may I have some water?"

The guard looked her over for a moment, then walked away. Alice heard sounds of liquid being poured. If she had any spit left, she knew her mouth would be watering.

He returned with a cup in his hand, the water spilling out of the filled vessel. She started toward him, her eyes hungrily on the cup.

"Stay back," he commanded.

She started and jerked herself backward.

"I will put it down, then you may drink."

Once he was a safe distance back, she dove for the cup and eagerly drank the warm water down in seconds. "Please, may I have another?"

The guard nodded, and the routine was repeated. Three times, Alice asked him for refills, and he obliged. When she had drunk her fill, she set the cup down at the bottom of the wrought iron door, within reach of the guard, and stepped back. He picked up the cup and, Ali assumed, started back for his station. "Wait."

He stopped and turned around to face her. If he gave her water, perhaps he would be inclined to give her information.

"If you please, sir why am I here? Who brought me here?"

The guard paused. Ali was sure that he was silently deliberating on whether to speak to her at all. Finally, he opened his mouth.

"You should consider yourself fortunate. He did not want you damaged." With no emotion, he turned and walked away.

The guard's words confused her. Her breath came in shallow spurts, and her vision swam so that the shadows mingled with the light. Afraid that her head would burst, she found her temples and held on. In an action that resembled more dropping to the stone floor than sitting, Ali paused and waited for the feeling to subside.

"Oh, God, no." Her desperate whispers mingled with her soft crying. "Please, no. Not this." Alice had never wanted her mother and father more. And what of Claudio? He would be desperate to find her. The reality of her situation bore heavily down on her as her shoulders heaved with each sob she released, sitting on the floor of the cold, dark cell.

Chapter Forty-Six

Alice did not know how she survived her first night in the Medici prison. At least, she assumed it was night. The occasional moaning in other parts of the prison settled down after a while. She awoke the next morning, believing a nightmare had haunted her sleep, but once lucid, she knew the dungeon was very much her reality.

Another guard replaced the one who had given her water—he made sure she was fed. In fact, he appeared surprised at the meal that had been dispatched for her: boiled meat, fritters, fruits, and spiced wine. Ali guessed that it was not the usual fare for prisoners, which led her to think that someone was trying, in their own way, to flatter her into submission.

If she were not so hungry, she would have refused the food. However, making herself too weak to think or act would not do anyone any good. So, she ate—it tasted good.

The guard watched as she finished most of it. The only thing left on her plate were two figs, which she kept for later—one never knew.

Time passed slowly. The minutes telescoped into endless hours. Despite having made her hay bed as comfortable as she could, every tiny noise served to rouse her, even when she had managed to nod off.

Faint sounds of snoring and cries sliced the silence every now and then, but none of the voices were nearby. She wondered if she was the only one in this part of the dungeon. In her solitude, her mind drifted, thinking thoughts of the torture and pain in store for her. The fear inside her mounted with each passing moment. At long last, she heard an outer door open and felt a breeze enter the stagnant air of her cell.

"Good evening, my lord." It was the young guard's voice again.

He said my lord! It's Claudio! "Claudio! I am here!" She leapt from her spot on the hay bed, bounded to the door, and thrust her arm through the bars, never doubting for a moment that it could be anyone but Claudio coming to rescue her from this place. Ali pushed her delicate face against the bars to get a better look at her soul mate, but instead of a cry of joy, she uttered a strangled gasp.

Bruno stood before her.

Alice stumbled back and shrunk against the rear of the cell, her hands spread against the back wall. She was like a caged animal with nowhere to hide from its hunter, unable to catch enough breath.

"Obviously, you are mistaken in your assumption, Elisa." Bruno's drawling voice was enough to make her stomach turn. "It is not Claudio who has come to save you—it is I."

Not knowing how to answer him, she opted to remain silent.

"Guard." Bruno motioned to the door.

Without delay, the guard unlocked the door. His gaze caught Ali's, but only for an instant. Once Bruno was in, he turned to the guard and said, "Secure the door and go."

Ali felt an invisible hand close around her throat as she remained motionless against the wall, her heart pounding. The guard locked the cell and bowed before turning on his heel, leaving her alone with Bruno.

A chilling, black silence surrounded them. For the longest few moments of her life, Bruno said nothing to her. He only looked her up and down, as one would evaluate meat in the window of a butcher shop.

"Wh-what do you want of me?" she managed to stammer out. "Why are you doing this?"

"Is that not obvious? I want you." His mouth curled up at the ends, but it was the furthest thing from a smile that Alice had ever seen. "Utterly and completely."

"Why me, my lord? You are heir to the throne—you may have any woman you wish."

"But it is you that I want. I knew when I first saw you that I had to have you. No maiden has ever refused me."

"But I love Claudio, and he loves me."

"All the more reason to have you." He took a step toward her.

"But was he not your friend, my lord?"

Bruno let out a snort and a guffaw. "My friend? Oh, you do have a sense of humor, darling. We were once, but he has chosen a different path. Besides, do friends not share?" He took another step, enjoying the agony his every action brought to Alice.

"That is disgusting—and I do not wish to be shared. I am not a thing you can pass around. I am a person."

"Mind your tongue," he said through clenched teeth. "That is of no consequence to me."

He was very close—so close that she could smell the sour aroma of wine on his breath. Ali moved swiftly to the other side of the cell, almost stumbling in her haste. Bruno stopped his advance. His jaw loosened, and his breathing became deep.

The hair on the back of her neck began to tingle.

"Darling, you need not worry yourself about my wanting

you forever." His wicked smile was back. "You would be kept lavishly, Elisa. You could have elegant dresses, such as the one I gave you as a gift for being my guest here." He chuckled softly at his humor. "Jewelry, gold, and all the other things a woman covets could be yours—if you would indulge me."

Alice felt ill. How could he think she would agree to such a repulsive proposition? She shook her head from side to side.

"One day, if you agree to be my consort, you may even be the mistress of the next ruler of Florence. And if I have my way, that day shall arrive sooner rather than later, my pet. All I ask is that you help me show Moro the futility of his efforts to influence my uncle. Would that not please you? To be the mistress of the future Duke of Florence?"

"My lord." Ali forced a smile. Was she hearing him correctly? Was he alluding to an imminent succession? "I could no more betray Claudio than tell my heart to cease to beat."

Bruno's expression took on a sinister quality, and Ali's heart sank. "Please, my lord, try to understand—I could not. Never." She swallowed, but her mouth was a desert. "I will always be only for him."

Bruno paused, not taking his eyes off her as she stood at the door, ready to spring to the other side of the cell.

Frustration hovered in his eyes, then in an instant, his features shifted from menacing to favorable. "I see now, from your poignant and tender words, that my patient pursuit of you has been in vain." He bowed to Ali, disarmingly. "It has caused both yourself and my friend great hardship, and I realize that you shall never acquiesce to my advances." His body language changed entirely, as though he were another person. "If you move away from the door, I shall call the guard, and have you released—on one condition—this little diversion, this escapade will be our secret—agreed?"

Alice felt cautious relief at his sudden change of heart. As Bruno backed away, his body still inclined in a bow, she moved forward to allow him to leave, but as she stepped into the middle of the cell to let him get to the door, he sprang from his bow like a snake uncoils to pounce on its prey.

He grabbed her hand roughly and wrenched her toward him. In a heartbeat, he spun her around and pushed her to the bed. She tried to scream, but he put a hand over her mouth.

"Silence!" he snarled at her, his eyes bulging and spittle flying out of his mouth. "You can either surrender and make it easy on yourself—or not. I tried to be cordial. Now I must insist. If you do not assist me in getting rid of Moro, I shall have to kill you—after I have had my fill of you, that is." His hand squeezed her mouth so that her lips hurt against her teeth.

With fearful images building in her mind, Ali nodded. Could this buy her a few moments?

He loosened his grip on her mouth. "Do not try to trick me, or you shall pay for it."

She had to try to reason with him. How could he think that he could get away with treating her like a piece of meat?

"Please, my lord, I implore you...when Claudio finds out, he will be furious. He will not rest until—"

Bruno wasn't listening. "I will have him arrested again," he growled, "and both of you shall perish in the dungeons. This time, I have reason to arrest you. Discussing the efficacy of the duke will cost you, and your dear Claudio, your freedom." He laughed contemptuously as he put his hand on her.

With her one free hand, she felt around for something—anything—to get him off her, but all she could find was dirt and pebbles.

"I do not know what or who has put these ideas in your mind, but they are not true."

"What does truth have to do with anything?" he scowled.

This is it, she thought. *Do it now.* She grabbed a handful of dirt and lifted her arm slightly to throw it in his face, but he was too fast.

His hand moved swiftly and grabbed her right wrist in a tight grip, slamming it against the hard floor. He leaned over her and grabbed her other wrist. With both her hands in his control, he was almost on top of her.

"Get your filthy hands off me," she said through clenched teeth, struggling to break free. The fear in her eyes had turned to fire. "I swear, if you do not let go, I will hurt you." Alice knew this was about control, and Bruno wanted it back.

Ali was furious at her vulnerability to him. Twisting her head away in horror, she screamed, her legs and arms flailing and twisting wildly to get some leverage over him. She managed to work her slim leg through his as he straddled her on the scratchy hay bed. With satisfaction, she kneed him hard.

Bruno let out a yelp that would have befitted a coyote, doubled over, and held onto his crotch to assuage the searing pain.

"You bastard!" Ali screamed. "You horrible person!" She clambered away from him, breathing hard, the blood pounding in her ears. "How dare you do this to another human being."

Bruno, too, was panting, and his pain was blisteringly evident. The feelings that resulted for Ali were so familiar, so awfully recognizable, that she felt she was going to be sick. It was Bruno and Enzo in the Great Hall all over again, but this time she would not stand for it. Her dress torn and blood on her lips, she stood defiant against the back wall of the cell.

"Get out!" she screamed. "Get out!" This brought the guard back, without being ordered by his lordship. When he saw the scene, and the condition Bruno was in, he swiftly opened the door and went to tend to him.

"May I assist his lordship?" His hand extended to help Bruno rise, but instead he was rebuked.

"You dare attempt to touch me?" Bruno managed to get to

his feet on his own, but he was rather shaky and still doubled over. He turned to Alice. "For this, you shall pay—with interest. Enjoy your last day with the living."

Ali swallowed down a sob. She would never give Bruno the satisfaction of seeing her cry.

He got to the door on his own and skulked off, gripping the wall and the front of his breeches all the way.

The guard closed the door after him and locked it, but instead of leaving, he watched and waited until Bruno was out of earshot. "Do you wish some water?"

At this slight act of kindness, Ali's emotions broke through. The cries she had held back to spite Bruno flowed freely as the guard stood by.

Alice could only nod her thanks as she took the cup of water with shaking hands and drank. Her mind kept going back to Claudio. Was he safe? Or had Bruno gotten to him, too?

Chapter Forty-Seven

Gabriela confessed everything to Clarice.

Even though Clarice still did not see what was so special about Elisa, and she felt the girl was an inconvenience, the maid certainly did not deserve to be imprisoned because of Bruno's nonsensical pride. It was all so clear to Clarice—the scullery maid was not interested in him—she had spurned him for Claudio, and Bruno could not accept that, the fool.

If he had arranged for something to happen to her to get to Claudio, it was not only undeserved, it would also put the duke in a very precarious position. Clarice had to warn her uncle, but he was on that silly hunting trip with Ambassador Castiglione and the Baron Tondini. The Medici had only just come back to power in Florence over the Borgia and the Spaniards—and though there were many in the prison that did deserve to be there—neither Claudio nor the girl did.

In addition, Bruno would risk raising the ire of the city and court of nobles if he falsely accused a well-respected courtier such as Claudio. In earnest, she did not understand how he could think of getting away with the entire scheme after the rousing celebration of the count's innocence at the hearing last month.

"So, what to do?" Clarice was in her apartments, her hand on her chest as she puzzled over the dilemma. Her brother would hardly speak to her. "Perhaps I should ask Aunt Filiberta for advice," she mumbled. "Yes, What a perfectly splendid idea —she will know what to do."

Clarice set out in search of her aunt and found her in a most peaceful and tranquil spot, enjoying one of the first few days of autumn in the palace garden. The morning sun was delicious, and the aroma of ripening citrus in the garden was intoxicating. There were a few ladies around her as she sat in the shade of a fragrant lemon tree reading a book. When the ladies saw Clarice they curtsied, to which Clarice perfunctorily nodded her acknowledgement, and then sped directly to her Aunt Filiberta's side.

"Good morning, Auntie," cooed Clarice as she kissed Filiberta on the cheek. "Are you enjoying the sunshine?" Best to ease into the matter with some pleasant conversation.

"Yes, thank you. And how nice of you to seek me out for company. I do miss having the frequent companionship I was accustomed to with Countess Maria, but I do not dare rob her of the happiness that Counselor Filippo's friendship brings her."

"You are too kind, Auntie." *Enough niceties for now*, thought Clarice, then turned to the ladies-in-waiting. "Please leave us. I must have a moment with the Duchess in private, but do not leave the garden. I may require one of you before long."

"What is it, my dear?" Filiberta barely took her eyes off her book. It was not unlike Clarice to urgently require a moment with her aunt now and then.

"Auntie, I fear we may have a situation that requires immediate attention on your part." Clarice looked around to ensure no one was listening. "You recall the hearing last month? Count Claudio and the scullery maid?"

"Of course, how could I forget? What a raucous evening that turned out to be. What was the maid's name? Elisa Beatrice?"

"Yes, Auntie. She is precisely why I am here—and Claudio, too."

"I thought the girl had left the palace."

"Hmm, but I have it on good information that she has returned to a nearby village."

Duchess Filiberta closed her book with an irritated snap. "Oh Clarice, please do not tell me you are embroiled in another scheme to thwart those two. It is below you to continue—"

Clarice let out an impatient sigh. "No, Auntie, not me. I know when my dignity is at stake, and I promised myself, after much reflection, to refuse to let anyone or anything come between myself and my pride ever again." Clarice shook her head and pursed her lips. "It is Bruno. I fear he cannot do the same. His pride knows no bounds, I am afraid."

"Come. Sit. Tell me what it is that has you troubled." Filiberta put her hand on Clarice's while she recounted the events to her aunt. Filiberta shook her head and looked at the ground.

"Oh dear. We do not want another situation to upset the tranquility of the duke's serene reign. And we especially do not want a reason for an uprising from the nobility. How could Bruno think, for one moment, that he could get away with another exploitative act such as this?"

The Duchess turned, and with a wave of a hand one of her ladies was at her side. "Costanzia, go and fetch Gabriela, please. Advise her that the Duchess wishes a word."

Not long afterward, Gabriela appeared, flushed and out of breath, hurrying along the pebbled path, her skirts hoisted above her ankles. The lady who summoned her followed farther behind, equally winded from the dash through the palace.

When Gabriela observed who was sitting with the Duchess, she took two steps back, and her face took on a fearful look.

Summoning up all her courage, she took the remaining steps to begin her audience with the Duchess of Florence slowly and with her eyes downcast. Her body language revealed her sentiments. "Your Grace," Gabriela said as she curtsied deeply to Filiberta. Then to Clarice, "My lady."

"Good afternoon, Gabriela," said Filiberta graciously. "Due to the urgency of the matter, and the supposition on my part that a young girl's life may be in jeopardy, I shall not dally with frivolous conversation and get right to the point. You need not worry about reprisals from Bruno, if that is your concern, I shall take care of that. Answer yes or no to my queries, that is all you are required to do, and you shall answer honestly. Do I make myself clear?"

"Yes, Your Grace," Gabriela gulped.

"My niece tells me that Bruno and you may be involved in a plot to somehow interfere in Count Claudio's friendship with a certain maid who once worked at the palace. Remember, you shall be safe. Now, answer yes or no."

Clarice's eyes darted from her aunt to her lady-in-waiting.

"Yes, Your Grace."

Filiberta's smile was warm and encouraging, making Gabriela's tenseness seem to ease. This was not lost on Clarice, who, in turn, attempted to emulate her aunt. She mused that she needed to practice this method of speaking to servants, as it appeared to her the response to a smile was more favorable than one to a scowl.

"Very good. Is the count aware of her whereabouts?"

"No, Your Grace."

"He must be beside himself with worry," Filiberta commented to Clarice before returning her attention to the maid. "And the girl is in the dungeons?"

Gabriela's face became red, and her eyes were once again

downcast. "She is, Your Grace."

"I see." Filiberta took a deep breath. "Is the girl still alive?"

Gabriela's eyes looked up from the ground and straight to Filiberta's. "She is Your Grace, but I do not know for how long she will remain so."

"Explain."

"When he first brought her there, Lord Bruno instructed me to bring her food from the palace. I believed to keep her happy, according to his reasoning. But when I returned last night with her dinner, the guard would not allow it. He said it was against Lord Bruno's wishes. I asked why, and he said that Bruno had tried to have his way with her. She fought him off."

Gabriela's last comment prompted a snorting laugh from Clarice and a gasp from the Duchess.

"Clarice, please. Go on, girl," urged the Duchess.

"As I was saying, the guard heard Bruno say that she would not live out another day. That was last night, Your Grace. I do not know when or if Bruno carried out his wishes, but if you plan on helping the girl, I would do so at your earliest opportunity."

Filiberta shook her head. After a brief pause, she pointed to Gabriela. "You know where this girl is?"

"Yes, Your Grace. I helped to dress her while she was sleeping. Her cell is in a very remote part of the dungeon—away from all the other prisoners. Lord Bruno said it was so that even if someone went looking for her there, she would not be found. Only he and his men know about her. They arranged it, so no one was there when they brought her in, and a guard is posted there with orders not to let anyone pass him."

Clarice and Filiberta exchanged glances.

"Costanzia," the Duchess snapped her fingers, "bring me several parchments, wax, and a quill." To another lady in waiting, she ordered, "Teresa, go and fetch Rubio, my guard." To Gabriela she added, "You stay here until I am ready for you to go to the prison with a letter and my personal guard." Filiberta regarded her niece with fondness in her eyes. "You, my dear, must find Bruno. It is early therefore I can only assume he is still asleep. Keep him occupied until I send for you. The duke and I shall deal with him later. We must stop this barbarism at once."

Clarice nodded. In her heart, she felt a pleasant kindle of warmth.

"What are you intending to do, Auntie?"

Filiberta looked as though her mind was hard at work. "The girl needs to be removed from the situation. I only hope that we are not too late."

Costanzia returned with the writing instruments and handed them with a curtsy to her duchess.

"I shall write a letter to Abbess Augustine at the Convent of the Infant Jesus introducing Elisa Beatrice and explaining her unique situation. I shall also write a general order to the guards with strict instructions to afford Rubio access to every part of the dungeon. Ah, Rubio, there you are."

An imposing, large man emerged from the palace, wearing full armor. He strode directly to the Duchess and bent to one knee before her, placing his sword vertically over his face in a salute. "Your Grace," he said.

"One moment, Rubio." He arose and waited.

As Filiberta finished her letters, Costanzia let a few drops of heated wax spill onto the folded flap to seal them. Filiberta pressed them closed, stamping them with her monarch's ring. Once finished, she spoke to her guard.

"This one is labeled Abbess Augustine, this to the guards in the dungeon—and this to Count Moro of Elba. Rubio listen carefully. Gabriela shall accompany you to the prison to procure a certain prisoner—a girl. Gabriela will show you where she is. If you encounter any opposition, hand them this letter—make certain they see the seal. Send one of your men with the swiftest horse to find the count. I should venture he is in or about the Tondini hamlet." Filiberta explained her plan to both Gabriela and the guard.

When finished, Filiberta turned to her niece again. "Now, Clarice, you must go and find Bruno. Keep him busy so he does not go to the prison. I hope he has not left orders to—"

"I shall go now." Clarice interrupted. She turned on her heel to run back into the palace, but her aunt grasped her hand and squeezed it. Clarice was surprised at this and gazed at the Duchess questioningly.

"I shall tell you that I have never been more proud of you, Clarice." She smiled. "Your show of mercy is quite refreshing."

Clarice smiled back and swiftly headed into the palace.

Chapter Forty-Eight

Claudio had never felt so weary. It was early afternoon of the third day since Alice had disappeared, and he had not slept since the night before last. Yet, he dared not sleep, for this would take time away from his search for her. He, da Vinci, and some of Francesco's men had split up to cover as much of the area surrounding the manor house as possible.

The search had taken the Baron and his skilled horsemen to the surrounding villages and the countryside, over mountains and the lush Tuscan landscape—but there was no sign of Ali. They had searched as much of Florence as they were able to, but it was in vain—they had even combed the palace, upstairs and down, and the Medici prison, believing that by some wild incident someone may have put her there, but nothing proved fruitful.

Almost at the threshold of despair, Claudio decided to return to Francesco's house to allow the stable hands to feed and water Spirit—she was exhausted and hungry.

As Claudio sat at the table in the dining area of the Baron's house, he thought how maddeningly frustrating this was.

Under the skin of Ali's arm this whole time was a microchip able to indicate her location across the globe, with pinpoint accuracy—but without the technology to find her it meant nothing.

"My lord, you must eat something," Caterina said, pushing a plate of mutton stew under his nose. She looked every bit as haggard as Claudio felt. "You must be strong, to keep up the search. It will do you no good to starve yourself." She nodded to the bowl in front of him.

He picked up the spoon and shoved some of it into his mouth, not tasting anything. It took him little more than a few moments to finish his meal, after which he pushed the plate away and took a long drink from his tankard of ale.

"I must go," Claudio said, rising from the table. "I cannot take the chance of leaving any stone unturned. Francesco, my friend, may I have a fresh horse? Let Spirit rest." He had barely gotten all the words out when he suddenly felt like a white light had blinded him. He fell into his chair, and da Vinci, seated next to him, tried to steady him as he wobbled.

"You shall stay here for a short time and sleep, Count." Francesco's voice was stern, yet sympathetic. He took an hourglass from the cupboard and set it on the table. "I shall leave word with one of the stewards to wake you when this timekeeper's sands run out."

"And I shall fetch some herbs from my satchel to help you to sleep, perhaps a Bella Donna blend, or essence of oleander." Da Vinci nudged Claudio. "Just a drop will ease the maelstrom you must have raging in your mind."

"I will ingest no such thing and run the risk of sleeping clear through until tomorrow. God only knows how she is suffering. I must keep going." Again, he tried to stand, but after a bout of severe vertigo, he sat back down. "How long is that thing?" He gestured to the timekeeper and then looked back over to his friend.

"I promise not long. Rest, and you will feel more refreshed and be more effective because of it."

Claudio surrendered. He closed his eyes and put his head down on his crossed arms over the tabletop. The rest of them had managed to rest, but Claudio had insisted on searching the countryside all night, fearing Ali may have been lost in the wooded areas about the hamlets and grown so cold as to suffer ill effects to her health.

When Leonardo was certain that Claudio was asleep, he moved to sit by Francesco as he finished off his ale. "What are you thinking about this terrible thing, Francesco?"

The Baron arched an eyebrow. "I am thinking that I smell Bruno all over this."

Da Vinci nodded his agreement. "But without proof, how can one even begin to accuse him of any involvement?"

"This is what I am thinking."

A rapid knock interrupted the relative calm of the morning.

"Dioneo," said Francesco.

"On my way, sir." The young man moved to the door. There were voices and footsteps.

"What is it, Dioneo?" Francesco shouted out.

"Edoardo and Lipari think they found something."

The sound of scraping chairs against the stone floor and multiple boot steps to the entrance broke the silence.

"What is it?" Claudio was first to the door.

"Look." One of the men held up a small piece of fabric.

Claudio took it in hand and examined it closely. "Strange...'tis a patch of cloth," said Caterina.

"But look on the other side," said Lipari as he turned it over.

A cold hand wrapped around Claudio's heart. "The fleur-de-lis—worn by the Medici guards."

"This is true, my lord. And where we found it aroused our suspicions," answered Edoardo.

"Let us go, then." Claudio was out the door.

"Show us where you found it." Francesco clapped them on the back.

"Let me know what comes of this," Caterina shouted after them.

Claudio dashed to the stable with da Vinci and Francesco on his heels. He mounted Spirit, who snorted her protests. "Sorry, old girl," said Claudio as he snapped the reins. "But this is more important than your sleep."

Edoardo and Lipari leapt onto their mounts and met up with the others who were just emerging from the barn. "You go," Claudio heard Francesco shout. "We shall follow you."

With a nod and a gentle kick to their horses' sides, they were off in a full gallop. Francesco's men led them up the gently sloping hillside, to the same clearing where Claudio and Elisa had observed the hamlet and the manor house a few days earlier. The two men circled around and dismounted.

"Here. We found it lying on the ground. Must have caught on a tree branch or something and was torn off."

"I was here yesterday...I found nothing unusual," said Claudio.

"Look there, my lord." They pointed to a spot under a tree. "Perhaps in your haste to find Elisa, you overlooked it."

Claudio followed their indication. There was an inordinate amount of hoof prints on the moist soil under the tree, along with several horse droppings. A few horses had been there only a few days ago. The clues struck Claudio like a cuff to the side of the head with a sword hilt.

The fleur-de-lis, horses gathered in one place...but what confirmed his reasoning was that he remembered who it was he had glimpsed in the village the other day when he, Ali, and Francesco were there—the old servant woman from the palace.

"Of course," his face flushed with rage and his teeth clenched, "it all makes perfect sense now." Claudio's jaw tried to work, but his breathing took away the words. Angered beyond consoling, he bellowed, "Clarice! If she dares harm her—"

Da Vinci grasped his arm.

"What do you think you are doing?" asked his teacher. "How do you know she had anything to do with Elisa's disappearance?"

"I still do not understand." Francesco looked dumbfounded.

"It all fits. The uniform, the horses, the old woman in the village..."

"What old woman?" asked Francesco.

"When we were in the village, I thought I saw someone I knew, but I could not place her. I just remembered who she is —the old woman who conspired with Clarice's maid. It all fits together. Elisa is probably at the palace as we speak. A prisoner somewhere. God only knows what they have done to her."

Thundering hooves in the distance halted the conversation. The men turned to see a royal messenger racing toward them. Claudio recognized the man, though he did not know his name. He eyed him with caution.

The messenger slowed his horse in a cloud of dust and approached Claudio. "Your lordship, Count Moro. I have been dispatched by Her Grace, Duchess Filiberta. If you please, my lord." He held out an envelope sealed with the Duchess's royal stamp.

"What is this?" asked Claudio impatiently. He broke the seal and swept over the message with his eyes, widening with every line he read. "Everyone—to the Porta Rossa!" He snapped Spirit's reins and sped off in a cloud of dust toward Florence.

Chapter Forty-Nine

"Guard!" Alice cried. "Is there anyone there?" She paused, pushing her face against the bars of the cell door, and strained to hear a response, but there was none. Her voice was hoarse from calling out. She was alone—completely and utterly alone. Frustrated and tired, she grasped the bars in a fit of anger and shook them with all her might, trying to loosen them to no avail.

No one had been to check on her for a long time. The guard had left shortly after the horrible incident with Bruno and had not returned since—that was many hours ago, possibly a day. Alice could not determine the passage of time, or if it was night or day; she had not the benefit of a window to be able to gauge it. In addition, since her sleep was sporadic after she had been kidnapped her body clock was completely off, and she could not trust that either.

Her body craved food and water, but none had been delivered. Were they planning on starving her to death? With her head down, she paced around her cell, feeling like a trapped animal—alone and afraid. How long before her fate would present itself? Bruno had said she would not live to see another day. She shuddered as invisible icy fingers ran down her spine.

"No, way," she whispered. "I will not let this happen. I will not be victimized by that creature." Her jaw clenched. "The only way to get away is when they open the cell door. But how can I overpower guards in armor—with swords and God only knows what else?"

With these thoughts in her mind, she felt her throat tighten. "No, you will not panic. You will stay calm, and you will breathe, and you will think this out. What's in here that I can use? Dirt and hay." She rolled her eyes and sniffed. "Not very effective. If only I could pry one of these bars loose and use it as a weapon." She grabbed hold of one of the iron rods, and with all the anger and frustration she could muster, she pulled and pushed until her hands ached. "Damn," she took a deep breath, "well that's that."

Ali ambled to her hay bed and sat. "Think of something else," she whispered as she sat upright, her back resting against the cold stone of the cell and her knees drawn up underneath her chin.

With her eyes closed, she rested her head on her knees and began to hum. It was an old song that Mamma used to sing to her when she was a little girl—a song from when her mamma was a child. The memory of the soft lilt of her voice and the comforting cadences made Ali forget, at least temporarily, what may transpire at any moment.

How can Bruno be so cruel? Why is he hell-bent on destroying Claudio and me? Ali looked up at the shadowy darkness outside her cell and wondered if her parents were thinking of her. How could she have thought that it would be so easy? Had she been so convinced of her own invincibility, or had she allowed her love and worry for Claudio to cloud her judgement?

"Guilty on all counts," she whispered and closed her eyes, so she could envision her family and Claudio and dream that she was with them instead of in this loneliness.

As her whispers faded like smoke in the silence of the cell, the sound of a distant clang emanated from somewhere in the dungeon, causing her to start.

She jumped to her feet and stood flat against the wall, rooted to the spot, silent and listening. The reverberation was soon followed by the echo of faint footsteps and muffled voices. Was this it? Were they taking her to have Bruno's last vile promise to her fulfilled?

Her breathing increased, unable to take in enough air. The footsteps stopped. Another clang sounded, but louder—they were getting closer. Their conversation was more audible.

Ali felt in her heart that this was it—they were coming for her.

The voices—she knew the voices. One was the kind guard who had offered her water after Bruno's attempted assault. She could not make out the other male voice, but in the middle of the mix, she thought she heard a woman. It was a soft utterance, but Ali was sure. *It must be a nun come to give me my last rights or something, before they behead me, or whatever they do.*

"Oh my God...what do I do?" Her hands covered her mouth to keep a scream from escaping at top volume. The steps and voices got closer. Finally, the clang that she was dreading. The final one at what she could only assume was her end of the dungeon, rang ominously, and the sound of metal-on-metal scraping, signaled that a door had just opened.

"It is just this way," the woman's voice said. The disconnected sound of clicking boots and heels on the cold stone floor accompanied the declaration.

"Why is she so far down in the dungeon?" asked the strange voice.

"Lord Bruno did not want her found. He was certain that Count Moro would come looking for her."

Alice gasped, choking on a cry.

"I believe he did," the kind guard confirmed, "but he was not brought to this level of the dungeon."

Thank God! Alice thought, her spirit lifted at the words spoken by the disconnected voice. Elation took over. If Claudio was searching for her, he was out there somewhere and alive.

"The closest he got was the level before this, upstairs. The door is plain wood. No one would think there was a level below if one was not already aware."

Almost here. There must be something I can do. I will not stand here waiting for them to take me to my death. And there's no way in hell I'm going to make it easy for them. She grabbed an armful of hay.

If I throw this in their faces, maybe I can distract them enough to be able to escape. God, please let him leave the door to the upper levels open. If not, maybe I can grab the keys. I'm small—I can slip right by them if I'm fast enough.

Thoughts raced in Ali's mind as she slid slowly and surreptitiously against the wall adjacent to the cell door, the mound of hay in her arms at the ready. The key in the lock turned over.

The unfamiliar woman cleared her throat. "True," said the strange voice, "the only reason I know about this level is—"

Ali cried out a deafening scream that reverberated against the cavernous dungeon. From her vantage point, all she could see was flying hay and scuffling, confused feet: one set with silky shoes and the other two with leather riding boots.

The woman screamed as Alice threw herself against the two men with the full force of her body, not even considering that they may have had drawn swords. Glancing sideways for a split second, she saw the woman on one knee, half on the ground and leaning against the wall. The two men were taken completely off guard, and Ali easily slipped through them.

Her adrenaline pumped madly as she bounded through the cell door and turned left on impulse. With no notion of where she was going, relying solely on instinct, she sprinted through the prison corridor. When she reached the closed door of her section, she pulled at it and sent a silent prayer of thanks when she found it unlocked.

As she flew up the stairs to a wooden door at the top, she heard them following her, but did not look back. Ali climbed the stairs, two and three at a time, faster than she ever thought herself capable.

Please be open. Please be open. Her fingers wrapped around the handle, and with an immense tug she tried to turn the heavy iron doorknob, but it would not budge. She tried again, pulling with both hands—still nothing. Alice screamed as rage took hold of her to her very core, and she tried again with all the force she could muster.

Broken, she let herself slide to the ground, still holding onto the door handle, sobbing.

A moment later, she felt an unexpectedly gentle touch on her shoulder. "Miss." The man with the strange voice gave her a soft shake.

"Miss, you had best be stopping the uproar or we will be giving ourselves attention that we do not wish to have right now." The kind guard was speaking, but Ali still did not move. Her sobbing was all she wanted to concentrate on.

"Miss, my name is Rubio. I am Duchess Filiberta's personal guard."

She hiccupped a cry and turned her head to look at them. The woman—a pretty girl, who was busy brushing the dust and hay particles off her dress with one hand—grasped parchment envelopes in the other. Ali recalled her face, but she could not remember from where.

"Maid, I am Miss Gabriela." She stood poker straight, her face pinched, looking extremely worried. "Her ladyship's lady-in-waiting. We are here to rescue you. Now, stop weeping and rise so we can make haste."

Not being entirely certain that she should believe them, Ali gazed at them with skepticism.

"Gabriela." Ali allowed one hand to slip from the door handle and wiped her tears away. "I remember what you did—you and that other horrible woman." She sniffed and shifted her gaze to Rubio before coming back to Gabriela. "Why should I trust you? You are more likely to lead me to the gallows than out of this godforsaken place."

"On the contrary." Gabriela sighed impatiently. "We have been dispatched by Duchess Filiberta in an effort to free you and return you to the count."

"He is still alive?"

"Of course, at least for now." Gabriela raised a brow at Alice's strange comment. "But Lord Bruno has plans for him."

"That makes no sense at all. He would kill Claudio because he cannot have me?"

"You ask me questions for which I have no answers." Gabriela reached down and pulled Ali up by the arm. "Do you want to take your leave of this place, or do you not?"

"Obviously, I do."

"Then we must be quick about it, Miss. You must trust us," said Rubio.

The kind guard reached over Ali, inserted the keys in the door, and opened it. Rubio exited first, followed by Alice with Gabriela in their wake. The guard nodded his acknowledgement to Rubio and closed the door behind him. "Come now, hurry. We have only been able to secure a safe passage for a short time. It is imperative that we leave here promptly." Rubio grasped Ali's hand as the women struggled to maintain his pace.

"Where are we going?" asked Alice, as she held up her gown to keep it from tangling in her feet.

"To the stables, then to the Infant Jesus Convent." Rubio's tone had a confidence that Ali trusted. "The sisters will look after you and keep you hidden, by order of Duchess Filiberta, until we can find Count Claudio. We hope to have you and Moro reunited by tomorrow—the rest is up to you—and him."

"Hmph," Gabriela snorted out a laugh between gasping for breaths. "May I suggest you and the count find sanctuary far away from here? I doubt that Bruno will abandon his pursuit of you indefinitely."

They reached the outer door. Rubio put his finger to his lips before motioning for both the women to remain against the wall. He checked to make certain the way was clear.

"It is safe to proceed. Our next destination is the palace stables." Rubio turned to Gabriela. "The letter, miss."

Gabriela handed over a parchment envelope sealed with red wax.

"This is where we part, Elisa." She took a step back. "If it is worth anything to you, I do regret all this. It was not that you are undeserving of respect. From what I hear, you made quite a case for yourself and the count at the hearing last month. But I needed to ensure my survival. In the palace, cultivating powerful allies is the best way to assure oneself of a continued existence in the way one has had the pleasure of becoming accustomed."

Ali gave her a black layered look. "As women, Gabriela, we should try to ally ourselves so that we help one another, instead of betraying each other. Only in that way can we *all* survive."

The lady-in-waiting smiled and inclined her head to Alice. "I shall consider it." With a swish of her skirts, she turned briskly and proceeded across the courtyard into the servant's entrance.

Ali was feeling more and more confident that her escape was imminent. Soon, she would be reunited with Claudio, and they would hopefully be on their way back to 2029 and her parents.

"Come on now, Miss." Rubio grasped her arm. "The stables

are just that way. We must get to a horse and ride fast to the convent."

With renewed energy, Ali managed to keep up with the guard's giant strides as he led her across the courtyard, past the well, and to the stables.

Chapter Fifty

"Bruno! Brother, are you there?" Clarice pounded on her brother's door with her little white fist, her bony knuckles turning red from the knocking. "Bruno!" she shouted. She had nearly given up hope when she heard a grunt from the other side of the threshold. "Bruno?"

"Come!"

"Praise to Bacchus, he is still here," she whispered to herself. Upon opening the door, she saw her brother rolling onto his back on the daybed.

"Clarice, why are you here at this time of day? What time of day is it, anyway?"

Clarice noted that he was still sporting his clothes from the night before.

"Do you not ever change for bed, my brother?" She sniffed and rolled her eyes as she closed the door to his apartments behind her.

"I did my fair share of drinking last evening." He rubbed his eyes. "I was rather angry that certain events did not go as I had planned." Wincing, he arose from his daybed. "Speaking of which, I have some business to attend to. Leave here so I may wash. I have made plans for a certain lady." His gaze was focused on the intricacies of the rug on his floor, but his smile defied evil.

Clarice could only imagine what was running through his mind. "A new conquest?" She asked casually.

"No. An old one who does not know what is good for her." He walked to the servant's bell, gave it a tug, and sat back down to wait.

"Really? Someone from the palace?" Clarice had never been this interested in Bruno's personal life—she had better draw back a little.

He shot her a quizzical glance, then chortled without any humor. "Since when do you give a fig in whom I am interested?" He rubbed the back of his neck.

"I am only curious. You are the one who mentioned it in conversation, not I."

"Hmph. No, not from the palace," he replied vaguely. "Clarice, why are you here?"

"Aunt Filiberta wishes to speak to you—immediately. Without delay." Her smile was perfunctory, and her voice rang with command.

Bruno's face twisted into a grimace. "Aunt Filiberta? About what?"

"She is not in the habit of discussing matters concerning you, with me." *I wonder if they have at least been able to gain access to the prison by now.*

"Since when do you deliver messages for Filiberta?" He let out a rattling breath, coughed, and raked a hand through his hair.

"Since I strolled into the garden and exchanged pleasant conversation with her. I advised her that I was going back indoors, and she asked if I would mind fetching you. She is still waiting in the garden."

Bruno measured her with a cool appraising look. "Very well...my plans shall have to wait."

"A wise choice, my brother." *Surely, they must be well on their way to finding her by now.* "I shall attend outside. She asked to see us together."

Her brother cocked his head and narrowed his eyes. "Which is it, my sister?" A decidedly mocking tone had entered his speech. "Both or just myself? You said a moment ago that she wanted to see me."

Clarice slanted her head in a similar fashion and pursed her lips in anger. "Both of us. Now hurry and dress." She wondered if she sounded angry enough. "And stop acting like the spoiled brat you are."

His gaze became less suspicious at her usual tone of voice.

"Very well," he conceded. "Give me a moment to ready myself."

∾

"Not that one," Bruno growled impatiently at the footman. "I am preparing for an audience with the duchess, not dressing for an afternoon in the garden."

His servant bowed his head. "Begging my lord's pardon, but the duchess is presently in the garden."

"How convenient that you should know. Were you in the garden taking a stroll instead of polishing my riding boots?" His sideways glance smacked of sarcasm.

"No, my lord. I was on my way back from the livery. I required the polish for your boots, and I happened across the rear of the garden when I noticed some unusual activity." He assisted Bruno to disrobe, then scurried off to collect the water and basin.

"No doubt, they required the services of a man to be rid of a particularly large spider." Bruno finished up by splashing water on his face and taking a towel from his footman's arm.

"No, my lord. From what I could glean from the exchange, the duchess sent a house servant to find the duchess' personal guard, as her lady-in-waiting was in an awful hurry to obtain Duchess Filiberta's wax and stamps."

Bruno stopped wiping his face and looked at the servant with narrowed eyes. This was all rather curious.

"Did they return with the personal guard?" Bruno pushed his arm into his day jacket and turned to look at his footman. "And did you happen to note who was with the her in the garden?"

"Why, yes, my lord. There was, Her Grace's ladies-in-waiting, her ladyship, Clarice, and her lady-in-waiting, Gabriela."

Bruno halted his actions as the realization washed over him. He took care not to raise a hint of wariness from the servant about his suspicion—he did not trust anyone.

"That is interesting, Simon." He pulled on the sleeves to make them taut and continued in his casual conversation. "Did you notice anything unusual afterward?"

The footman paused for a moment with his master's riding boots in hand.

"The assortment of people engaged in the garden was not particularly unusual, my lord," said the footman.

It was obvious to Bruno that his servant's self-importance had just risen by leaps and bounds.

"It is what transpired afterward that was rather curious."

"Well?" Bruno rolled his eyes as he pulled his riding boots up over his pantaloons. "On with it." The footman conveyed the details of the activity he had witnessed in the garden as he completed readying Bruno. At every new detail, Bruno's lips pressed together tighter and tighter until they were a thin white line on his red face.

"Letters you say—to whom?" asked Bruno.

"I could not say, my lord. She spoke to the maid and her guard at length. Her Grace then pointed to the letters as though they carried something of great importance, before sending them off in haste."

"Do you recall which direction they were headed?" asked Bruno, adjusting the ruffles of his linens over his jacket. His voice was calm, but inside he was seething with anger. He knew where they were headed. That insipid girl had surrendered to her remorse and allowed her guilt to take over her actions.

"As I have said before, my lord, I do not usually concern myself with matters of the nobles and their servants."

"Yet you were nearby long enough to gather plenty of information."

Simon smirked and bowed his head.

"Where were they were headed?" He repeated. He was certain that Simon knew the answer.

"Rubio and Miss Gabriela entered the palace, then took the hall to the Great Room. There are only three places to proceed from there, sir. Upstairs to the living quarters, passed the Great Hall and to the kitchens and the servants' area, or to the outside courtyard and the guards' quarters."

"Which leads to the prison." Bruno's voice was gravelly. Huffing breaths punctuated each syllable as he adjusted his shoulder belt and scabbard around his waist with unnecessary force. Without another word to his footman, he grasped his sword and thrust it into its sheath. Muttering curses under his breath, he swung open the door and stomped past Clarice, who was seated on the daybed.

"Why are you blaspheming?" she asked.

"I am surprised at you, Clarice." Bruno's boots stomped out his anger with every step he took. "You, above all other people, should understand my motives for doing what I did."

Clarice had to work her legs twice as fast as Bruno to keep up as he turned his apartment upside down. "But I do, and I tell you, Bruno, it is not worth the effort. What good will it do to avenge your pride?"

"My pride may be all I have left after your Count Moro has his reign in Tolfa and the alum mines. Of course, he will excel at it. He excels at everything. Everything I desire, he acquires." Bruno turned and searched his bureau and dressing table for his knife. It was honed to reveal a glistening, sharp edge. He thrust it in its covering and attached it to his holster next to his sword. "Everything that is mine to have, he takes with ease. Business, talent, education—women."

"Bruno, why can you not see that it will do you no good to pursue this? It can only bring you humiliation. Leave Claudio alone. You can have any woman you wish."

"I know where your maid and that guard are headed. Elisa is not to be released."

"She will be," said Clarice defiantly. "By order of the duchess."

"I do not care. She will stay until I say she can go. I am sick of being usurped."

"Stop this madness, Bruno, and listen! Auntie can, and will, counter your order. She is the duchess!" Clarice's voice had reached a shrill pitch. "Why can you not let things go?"

Bruno whirled around, grasped his sister by the shoulders, and pierced her gaze with his scowling eyes. "Because I cannot. I will not." He released her and whispered in a voice barely audible. "Weakness is unacceptable. If I allow this to happen, I will be perceived as weak. A future monarch cannot vacillate." He stomped out the door, rounded the corner, and strode to the staircase leading to the Great Hall.

Clarice ran after him into the corridor, hoisting up her silken skirts. "Stop Bruno. You shall regret this." But he did not listen. He was already on the landing and halfway down to the main level of the palace. Clarice shook her head slowly from side to side, leaning on the banister. "You poor, misguided fool.

Mercy is not weakness. I am beginning to understand, instead, that clemency is might."

"You can believe whatever you wish. I know what I want." With this last word, he stormed down the stairs and disappeared into the Great Hall.

Chapter Fifty-One

"Blast! Why does being good have to be so complicated?" Clarice wasted no time.

Her brother had dashed off toward the prison, but she knew that Rubio and Gabriela had certainly had enough time to pluck the maid out of her cell and must be on their way to the stables. That was where she needed to go next—to warn them that Bruno had discovered their plot and to watch for his appearance.

Her silken-covered heels switched from clicking echoes on the marble floor to reverberations against the cobblestones outside as she raced to the massive palace stables.

As Clarice darted to the barn, a feeling of empowerment filled her, along with thoughts of how she was having more fun than she could remember. Though she was gasping in breaths of air, she felt more alive and purposeful than ever. "This is where Uncle's insistence on riding lessons will prove useful."

"Boy," she shouted to one of two stable hands, "did a large guard and a young woman come into the barn?"

"Yes, milady," he answered timidly as he hastily bowed.

"They were here a few moments ago requesting a horse. I think they should not be very far."

"Oh, thank heaven. Fetch me a ready horse immediately!" The boy set down his pitchfork, scrambled to one of the geldings in the nearest stall and grasped the reins to lead him out. He held out his folded hands for Clarice to step on. She gracefully clambered onto the horse and grabbed hold of the reins.

"Go immediately into the guard compound and advise the captain-at-arms that, by order of Clarice de Medici, a contingent is to meet me at the Porta Rossa forthwith." She guided the horse deftly toward the barn door. Thinking of one more thing, Clarice pulled on the reins to turn the horse about. "And you, over there," she called to the other stable hand who stood open-mouthed. "Take all the saddles off the other horses, at once!" *That should slow Bruno down a bit.*

She paused a moment and wondered what she forgot.

It came to her suddenly. "Uhm. Thank you!" she called out, then headed out the stable doors. This prompted the boy to produce an appreciative grin.

Without further delay, she was off to the meeting place according to Auntie Filiberta's plan, the Convent of the Infant Jesus, to warn Rubio of her brother's impending pursuit.

Rubio and Alice raced through the crowded streets to reach the convent in the center of the City. Duchess Filiberta's personal guard offered no mercy to those in his way. He navigated the black gelding, carrying himself and his charge, through the narrow, congested avenues at this extremely busy time, after the midday resting period and right before the evening meal.

There were vendors aplenty displayed their wares in the marketplace. Carts bearing fruits, vegetables, nuts, wines, and ales of every kind cramped the already small spaces, creating an abundance of obstacles for the expert rider to overcome.

"Move, I say! Remove that blasted cart from the center of the street, old man."

Ali sensed that Rubio's frustration was approaching the boiling point. She knew that the longer it took to reach the sanctuary of the convent, the greater the risk of being caught if Bruno realized her escape. As the guard plowed through the throng, Ali looked back nervously to check behind them, wondering if the bold plan would work.

A few smart maneuvers from Rubio and they were out of the milieu, though they had lost precious time in making it through only a few city blocks. Rubio halted the horse a short distance from the convent gates and turned his head toward his charge.

"Let me speak to the abbess first, miss. I have a letter of introduction from the duchess and—" But before he could complete his sentence, a familiar high-pitched voice pierced the air over the clamor in the street.

"Rubio! Halt!"

"Oh no," said Alice, her voice barely a whisper. She felt the blood drain from her face. "Clarice."

Rubio swiftly turned the horse in the direction of Clarice's voice, his neck craning to catch sight of her. Alice spotted her bobbing head; she appeared from one of the side streets, attempting to navigate about the crowd on a horse almost as large as hers and Rubio's.

"Rubio, please, do not stop!" shouted Ali. "She has come to take me back. Clarice despises me."

"You are wrong, miss." With puzzled eyes, the guard's voice held a quality of conviction that was difficult to misinterpret. "Lady Clarice is the one who, together with Her Grace, planned your escape."

Ali grimaced and tried to scramble free to flee from the

danger that she was only too accustomed to when dealing with the Medici royals.

"No, not her." Ali pushed herself away from Rubio to give herself some space and swung her leg up and over, hastily scrambling off the horse and nearly falling over in the process. "I do not trust her for a moment."

Clarice, finally clear from the crowd, raced to catch up to them. "Stop her Rubio! We must get her away, Bruno knows." Clarice was shouting as she sped closer to them. "Take her to the—"

Alice was not interested in what Clarice wanted for her. The mere mention of Bruno made her skin crawl. "Bruno." Ali nearly choked on the name. She pulled up her skirts and broke into a run, heading intuitively for the crowd.

"Do not let her get away!"

Ali managed to wind her way back into the crowded marketplace, but Rubio and the horse were too fast for her. He rode mercilessly into the throng, dipped down, and reached his massive arm around her waist as he rode by, plucking her up like a rag doll.

With Alice wriggling in his grasp, the hulking personal guard had stirred such a scene that the people at the market had stopped to watch the scene. He lifted Alice as he would have lifted an infant, moved back on his saddle, and plopped her in front of him.

"You dare to handle me in such a manner!" Ali's lips curled with rage. "Let me go, you overgrown son of a—"

"Stop that, Miss," Rubio said calmly.

"You idiot!" Clarice shouted at Alice as she caught up to them, a look of exasperation on her pointed face. "Do you not see we are attempting to set you free!"

"You? Rescue me!" Ali's face was on fire, her mouth twisted with anger. "Ha! That is comical, considering you tried to have me thrown in prison only last month—a thing your brother succeeded in doing most recently. Do you not have anything better to do with your life than to meddle in mine and Claudio's?"

Rubio paused for a moment as he looked from Alice to Clarice.

"Miss Elisa, I should advise you to stop that kind of talk lest you should anger milady."

"Good advice, Rubio." Clarice spoke in a calm tone, but her jaw clenched as she drew closer to Ali and looked deeply into her eyes. "I shall consider your reasoning affected due to your situation and the fact that you are beyond worry regarding Count Moro. In that regard, I shall overlook your disrespect. However, an outburst such as that shall only be tolerated once." She straightened up. "Hear me, maid, before you act, then if you so choose, you may go your way."

Alice pulled away from Rubio's grasp and lifted her chin defiantly. "I am listening."

"I have just come from the palace." Clarice licked her lips. "Bruno is aware that you have escaped. It was my intention to warn you so that you would leave Florence altogether. It is too dangerous for you here—and for that matter, the count. You should both leave as it is evident that my brother will not surrender his obsession for you or for the throne."

"Where do you suggest we go?" Ali angled her head, still skeptical.

"Before we discuss that, I should think we must get you out of the city," counseled the guard.

"I agree," said Clarice. "If we—" Clarice stopped in mid-sentence.

Alice heard it too. In the distance, thunderous hoofs clattered against the cobblestone streets, sending echoes every which way.

"Blast!"

"Get us out of here, Rubio!" shouted Ali.

"To the Porta Rossa!" ordered Clarice. "We may have friends there, already."

They turned their horses from the crowd, which was beginning to part to allow the team of oncoming horses through. The clatter from their hoofs only added to the confusion as they sped to the arched piazza up ahead, which opened to the city gate.

They did not have far to go before they reached the Porta Rossa. Alice had begun to believe Clarice—that she was really trying to help her—but when they reached the piazza, there was only them, no help as Clarice had mentioned.

"Where are your so-called friends, my lady?" Alice's voice dripped with derision.

"You dare to question me again?" she countered icily.

The horse-hoofs grew louder, and the crowd around them scattered.

"Stop that girl!"

Alice heard a shout from behind as the massive gate stood looming up ahead of her. Two sets of gates separated her from the outside, each positioned a healthy measure apart—plenty of room under the arch of the great city wall for the guards to eat, keep warm, or even sleep while serving sentry duty.

Ali looked back. Bruno and his men were catching up; he was quickly approaching with his gaze directed at the top of the towers.

"We must hurry! He is upon us!" she cried.

"Ali!"

Her heart jumped. That one word was clear and loving and safe. She craned her neck to look through the entry of the gates, and her eyes found him.

"Claudio!" Her heart leapt at the sight of him. "I'm here! I'm here!"

"I will get you through," Rubio said. He steadied his horse and moved it toward the iron partitions.

"Open the gates, now!" Claudio shouted to the sentries, signaling. He peered through the gates at Ali, his eyes wide with anticipation. "I see you! I will be right there. Is that Clarice with you?"

His entire aspect changed from absolute joy to hasty panic. "Hurry up!" Claudio's eyes turned wild.

He must have seen Bruno now, too, thought Ali.

"Open the blasted gates." The command came from da Vinci, directly behind Claudio. The guards hurried to the heavy iron bars barring the entry from possible invaders and extracted the barrier to let Claudio and his party through.

"Hurry now!" came a command from Francesco.

"Hurry! Open the gate!" Clarice's voice chimed in with the men on the other side.

"I said, stop that girl! Do not let her through!"

Alice heard Bruno's growling bellow coming closer. Thinking that at any moment the sentries would hear his command and lock up the passage again, she scrambled off the horse and sprinted to the small opening in the gate. It was not wide enough to let a horse through, but it was large enough for her. The space between the two gates may as well have been a chasm as Alice dashed to the other side of the mammoth threshold.

Claudio was waiting on the other side, but instead of joy on his face, there was horror—she sensed someone behind her. The guards were working on the outer gate and managed to open it just enough to allow him to slip through. Immediately, Claudio pulled his sword from its sheath and held it high.

Alice reached out her hand and felt the tips of Claudio's fingers touch hers as he tried to grab hold of her, but only for a split second. In the next instant, an arm wrapped around her waist, and the very breath was wrenched from her lungs as a harsh yank pulled her away from Claudio's saving grasp.

Chapter Fifty-Two

A jarring pull dragged her from Claudio and then hurled her like a ragdoll to the flagstone floor. Ali winced in pain as she tumbled onto her side, rolling over twice before thudding to a stop against the inner wall of the Porta Rossa, her face coming to rest against the crook of her elbow. Barely able to maintain awareness, she drifted in and out of the dark waters of unconsciousness.

"Alice, my love!" Claudio's caress finally found her as she felt his presence kneeling over her. "Are you hurt?" Gentle hands stroked her hair.

"No," Ali whispered. "I don't think so." In her dim state, Alice still recognized the unmistakable sound of the scrape of a sword being drawn from its casing.

"You drew first, Moro," Bruno's voice drawled with arrogance and superiority. "Now arise like a man, and let my sword find its mark!"

"You bastard!" Claudio's voice thundered. "You dare put your filthy hands on her!"

One last caress was followed by a howl of strangled rage and clashing swords.

"If you are a man, you will agree to have it out, here and now, without the assistance of your dogsbody!" Claudio's tone egged Bruno on.

"You shall pay for that, Moro. When you are dead, the girl will be mine!" Bruno's voice was an animalistic snarl, yet low enough that only Claudio and she could have heard him. "I have a witness who will swear she heard your plot to usurp the duke."

"Again! You are a mad man!" growled Claudio.

"Claudio," Ali whispered, too weak to be heard. "No." In the midst of her dreamlike state, a mix and multitude of voices from every direction pelted her ears.

"Bar the gates!" Bruno ordered. "Nobody enters or leaves until one of us draws first blood!"

The thud of the heavy iron bars dropping into place echoed ominously in the cold harshness of the stone archway. A crashing sound of metal against metal rang in Alice's ears as they engaged their swords, scraping and scouring, thrashing and hammering rhythmically. She lifted her head slightly and saw guards at both gates keeping those outside from entering.

"You should be so fortunate to only have a flesh wound after this, Moro."

A gnashing of swords and thrashing filled the space. Alice could only watch, huddled on the ground, still winded from being hurled to the stones.

"You would murder a noble without just cause, you son of a jackal!" snarled Claudio.

"No! Count do not engage him!" Leonardo's voice penetrated the sounds of their scuffle. "It is not worth it!" Francesco cried out.

Clashing steel pierced the arch as the two men locked swords close to where Alice lay. "Your death shall be avenged by your followers who, in return shall kill the duke." Bruno was taunting Claudio with this talk, his voice barely perceptible when they locked swords. "Leaving the throne to the next righteous successor."

"You are dreaming with eyes open, Bruno. My men would go after you, if anyone."

"Their continued existence is a mere detail. After they are found responsible for Giuliano's death, they will not have time to do anything but confess before the gallows."

"Bastard! I will never allow it!"

"Let us through in the name of the Duchess!" Rubio's thunderous shout could be heard. "We must get to the girl!"

"You would have done better to have left the maid to me that day in the Great Hall," sneered Bruno.

All the while, sounds of grating and hitting metal prevailed. Seconds felt like hours as Ali watched from her place on the ground, stunned and dazed into submission.

Swords in a fight...in a duel...Claudio and Bruno. No, no. With unambiguous finality, the clarity of the situation descended on Alice, seizing her every sense like a vacuum and leaving nothing in its wake. This was it—the very thing she had tried so intensely to prevent was happening right before her—because of her. The duel that Castiglione referred to in his letter.

Get up! Get up now, dammit! Go stop this! You did this—you fix it!

With great determination, she willed herself to push her pounding head up and, slowly, first on her knees and then leaning against the cold brick wall for support, to her feet. She brushed her tangled hair away from her eyes. "Claudio, please stop. This is it. Do you not see?"

"I should finish you here, for all that you have done to her." Claudio's breath was coming in great gasps. Grunts and groans filled the air as each man chopped, blocked, cut, and struck to mortally harm one another, metal against metal, again and again. Claudio was relentless, thrusting forward, then backing up, his rage spurring him on.

Alice was in a no man's land under the mammoth arch and

in between the city gates. Her frantic gaze looked beyond the gates to Rubio and Clarice, who were being held at bay by Bruno's contingent so that they could not interfere. She looked to Leonardo, Francesco, and the rest of the men, who were also held behind the barred iron gate.

"Please, stop this madness!" she cried out, but Claudio did not respond—his rage was too great. Months of frustration and fury toward Bruno finally spilled out of him. Ali put her hands at her temples and turned to Leonardo. Da Vinci was rifling around in his satchel. He signaled her to hurry over, and she complied, sliding flat against the wall to reach him, trying her utmost not to attract the guards' attention. Engrossed as they were in the fight, it was unlikely they would notice at all.

When she reached the gate, she turned her head slightly, so she could hear da Vinci, as he was speaking in a hushed tone.

"Hurry, take this." He held a small green flask in the palm of his hand.

Ali furtively slipped her hand through an aperture in the gate and accepted it, holding it tightly in her palm.

"It is a remedy—for Claudio. You must make him drink it. This potion will—"

"You there!" Damn, she was found. One of Bruno's men pulled Ali away, pushing her against the far wall. "Away from the gates!"

Alice lurched forward, but kept her balance, not wanting to fall and risk breaking the little bottle of medicine. The master had thought of everything—a sort of tonic to strengthen Claudio as he raged in battle. But how was she going to get it to him? She said a silent prayer for an opportune moment to present itself.

As she watched in desperation, the two men wielded their heavy swords with skills beyond anything she could have imagined. Though she was horrified at the display before her, she could not help but marvel at how Claudio was strong and skilled in the art and handling of the foil; he attempted to disarm Bruno with a series of leg and shoulder strikes, but he was equally skilled.

Bruno gestured to one of his men to come closer to the gate.

"Stop!" the guard shouted at Claudio. "Move away." Claudio relaxed his sword and turned, soaked in sweat as though he had fallen in a watering trough, and hurried to Ali's side.

"My love," he gasped, trying to catch his breath. "Thank God you are safe." His arms wrapped around her and held her close to his heart. She felt his body shaking with exhaustion. Francesco started to run for the gate with a flask in his hand for Claudio.

"No, nothing for him," growled Bruno. At this, two of the soldiers on Francesco's sidestepped forward, their rapiers drawn to block the Baron's way. Da Vinci grasped Francesco's arm and pulled him back to the others in their ragtag party.

"Cheating jackal," Francesco snarled as he backed away.

One of the soldiers on Bruno's side of the gates hurried to his horse and came back with a flask. Bruno grabbed it from the soldier's hand through the gate and drank it greedily.

This is it, thought Alice. *The medicine*. She placed the little green bottle in Claudio's palm.

"Quickly," she held him close, whispering in his ear. "Take this before they see you or they will take it away."

He wiped his brow with his sleeve and blinked at the green bottle in his hand.

"What is it?" He flipped the cork off and gulped it down.

"Leonardo said it would help you—"

"Get away from there!" One of the guards thundered. He thrust up the barrier on Bruno's side and forcefully opened the gate. With two other soldiers armed with spears in tow, he grabbed Ali's arm and dragged her out while the other two pushed Claudio away.

"Leave me alone!" shouted Alice, struggling madly to break free of his grasp. From the corner of her eye, she saw Rubio scramble off his horse and rush to her.

"I will ensure she does not interfere." His voice was steeped in authority. The soldiers nodded and passed her off to him. He took her by the arms and nearly carried her to his horse, which was alongside Clarice's.

"Now, be silent," he said in Ali's ear. "We will find a way to get you both out of the city. They cannot be at it for much longer—they are both tired. When first blood is drawn, the duel will be called. We can only wait until then."

Clarice offered her version of an encouraging nod.

Alice choked on a sob, finding the courage to hold it back. "I know they are supposed to stop at first blood, but Bruno is so angry...he is liable to do Claudio real harm."

"They are both very skilled swordsmen who have done this before, many times," Rubio said hearteningly. "They know."

And so, she waited.

With a torturing curl of despair in her stomach, Ali watched. History was already written. The best she could hope for was that Claudio would get out of this alive, so they could fake his death before traveling back to 2029.

Having finished his drink, Bruno returned to the center of the archway, refreshed and renewed to fight, but Claudio appeared even wearier than before. Ali prayed silently for it to be over soon, so Rubio could take her to him.

Bruno brandished his sword in an unsettling fashion and with quick, fluid steps crossed to Claudio's chest to cut, but Claudio blocked it and pushed the weapon away, jabbing to Bruno's right arm.

Block, jab, and dodge. Again, and again, over and over.

But suddenly, Claudio shook his head and backed away.

"Come now, Moro, you have given me no satisfaction at all."

Bruno advanced on Claudio and tried to strike, but Claudio

ducked and twisted, ending up against the wall, stumbling and faltering.

Relentlessly, Bruno raised his sword, and as Claudio gasped for air, leaning against the wall for support, Bruno sliced the air with his blade, cutting Claudio's shirt sleeve clean through and slashing him across his right forearm.

Alice screamed and tore herself from Rubio's grasp, running for the gate. The crowd drew a collective breath as blood-stained Claudio's shirt sleeve a bright crimson red.

"Claudio!" she cried. Not satisfied with this work Bruno lifted his sword again and brought it down diagonally across Claudio's chest, cutting the skin.

Ali watched, unable to get to him as Claudio dropped the sword from his hand. He staggered away from the wall, eyes glazed over as though he was already dead. Bruno stood back and watched, a triumphant grimace taking over his face.

Disoriented and confused, Claudio's breathing came in gasps.

Ali pushed her arm through the iron bars. "Here, Claudio, I'm here!" she shouted out to him.

When he heard Ali's voice, he staggered toward it, his eyes vacant. One...two steps. Three.

But before he could reach her, his eyes rolled back, and he collapsed in a heap.

Standing over him, the look of intense satisfaction on Bruno's face turned to bewilderment.

For Alice, time stood still. The love of her life's face was gray, his body lifeless, and from where she was, she could not tell if he was breathing.

A strangled sound came from the very depths of her soul, a visceral cry, primal in quality as she gripped the iron bars of the gate and shook with all her might. The guards from both sides of the gateway hoisted up the massive iron barriers, allowing a frantic Ali and all interested parties into the archway to observe the carnage.

"Claudio!" sobbed Alice as she slipped through the barely open gate. Her hands took his face tenderly and propped it on her lap. She felt for his pulse in his neck but could not find it. Hurriedly, she looked in his eyes for signs of life.

Nothing.

A raw primitive grief overwhelmed her. "No! No!"

Chapter Fifty-Three

Anguished, a sensation of intense desolation swept over Ali.

She held onto Claudio, the blood from his chest and arm trickling onto the flagstones of the archway. Through her haze of despair and tears, she heard voices around her commenting on the outcome of the duel.

"Bruno, what have you done?" Clarice's voice pierced over the mingling crowd.

CPR—I'll do CPR! Desperate, Alice lay her hands, one over the other, upon his heart and pushed down in a rhythmic pattern before breathing into this mouth. She watched his chest and felt his pulse. Again, she pressed on his chest and tried to breathe life into him, but he was not responding.

How could this be? The cuts aren't deep enough to kill him.

"Away from him, all of you!" Leonardo called out as he pushed his way toward Claudio.

Ali's trembling hands were scarlet with Claudio's blood.

"Someone get the girl—she is frantic with grief," Francesco said. "I will take care of him."

"The wounds are not grave enough to kill him," Bruno's horrid voice proclaimed. "Let me see."

She felt hands on her shoulders as she cried.

"Have you not done enough, here? Are you not yet satisfied? You have killed him." Leonardo leaned in close to the body.

Ali's struggle to stay with Claudio was in vain. A force picked her up and pulled her from the lifeless body of the only love she had ever known. "No! No!"

"Elisa, it is I, Rubio." He was taking her away. "Let us go away from this place."

Why would Rubio take her away from him?

Alice looked up from her misery and saw Duke Giuliano, Castiglione Baldassare, and the elder Baron Tondini, all riding up to the Porta Rossa gate on horseback along with the rest of the hunting party. They took in the bloody scene before them.

"See here. What is all this?" questioned Duke Giuliano.

"Your nephew murdered a count who also happens to be one of your most faithful courtiers. Count Claudio Moro," da Vinci called out, rage settling into his face.

Giuliano licked his lips and glanced sideways at Castiglione whose eyes were on Ali. Covered in Claudio's blood, she was trembling and struggling against Rubio's hold.

"Let me see this for myself," Bruno scowled, still out of breath from the sword fight.

Alice felt her heart split between rage and grief. "Don't you dare touch him!"

But Bruno pretended not to hear. He sauntered up to Claudio and put a hand to his chest, then recoiled, his eyes darting to his uncle.

Obviously not satisfied, Bruno put the side of his hand under Claudio's nose to feel for his breathing. Finally, convinced that Claudio was dead, Bruno looked up, bewildered. "I do not understand. It was a cut. A flesh wound, not a mortal injury."

Castiglione and Tondini descended from their horses and

moved toward the archway, their guards and valets following behind them. As they got closer to Claudio, they removed their caps. Da Vinci pushed Bruno aside and felt for Claudio's heartbeat. When he was satisfied, he turned to Duke Giuliano and spoke with a dark quality to his voice. "He is dead, Your Grace. At the hands of your nephew."

"But I thought this business between you and Moro was over and done with, Bruno," said the duke, annoyed and bewildered at the same time.

"His friends would have you believe he is innocent, Uncle, but he is far from such. If I had not taken care of him, he would have no doubt gone through with his plan to usurp your throne. He would have been in Tolfa, but his designs were on your Duchy. I have it on good confidence that—"

"Silence." Giuliano's eyes narrowed as he focused his glare on his nephew. "There shall be an investigation. In the meantime, Bruno, I suggest you ready yourself for Tolfa. Clearly, young Claudio will not be taking the position."

Bruno bowed deeply to his uncle, as a wide grin split his face.

Castiglione's eyes widened at Duke Giuliano's decision, as did the elder Baron Tondini's, both their faces reflecting confusion.

"Do not feel you are out of danger yet, nephew. This might have been a consensual duel, but there should not have been a death. First blood drawn would have been the civilized way to settle this matter once and for all." He gazed at the blood on the cobblestones and grimaced. "Now I shall have the tedious task of salvaging what I can of your belligerent character to the nobility, yet again. Come, Clarice, we must inform the Duchess of this unfortunate development."

Putting a finger to his lips, he spoke as though musing out loud of the next inconvenient chore awaiting him. "Oh, blast Bacchus, Countess Maria will be quite beside herself over the news. Bruno, why do you insist on ruining a perfectly glorious end to an exceptionally grand hunt? Off with you now, to the palace with your guards," said Giuliano, waving Bruno away. "Ready yourself for the journey to Tolfa."

Clarice was nearby, crying softly, and listening to her uncle while her onetime object of affection lay lifeless on the stone floor of the archway.

"Duke Giuliano, may we take the body to be cleaned and prepared for the boy's mother?" asked da Vinci.

"Yes, yes, of course." Giuliano closed his eyes tightly and pinched the bridge of his nose with his fingers. He drew a deep breath and then let it out in a huff. "Where are you taking him?"

"To the abbey, Your Grace—for a proper funeral."

Giuliano nodded to acknowledge da Vinci's plan. "I quite agree," he said, then glanced again at his niece. "Clarice, dear, come with us. There is nothing for you here."

Quite limply, she sniffed back her tears and dabbed at her face as she glanced at Claudio. "I am afraid that you are correct, Uncle." She swallowed hard and pulled on her horse's reins to guide him to join Giuliano's party. With a fleeting look of measured compassion directed at Alice, she spoke again. "Regretfully, though I tried, I feel that I did not do enough."

Giuliano raised a brow and addressed his hunting party. "Gentlemen?" He turned, and his entourage shadowed his moves, but Castiglione and Baron Tondini stayed behind.

"Francesco, my son," said Francesco's father,, scrunching his cap. "I am sorry for your friend. He was a good man."

"Yes," Castiglione agreed. "A good young man—wiser than his years. It is a pity. I feel we would have been fast friends." He gave Claudio a last look and started back for his horse.

"We need to move him, now," urged da Vinci. "Come, help me to get him onto Spirit."

Ali felt an emptiness take hold of her that was beyond this

world. Her crying had stopped, yet her throat was raw with unuttered curses and screams. Still stunned and not knowing how to react to the decisions being made, she only shuddered. She held her hands up to her face, her eyes seared with the vision of her bloodstained fingers. With painstaking care, she touched them to her cheeks, then her neck, and finally her heart. Claudio's blood marked her a bright crimson red.

"I will come back for you, Elisa," da Vinci said to her as he and Francesco gathered up Claudio's body. "I will come back as soon as I can and bring you to the abbey. Francesco and I have not forgotten you. We shall endeavor to set you on your path home soon enough."

She did not respond. His words were as if they were spoken under water. Strong arms wrapped around her, and Alice allowed herself to be led by Rubio to his horse. The crowds were starting to dissipate now. The spectacle was over.

A short ride on horseback and soon they were at the convent gates. Rubio took her with him to the door. More blurred words were exchanged with a nun, and a letter was presented. The nun read it and readily accepted Alice into the convent.

Once inside, she sensed someone with a gentle and kindly hand helping to wash the blood off her face and hands before being put to bed. She did not utter another word. Her body, mind, and spirit were not her own anymore. Alice was an empty vessel, rapidly filling with grief and heartache for the love she had lost.

Chapter Fifty-Four

"Here! Quickly! Place him here," da Vinci ordered with desperate urgency as he swept his arm over the top of his worktable, spilling everything onto the floor. Francesco held onto Claudio's shoulders while his stewards, Edoardo and Lipari, held his legs and feet. They managed to rush him back to the monastery on Spirit's back and were now carefully placing Claudio's body on the hard surface.

"Master," Francesco had a huge lump in his throat, "allow me to assist you to wipe the blood and cleanse him off."

"You lads—you can go." Da Vinci waved the stewards away as he scurried to a shelf and reached into a basket, pulling out some linens. He opened and closed drawers, searched various vials and ointments.

Francesco's men glanced at him for permission to leave. He nodded warily as he watched his master bustling about the room, sticking his hand into one ceramic pot, then the other.

"Go ahead...go back to the manor. There is nothing more you can do here." Francesco grabbed a flask of water and poured some on the linens that da Vinci had tossed on the table. "I shall follow—nay, rather after this I should like to visit the countess..." His eyes shifted to his friend lying on da Vinci's worktable, and almost instantly his tone took on one of anger and frustration. "And Giuliano. I plan to press him to charge Bruno with the murder of my friend."

"Ah, here it is," the old man chortled.

Edoardo shook his head, baffled at da Vinci's behavior, and Lipari raised a brow. Da Vinci cut some strips of cloth from the linens and began bandaging the wounds, applying a fair bit of pressure. The men gave the old master a last parting glance, after which they nodded to their Baron and offered a quick bow before departing.

"Sir," continued Francesco. "Is that necessary?" A sympathetic look gave away Francesco's assessment of da Vinci's actions—he clearly could not accept that his apprentice was dead. "Master da Vinci, his mother will want to see the body—"

"Precisely, my boy. We must stop the bleeding. Here now," the old master handed his student a piece of cloth. "For his arm, there." He motioned to the gash on Claudio's limp arm.

Francesco took the cloth, grimacing at his master's actions. "Master da Vinci, I am deeply saddened...torn by this...but you must be strong and face the truth. Claudio is dead. There is no need to—"

"Oh, but there is a need, boy. Do it now."

He shot a glance at Francesco. A glance that told him that his master was deeply serious. Francesco did as he was told, applying pressure and tying up the linen wrapping.

With a look of satisfaction that Claudio was properly looked after, he grasped a small flask, much like the one he had given to Elisa earlier that horrible afternoon. He took Claudio's head in his hand and put a drop of liquid from the flask onto his lips, letting the drops flow into his mouth, being careful not to allow too much. He dropped another, then another, and tilted Claudio's head up so that the tiny drops of elixir flowed into the body.

Francesco watched all this with fascination, wondering what his teacher could hope to accomplish—even he knew that the master did not have the power to bring a dead man back to life.

Aware that time was passing, but unable to care, Ali existed within the vacuum of her emotions. Whispers and hushed tones drifted into her conscious mind, but her brain could not process the meaning of the words. She felt nothing, only emptiness—a chasm would have had more substance than Alice's soul. Time was a haze of disunited events as she slipped in and out of nightmarish consciousness, in a trance of grief and anguish.

People attempted to entice her to eat. They tried to feed her broth and sweetened tea, but Ali took only a little. She did not refuse, though she did not feel hunger or thirst. She neither wanted to decline nor accept. Her grief was so acute she felt physical pain...so much pain for Claudio. Even thinking his name made her limbs ache, her chest burn, and her eyes sting anew with tears. Her body, mind, and soul were alive by the involuntary systems of biology that breathed for her and set her heart to beating.

One night, as she dreamt of watching the sun set near San Miniato Castle, where she had admitted her deep love for Claudio, she heard an angel's voice singing. It echoed across the valleys dotted with olive trees and carefully landscaped grape terraces. The angel's song was clear and pure—its cadences so faultless, its pitch so perfect that Alice thought she had departed this life to follow the welcoming hymn as she passed to the other side.

"The angels are so happy for us, my love—do you hear them singing?" said Claudio, his voice so much sweeter than that of any spirit. The song became clearer and more pronounced.

Well-defined and exquisite. So much so that she could sleep no longer.

Her feet touched the stone floor as she unsteadily balanced herself to a sitting position on the edge of the firm, utilitarian bed. It was night-time, and she felt suddenly cold, so she grabbed the blanket that had covered her all this time and wrapped it around her shoulders. A glance down at her body revealed the plain cotton nightshirt she wore. A single flame flickered in the lantern placed on a desk at the opposite wall, casting quivering shadows as she draped the coverlet over her nightclothes. Slowly, she glanced around the room, really looking at it for the first time.

Why am I here? Oh yes, I'm waiting for Leonardo to collect me when the chamber is ready, so I can go home. Not that it matters anymore. Claudio is dead, and I will return alone. I failed. Failed in the most profound way.

She willed her feet to move, managing to put one foot in front of the other and followed the sweet song. Treading softly, she reached down to grasp the latch on the door, pushed it up over the catch, and opened it. She poked her head carelessly into a long hallway to try to figure out from where the heavenly sound was coming, noting the rows of identical doors that lined the hallway on either side.

Right, I'm in the Infant Jesus Convent.

Alice stepped out of her cell and bore left, following the notes of the chant as though she saw them drifting in the air. Softly, she hummed under her breath in unison with the voice, echoing the recitation. It was important to focus on her steps: one foot then the other and humming, gently, one foot then the other and humming.

The song was close, coming from a nearby cell, and the chant was set to repeat. Becoming more confident in the hymn, she sang a little louder. The singing stopped, and Ali stopped, too. She stood still and waited, but she heard nothing. The angel had finished her chant.

Ali did not feel the need to investigate further. The song was gone, and so was her reason for getting up. She turned and went back, slid into bed, and prayed that sleep would once more take her from her grim reality.

~

"Abbess, the door to the girl's cell was wide open this morning."

Sister Clement, a novice nun at the Infant Jesus Convent, was not usually in the habit of raising her voice in excitement, but Abbess Mother Augustine detected a hint of enthusiasm.

"She must have been up and about last night." Sister Clement stood anxiously and waited for a response.

When the maid was carried into the convent by Duchess Filiberta's guard, half of the convent had been frightened out of their wits by the blood spattering the lady's clothing. Clement and a few of the older nuns had bathed and dressed her in clean clothes. Discovering that she was physically unharmed, they all wondered aloud where the blood had come from.

They tried to feed her warm broth and strengthening herbal teas, but the girl remained silent and still, at times her eyes open but unresponsive—as though her body was without a spirit. Mostly, she slept.

The abbess pursed her lips and drew her hands to her mouth, clasping them, saying a prayer of thanks. Tilting her chin so that her habit adjusted with her movements, she looked directly at her novice.

"Has she spoken?" questioned the Abbess, her voice even and stoic.

"No, Mother," answered Clement eagerly. "Not yet."

"Stay close to her, Clement."

The novice took a few steps toward her superior.

"I will, Mother. I will take good care of her." The novice's face broke into a guarded smile. She bowed and turned to leave, but hesitated. "One more thing, Mother—what is she called? Do you know the girl's name?"

"I do. She is Elisa Beatrice. A girl who never knew her mother and father."

"Then she is much like me, Mother."

"No, Sister Clement." The Abbess sighed deeply. "I am afraid she is not like you at all."

Chapter Fifty-Five

Alice recognized the place up ahead—it was Anna and Dario's villa in San Miniato. The driveway, lined with swaying cypresses, led her to the four-storey house that was nestled in a knoll at the top of a hill, surrounded by olive trees and grape vineyards. It felt like home, safe and familiar.

As she edged closer to the house, she saw Claudio walk from the rear of the building. She smiled at him, her love and her champion. He was smiling back at her—his beautiful smile —but as he got closer, his lips turned down in a frightening grimace, and his clothing started to ooze red. He was bleeding through his shirt and jeans. There was blood everywhere. Her feet were rooted in place. She could not move to help him, and as he got closer, he became weaker and weaker.

Ali stretched her arms out as far as they would go to grab him before he fell, but they barely brushed, and then he was gone. Only a pool of blood left on the ground. A cry of pain and sadness swelled in her throat for her lost love. She cried out and then suddenly awoke. Hands on her shoulders shook her awake.

"Elisa, wake up." A young woman dressed in nun's garb was

sitting on her bed, grasping her shoulders. "It was a dream—a bad dream. Wake up."

Ali wiped her eyes. She had been crying. The nun looked at her warily.

"Are you the one who was singing the other night?" Alice asked stoically. Her directness had taken the girl entirely by surprise as her eyes were like saucers, her mouth working hard to try to speak.

"Y-you have found your voice, miss." The nun managed to sputter.

Alice tilted her head and waited for an answer. "Were you the one singing?" she repeated, hoisting herself up on her elbow, her eyes focused on the young woman who had returned to the chair by Ali's bedside and placed her hands in her lap underneath her nun's scapular.

"No, miss, it was not I. However, I do know of whom you speak." Her eyes smiled, and her cheeks blushed. "If I may be so forward, miss, my name is Sister Clement."

"Sister." Ali nodded her acknowledgment. "You will forgive me if I am not that interested in conversation. I was merely curious to know if it was you I heard." She paused for a moment and shook her head. "Or at the least, I thought I heard. It was like...like an angel was singing." She lay back down and stared at the ceiling.

"You are suffering from a terrible loss, Miss Elisa. I know the Abbess has—" Her words trailed.

"Claudio. His name was Claudio."

The nun nodded.

"Yes, Miss Elisa. He is—was a count in the House of Medici."

"Was," Ali said softly. "It is very difficult to believe. Was." She put her hands to her face. "I want to go home. Can you please take me to Master da Vinci? He is at the Monastery at Galluzzo."

"I cannot," Sister Clement said, her eyes downcast. "Abbess Augustine has told us we must wait until he sends for you."

The lump in Ali's throat returned. A piece of her heart was gone, and all that lay in its stead were ruins of a great love now lost. Her mind had been in 'safe' mode the last few days. It was her brain's way of coping with Claudio's death, so she wouldn't go completely insane with grief.

"I need to go home. Can you please speak to your abbess and ask if she will let me go to Galluzzo?" The tears spilled from her eyes, into her hair, and onto her flattened pillow.

"I am sorry, miss, but we have our orders."

Alice sniffed, wiping the flowing tears with her sleeve.

"May I please bring you some tea or warm broth?" She said, as she hopped up to retrieve a tray containing two wooden cups from the dresser. "You will feel better if you eat a little. It is time for your morning meal. You see, I brought it to you in case you should awaken, and indeed, you are awake."

Alice shook her head. "I could not eat or drink a thing, thank you." She turned away and lay down to face the wall.

"But you must eat." The novice sounded distressed. "If you do not, you shall become ill with the coughing sickness or worse. Then we shall have to bleed you and all sorts of unpleasant things. You do not want that, do you?"

Alice took in a deep breath and thought of leeches all over her body. "Very well." She turned slowly to face Sister Clement. "Perhaps some tea for now."

The novice had a valiant look on her face, as if she had succeeded in overcoming a tremendously significant obstacle. Ali took the tea and sipped. It tasted good, though she hated to admit that anything could give her pleasure, even a good cup of whatever tea they were giving her.

"You still have not answered my question, Sister. Who did I hear singing in the night?"

Clement laughed softly and tucked her hands in her scapular. "That would be Sister Celestine. She often sings at the most inappropriate times. In the middle of the night, during vespers —really whenever the fancy strikes her." Her face held a look of mild disapproval that was tempered with kind understand. "Celestine has her own—personality, shall we say."

"Oh? In what way?"

"In the way that she is not like the rest of us. She is different. Her mind is that of a child, though she is much older than I."

Ali was beginning to understand. "I see." She took another sip of the warm liquid. "She may be different, but she certainly has been given a unique gift. Her voice is that of—"

"An angel, yes, we know." Clement finished Alice's sentence. "If only she could put that gift to good use. She cannot, or will not, follow a chant and refuses to sing when asked to do so. It is as though she only wants it for herself."

Alice's lips curled into an almost imperceptible smile. "Does she speak to anyone?"

"Yes, at times. But mostly she just looks at people and is there—just there, with the rest of us. Abbess Augustine takes care of her. We all take care of her."

Ali managed a small smile in response to Sister Clement's pride in informing her of the abbess' charitable work.

"Do you think you may arise and come to chapel with us?" The novice asked with measured enthusiasm.

"I shall try."

Alice struggled to act like a human being the rest of the day, to acknowledge people's presences, and to nod 'hello' when appropriate, when all she wanted was to go back to bed and sleep forever in a banal limbo.

There was a bright spot to the day, though, when one of the nuns appeared in the courtyard of the convent where Ali sat staring at an anthill, fascinated by the business of its million occupants. She had a visitor—Caterina. Ali was pleased to see a familiar face but dreaded having to engage in the inevitable conversation. She was not ready to deal with pity.

Her dear friend entered the courtyard and rushed to throw her arms around her. "Oh, my poor darling Elisa. What have they done to you now? They have managed to kill the only decent man that ever walked the halls of that cesspool of a palace." Caterina's tears flowed as she spoke. She pulled herself back to look at Ali, who was beginning to tear up anew. "I am truly sorry for you—and for that poor man, Count Moro."

Alice nodded, wiping the tears from her cheeks. She felt a thousand times worse than she had when she realized, on the plane home last summer, that Claudio was dead five hundred years in the past. But here—in this moment, he had just lived, breathed, laughed, and loved. In an instant he was gone as she had stood nearby, helpless to save him. It was difficult for her to carry on even the most cursory of conversations, but this would be hers and Caterina's last.

"Thank you, Caterina. And thank you for coming to see me. I am sorry that I have not been back to the manor house, but the duchess had me brought here for safety's sake. And truthfully, even if I was able to amble there under my own power, I fear that I do not have it within me to set my eyes on places he and I shared together."

Caterina nodded sympathetically. "Yes, of course, my dear. I was told by Baron Francesco of your whereabouts. I came every day asking for you, but the nuns told me you were as though dead. I was so happy to hear you were up and about today. My poor girl—suffering so, you were."

"They have taken good care of me," Ali assured Caterina.

"I see." Caterina's face brightened. "But now that you are better, you must come home with me."

"I do not think so, my dear friend. I fear that soon I shall be departing—perhaps venturing even further than Prato, if I can find a position."

In fact, she would return to a life so different from the one she had lived for only a short time. She had lived here awaiting a passage home, but without Claudio, home would not be a place she could find anywhere or anytime on earth.

"But, why? Why can you not stay here? Baron Francesco will gladly take you in. You were his dearest friend's intended, after all, and there is so much room at the manor house."

"Caterina, you are very sweet to think of me, but I must go. I cannot live here. His memory is everywhere I look. Every field, every meadow, every street in Florence. Staying here would only bring me pain. I must start a new life elsewhere, far away from Claudio's memory and Bruno's influence." Alice's eyes looked far beyond the fountain in the yard upon which her gaze was fixed. "I shall go from here, with a letter from the Baron and from Master da Vinci, to Lucca or Pisa or even Milan to seek out a new situation."

Caterina pressed her lips together and looked intently at her friend. "I do not know what you are running to, but I understand who you are running from." Standing, Caterina, the girl who had practically raised her as her own sister, wrapped her arms around Ali and held onto her for a long time. "Promise me that you will take care of yourself. That you will fall in love and have many children. Promise that you shall try very hard to find happiness. And if the Fates allow, that we shall see each other again."

Alice's eyes stung with tears, knowing full well that she would never see her protector again. "You as well, my dear, dear friend. Thank you for everything you did for me."

It was a long goodbye hug, one that would have to last the two friends throughout the ages. One that Alice would cherish forever.

Chapter Fifty-Six

The sinking sun splashed a lavender hue across the fields of golden grasses. Olive trees and neat lines of vineyards curved across the rolling hills below San Miniato. Ali stood by Claudio, their feet on the fence, staring out at the lush scenery before them. A calm peacefulness swathed her. She was safe in her knowledge that he was by her side. A clear and melodic voice sang its sweet song to the setting of the evening sun. Tranquil and pastoral, it lulled them both.

Soft footsteps accompanied by a jarring "Shh", forced Ali to awaken. It was dark, save for the lantern in its place on the desk.

"Sister, you will wake the girl."

There was silence, then padding footsteps softly fading into the hallway.

How lovely, Alice thought. *If I could just sleep and dream, he would still be there. Will it always be this way?*

'Time is the greatest healer,' she had heard someone say once. Ali hoped the words were true. However, as much as she wanted to slip back into her dreams, the curiosity about who was on the other end of that melody was unsettling. Plus, it had become uncharacteristically hot for fall, and the convent air was stifling. Ali bit her lip as she deliberated, then made up her mind.

She pushed off her thin coverlet, slipped her feet into a pair of crudely finished mules, and walked to the desk to take hold of the lantern. In her mind, Ali believed the woman was the most beautiful in the world and that Sister Clement was mistaken about her origins. Perhaps she had been banished here by a wealthy family because she had refused to marry the man chosen for her. Instead, she wanted to run away with her one true love.

Alice grasped the latch on the door and opened it, causing the flame in the lantern to flicker and dance on the walls opposite her. The air was cooler in the corridor, and in the stillness of the stone inlayed hallway, she could hear the hum of the voice, continuing to sing, but softer, to keep from being discovered by the 'shusher'.

Quietly, Ali made her way down the corridor to the where light spilled from under a door. Standing near it, she placed the lantern on the floor beside her, closed her eyes, and listened. Her breath took on a rhythm equal to the ebbs and flows of the low Gregorian chant floating toward her from the other side of the door. The song finished sweetly on a pleasing cadence.

Alice did not move. For a long while she stood quietly, wondering what would happen if she opened the door and made contact. She willed herself to take a chance as her curiosity would not let her rest until she saw who the voice belonged to—who this poor individual was who needed to be cared for by the nuns in this convent.

The low hum began again, and Alice decided to act. Cautiously, she brought her fist up to the wood and struck lightly. The humming stopped. Alice waited, then tried again, softer this time.

Putting her cheek close to the door, she whispered, "Hello?

Sister?" She was met by silence. "Sister, my name is Elisa." Her voice was low and composed. She heard shuffling and rustling, followed by more silence. "Sister? May I enter?" Ali pressed her ear to the door and heard subtle footsteps moving closer. "I am moved by your voice. It is like none I have ever heard."

When the nun failed to answer, Ali continued, "I must tell you, Sister—may I call you Sister?" Ali felt a natural affinity to this mysterious woman. "I am here at the abbey because I am very sad and away from home." The footsteps sounded like they were moving closer. "Your song comforts me." Alice stopped and waited for a reaction. Anything.

A click of the latch gave Ali some hope that she would be allowed to enter. "Would I be able to just speak to you? Will you let me in?"

At long last, a slow pull on the door pierced the hall with a thin streak of golden light from inside the room. The door opened just a crack.

"Are you alone?" The small opening revealed a middle-aged woman's face framed with salt and pepper shoulder-length hair flowing loosely about her shoulders. At first, she peered at Alice with suspicious eyes, but after catching a glimpse of her, her face broke into a welcoming smile.

"Good evening."

The nun opened the door wide. She wore a loose-fitting oatmeal colored nightshirt that touched the floor. "Good evening, Your Grace." She curtsied deeply, still holding the door latch.

Her greeting brought an unexpected smile to Alice's face.

"You may call me Elisa. And I am not a royal—far from it, in fact," she said softly. "Please rise."

The woman did as she was told and stepped back.

"You are Sister Celestine?"

She nodded and stood aside, motioning to Alice with a sweep of her arm that she was invited into her cell.

"Close the door behind you, Your Grace."

Ali obliged, then held up her lantern and looked around the cell. It was the same as hers—same bed, desk, and crucifix in the same spot. The only difference was that the sister had hundreds of sheets of parchment strewn over the terra cotta tile, with what looked like rudimentary musical notes. Was she recording her chants on music paper, like a Renaissance version of Hildegarde von Bingen?

After a moment of awkward silence, during which Celestine's eyes never left her visitor's face, Ali spoke. "I came to see you because I wanted to tell you how much I enjoy listening to your singing. You have a beautiful, soothing voice. Like an angel."

Celestine shyly shook her head from side to side. "Your Grace is too generous with her words. It is she who is the angel —the face of heaven in the expression of an earthly woman." She curtsied lower than the first time. "My song is an offering to the Lord, but I am happy it pleases Your Grace."

"Celestine," Alice's brows arched, repeating in a patient tone, "I am not of a royal family." Reaching down, she grasped the older woman's hand and helped her up, but when Alice touched the nun, she took her hand and kissed it.

"But you are, Your Grace," Celestine insisted, a bewildered quality overtaking her face. "You are as much a royal as your father, Lorenzo, the Magnificent."

Alice was intrigued by the nun's ramblings. If she remembered her history correctly, according to the nun, she was the daughter of Lorenzo de Medici, the ruler of the Florentine Republic during the 1470s or so. What would be next? The heir to the House of Windsor? In addition, poor Sister Celestine's sense of time was totally off. According to her 21st century history books, "Lorenzo the Magnificent" died around 1492, before she was even born.

"May I sit, Sister?" Ali placed her lantern on the desk alongside Celestine's and sat on the edge of the bed. "Tell me more about your music."

Celestine gently took one of the music sheets in her hand and passed it to Alice. She ran her fingers over the notes, marveling at the perfect placement.

"The sisters sing every day. As such, I have taken to creating music as a symphony for angels praising God. I believe, Your Grace, that God is best worshipped by the exquisite weaving of body and soul. In singing and playing music, we integrate mind, heart, and body. With a profound unity of voices, we sing the praises of God, here on earth. It is beauty in sound for the Heavenly Father."

Ali sat in quiet thought for a long time, admiring Celestine's eloquent wisdom. She was a bit eccentric maybe, but mad? No. How could they think she was mad?

"Your words are like poetry, Sister," Alice said as she smiled at her. How odd it was to smile again. "Thank you."

"Oh, no, Your Grace. It is my lady to whom I should offer my gratitude—for her visit. Good night, my lady Beata."

Ali laughed softly, shaking her head. "Sister, I do believe you have me confused with someone else. My name is Elisa."

Celestine's attention was drawn to her sheet music, running her fingers over the inky notes, as if touching them would make them come to life.

"Oh, no, my lady. It is you." She spoke the words with eerie conviction. "Many years have passed, but I know it is you. As certainly as the sun climbs the sky on the morrow."

Biting her lip, Alice thought that she would not press the issue. "Please, come and visit me to—"

She barely got the words out of her mouth when Sister Celestine whirled around, her eyes wild.

"I cannot leave my cell, Your Grace." Her voice held an anxious, heightened quality. "It is dangerous out there." Her head motioned to the hall. "There are many who do not wish me here."

"Shh...please, Sister." Ali got up when she heard a loud snore from another cell end abruptly, probably due to the volume of Celestine's voice. "No, you are mistaken. No one would hurt you."

Celestine shook her head wildly and began to wring her hands. "I cannot go out there. I cannot." She started pacing about the cell.

Ali watched the sister go from relative tranquility to high anxiety in a matter of seconds. *I'd better diffuse this before she goes over the edge, and I can't bring her back.* "I will come here, then. You need not leave, Sister. I will come here."

"As you wish, my lady." Celestine curtsied to Alice and turned to put her sheet music away.

"I should go back to my cell now, Sister." Alice said, furrowing her brow. "I will come back tomorrow to visit."

A brightness returned to Celestine's thin, grey lips. "I would be honored, my lady Beata. And please, close the door behind you."

Chapter Fifty-Seven

After four days in the convent, Alice was growing restless. The heat and humidity were building, and she wanted nothing more than to go home. How could these people stand not being able to communicate, even by that landline phones they used to use when her parents were young?

She needed to get to the abbey to press Leonardo to work faster. There was nothing left for her here. The time had come for her to stop wallowing in self-pity and to pick up the pieces of her life. Feeling sorry for herself would serve no purpose. She had to find the strength within her to help herself. Claudio would have wanted her to do that.

"Good morning," declared Sister Clement as she carried in her morning meal. "Did you sleep well?"

"Thank you for that." Alice motioned to the food and forced a smile. "Unfortunately, I did not sleep well. I fear I shall not sleep well for some time to come." She picked up the tea and took a sip. "I would like to speak to Abbess Augustine today about seeing Master da Vinci at the monastery." The words spilled out of her mouth as she stood in the middle of the room, cup in hand.

Clement looked surprised. "I believe that Mother will see you when you are called by the Master or by Father Federico. It is not everyone who can speak with Mother."

"I will see her now, Sister." Alice wanted control of her life again. Her visit with Celestine, and the subsequent restlessness, had crystallized that in her mind. "Tell me where I can find her, and I will go to her myself."

Clement hesitated.

"Tell me now." Alice stepped toward the young novice, her face determined and her tone resolute.

Clement's mouth had trouble getting the words out, but she finally succumbed to Alice's request.

"Please, Abbess, I must go to the monastery. It is imperative that I speak with Master da Vinci concerning the departure back to my home."

The Abbess's eyes stared at Ali as though she could not tear her gaze from her. "I see you are feeling much better." The older woman turned her face to the window. Gray clouds had overtaken the hazy afternoon sky. "In future, I request that you refrain from frightening my novices and—"

"In future," Ali interrupted, "I hope to be in my own home and not disrupting your convent, Mother."

Augustine inclined her chin slightly in acknowledgement. "I will dispatch a message to Abbott Federico regarding your wishes. I do not anticipate you shall be denied your request, lest there is good reason." She paused, still surveying Ali. "Are you not comfortable here?"

Alice shook her head and walked to the window behind the Abbess's large desk. An ornate hand-painted bible lay open on a pedestal.

"It is not that. Sister Clement has been welcoming and has

taken good care of me. I am thankful to you for allowing me to stay here, at my most vulnerable, and away from danger." Alice turned to look at the abbess. "I am forever in your debt, Mother, because this abbey cared for me after my very heart and soul were taken from me."

Augustine's piercing eyes caught Ali's, and Ali clasped her hands in supplication. "But you must know I will get away from the clutches of that horrid Medici family."

The Abbess's demeanor changed. She broke eye contact and cast her gaze to a distant place, well beyond the wall bearing the simple rosewood crucifix. Augustine stared at the icon with her hands folded to her mouth for a long moment. "Sister Celestine tells me you have been in communication with her."

"Yes. I hear her singing at night. Her voice is very comforting." Ali was growing impatient. "Should you not send a messenger to the abbey, Mother?"

"I already did—earlier this morning when Clement advised of your improvement in health."

"If that is so, why did you not tell me?"

"It does not matter. Your place is not here with us. It is with people of your kind. I think you shall do well in Milan—you may decide to take the veil yourself."

Alice was taken aback at her candidness. She was not lacking in classism, that was for certain.

"How much has Sister Celestine told you?" asked the Abbess coolly.

Ali stopped her pacing and sat across from the abbess, hoping she did not get Sister Celestine into trouble. "We talked of her love of music, mostly. It is clear that she prefers to stay in her cell, rather than go about with the other sisters. And oh, yes," Ali laughed softly, "she insisted on calling me 'Your Grace' and referred to me as 'my lady Beata.' She is clearly confusing me with someone else—Mother, are you quite well?"

The Abbess's face turned ashen grey. Her hand curled into a limp fist as she brought it to her mouth.

"Abbess Augustine?"

The nun sat silently, staring at the cross on the wall. With fresh resolve, she faced Ali. "You are correct in assuming that Sister Celestine has you confused with someone else. You are not Lady Beata de Medici."

"Well, of course not. I never thought for a moment that I was."

"My lady, you are not Beata—you are her daughter, Lady Elisa Beatrice de Medici."

Alice sat quietly, her mouth half-open with unspoken words. She frowned and slowly shook her head. "No," Ali's voice echoed in the sparse room. "No, I am not."

Augustine squeezed her eyes closed, a look on her face as though someone had sliced open a healed wound. "There is more, my lady. You are a Medici, to this I will swear. The granddaughter of Lorenzo the Magnificent and Clarice Orsini—"

"No!" Alice hissed.

"I tell you in earnest, my lady." The Abbess' voice held great remorse. "After these many years of keeping the secret, against my faith and beliefs, you are the daughter of Beata de Medici."

"You are mad." Alice's voice was a hoarse whisper.

"I speak the truth."

"Why should I believe this is the truth? I have been living with this unknown my entire life. Burying thoughts of feeling unwanted and unloved with the certainty that it did not matter because the love of my adoptive parents was all I needed, and now, you tell me this? Tell me, Mother, why should I believe you?"

"Because it is the truth. I cannot hide it any longer. I cannot let your mother's legacy be forgotten."

"And pray then, who is my father?"

The Abbess breathed deeply. "He was a marshal, in charge

of the duke's mounts. After Lorenzo's death, Lady Beata was devastated. She and the marshal found love. In fact, they were very much in love, but her Uncle Piero, Lorenzo's successor, would not hear of the union. The marshal suffered Piero's wrath because of it, for there was a great conflict due to their difference in society. The new duke had him killed, believing that the family name would be sullied by such a scandal, and he sent his niece here, under the guise of her wanting to take the veil. Instead, she bore a beautiful baby girl. You are that girl, my lady."

Ali listened to the Abbess, each spoken syllable drawing her deeper into a haze of confusion and surrealism. *This woman is delusional. Things like this don't happen in real life, only in faerie tales.*

"She did not live long after she set eyes on you. Your mother was very ill in the last weeks of her time. After she gave birth, she kissed you dearly, said she loved you and that you were the most beautiful baby she had set eyes on. Then, sadly, she drew her last breath, the poor dear, and quietly passed away. Afterward, I visited His Grace, Piero. I believed he may have wanted to set things right, but instead, he took you and placed you with servants, and proceeded to spoil his two children, Bruno and Clarice. No one ever knew about you. I was sworn to secrecy by Piero—a burden I have born for eighteen years." She shook her head, as though trying to deny the truth in her words.

"Your adoptive parents were named Monica and Enrico de Povri, though they were not your parents for long, as they were killed, too. They were wrongly accused of treason shortly before the Borgia seized Florence. I truly believe they were put to death to hide the fact that they may have known who you really were. You remained in the palace as a maid, your birthright unknown to spare the current duke embarrassment. After the Medici came back into power, your history unknown and your mother all but forgotten, you remained a maid under the rule of Giuliano de Medici, your other uncle. Piero kept his secrets well, and unfortunately, so have I—until now."

"You, Elisa, are a Medici. And now, here you are, once more in my convent." Her voice trailed, her face weary. "I pray God will forgive me my transgressions and that you may salvage your life in some small way now that you know. You are a royal, my lady, a true blood royal."

Ali listened, not knowing if the Abbess was playing a cruel joke on her or if she was mad. There was no other explanation for this absurd story, too outlandish to be real. Clarice and Bruno, her cousins...impossible!

"Abbess, you will forgive me if I say I do not believe you. I do not know to what end you are playing at, but rest assured that—"

"I am not playing at anything, my lady—"

"Please." The information was too much for Alice to process all at once. "Stop calling me that! I am not—" She put her hands over her ears to block everything out, but the words resounded in her head just the same. *Your mother is Beata de Medici. Your father, a Medici marshal. You are a Medici and a royal.*

"Go, then, and ask Celestine, if you do not believe me." Augustine's voice was quiet. Her eyes reluctantly met Ali's. In them, there was anguish and guilt. "She assisted at your birth. She and I brought you into this world." Her voice took on a pained quality, "and she is the only other person alive who knows the truth."

Chapter Fifty-Eight

As was her habit, Sister Clement brought Ali her lunch, but when she did not engage her in conversation, the nun shrugged her shoulders and left. Ali did not have it in her to make small talk. And she could not even look at the tray of food. She was still trying to digest the information that Abbess Augustine had force-fed her that afternoon.

This was a cruel turn of events, indeed. Though she had been raised by loving parents, she was still an orphan. And although she would never admit it to herself, or to Reno and Barbara, in not knowing who her biological parents were, her life-story had always felt a little incomplete.

Even the couple she had thought were her parents, Monica and Enrico, was a lie. The fact that she was a product of a union between the daughter of one of the most powerful and influential historical figures of the sixteenth century and a mere marshal—barely a step up from a stable boy—was all too surreal. Was she ever going to have a normal life?

Regardless of her birthright, all Ali felt was a deep desire to go home and hold onto Barbara and Reno, the only mother and father she had ever known. She wanted so badly to grieve, talk to her mother, and then maybe begin to heal. Ali's perception of justice had not changed—only the innocence in thinking that it would always prevail had taken a beating.

Although she had been lost in these thoughts most of the day, Ali did take time to notice that the clouds had been building all afternoon into twisted, angry thunderheads. By early evening, the tempest outside her window was in full force. Da Vinci must be beside himself with anticipation, Ali thought. Hopefully, a lightning strike will reproduce the wormhole passage to 2029 in the chamber.

Ali's pacing quickened with each roll of thunder and every drop of pelting rain against the wooden shutters of her window. Walking in a circular pattern around the room did not help, and if she carried on until the morning, she knew that she would drive herself insane thinking about it all. There was too much to consider.

Yet, even though she was loath to think of herself as associated with Bruno in any way, she was intensely curious about her biological parents. She desperately wanted to talk to Sister Celestine about the circumstances of her birth - but she did not want to upset the fragile nun, either.

A loud clap of thunder made her jump. She opened the shutters to see if she had a view of the abbey in Galluzzo, but her window only offered a vista of the inside courtyard. Ali hurriedly closed the shutters, so she would not get soaked by the sideways rain, and walked pensively to the door.

In the end, curiosity won. Alice took a deep breath, lifted the latch, and strode through, ready to accept the truth in whatever form it would greet her.

～

There was no singing from Sister Celestine's part of the corridor.

Tap, Tap. Ali knocked lightly so as not to startle her. She heard a flurry of shuffling before the door abruptly swung open to reveal Sister Celestine in her full nun's habit. Sister's hand reached out, and quite literally, pulled her into the room.

"Thanks to the blessed Lord, someone has come to sit with me." Though she was dressed, her habit was askew and her headpiece terribly disheveled. At the sound of a thunderclap, Celestine covered her ears and scurried to the far corner of the room, the one furthest from the window. A sympathetic smile was dying to take over Ali's lips, but she dared not let it loose for fear of offending the poor dear.

"Sister, what is troubling you this day?" Ali asked compassionately.

"The noise." She pointed to the window with a shaky finger. "I cannot bear the noise. I am afraid of it. The light and cold fire that follows affects me to no end."

Cold fire, Ali mused. *Now there are some new words for lightning I've never heard before.*

"Do not concern yourself, Sister. It will not harm you. The cold fire is far away."

"Hmm. I am not convinced of this, my lady Beata."

Alice bit her lip and sat on Celestine's bed. *Okay, so there's the segue.* "Sister, do you remember when I was here before? I was with child." Ali's tone was on edge, but she tried her hardest to maintain her equanimity.

Celestine stopped her rocking, and her eyes locked onto Ali's hands, not making direct eye contact. "Certainly, my lady, as if it were yesterday." Cautiously, she moved toward Ali and sat beside her on the edge of the bed.

A tight knot settled in Ali's stomach. It was becoming more and more difficult to disbelieve the Abbess's confession.

"You were just as you are today," Celestine added. "So small and pretty, but you were not well. The baby took much from you, I am afraid, as some babies do. It was difficult for you, my lady." She looked away. A distant rumble made her flinch.

"Remind me, Celestine, how long was I here, at the convent?"

"Your uncle, Piero, brought you here when there was only a gentle swelling of your belly. On any other woman, it would have been barely noted, but because you are so slight..." Her voice trailed as she looked at the wooden shutters covering her window, lost in her thoughts.

"Yes, Sister, go on."

"You stayed for several months until it was your time to give birth. Every now and then, your sisters would visit, incognito, of course, to avoid scandal." Her brows rose in mild disapproval. "It was complicated. You were forbidden from seeing the marshal when it was discovered you were with child. That is when His Grace had you brought here. The Abbess and I were forced to hide your identity. When your time came, we sent word to the palace. You had a beautiful baby girl, born with honey-brown curls, just like yourself. A cherub, she was."

Alice listened intently, with a bittersweet tumult inside her.

"You barely had strength to hold her. You kissed her curls and loved her for all too brief a moment...and then..." Celestine shook her head slowly. "Then, you left our world with her name on your last breath...Elisa."

Ali felt the knot in her stomach unleash itself into a silent barrage of emotions. Sadness, rage, love, and grief for her lost birth mother competing with resentment for the Medici family. Not to mention the sense of loss for a father who had never known she existed.

Abbess Augustine was telling the truth. Ali was a Medici.

"Thank you, Sister Celestine." Ali sniffed. "You have helped me a great deal."

"You are the baby, my lady, are you not?" Celestine's eyes finally locked onto Ali's.

Ali drew a deep breath and tried not to cry. Her mother must have been a sweet and kind individual to elicit such feelings of loss from this woman after so many years.

"Yes, Sister Celestine," Ali answered in a quiet voice. "I am the daughter of Lady Beata de Medici and her marshal—Elisa Beatrice de Medici."

Chapter Fifty-Nine

A quick hug from Sister Celestine was all that Alice could garner before going back to her cell in a zombie-like daze. The nun's beloved music sheets caught her eye after what was, for Alice, an earth-shatteringly revealing conversation.

Alice lay on her simple bed, thinking of where her journey back to Renaissance Florence had brought her emotionally and mentally. In the act of trying to save her beloved, she had been the cause of his demise—of this she was certain.

Maybe she should not have come back to warn him? Then again, perhaps it would have happened anyway, and this was the universe's way of saying that no matter how hard one tries, one cannot change what is meant to be.

All she wanted was to go home. To let herself be wrapped in the love of her parents. To eventually heal her wounds, to bleed out the grief and misery of her loss and rebuild. There was no doubt that she would, it would just take time. Time is the greatest healer.

A sharp knock at the door startled her out of her philosophical reverie.

"Miss." Sister Clement's voice carried through the wood.

Ali forced herself to rise and answer.

"Your guide to the monastery has arrived. One of the brothers awaits you at the entrance outside the gate." The novice's demeanor was timid.

"Thank you, Sister," replied Ali. "Clement. I must apologize for my way of speaking to you yesterday. I am not in the habit of depending on others. Of not being in control of my own destiny."

Clement grimaced. "I am not a wise woman, nor a learned one, but even I am aware that at times one must believe that destiny will find its way to you."

"Perhaps. I only know that I cannot stay here," Alice mumbled under her breath. "Right then, Sister Clement, I am ready."

She strode out with the nun to the end of the hall and turned the corner to the main hallway that led to the front entrance. Abbess Augustine was waiting with a chestnut brown vestment draped over her arm. The two girls halted in mid step.

"The brother has requested that you circle to the rear exit. He has provided a monk's cloak to cover you. Wear it with the hood over your head to conceal your identity. It will make your passage to the monastery safer. Clement will accompany you." Mother handed the novice an ancient-looking, oversized key. Nodding to Alice, she raised her hand in a blessing. "May God be with you, now and every day, hereafter, guiding your steps in your journey."

Alice bowed her head as she made the sign of the cross, then took the cloak from the abbess.

"Thank you," said Ali, as she wrapped the hooded cloak about her shoulders and fastened it under her neck. Alice's eyes met Abbess Augustine's as she slipped the hood over her head. "I want you to know that I bear no ill feelings toward you, Mother."

Silence hung in the air as she waited for a response; Clement's eyes darted from Ali to the Abbess and back again. Augustine drew in a deep breath, took Alice's hand, and touched it to her forehead.

"May you enjoy a long and happy life, my lady, wherever you choose to live it." She bowed slightly, then turned. Her robes swirled behind her as she briskly walked away, disappearing into the shadows of the corridor. The two young women watched her, Clement looking a bit bewildered. She turned to Alice, handing her the robe.

"Shall we, then?"

Adjusting the robe around her shoulders, Ali answered, "You lead the way—I shall follow."

Alice trailed behind Sister Clement as she wound her way through the convent's labyrinth. In due course, they reached a staircase that led them down to a thick wooden door. Clement opened it, and they stepped into the muggy, Tuscan afternoon air. It was still cloudy, and the ground was soaked from the earlier downpour. They followed a path through the garden that bore the last of the late summer vegetables.

This was it. Her final hours in 1512 were upon her, and she would not even able to attend her beloved's funeral. She was scuttled away like an undesirable, just as she had been at birth. Had she thanked Clarice for trying to make things right in her own way? Did she thank Rubio for protecting her during the horrific exchange at the Porta Rossa? How could she ever repay Duchess Filiberta for orchestrating her rescue from the prison?

These were all people who, in a very special way, had sacrificed themselves to set things right. She made up her mind to send word through Leonardo to them—to tell them how grateful she was for their kindness. Alice also hoped that Francesco was at the monastery, so she could offer her thanks to him for supporting Claudio as his colleague and his friend.

The little path led the two girls behind a barn that was at

the outermost perimeter of the convent grounds. The entire complex was surrounded by an ornate wrought iron barrier. They stopped at the gate, beyond which Alice spotted a monk sitting on horseback. His shoulders were hunched, and his face was covered by a hooded robe, just like hers. Sister Clement paused and looked at the monk before inserting the key in the lock. The novice looked back at Ali and clasped her hands in prayer.

"May God be with you."

"Thank you, Sister. And I am sorry if I acted strangely. I just want to go home."

Clement nodded. "Perhaps it is wise to keep your hood about you and cover your face, miss. One never knows who may be watching." Clement gave her one last sweet smile as Ali walked through the gate, pulling her hood over her head.

Alice looked at the hooded monk and furrowed her brow. "Good afternoon, Brother."

Silently, he nodded his acknowledgement.

The horse whinnied, tossing its head up and down. She thought how much it looked like Spirit, but how could that be? "Spirit, is that you?"

The monk tightened the reins to control the horse's movements and kept his head down, adjusting the hood around his face.

"Are you here to bring me to the monastery at Galluzzo...to Master da Vinci?"

He nodded again and held out his gloved hand as a signal to come closer. Ali paused, not knowing whether she should trust him, but with no other alternative, she grasped his hand. He returned her grip with a gentle and effortless pull, and she swung her leg up and over the horse's back in a swift movement.

She held onto the back of his robe instead of wrapping her arms around his waist, as she had with Claudio.

Claudio.

Listening to the *clip clop* rhythm of the horse's hoofs on the cobblestones, she thought of him: their meetings in the palace garden, riding on his Vespa over the Ponte Vecchio under the hot Tuscan sun, walking through the village. His goofy sense of humor, his incredibly delicious, crooked smile.

Everywhere she looked, wherever she cast her eyes, she found a memory. Claudio was a part of her, yet she had to come to terms with the fact that she would never again gaze into those eyes, so warm and sweet and loving. She would have to accept that anywhere her destiny brought her, in the past or in the future, she would be tormented by the ghosts of their love.

Clip clop. The horse carried on, and her musings continued. Before she realized it, they were almost at the Porta Rossa. This she could not bear. Alice could still envision Claudio lying there, bleeding on the cold, hard flagstone floor while that brutal animal, Bruno, stood over him.

A precarious façade of strength soon gave way to a familiar lump rising in her throat as she remembered his last breaths, unable to help him, his body going limp and lifeless. Tears welled up, and her breathing became ragged.

"Please, Brother." Ali hiccuped a sob as she spoke. "Hurry away from here. I cannot bear to see this place."

Her tears brimmed over and began to fall down her cheeks. Crying softly, she brought her hand to her eyes to wipe the tears, but to her surprise, the monk reached behind him and blindly sought out her other hand.

He held it tightly, and Alice thought it odd, but then again, he was a member of the Church, and it was his calling to comfort those who were suffering. His hand around hers felt calming, almost otherworldly.

Once out of the city gates, the brother gave the horse a gentle kick, and it increased its speed to a light gallop. As they rounded the corner to head onto the road to Galluzzo, they cleared the treetops, and Ali saw the monastery high up on the hillside overlooking Florence, its imposing presence keeping watch over the city. She had managed to ease her crying, trying hard to keep from drawing attention to herself.

The brother veered off the main path and steered the horse into a wooded area away from the road. A flutter of apprehension overtook her. "Why are we going this way? This is not the way to the monastery."

The brother halted the horse but did not turn to face her. "This is as far as we go for now my lady."

Ali's heart jumped. She knew that voice.

The brother slipped the hood off his head. She only glimpsed the dark hair...the curve of his ear...the outline of his jaw. Ali gasped and felt a thunderbolt go through her heart.

"Oh, my God." The words came out in a trembling whisper as her thoughts raced out of control. *Is it? No! I'm hallucinating. I'm losing my mind. Is it...*

He turned to face her, and her heart nearly stopped.

Chapter Sixty

"Oh my God! It's you." Claudio was alive and breathing and smiling, and Ali thought she would die with the shock of it all.

In one fluid movement, he swung his leg over and slid off the horse. Grasping Ali around the waist, he helped her down. Her hands slid up his arms, over his shoulders, and clung to him as he held her in his arms, spinning her around before setting her on her feet again. Their eyes met, and a thousand words passed between them without a sound.

"Alice, my love. My angel."

"Claudio." Ali held his face, framing it in her hands as she eased back to look at him. "I can't believe you're here. Are you real?" Her hands grasped his arms to make certain she was not embracing a ghost.

"I am."

He kissed Ali's forehead and buried his face in her hair as she set her cheek firmly against his chest, and listened to his heartbeat. The wonder of it all but drowned her.

"Do not cry. I am so sorry to have put you through hell, my darling, but I—"

"Quiet, Claudio. Just...hold me. Let me listen to your heart."

She had to understand that this was really him—that she was not dreaming. That her senses were not playing a cruel trick on her. Claudio's hands glided gently over her back, soothing her. Alice, her eyes squeezed shut, allowed her senses to convince her that he was real—the smell of his skin, the feeling of his lips against her forehead, the rhythm of his breathing, and the beating of his heart.

Finally, Ali felt confident enough in her own state of mind to step back and carefully study Claudio's face. She wanted to see him, his loveliness and familiarity. Ali brushed at the strands of hair that fell over his forehead, then ran her hand from the curve of his jaw to his lips, feeling them with her fingertips. He took off his gloves and clasped her fingers. Gently, he kissed her palm, then placed her hand against his face—gestures that were so familiar.

"It is you."

His hands were covered in cuts and scratches from the fight, but they were tender and gentle as ever against hers. She drew close to him and brought his face down to her. They kissed, as they had the first time in the garden, with the purity of unconditional love. Alice and Claudio held one another and let their love spin around them.

When the kiss was over, Claudio looked into her eyes as the last glints of sunlight glowed on his face.

"What happened? I saw you die," was all Ali could manage. "How? What?"

"Listen," he said, "we have but a few moments before we must go." He pushed up his vestment sleeve and revealed cloth bandages on his forearm. "See here." He pushed his robes aside and indicated strips of cloth wrapped diagonally across his chest. "The injuries did occur, but my death was a ruse devised by Master da Vinci to buy us more time. I, like you, had no idea there was a diluted derivative of the oleander plant in the flask

—poison. A small amount is ideal to help one sleep—a larger amount simulates death. Even more, can kill."

"Why would he do that? I thought the duel was only to first blood drawn."

"If he had not, Bruno would have killed me for certain. Da Vinci knew that he would not have stopped at first blood. Essentially, the oleander did kill me. I was in stasis. My breathing was undetectable, and my heartbeat was almost non-existent. For all intents, I was dead. It was the only way I could have survived that duel. Bruno would have settled for nothing less than my murder—be it sooner or later. This way it was on our terms—da Vinci made certain of that. So basically, he got away with murder. He is a Medici, and they are untouchable, my darling."

Ali felt a twinge in her stomach. Feeling the heat of a flush working up her neck mortified her. She was a Medici—she had to tell him, so he could make an informed decision about his love for her.

"He would have ignored you if I had not come back," Ali asserted. "I put him over the edge when I showed up again."

"That is where you are wrong, Alice. Never blame yourself for this. He had every intention of getting rid of me when I was offered the position at Tolfa. He could not stand the fact that his uncle trusted me more than his own nephew. I overheard the entire conversation at a function at the palace."

"Oh my gosh! Your mother," Ali gasped, imagining the countess' heartache. "She must be beside herself with grief."

Claudio smiled with a hint of sadness and shook his head.

"Do not worry, she knows."

Ali released her breath, relieved that she was not responsible for his mother grieving her lost son. "Leonardo contacted her shortly after he brought me to the monastery. She was secretly assured that I was only injured, not dead. We were able to say our goodbyes earlier today, and she understands that I cannot be seen in Florence again. I am dead to all, and I shall remain that way. It is a *fait accompli*."

"But how can she be satisfied without any contact from you forever?"

"The Master and Francesco are planning to travel to Milan, perhaps even France. I have told her that you and I have agreed to accompany them, so we can start a new life and be free of Bruno's wrath for good. Francesco suggested to me that he would correspond with my mother in my stead on a regular basis, this way she still has a connection to her son."

"But in actuality, you're coming with me, back to 2029." Alice's face lit up. "The timeline is not tainted, and you are allowed to live out your life." She thought again of Countess Maria, and her brow furrowed. "But I feel so guilty that you are being taken from your mother and your friends. And Leonardo —you will miss him so."

"My mother has the satisfaction of knowing that I will live a full life in the field that I have chosen, and she will not be alone. She shall marry Counselor Filippo soon enough, just as Castiglione had outlined in the letter you found." Claudio smiled soothingly and cupped her chin in his hand.

It struck Alice that she had forgotten to ask a most important question. "And the chamber? Did a lightning bolt strike?"

Claudio raised his chin and pulled her close. "It did. We were able to establish another wormhole, but it is weak. I am uncertain how long it will remain active. We think Luca's laser may have compromised the passage, but if we act fast, we could take advantage of the temporal wake which will protect us from any ill effects in the passage to 2029. Now, we really must go. Master da Vinci and Francesco are—"

"Wait, Claudio. Before we go, I must tell you something very important." She pulled away slightly and dropped her gaze, reluctant to see his expression when she dropped the bomb about her pedigree. "I want you to know before we go any further."

"Of course."

"You must decide if you still want me after I tell you." She turned her face up to him.

An expression of puzzlement swept over Claudio's face.

"I am a Medici."

Claudio's features went from a grimace to a smirk.

"It's true. Abbess Augustine told me. I'm the daughter of Beata de Medici and a commoner, the Medici's stable marshal. Piero de Medici had him killed because of it. They had an affair, and I was the result."

"How can this be?"

She exhaled a breath and went on to explain how the abbess had revealed the truth to her, which had been corroborated by Sister Celestine. "I am a Medici, Claudio. I have their blood running through my veins." She turned her head and looked up him, her chin balanced on his collarbone. "Have your feelings for me changed?" The words from Ali's lips floated in the twilight like so many fireflies. "Can you still love me?"

Claudio appeared speechless. He shook his head and tried to make his mouth work. "I do not care where or who you come from." His crooked smile was back, and his brow was smooth again. "I fell in love with you, not your lineage."

Alice searched his eyes. He encircled her shoulders with one hand and reached up to cup her face with the other and traced her chin and lips with his thumb. In her heart, Ali knew that Claudio's feelings did not change—she believed him.

"I will always love you."

Ali's hands slipped around the back of his neck and took hold of his hair—it was as it had always been. "I kind of thought so, but I still had to ask."

When they drew apart, Claudio glanced at the low sun in the sky. "And now we really must make haste. It is getting late."

～

Spirit raced effortlessly to the monastery as Ali held tightly to Claudio. She was still trying to convince herself this was not a dream, and that he was real, alive, and in her arms again. The mare halted in front of the monastery, and they dismounted. After ensuring their hoods were pulled low over their faces, Claudio knocked on the door. In seconds, the massive door opened, allowing the two and Spirit into the courtyard of the imposing structure.

"Thank you, Anton—you are not Antonuccio," asserted Claudio, as he hastily turned to thank the brother. Alice still had her hood wrapped securely, hiding her face.

"I am not, Count—he is elsewhere."

At this, Claudio shrugged and continued. "Please, let Brother Antonuccio and Abbot Federico know we are here."

While Claudio spoke to the monk, Ali stood close to Spirit, rubbing her nose and trying to appear at ease in her surroundings. When the monk left to deliver his message, Claudio turned his attention to Ali and Spirit. The mare gave him a gentle nudge with her snout.

"Aw," whispered Ali. "I forgot about Spirit. Who is going to take her?"

"Francesco will." He rubbed the mare's nose and gave her a last pat. "You know, old girl. I know you do. Do not worry, Spirit. You will be very well taken care of." He gently led her to a corner to the watering trough, where she began to drink.

Claudio's eyes met Ali's, and she knew that it was time. They both turned and hurried toward da Vinci's studio.

Chapter Sixty-One

With her hands tucked in the widely brimmed sleeves of her monk's robe and crossed over her chest, Alice felt a shiver of excitement work its way from her stomach to her throat. She and Claudio walked rapidly around the corner to the north wing of the abbey and descended the familiar stairs to the master's apartments.

"I feel like I'm watching me do this," blurted Ali. "Like I'm floating above and taking all this in."

Thoughts chased each other in Ali's head. How she had come full circle and she was ready to reconcile her past with her present and prepared to tackle the future with new information about who she was and who she had the potential to become. She, a scullery maid, who had fallen into a forbidden love with a highborn member of the Medici court in 1512 Florence, finding that her own mother, a Medici princess, had fallen for a commoner. The irony was almost too perfect.

Time slowed, and she sensed the air growing electric around them as their anticipation grew. Would they finally have the chance to allow their relationship to flourish and grow instead of constantly having to overcome obstacles that kept them apart? Ali sighed at the prospect of having just one simple, normal date with Claudio—a luxury they had only been afforded a handful of times.

Claudio looked back at her as they stepped closer to Leonardo's apartments. "Come on," he urged, as they got closer to the hallway leading to da Vinci's outer chamber. He checked to ensure they were alone, grasped Ali's hand, and broke into a full run that caused their hoods and robes to trail in flight behind them.

As they rounded the corner to da Vinci's hall, they spotted Abbot Federico and Brother Antonuccio, hurrying toward the master's quarters.

"Father! Antonuccio!"

The monks halted and turned at Claudio's cry.

"I feared I should not see you before I depart. In earnest, we would not feel at ease if we did not have the opportunity to thank you." Claudio's voice held a mix of surprise and relief. He and Ali continued to move past them to get to Leonardo's door.

Alice offered a grateful smile to Antonuccio, who proceeded to blush red as he and Abbot Federico followed in the couple's wake.

"I should not miss a final farewell and the opportunity to offer a last blessing." Abbot Federico said breathlessly.

"Hence, with haste, we must go to the Master's studio, Father."

The four dashed through the halls, their sandals thudding on the stones beneath their feet. Antonuccio had no trouble keeping up, but when Ali turned around, she noticed that Father was lagging.

"Go on, child," he wheezed, gasping for air and holding his right side with one hand while resting the other on the wall for balance. "I give you my blessing. And I shall pray for your safe journey home. Go now, for you are in good hands." Federico nodded toward the novice monk who had already disappeared around a column. Claudio and Ali complied, shouting out a last, "Thank you!"

"H-here we are!" The monk was the first to get to da Vinci's apartment door. In an instant, Francesco tore it open.

"Thank God you two have arrived. What kept you?" Francesco was flustered and perspiring, which in turn made Ali very nervous.

"Francesco, what is the matter?" she asked, stepping around Antonuccio. Francesco peered over Ali to the novice monk.

"If you please, Brother Antonuccio, we require a lookout at the top of the north staircase, in the event that any of the other brothers should wander close to the Master's apartments."

Antonuccio nodded. "Y-yes, sir." With a triumphant look of satisfaction on his face, he set off to his sentry position.

Ali and Claudio stepped into the main studio, and Francesco closed the door behind them.

"The spiral in the chamber...it is fading." Francesco croaked out the last three words.

"No." Claudio grimaced. Fear, stark and vivid settled in his eyes. "No. It was strong enough when I departed."

"This cannot be happening," Alice whispered her words. Panic was rising inside her. "There must be some way we can fix this."

"I am afraid that is easier said than done, child." Da Vinci appeared in the doorway that led to his studio.

Alice could see beyond him. She studied the familiar work-tables, glass containers, brushes, and easels strewn about the master's workspace in the antechamber room.

"Francesco and I have attempted all that we know and some things at which we could only speculate."

Claudio wasted no time dashing for the portal. The faint outline of spiraling arms deep within the chamber was still visible, but as they watched, they pulsed dimmer and dimmer. Despair eased up Ali's throat.

"There must be something we can do—we cannot just let it fade away." Alice's gaze alternated between the three men in the cluttered space.

"Is the copper attachment still intact?" asked Claudio.

"Yes, but are we to wait for another storm?" asked Francesco.

"I fear we do not have that extravagance, my boy," da Vinci sighed. "If only I was in possession of materials from your time, Elisa. I should think we would possess enough ingenuity to set things right. But I fear that we have exhausted all our alternatives." His gaze dropped to the floor. "I am sorry."

Alice turned from da Vinci to Claudio, open-mouthed.

"It is the basic law of science, Alice," Claudio tried to explain. "When you compress something, it heats up. The density of the chronometric particles stabilized the wormhole. Without compression, it essentially cools and loses its fuel— that is what is happening at present. We have no choice but to wait and try again later. Do not worry, my love. I will get you home somehow."

Alice looked deep into those dark eyes and wished she could lose herself in them. His voice sounded confident, but his gaze gave his uncertainties away. She sensed Claudio's desperation and frustration at having triumph ripped from their grasp. Her eyes drifted momentarily back to the chamber and saw the last faint glimmers of light disappear into infinity. All that remained was an empty box—an ordinary, copper box.

Oh babe, I know you're lying to me. You're trying to be brave, but I know the variables are wildly against our favor right now. Her thoughts of a safe haven for her and Claudio were vanishing along with the chamber spirals.

She distractedly rubbed the subdermal chip under her skin, suspecting that her mother and father must be freaking out by now. An overwhelming feeling of frustration and guilt descended on her like a suffocating, dark cloak. "Oh my gosh." She shook her head and gazed into the empty chamber. "My parents will be beside themselves with worry."

"I am sorry, my darling," Claudio said, his voice throaty. "I promise—I shall not surrender. I shall not rest until you are safe back at home."

With all her might she willed herself not to stay strong. Every step of the way, she and Claudio, whether together or apart, had worked to overcome countless obstacles that had been thrown at them. And now, at what seemed to be the very last moment before they could be safe and sure of their future, another had been cast in their way.

What if they could not get the chamber to work after all? Her stomach tightened at the prospect of her and Claudio constantly looking over their shoulders, hiding their identities forever.

Alice's hand searched for his. She laced her fingers through his and pulled him closer as his gaze locked onto hers. With thoughts that were fleeting and dynamic, gossamer-like in their quality, she resolved herself to the awful truth. Her destiny was no longer in her hands but in the hands of random events over which she had no control.

Leave it alone. Let it go. Ali guided Claudio's bandaged hand around her waist, as she wrapped her arms around him. His heart was strong. She loved listening to it.

"In the meantime, where shall we go?" Ali breathed in deeply and smiled lovingly up at Claudio as he tucked a loose tendril of her hair behind her ear.

"We shall find a place," Claudio affirmed, but there was frustration in his eyes. He held her close and dropped a kiss on top of her forehead. "I am so sorry, my lady. I have failed you."

"You have done no such thing." Alice forced a smile as she

let her head sink onto his chest. "There is no other place I would rather be, than here with you."

"Here, I have something for you." He leaned back so he could reach into his pocket and held up his red neck-scarf that had been torn off Ali during the struggle with Bruno's men. "I promised I would get this back to you—whatever it took."

She gazed up into his loving eyes, then at the tattered piece of cloth and took it gently into her hands and tied it about her neck.

"Thanks," she laughed softly. "This got me through some rough times."

"Come now, you two," said Leonardo. "All is not lost. We may be able to scuttle you out and try again another time."

"Thank you, sir." Claudio sounded weary. "We shall have to hide until we can come back."

"Off with you both now, Count and lady!" said da Vinci. "Keep your hoods over your heads and stay down when you are on the—"

In that instant, an intense burst of light exploded in the chamber and a thunderous crack split the air like a giant's blade.

Francesco made a sound—perhaps a scream. Da Vinci started back and howled in pain as Claudio shielded Ali with his body. But everyone in the room winced at the reverberation and shielded their eyes from the powerful radiance.

Ali felt her skin tingle with the sensation of a million pinpricks, while a charged smell of ozone permeated the air. There was no storm, no thunder or lightning.

The bolt came from the other side of the chamber.

Chapter Sixty-Two

"What in the name of..." da Vinci's voice faded. The light from the chamber dazzled the senses and kindled anew the sense of wonder at the phenomenon before them. It crackled sharply as the particles began to settle and stabilize.

Ali was the first to react.

"Luca!" she shouted with delight. "I knew he could do it! He must have realized the spirals had faded and used the laser to reactivate the chamber. Our plan did work." Elated, she wrapped her arms around Claudio's neck and whooped with delight.

"I always knew he had it in him," Claudio beamed as he looked lovingly at Ali, returning her embrace.

"So," she pulled away and held him at arm's length, studying his eyes. "Are you ready to start anew? This will be forever—you in 2029. Are you prepared to commit?"

"I could not want anything more." Claudio's smile never failed to make her knees buckle.

"I think a trial is called for?" Francesco interrupted the

joyful exchange. "To ensure safety?" His question was directed at da Vinci who nodded his agreement.

"I concur," replied da Vinci. Francesco moved to the chamber and slowly put his hand in. The tips of his fingers slid into the infinite spirals. Ali moved closer to the charged array and watched as his fingers disappeared into the darkness. She felt the electricity dancing on her skin.

"How does it feel, Francesco?" she asked. But instead of Francesco's voice, she caught a faint response from inside the chamber.

"Ali." Barely audible, but unmistakably clear. "Ali?"

"Papa?" Ali cried. In a few steps, she was at the chamber and if it had not been for Francesco's quick thinking, she would have fallen through.

"Wait!" shouted Claudio, grabbing her other arm.

"That's my father! Papa!" she shouted again.

"Alice, it's me!" Her father's voice warmed her heart. "But wait. Do not come through yet...stabilization is not complete."

"Okay, Papa, but hurry...and Claudio is coming with me!"

There was an agonizing silence from the other side of the chamber, followed by a faint, "I figured as much."

She turned to Claudio. A grin spread on his lips as he tried not to look nervous. Was he fearful of Reno? Her lips curled in an elfish grin.

Alice turned her attention from Claudio's anxiety at meeting her father, back to the chamber. "Papa?"

"Almost there." His voice was clearer, and the spirals were becoming more defined and less intense in brightness. It occurred to Ali that she and Claudio had only moments until they crossed to their new lives. She turned toward da Vinci and Francesco.

Claudio extended his hand to his friend, Francesco, and smiled with a look that spoke volumes. "My gratitude to you is boundless, my dear friend. I shall be forever in your debt."

Francesco clapped a hand on his back as the two exchanged a rough embrace.

"Do not forget to write to my mother as often as you are able. And take good care of Spirit."

"You shall be served, my lord. And my friend." Francesco moved toward Ali. Gently, he held her hand and kissed it. "A pleasure, as always, my lady."

"Please, give my love to Caterina and look after her." Alice beamed a conspiratorial smile. "You know, I very much think she is sweet on you."

Francesco blushed. Claudio extended his hand to the master —his teacher and mentor. Alice knew how hard this must be for him.

"Sir." Claudio choked on the word. With glistening eyes, da Vinci did not hesitate to embrace Claudio as a father would embrace his son. "You have been an inspiration, Master Leonardo, in ways you cannot imagine. A father to me when I needed guidance in seeking my way in life. For this, I thank you."

"You are too kind, my boy, indeed." After a brief clapping of hands on backs, the two released.

"Master da Vinci," Alice wrapped her arms around his neck, "It was an honor being in your presence, sir."

Da Vinci laughed softly, his eyes twinkling as he looked down at Ali. "The heart of a lion...."

"But the face of an angel?" Her voice held a knowing lilt.

"Yes." His eyes were pensive as he grasped his jacket lapels.

"Will you be all right here, sir?" asked Claudio.

"Do not concern yourself with me and trivialities of your past, Claudio. Your future is what you should be looking to."

"Ali." Her father's voice filtered through the chamber, still slight. "Are you ready?"

"Can we come through now?" Alice leaned in her head to hear her father better.

"Now is good." Alice recognized the certainty in his voice. "Come through, now."

Alice turned to Claudio. "Ready?"

His gaze went from the chamber to her. In one fluid movement, he lifted her up at the waist and kissed her.

"Every great love begins with a kiss," he murmured as he tenderly set her on her feet and caressed her cheek with the tips of his fingers. "And every journey, a leap of faith."

Ali and Claudio held hands. Their gazes never breaking from one another's, they stepped toward the center of the chamber, the pins and needles sensation increasing exponentially as they moved deeper into the spirals.

A sticky pull grasped them and pushed them to the other side, wisps of color and lines of light and dark flew past them as they were both pulled and pushed to the light at the other side. Whatever they were to encounter, they would face it together.

Chapter Sixty-Three

As Leonardo's empty, 21st century apartment came clearer into view, three figures also became distinguishable in the semidarkness of the portal. Ali's heart leapt as they crossed the threshold. Her father, Luca, and Father Donato were positioned around a sleek titanium device, at present not operating, but Alice recognized it from the laser specs.

"Papa!"

He was positioned behind the laser, similar to the 3D print they had manufactured to recreate the passage, but this one, to Ali, looked like the real thing. She ran to him as he came around Luca to meet her halfway. Ali threw her arms around him and wept openly with relief and joy.

"I thought I'd never see you again. You don't know what a relief it is to see you."

"Me too, sweetheart, me too," Reno said, equally tearful. He held her tight and patted her back to soothe her. "When all this is done," Reno sniffed, "you're grounded for the rest of your life." His laughter helped to break the emotional scene.

"Deal," said Ali, laughing softly.

Luca stood nearby but did not waste any time heading to Claudio. He offered his hand to his friend and received, instead, a rough hug.

"Damn, she got you after all." Luca laughed.

"My good friend," Claudio responded. "How can I ever thank you?"

Ali reached around her father's arm as he held her tight and grasped Luca's hand, squeezing it as an appreciative smile flashed on her lips.

"Luca. Father Donato," she said with delight. "You saved our lives. The wormhole faded on the 1512 side of the chamber."

"My biggest contribution was the praying." Donato smiled as he inclined his head in acknowledgement to Ali, his hands folded in his sleeves. "It was all Luca and your father."

"Yes, we saw," Reno nodded. "That's why we recalibrated and discharged the real laser—to reactivate the link." He gently let go of Alice and grabbed some industrial-looking gloves from the top of a workbench before moving to another device about the size of a briefcase. "Sorry, darling, we need to move fast."

Claudio awkwardly came forward. "Sir, I am Claudio Moro."

Reno looked in his direction as he worked and nodded a quick salutation. "I see you have made a miraculous recovery," said Reno dryly, shooting Ali a glance as he and Luca worked feverishly on the new device.

Claudio looked puzzled.

"I'll explain later," Ali mouthed to Claudio.

He shrugged and continued, "Mr. Ferro, the portal needs to be neutralized."

"Way ahead of you." Reno motioned to the device. "We found an instrument to counterbalance the wormhole and safely deactivate it."

Claudio moved closer to Luca and Reno as they worked.

"This container holds sodium gas, which has been cooled to

the lowest temperature ever recorded—only half-a-billionth of a degree above absolute zero."

"I read about these at the university," said Claudio, his eyes wide as he observed them working. "It is a near absolute zero temperature compartment. It would neutralize the residual energy of the lightning strike."

"Atoms move their fastest at high temperatures, a reflection of their energy," Alice chimed in. "And absolute zero is the point at which there is absolutely no heat energy remaining to be extracted from a substance, thereby freezing the wormhole and safely diffusing it. Genius, Papa."

"Correct. You've been listening to your papa." Reno smiled. Then he turned to Claudio. "Right now, grab a pair of gloves, Claudio, and help me and Luca get this into the chamber. Be careful, now, this thing has gas in it that will render any part of you a Popsicle in a split second."

Once they placed the device in the chamber, Reno set the timing release mechanism and stood back. "This should work pretty fast."

Alice marveled at the sight. In painstaking measured degrees, the cooled sodium gas was released into the chamber. It did not take long for the mighty spirals to begin to pulsate dimly, just as they had before, slowly dying away until they were but a shadowy mist in the darkness. With a last pulse, the spirals disappeared.

"It is done." Claudio said, still holding Ali's hand. "Both the laser and compartment worked brilliantly."

"I knew the laser would work," said Reno. "The calibration needed tweaking, but essentially, Luca and Olivia had the right idea."

"Where's Mamma?" It suddenly dawned on Alice that her mother must suspect something. "Does she know?"

"Yes, she is at the villa with Anna and Dario, waiting."

"What prompted you to come here? To come for me?"

"After a few days of not checking in, we called your aunt, and she was worried as well. We tried to find you through your microchip, but it was indicating non-locatable. That was a huge hint. Even if you're in a rural area, the transponder should still work. Your mother and I were both worried sick, so we hopped on the next available flight and..."

Ali nodded as her father's voice trailed. He looked over the top of her head at Claudio.

"Papa," she took Claudio's hand, "this is the boy I told you about."

Claudio offered his hand. Reno narrowed his eyes, looking Claudio up and down. Finally, he extended his.

"Pleasure to meet you," said Claudio.

"You are dressed as a monk," said Reno, with a deadpan expression. "And for that matter, so are you," he said to Ali.

Alice and Claudio looked down at their clothing and shrugged.

"I'll explain later. How did you end up here, Papa? In the monastery with all this stuff?"

"As I said, I couldn't get a lock on your microchip, and when you were late in contacting us, I called your aunt, who in turn put us in contact with Anna and Dario. Once they explained what was going on, I met with Luca and Olivia. We figured out the rest, and I called in a lot of favors to borrow this equipment." Reno exhaled. "1512 and 2030 shall forever be separate—and rightly so."

"It's 2030?" Ali asked with surprise.

"It is. Happy New Year. We have turned the page to a new decade." Reno crossed his arms and tried to look stern. "Now, you have some explaining to do, Alice Ferro," he said, his brows raised.

"Yup." Ali huffed out a breath. "So, have you got about a month?"

~

Leonardo da Vinci, Abbot Federico, and Francesco watched in amazement as the portal slowly went dim—the spirals diminishing and fading until there was nothing left but the empty hull of the chamber.

The Abbot shook his head slowly as he surveyed the emptiness in the copper box.

"I suppose that is it, gentlemen." Da Vinci squeezed his lips together and shook his head.

Federico folded hands under his scapula. "I trust you shall dismantle this object of peculiarity as soon as is practicable."

"We shall begin this task on the morrow, Father."

"If you are agreeable, Francesco, I should like to begin preparing to make a start for Milan, or perhaps France, within seven days," da Vinci said after Abbot Federico had departed.

"Agreed," replied Francesco. "I shall make the necessary arrangements. Will you require all your works, sir, or a select few, for now?"

Da Vinci put his finger to his lips and thought for a moment.

"Yes...bring the Lisa Gioconda canvas. That rogue of a merchant has not paid for his wife's portrait, and he shall not have it until he does."

"Yes, Master."

"Oh, and are we still in possession of the second Madonna of the Rocks?"

"Yes, sir, behind those canvases there." Francesco pointed to a place just beyond the worktables, where most da Vinci's unfinished works were stored.

"Make certain you have the workers load that properly." Leonardo's eyes twinkled with delight. "I do believe that I have an idea for the face of the angel."

Chapter Sixty-Four

Ali set her iPhone beside her on the ancient retaining wall overlooking the city of Florence from Piazzale Michelangelo. With Claudio's arms wrapped snugly around her waist, they watched the sun setting over the Arno River below.

The water was ablaze with a ripe orange sun, its reflection peeking triumphantly between the bridges traversing the old river. Slowly and teasingly, the brilliant orange ball sunk into the cityscape horizon, washing away the day with mixed hues of mauve, pink, and gold. A slow, romantic tune softly played on Ali's phone

"This is my favorite time of day." She sighed, and Claudio slipped his hand down to hers, linking their fingers.

"Mmm." His nose nuzzled her hair as he stood behind her. She sensed he was paying absolutely no attention to the sunset.

"Claudio, are you watching this with me or what? Look how beautiful it is."

"I would rather watch you. Turn around so I can kiss you." He spun her about, and Ali giggled as she continued into a three-sixty, much to Claudio's dismay.

"Come on now, my lady." He grasped her hands and gently turned her, so she was facing him. "Or should I say, Your Grace?"

Alice ran her hands up to his shoulders, feeling his strong arms underneath his white shirt.

As the two murmured their affirmations of love for each other, a car pulled into a parking spot near them. The radio was blaring the evening news, with a report already in progress.

"We bring you an update to the recent report of the DNA confirmation regarding the Medici heir. It was widely reported last year that a search was in progress for anyone who could prove they have a connection to the famed Medici family. Last winter, the last known direct descendant of the Medici, Prince Carlo Gregorio de Medici, died suddenly in the south of France. He was not survived by any immediate family, though there were distant relations in Italy and in the United States. The young woman who came forward earlier this year was tested using the latest, most sophisticated forensic technology, and she was found to be the closest match to the sample taken from a long-rumored, secret crypt of the Medici family that was discovered by scientists in 2004. The vaulted chamber was found under a stone floor behind the main altar of the Medici chapel in the church of San Lorenzo in Florence. A long-awaited press conference, introducing the heiress to the Medici mega-fortune, will be held tomorrow morning at Palazzo Pitti and will reveal the identity of the young woman who stands to inherit property and assets estimated in the millions of Euros..."

Ali turned her face to the diminishing sun and took in a deep breath, her stomach churning with anxiety and unease at the prospect of possibly living a fishbowl existence for the rest of her life.

"What is wrong, my darling?" Claudio asked softly as he

wrapped his arms around her waist anew. "Do not let it worry you. The lawyers will be speaking on your behalf."

"Yes, for the most part, but they're still going to expect me to say something." She burrowed her head against his chest. "I know my parents will be there, supporting me, but I just...I don't want to sound like an idiot."

"You?" Claudio laughed softly. "There is no chance of that, I am sure. Need I remind you of the hearing in front of Giuliano and his cronies? You could not have been more eloquent."

Ali inhaled deeply. "You'll be there, too, won't you?"

"Try to keep me away."

Ali's stomach began to settle. Her mind raced thinking of all that had happened since they had come back through the chamber. The lengthy explanations to her parents, their cautious but now, steadfast acceptance of Claudio, and the quick and silent dismantling of the chamber at the monastery by Claudio, Luca, and her father. Ali was convinced that her father needed to ensure it would no longer be used, hence he spearheaded the undertaking.

Upon hearing that the search was still on for an heir to the Medici riches, Alice applied on Claudio's dare before going home last January. A DNA sample was taken from her, after hearing of her extraordinary orphan-at-the-convent-door story, and a few weeks later, they called her in Boston to confirm she was the one. In fact, they marveled at the authenticity of the DNA match. "It is as though you were born only one or two generations removed from the Medici in the crypt. Astounding."

Inside, she had been laughing. *I probably am only a couple of generations removed from whoever was in there.*

"What are you thinking?" asked Claudio, gently kissing the back of her head. The sun had almost set completely.

"I'm thinking of how our lives might change after tomorrow."

"In what way, do you think?"

"Well, I know we're still going to see each other during reading week and the summer. You'll stay with us when you visit me in Boston, and I'll stay with you at Anna and Dario's, but I mean...this Medici thing is huge." Alice turned to look Claudio in his dark, mesmerizing eyes. "I don't want anything to change between us. I could never stand to lose you again."

"I am not going anywhere. I have checked the history data bases at the university and all remains perfectly as before. We are both in our chosen universities in September, so what is troubling you, my love?"

Ali shook her head, unsure herself. Of what could be worrying her. She reached up to caress his face, and tried to shake off the feeling. "Nothing. Maybe I'm just not used to not being in a crisis of some kind or being so incredibly happy and in love with the most amazing person I know."

They drew closer and their lips met—a tender kiss filled with irresistible love. Alice's head still spun when he touched her. Claudio opened his eyes and gazed into hers.

"Those eyes will never cease to bewitch me." He tenderly caressed her cheek. "Come with me. We will get a gelato at that place on the Via dei Calzaiuoli." He grasped her hand with both of his, brushed it gently with his lips, and led her to the red Vespa scooter. "Gelato makes everything better."

Her smile gave away her delight. "Only if you'll let me buy." Ali accepted the helmet he handed her and slipped it over her head, snapping the strap closed.

"Then after that, we can take a ride through the city before your big reveal tomorrow—one last night as a commoner, just you and me." Claudio flashed a teasing, irresistible smile. She mounted the bike and held on tight to his waist, laying her head against his back and taking in his delicious scent.

"Hey, I just thought of something. I'm a princess, now,

royally speaking, I outrank you." She laughed and wondered if she was allowed to be this happy.

Rolling his eyes and chuckling, Claudio started up the *motorino* then turned to Ali. "Who you are never mattered. I was a slave to your heart from the moment I saw you, my lady."

Alice tightly wrapped her arms around him. "And I to yours, my lord."

As they headed down the winding road into Florence, it occurred to Alice that their history and their present would stand as a testament to their future. It didn't matter who or what people assumed she was made of, she would always be Alice, and Claudio would always be hers, scullery maid, princess, count, commoner, or otherwise. Their love was five hundred years in the making, and if she had anything to do with it, it would last five times five hundred more.

Don't miss your next favorite book!
Join the Fire & Ice YA Books newsletter today!
www.fireandiceya.com/mail.html

❧

THANK YOU FOR READING

❧

Did you enjoy this book?

We invite you to leave a review at your favorite book site, such as Goodreads, Amazon, Barnes & Noble, etc.

DID YOU KNOW THAT LEAVING A REVIEW...

- Helps other readers find books they may enjoy.
- Gives you a chance to let your voice be heard.
- Gives authors recognition for their hard work.
- Doesn't have to be long. A sentence or two about why you liked the book will do.

About the Author

E. Graziani is a teacher/librarian by day and the author of the YA time-travel series, *Alice of the Rocks & Angel of Time*. *Alice of the Rocks* was named one of Barnes & Noble's Top Ten Young Adult Indie Summer Reads, 2023. She has written *Magenta* and *Everything That Was Us*. She is the author of *Breaking Faith*, a contemporary YA novel, listed on CBC Canada's Must-Read Books for Spring 2017, selected for the 'In the Margins' Book Award 2018 Recommended Fiction List, and one of CCBC Best Books for Kids and Teens. Graziani is the author of the YA historical memoir, *War in My Town*, also one of CCBC's Best Books for Kids and Teens, and a finalist in the Hamilton Arts Council 2016 Literary Awards for Best Non-Fiction. Graziani has also written the novella, *Jess Under Pressure*. E. Graziani appears regularly on CHCH Morning Live to discuss new releases in Canadian KidLit and has spoken at many school events and school book clubs. She loves to connect with her young and not-so-young readers. She resides in Canada with her husband and daughters.

Find Edy Online:
www.egraziani1.wixsite.com/egrazianiauthor
www.chch.com/tag/edy-graziani

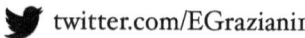 twitter.com/EGraziani1

instagram.com/e.graziani

goodreads.com/egrazianiauthor

Also by the Author

Alice Series

Alice of the Rocks

Angel of Time

Novels

Magenta